AFTER SUNDOWN

AFTER SUNDOWN

A NOVEL

LINDA HOWARD
and LINDA JONES

WILLIAM MORROW
An Imprint of HarperCollins*Publishers*

HarperCollins books may be purchased for educational, business, or sales promotional use. For information, please email the Special Markets Department at SPsales@harpercollins.com.

FIRST EDITION

Designed by Bonni Leon-Berman

Library of Congress Cataloging-in-Publication Data has been applied for.

ISBN 978-0-06-284263-3

20 21 22 23 24   LSC   10 9 8 7 6 5 4 3 2 1

Our very special thanks to Fran Troxler for ferrying us up and down Cove Mountain and along the quiet Wears Valley roads, and for answering all our questions about the community. She knows it well! The valley has a great asset in the Troxlers. Thank you, Fran and David, for all you do. It's deeply appreciated.

AFTER SUNDOWN

CHAPTER ONE

Ben Jernigan snapped awake at the first beep of his computer alarm. What felt like a lifetime of training had him moving and on his feet in front of the computer before his conscious caught up with his subconscious. He scrubbed a hand across his face and turned on a lamp as he focused on the information displayed on the computer screen in very tiny print. Swearing under his breath, he enlarged the screen—and then swore out loud.

His cell phone rang no more than ten seconds after he began reading. Very few people had his number and any call coming in at—he glanced at the time on his bedside clock—2:43 A.M. wasn't a call he'd ignore.

"Yeah," he said, trying to elevate his tone from growl to something intelligible. The abrupt awakening had adrenaline pouring through his system, tightening his muscles, sharpening his vision, his thought processes racing. He hadn't been shot at in over two years, but his sympathetic nervous system was still ready for action.

"You reading this?" The voice belonged to Cory Howler, longtime buddy from the military who now worked with the government in a somewhat murky job description that had him in position to know a lot of shit. People who knew shit were invaluable in every organization, no matter how large, or how small.

"Yes. Data?"

"Bigger than Carrington."

"Shit," Ben said softly. The Carrington Event was a series of powerful coronal mass ejections, or CMEs, in 1859 that had melted telegraph wires and set some telegraph offices on fire. Technology in the nineteenth century had been limited to telegraphs; now the developed world ran on technology, and the damage would be catastrophic. Satellites would be fried, the power grids—most of them, there were a few that had hardened security—would go down, gasoline supplies would vanish because the pipelines would be damaged, food supplies would dry up, and cities would become the sixth level of hell.

Small CMEs that had little or no effect on technology occurred almost daily, but those mild solar storms couldn't be compared to what was coming.

"What's the timing?"

"About thirty-six hours from now. We'd have had more lead time but one of the GOES satellites is down for maintenance, or malfunctioned and they don't want to say so. Bad timing," Howler said in wry understatement, given the magnitude of the impending disaster. "It's a series; we've seen four so far. The first one will hit the Far East in about twelve hours, but the ones behind it are bigger, wider, and traveling faster. The Middle East and Europe are going down."

Ben didn't miss the qualifier "so far." They expected more than four. The fourth one would hit the Atlantic, which would play hell with any ships at sea, but any CME after that would hit the American continents, making this a worldwide shit-storm. The thing with a series of CMEs was that the first one sort of cleared the way, cosmically speaking, for the ones behind it and they grew in intensity and speed.

"What are your plans?" he asked, because Howler had a family to take care of.

"I'm packing up the wife and kids right now and sending them south. I want them away from the city, and as far south as possible."

Ben grunted. The farther south they went, the more survivable the winter would be.

"What about you?"

"I'm making preps, but hanging here for another twelve hours or so. Then I'll meet up with Gen and the kids and we'll hunker down, try to survive. My guess is close to a year before the grid comes back up."

That was an optimistic guess, but not completely outlandish. "Will there be a warning?" He didn't assume there would be, because the government was so screwed up someone could persuade the head honchos that "panic in the streets" was somehow worse than actually making preparations. On the other hand, governments weren't the only entities who could see this thing coming. Word would get out, but sooner was better than later.

"It's being framed," Howler said. "Word is we'll hear something right after daybreak, but I'm betting it might not happen until this afternoon. The morons might think it could be a false alarm and wait until Japan is hammered. You know how it goes."

He did, unfortunately. "See you on the flip side."

"Take care, bro."

Ben ended the call and began pulling on his clothes. He was largely self-sufficient, but there were still things he could do to harden his position, expand his resources, safety measures he could put in place. He had solar panels to protect; his ham radio would be worthless for a while after the CME hit because the atmospherics would be fucked, but he needed to protect some of the components so they'd work when the atmosphere did settle down; he also had to protect his generator and get it topped off with propane, get extra gas for his truck and ATV.

There was no way to get enough gas to last for the duration. This wasn't going to be a short-term event. Both the corporate side and the government side had had their heads in the sand for decades, opting to do nothing because of the cost and gambling that a catastrophic solar storm wouldn't hit Earth, at least on their watch. Some of them had just run out of luck. The sun called the shots, and the sun had just lobbed the energy equivalent of thousands of nuclear weapons at them—no explosions, but enormous damage.

The people who were paid to think of events like this and the likely outcomes had predicted that the worldwide mortality rate would be at ninety percent by the end of the first year. Ben didn't think it would be that bad, because people were more resourceful than government entities gave them credit for being.

There wasn't much he could do right now, with dawn still hours away. On the other hand, neither could he go back to sleep. He went to the kitchen and made himself some coffee, then checked the thermal signatures on his security setup to see if any bears were wandering around in his yard, or even on the wraparound porch. Bear encounters here in the east Tennessee mountains were a fact of life, and he gave the bears the right of way.

There were a few small signatures, birds and what was probably a raccoon, but nothing bear-sized. He took his can of bear spray, a pistol loaded with shotgun pellets, and his coffee cup out on the porch looking out over the valley. Just because there wasn't a bear now didn't mean one wouldn't come along. Settling in a rocking chair and propping his booted feet on the porch railing, he sipped the coffee and looked out over the twinkling lights of Wears Valley, far below.

He'd lived here almost two years now; a military buddy from this area had steered Ben to the mountains, and though he'd initially thought about maybe building a small cabin tucked away in the mountains, when he'd seen this place he'd put in an immediate offer. It was larger than he'd planned, but the location was ideal, situated high on the side of Cove Mountain. The rudimentary driveway leading up to it was steep, impassable to regular cars, and even most pickup trucks couldn't make it unless they were jacked high enough to clear the big rock Ben had moved into the middle of the driveway as another deterrent. He could have put a chain across the driveway but then he'd have had to get out and unlock it every time he came and went, and for the most part he'd just be making things tougher on himself. Not many people ventured up here.

He liked being alone. He was more content this way. After years of combat and dealing with bureaucrats who didn't know their asses from a hole in the ground but were nevertheless in charge of life-and-death decisions concerning him and his men, he was done. He got out, and now he just wanted to be left the hell alone.

That meant he never let down his guard. He had a top-notch security system, monitors, alarms; he was serious about keeping people at a distance. A couple of times some nosy neighbors—or tourists, and he didn't know the difference because he didn't know any of his neighbors, if someone who lived over a mile away could be called a "neighbor"—had hiked all the way up here. His motion alarm had alerted him the moment they cleared the curve and set foot on the wide, flat area where his house sat, and he'd stepped out on the porch with his shotgun broken open and draped over his arm. Neither time had he had to say a word; just the sight of a big, muscular man with a dark scowl on his face and a shotgun in his hands was enough to send the trespassers the hell off his property.

Sitting here on his porch in the predawn darkness, listening to the nightbirds, the rustling of the trees, not a soul anywhere around him—this was why he'd moved to the Tennessee mountains. He didn't have PTSD—no nightmares, no flashbacks, no sweats of terror. Maybe some shrink would tell him that his extreme withdrawal was a form of PTSD, but that's what shrinks did: come up with diagnoses that justified their jobs. As far as Ben was concerned, anyone sane who had spent years dealing with the bullshit he'd dealt with would react the same way.

It wasn't that he didn't know people, or at least know their names. By necessity, he'd met some of the valley residents. People insisted on talking to him, even when he limited his responses to grunts. That was almost the only drawback to the area: Southerners were friendly. They talked to everyone. He didn't want to be talked to. Once an elderly couple he'd just met had invited him to supper; getting away from old people was almost as hard as escaping an ambush, because they were persistent with their offers of hospitality. He'd felt as if his skin was being peeled away, and all he'd wanted to do was duck and cover.

He hadn't even met any women he'd been remotely attracted to. Scratch that, his subconscious immediately said. Sela Gordon, the owner of the little general store / gas station on the highway . . . he'd noticed her. For one thing, she was quiet; she didn't bombard him with questions or try to draw him into conversation. He could go into her store and pick up a few items without feeling as if he were under attack. Maybe she was a little shy, because she didn't get real talkative with any of her customers. Shy was a bonus; she wasn't likely to start feeling comfortable around him and start up a conversation.

She was slim, quiet, dark hair and soft brown eyes, just curvy enough to leave no doubt she was female. She didn't wear a wedding ring—or any rings at all. When she wasn't looking at him, which was most of the time whenever he was in the store, he'd indulge himself by looking at her, though he was careful not to let her ever catch him at it. That was the only time in the past three years his dick had shown any signs of life.

Brooding, he watched a lone car on the highway far below, its headlight beams crawling from left to right. Okay, so maybe he did have a form of PTSD. A few years ago he'd have been all over Sela

Gordon, trying to score; the fact that he'd noticed she didn't wear a wedding ring said a lot. Still, his reluctant interest couldn't overcome his much stronger need for solitude.

The people down in the valley were still sleeping peacefully, for the most part. Maybe there were a few who didn't sleep well and were waiting for dawn the way he was, maybe there was even someone who had a NOAA space storm alarm on their computer the way he did, though he doubted it. Their lives were about to change in drastic ways. His, not so much. His income stream would dry up when the CMEs hit and he stopped writing columns for survivalist magazines; his military pension would accrue until such time as the government and banks were up and running again, but the hard fact was there wouldn't be any bills he needed to pay because utilities would stop working, and he'd be feeding himself with what he could hunt or grow. As an extra hedge, he had about a year's worth of freeze-dried food stored in a secure locker under the house, he had canned goods, and he had plenty of ammunition stockpiled to protect his food and property.

If the think tank people were right and only ten percent of the population survived the coming Very Bad Day event, then he intended to be one of the ten percent.

Business had been brisk, for a weekday. Sela Gordon's grocery store / gas station was located right on Highway 321, so business was usually good anyway. She wouldn't get rich off the store, but she made a decent living. The gas pumps were out front, in the center of the smallish parking lot. Inside, there were seven rows of shelves filled with basic goods. No one would do their regular grocery shopping here, but if someone in the valley ran out of a few things and didn't want to go all the way to town, this was where they came. Aunt Carol called it the "toilet paper and Spam" collection, and she wasn't all that wrong, though there were also chips, and cookies, and a few boxes of cereal, some canned goods, and a small section of staples such as salt and sugar and pepper. One aisle was dedicated to over-the-counter meds, bandages, and feminine products. The small floor-to-ceiling cooler in the back was filled with beer, soft drinks, and juice. She'd carried milk for a while, but it hadn't sold well enough to justify the necessary space. When it came to pricing, she couldn't compete with the bigger grocery stores in town, and the dairy sell-by dates came and went too quickly. Now she kept a few packs of powdered milk and some cans of condensed sweetened milk that sold mostly in the summer when people were making homemade ice cream.

Between the locals and the tourists, who either stayed in Wears Valley or passed by on their way to and from Pigeon Forge or Gatlinburg, she stayed busy enough to make this small venture profitable. She'd never own a private jet or buy her own vacation home, but she did okay, and okay was good enough.

Carol said Sela liked her small business because it was safe, and again, she wasn't wrong.

Taking chances, both personally and professionally, was for people who liked an adrenaline rush. Sela wasn't one of those people.

A big gray pickup truck, riding high on its chassis, pulled up to one of the gas pumps. She recognized a lot of the locals' vehicles, including this one. Ben Jernigan didn't come in all that often, though he did stop for gas now and then, and he'd run in for beer and cereal a time or two—but she recognized him because it was impossible to ignore him. Both the truck and the man were impressive, he more than the truck. He was big, at least a couple of inches over six feet, with muscles that strained the cotton T-shirt he wore. His arms were thick and roped, decorated with a few tattoos, his hands scarred and callused. Usually he was somewhat scruffy, with at least two days' growth of beard. He almost always wore sunglasses, though he'd slide them up on top of his head whenever he came inside, and his pale green eyes always had a remote, cool expression that cut like a laser. She tried to be friendly with her customers even though she wasn't an outgoing person, but with him she couldn't manage even that much. She stayed quiet, like a rabbit hoping the wolf didn't notice her.

She didn't like tattoos, but she couldn't imagine his arms without them. She was vaguely alarmed that she'd given his arms that much thought.

Whenever he came in, her heart pounded hard and fast for at least a few minutes after he'd left. Rabbit, indeed.

She watched as he left the truck and headed for the gas pump, but then he stopped and looked toward the store. Sela quickly glanced down, though she doubted he could see her through the reflection on the glass; she still didn't want to take the chance that he'd think she was watching him, even though she was. *Bold* had never been a word used to describe her.

He left the gas pump and started toward the store.

Right on schedule, Sela's heart started pounding. She concentrated on the invoices on the counter in front of her, even though she wanted to look at him. What woman wouldn't? She was definitely a woman, even if not a very adventurous one.

The chime sounded, and he walked past her without a word. She wanted to ask him why he hadn't pumped any gas but had left his truck at the pump, but she didn't. Only after he'd walked by did she look up, quickly glancing at his muscled back covered by a brown T-shirt, and while she was at it also noticing how well his muscular ass cheeks filled out his jeans. Her cheeks got hot and she returned her attention to the invoices, fiercely focusing on them, or trying to, anyway.

Her thoughts raced, refusing to concentrate on the invoices. He'd picked up one of the baskets on his way in, which was unusual. He never bought much, certainly not so much that he couldn't carry it in his two big hands.

Damn. Was her mouth watering? It was! The realization flummoxed her. If she was in the market for a man, which she definitely wasn't, Jernigan would be the last man she considered as an option. Sure, he had the looks, and the muscle. She darted another look at him. Those arms, that ass . . . just wow. But there was something about him that screamed danger, danger, like the screeching robot on that old TV show, and she knew she'd panic if he actually asked her out or even lightly flirted. It was a smart woman who knew when someone was more than she could handle.

Jernigan was usually quick and efficient in his shopping. He knew where everything was and walked straight to it, without fail. Today he seemed to browse, which was out of the ordinary for him. Hmm. He went up one aisle and down the other, then came to the counter with a full basket not to check out but to unload and go back.

Toilet paper. Aspirin. Canned soup. Blueberry Pop-Tarts.

He returned with another full basket, silently unloaded it, and nodded at her. For a fast, heart-stopping moment her gaze met his and that was all it took for the bottom to drop out of her stomach. His eyes were so striking, a predatory pale green, almost pretty in a face that wasn't pretty at all but was so masculine and intriguing that pretty didn't matter.

As always, she was the one who looked away. Silently she began picking up cans and scanning them.

She should say something, even if just "hello." She knew she should. That was what a store clerk did, make the customers feel welcome, and especially so when the clerk was also the owner.

"Is there anything else?" was the best she could manage.

"Thirty bucks in gas."

He normally just paid for his gas with a credit card, most of the time leaving without coming in. She nodded and keyed the computer to let the pump dispense thirty dollars' worth of gas.

She gave him a total. He pulled his wallet out of his back pocket and withdrew a stack of bills while she finished bagging. There were a lot of bags, and if it had been anyone else she would have offered to help him to his truck, not that he would have any problem at all, but if he were any other man she'd still have offered. She made change, which he stuffed into his front pocket before he gathered all the bags and headed for the door.

Sela breathed out a silent sigh of relief as he reached the door. What was it about him that put her so on edge? She hoped she wasn't so shallow that it was just his looks. Or his body.

Then he stopped at the door and for a split second she wondered if he was having trouble opening it; she started out from behind the counter, saying, "Let me get that door for you," but he turned and looked at her and those laser eyes stopped her in her tracks.

"You might want to put a few things back for an emergency, just in case."

Emergency? Startled, Sela looked out the windows, expecting to see storm clouds or something, but it was a typical September day, the sky blue against the green mountains, the weather still hot, no forecast of a hurricane roaring up the Gulf that would hammer the region with heavy rain. Snow was months away. So—?

"The news hasn't hit yet," he continued. His voice was deep, a little rough, as if he didn't talk much and needed to clear his throat. "But it will, maybe in a few hours, maybe tomorrow, depending on how on the ball those responsible for the alert are." Small muscles in his neck and jaw clenched a little. "They're pretty much never on the ball, so—" He shrugged.

She still had no idea what he was talking about. "What news? What kind of alert?" she asked.

"There's a solar storm headed our way. A CME."

"A what?"

"Coronal mass ejection." The words were clipped. "A big one. If it's as bad as predicted, the power grid will go down."

"We'll have a power outage." They lived in the mountains. Power outages were a fact of life, though their local utility was a good one.

A hint of impatience flared across his expression. He looked as if he already regretted stopping to talk. "A power outage that will likely last for months, if not a year or longer."

She almost recoiled. And there it was, the big flaw, and one she hadn't expected. Drink too much, financially irresponsible, smoke too much weed—those were things she saw every day that kept her from accepting what few invitations came her way. This was way out there. He was a survivalist / conspiracy theorist. No fine ass or muscled, tattooed arms or even pretty eyes could make up for that fault.

"Get all the cash you can," he continued, his reluctance so obvious it was as if he was having to push the words out. "Stock up on staples, canned goods, batteries." Then he'd evidently had enough because he ended with an impatient, "Just Google it."

The back door opened and behind them Aunt Carol called out a friendly "Hello." Jernigan's gaze flashed to her and evidently that was his cue to leave, two people being one too many, because he pushed through the front door and headed for his truck.

Well, that had been weird.

Carol glanced through the front window as Jernigan stowed his groceries in the truck cab then began pumping his allotment of gas. "Man, I just missed the hottie. I shouldn't have taken so much time with my hair." She flicked her fingertips at her short bleached blond locks that were highlighted with a streak of cotton candy pink, and batted her blue eyes. And then she laughed. Carol had a fantastic laugh, rollicking and infectious; she put everything she had into it.

Sela cleared her throat. "He just told me we're about to get hit with a solar storm that might knock the power out for months." It sounded just as ridiculous coming out of her mouth as it had coming out of his. And she didn't refer to him as "the hottie" even though she agreed with the description, because that would only spur Aunt Carol to start prodding her to ask him out, as if she'd ever asked out a man in her life.

Carol made a snorting sound as she retrieved a broom from the utility closet. She helped out at the store on occasion, usually early in the day before Olivia, the fifteen-year-old granddaughter she'd raised from the age of five, got out of school. As she began to sweep, she sighed. "Damn it. Why are all the good-looking men nuts? I should have known he was one of those when he bought that old place on Cove Mountain. Who wants to live in such an isolated place alone? Why? And then he trucked up all those solar panels, and I hear he has a ham radio." She glanced up at Sela. "Don't judge me. I'm not a horrible gossip, but people talk. And I listen."

Sela wasn't sure when having a ham radio had become a sign of being a nut; she knew at least one other person in the valley who owned one. The thing was, Jernigan had never seemed like a nut to her—the opposite, in fact. He struck her as a man who had dealt with some hard realities.

She leaned on the front counter while she tried to square her instincts with her doubts. What if—? "What if he's right?" It was an alarming idea, one she hesitated to voice. Immediately she had to fight down a sense of panic, because she couldn't even imagine what life would be like without electricity for months.

Carol stopped sweeping and leaned on the broom. She wasn't much wider than that broom, truth be told. She rolled her eyes and made a face. "I still have my Y2K windup radio. You were a kid when the calendar went from 1999 to 2000, so you might not have paid any attention to all the hysteria, but seriously, there were people who thought the same thing would happen when computers tried and failed to make the switch. Banks would collapse. Power plants would go offline. Chaos! Pfft." She started sweeping again. "Nothing happened. I'd stocked up on enough toilet paper I didn't have to buy any for a year. And I have a nifty windup radio for emergencies, not that I've ever needed it."

Maybe Carol was right, and nothing would happen.

Then again . . . what if it did? She'd be silly if she acted on the warning of a man she barely knew and nothing happened, but if she didn't act and his warning was right on target, then she was stupid.

She'd rather be silly than stupid. Silly was embarrassing at worst, while stupid could be deadly. That wasn't a chance she was willing to take.

She grabbed a shopping basket and started filling it with a few essentials. She wouldn't clean off the shelves, wouldn't lock the front door and close for the day, but it wouldn't hurt to have a few things set back, things that she'd need anyway, even if they weren't used right away.

While Sela was grabbing some tuna and canned chicken, Carol decided to sweep down the canned meat aisle. After watching her for a few seconds, Carol made another scoffing sound. "If you're preparing for doomsday, don't forget to pick up some mayo."

"I won't. I'm just getting what we'll use anyway. If nothing happens, then no big deal. I can put everything back on the shelves."

She walked up and down the aisles, her mind buzzing. She liked to be organized and controlled, but abruptly she felt neither. Everything around her was the same, but she felt lost. She didn't know what to do, couldn't get her mind around the scope of what he'd said could happen, so she concentrated on what he'd actually said. She had some cash, but not enough to get them through a long-term disaster. What good would cash do anyway? But he'd said get cash, so she'd get cash. If the solar storm happened and the grid went down, the way Jernigan said it might, she wouldn't be able to access her bank. The credit and debit card charges she had in her cash register would be worthless.

"Just for today," she said in a voice just loud enough for Carol to hear, "we'll take cash only. Tell everyone the credit card reader is out of order." She hadn't taken checks for years, so that wouldn't be a problem.

"What about the gas pumps?"

She thought about it for a minute. Tourists would be headed for home, if Jernigan was right and an alert went out. At least, she assumed so. She would, if she was away on vacation; she'd burn the highway up getting home. The tourists would need gas. Everyone would need gas. "We'll leave them, for now." She didn't want people who didn't have enough cash to fill their tanks to end up stranded in her parking lot, or down the road. It was a decent compromise, at least for now. That would change if there really was a warning.

Again she felt a sense of unreality as she tried to deal with the realities of the possible situation. Civilization and culture as she knew it, as everyone knew it, would vanish in an instant. This was too big. There was no way to prepare.

She headed for the cookie aisle. Carol called out, "If anyone else had told you to prepare for Armageddon, would you have taken it seriously? Or are you stocking up for the coming apocalypse because Hottie McStud is the one who told you it was coming?"

"I don't know," she said helplessly. "I don't know that I believe him. It's just . . . why gamble that he's wrong?" She took a deep breath. "And it isn't just me, it's you and Olivia, too."

That was what terrified her, she realized. They were family, she and Carol and Olivia, and they didn't have many other relatives. There were a few scattered cousins, and Olivia's older brother, Joshua, who was in the military, but here it was just the three of them. If anything happened to Carol or Olivia because she, Sela, hadn't been prepared enough, she'd never forgive herself.

They'd suffered enough loss, all of it in the past ten years. Olivia's parents—Carol's daughter and her husband—in a senseless car crash. Sela's own parents of natural causes—a slow cancer and a quick aneurysm—three and five years later. Carol's husband had died after a heart attack four years ago, less than a year after Sela's divorce.

She'd lost enough. She would damn well do everything she could to keep what remained of her family safe.

Their lives were so entwined she couldn't imagine being any other way. They lived in a small subdivision within easy walking distance of the store and each other, in houses that were similar on the outside, though wildly different inside. Sela was a minimalist. Carol never met a knickknack she didn't like. Most importantly, Carol wasn't prepared for more than a couple of days without power. She'd decided that she didn't need a generator, because Sela had one, and if there was a power outage she and Olivia would just stay with Sela until the power came back on. Both houses did have fireplaces, though Carol hadn't had a real fire in hers in years. That might be about to change.

Suddenly it seemed to Sela that she could take everything in her own store and not have enough for them, not for months. And it wasn't just Carol and Olivia. What would happen when a friend or neighbor showed up, and they needed something? Her family came first, but it would be damn hard to turn people away. Shit. She stared at the pitiful stash she'd accumulated.

No way was this enough.

She took a deep breath. "Of everyone here in the valley, who would you choose to believe when it comes to surviving a catastrophe?"

The two women stared at each other, and Sela knew they were both picturing their friends and acquaintances, and measuring them against the tough, grim, hard-muscled man whose eyes said he'd seen more than they could ever imagine, or want to imagine.

"Hot Buns Steelbody," Carol said reluctantly, coining a new term for Jernigan.

They shared another look, then Sela said, "Watch the store for a while." She put the last of what she'd gathered in the office. "I'm going to town."

"For what?" Carol asked.

"Smart things we need to do. Call your pharmacy and get refills on all your medications, and I'll swing by and pick them up."

"They aren't due, insurance won't—" Carol began, then said, "Oh. Forget insurance, we'll pay for them ourselves. Right? Will pharmacies do that?"

"Don't see why not, as long as it isn't narcotics. Call and find out, and let me know." Sela grabbed her purse out from under the counter and headed for the door, already organizing a list in her head: cash from the bank, more supplies from the grocery store, the prescription refills for Carol, batteries, fuel for the oil lamps—more and more items occurred to her, so many she felt overwhelmed. She couldn't think of everything, she couldn't get everything . . . but everything she did get was a small step toward keeping them alive and safe.

Maybe Jernigan was totally wrong, maybe he was nuts, or possibly a decent but gullible guy who'd been given bad information. An image of him flashed to mind. No, scratch "gullible" from any description applying to him. He didn't strike her as a man who trusted easily.

Someone was always hyping that next Tuesday, or next year, or a date on an ancient calendar, was going to be the end of the world. Knock on wood, so far they'd always been wrong.

That wasn't Jernigan. He didn't seem either gullible or nuts. She didn't know him beyond the most superficial acquaintance, but of all the people she could think of he struck her as the one who would know the most about what was going on in the world beyond Wears Valley.

He had seemed almost reluctant to warn her, but he had, and suddenly she wondered why. Was he telling everyone? Was he doing a Paul Revere, up and down the valley?

"When will you be back?" Carol asked.

"I don't know for sure, but before Olivia gets off the bus. Hold down the fort."

CHAPTER TWO

Sela was in the grocery store before she realized that except for canned soup and more instant coffee, she had little idea what to get to prepare for such a long time without power. Even more disconcerting, the store wasn't particularly crowded. Surely something of this magnitude couldn't be kept secret, even though there hadn't been the official announcement that she'd expected to see on her phone or on the radio or even an emergency siren sounding on the town's loudspeakers. So whatever was going to happen—if it was going to happen—not many people knew about it yet.

She started to bypass the produce section. There was no need to buy anything perishable. But still, as she passed the bananas she grabbed a bunch. They'd get eaten in the next couple of days, and damn it, if Jernigan was right they might not be able to get bananas for a while. And oranges. They'd need the vitamin C.

It had to be a false alarm. She prayed it was a false alarm, that nothing at all was going to happen. Halfway down the aisle she thought, "Bull, I'm not doing this," and turned around to replace the bananas and oranges because no way could she just walk off and leave a shopping cart for someone else to deal with, but then Jernigan's grim face flashed to mind and her heart started pounding and she returned to shopping. What would a couple of years' supply of canned chicken hurt, anyway?

Something about him inspired trust. Even though she couldn't say she actually believed a catastrophe was going to happen, because he said it would she had to tilt to at least 60/40 in his favor.

What did one buy when faced with the end of the world as she knew it? Chocolate?

At the end of the aisle, with nothing but bananas and oranges in her cart, she pulled her cell phone from her pocket and searched "survivalist necessities." Several prepper websites came up, and she picked the top one, which provided a long list of specialty items she couldn't possibly find in Kroger. The second site she chose was more practical, for her current situation.

Bleach, matches, water, candles . . . Okay, those were doable, and not even unusual. There were several items on the prepper's list that were more camping gear than anything she was going to find in a grocery store, but there were also some practical suggestions. She might be able to find some of the more expensive survivalist items at an outdoor goods store, but there was nothing close, and besides . . . this was just in case.

Prepare for the worst, expect the best. In this case, expect nothing.

She grabbed more toilet paper and canned meats—Spam, salmon, chicken, beef, multiples of each. Four big jars of peanut butter wouldn't last long, so she made it six. She made a quick trip down the feminine hygiene aisle, then got some first-aid items: aspirin, antiseptic cream, bandages, Vaseline. She grabbed anything that looked like it might be useful, as she walked through the pharmacy section. While waiting for Carol's prescription refills, she made another trip up and down the aisles, got more adhesive bandages, and an Ace bandage. More adhesive bandages. Another Ace bandage. No, make that three.

By the time the prescriptions were ready, her shopping cart was full.

She looked at the collection of stuff and blew out a big breath.

She'd gotten only things they'd eventually use anyway, so she didn't feel bad about her shopping spree. She had hedged her bets and done something. Did she have enough supplies for several months? No. Was she better off than she'd been when she'd started? Absolutely.

According to the sites she'd checked out, she should have a water filtration system for safe drinking water, heirloom seeds for growing her own food next summer, and enough freeze-dried food to get her by until then. She didn't.

Jernigan probably did, though.

When she checked out she paid with a credit card. Nothing she'd bought was very expensive, but she wanted to conserve her cash.

If they were without power for months, would cash be any good? Perhaps. As long as people saw value in pieces of green paper, it would be. Cash would be a way to get items they needed and didn't have. The bank was on her mental list of places she needed to go. She'd withdraw a nice bunch of cash from both her personal and the store account. If nothing happened she could re-deposit the money in a couple of days.

Feeling like a crazed squirrel, she darted from place to place, completing one errand after another.

As she drove home just after lunch, exhausted from the stress of hurry hurry hurry, she suffered a passing second thought. If Jernigan had been pulling her leg, if he was crazy, or even, hell, if he'd just been given bad information . . . she was going to be so pissed, maybe even pissed enough to get in his face and tell him about it, though confrontation wasn't her style at all.

But if disaster did strike, she'd really be pissed because obviously anyone in the electric energy business should have known this was possible and taken steps to make sure it didn't happen. Yes, definitely pissed, and deeply grateful, because without the chance to prepare she would've been in no better shape than anyone else. As she drove back into Wears Valley she glanced toward Cove Mountain. "Thanks," she said aloud. "I think."

Carol rolled her eyes a bit at Sela's haul of groceries, but helped her get everything organized. "You think you got enough Spam?" She busied herself stacking the oblong cans, her lips twitching in a smile.

"I'll remind you that you said that, if this thing happens and you run out of food. Besides, I got stuff that we can put on the store shelves if nothing happens." Sela and Carol both knew that whatever one of them had belonged to the other, too, because family took care of family. If Sela had Spam, then Carol had Spam.

They got the supplies divided, added things from the shelving, and Carol loaded everything into her car to take to their respective houses. Customers came and went, enough that Sela stayed busy, and none of them looked worried or said anything about an imminent disaster. Carol returned, and went into the office to watch TV while Sela puttered around cleaning, straightening, waiting on customers. The old-fashioned Kitty-Cat clock on the wall, which she kept because she liked the swinging tail, clicked past one P.M. Surely if anything was going to happen whoever was in charge of getting out the warning would have gotten it done already.

With every passing second her doubt grew stronger, and she began feeling more and more like a gullible fool. Word should be getting out—if there was any word—around the world. Astronomers would know, NOAA would know and might even have it up on their website, in which case Twitter and all the other social media platforms should be exploding with the news . . . if there was any news. If, if, if! Maybe she should go to the NOAA site herself and see if anything was there—

The store was empty of customers and she was just reaching for her phone when it sounded a high-pitched alarm, like that for violent storms. She jumped and automatically turned to look out the window, just as she had when Jernigan had first mentioned an emergency, but the sky was still a beautiful September clear blue. There wasn't a cloud in sight.

Her mind raced with other possibilities. It could be an Amber Alert, or a monthly test. There were plenty of options, but her heart was suddenly pounding and she knew damn well it wasn't any of the usual emergencies that caused the alarm. From the office, where Carol was watching TV, she heard Carol's cell phone start bleating its own alert and the hairs on the back of her neck stood up.

She grabbed the phone from beneath the counter and there it was on the screen, the alert she had both doubted and expected. She and Carol both got their alerts via Sevier County's CodeRED system, so she knew Carol was reading the same thing: NOAA ALERT GEOMAGNETIC STORM K-INDEX 9 PREDICTED 3PM TOMORROW. PREPARE FOR EXTENDED POWER AND COMMUNICATION DISRUPTION.

Another alert, another message flashing on the screen: THIS IS NOT A TEST. REPEAT, THIS IS NOT A TEST.

Carol came out of the office, clutching her phone, her eyes wide. "Shit," she said softly.

Sela's mouth was abruptly dry and she tried to swallow. She leaned against the counter. "Double shit."

"I take it back about the Spam."

Twenty-four hours. They had approximately twenty-four hours in which to prepare, which meant Jernigan had been right not only about the danger but about the timing. Good God. What could they possibly do in just twenty-four hours that would get them through an "extended power disruption"? They needed months to get ready for something like this.

"Looks like you were right to listen to Jernigan," Carol added.

Her eyes looked a little wild, and her face had lost color. "Holy moly. But—they could be wrong, couldn't they? I mean, it could be like the big thunderstorms or ice storms they predict that never happen. We could dodge a bullet, isn't that what the weathermen always say when they're wrong?"

"I don't think a geomagnetic storm is like Earth weather, where a system can slow down or break apart." She wished that could happen, but she wasn't going to bet her life—or Carol's and Olivia's lives—on it. Her stomach clenched as she was overwhelmed by a sense of urgency, an adrenaline shock as her primitive survival instincts kicked in. Thank God, despite her doubts, she'd gone to the bank and the grocery store before everyone else knew what was going on. "Think! What else do we need to do to prepare?"

Carol just gave her a blank look. "I thought we were already prepared."

"We're a little better off than a lot of people, thanks to Jernigan. We have food. But what about wood for the fireplaces for this winter, what about oil for lamps? I meant to get oil and forgot. I picked up some candles, some batteries. If this goes on for a year or more—"

"A year!" Carol looked horrified. "You don't think—that isn't possible, is it?"

"I don't know. I don't think anybody knows." Except maybe Ben Jernigan, who was more likely to have a better idea than anyone else she knew. "He said months, possibly a year or longer." No need to specify who "he" was.

Carol sucked in a deep breath as the huge ramifications began washing over her. "Then we need ammunition. And whiskey."

"Ammunition?" Sela gaped at her aunt, but she wasn't questioning Carol's choices; she was horrified by the realization that they'd very likely need ammunition . . . and whiskey. Society as they knew it was built on electricity. There wouldn't be any going to the grocery store to pick up something for dinner. They might have to do what their mountain ancestors had done and hunt their food—except she didn't know how to hunt and felt nothing but anxiety at the possibility of having to learn. She did own a .22 rifle—she and Carol both did because she lived alone and Carol had Olivia to protect—but she'd shot it only a couple of times and was a long way from being capable of hunting.

She felt dizzy and her ears rang a little; there was that adrenaline rush again as another realization hit her. Shit. Carol and Olivia were her responsibility. They'd need her if things really did get bad. Carol was in her late sixties, and while she was in general good health she wasn't quite as active as she'd been just a few years ago. Olivia was fifteen. Enough said there.

Sela looked around the store, taking mental inventory and looking at the supplies on the shelves, thought about what she had stored in back. She tried to calculate what they'd need, and how much, but she couldn't make herself grasp what a year without power would mean, or decide what she should do.

Her immediate dilemma was that she could keep the store open and try to help her neighbors, or she could focus on her own family. Her shelf space was limited and she carried only basics, plus snacks; she'd be cleared out in no time, leaving nothing but the supplies she'd already set aside for their own survival.

Maybe she was a complete shit, but she decided with only a few seconds' thought that her focus had to be her family. Family first, family always.

She needed a plan of action. Almost any action was better than none.

She stuck her phone in the back pocket of her jeans as she walked out from behind the counter. "Olivia will be here soon," she said to Carol. Normally Olivia hung around the store for a while after the school bus dropped her off. She'd have a soft drink, maybe a candy bar or some chips. Sometimes, if they were lucky, she'd tell them about her day. Most afternoons she sat in the office near the back door and texted her friends before heading home. "I want the two of you to take what you can carry and go home. When you're there, start loading up the ice chests with ice, so the ice maker can keep working."

"Ice?"

"We have a day, maybe a little more, to collect ice to keep what perishables we have fresh." Some of it would melt, but the more they added to the ice chests, the better it would keep.

"You have the generator—"

"We'll need it more when winter gets here than we do now." Her generator was a small portable one, but it was strong enough to run the heat when the weather turned cold. What it wouldn't do was run a whole house; as far as that went, it wouldn't run at all when they were out of fuel for it. No matter how she looked at it, she was afraid they didn't have enough of anything.

For a few moments, Carol didn't move as she stared into the middle distance, doing the same thing Sela had done before, trying to come to terms with the awful possibilities.

Through the store windows they watched a car speeding down the highway, a blur headed out of town. It had been quiet before that, just a handful of vehicles moving at normal speed. Was the speeder leaving because of the alert? Word was definitely out, likely on television as well as through the national weather service, maybe by radio, if anyone listened to radio anymore.

Of course. The tourists that were the lifeblood of the Smoky Mountain towns would want to get home. In a rental cabin they'd have no long-term provisions, no way to hunker down for more than a few days.

And if they'd left family at home, they'd want to be there. Family would come first for almost everyone, just as it did for her.

An SUV with parents seated in the front seat and two young

children in the back pulled into the lot, moving too fast. The lurching vehicle pulled to one of the fuel pumps and stopped with a jerk. The man who'd been driving jumped out, swiped a credit card, and pumped ten dollars in gas before taking off again.

"Shut down the pumps," Carol said, rousing herself, but Sela had already done so.

She grabbed some plastic bags and went outside to the pumps, covering the nozzles, the usual signal that there was no gasoline available. Her supply was small to start with, and if she wasn't careful it wouldn't last long. Once the power was down the gas would have to be pumped out of the tanks by hand. It wouldn't be easy, but it could be done.

Her family was the focus, she reminded herself; they were most important in any crisis, but she did care about her friends and neighbors. She wouldn't hang them out to dry. About half the generators in the valley were fueled by gasoline. Some were propane-powered, but not hers, and not her closest neighbors'. Before the power went out she'd need to go online and research how to access the gasoline in the tanks.

Jernigan would know how.

She dismissed that stray thought. Not only was he not approachable, but she needed to know for herself; she needed to stand on her own two feet. She'd learned that the hard way, after her ex-husband walked out. A lesson learned hard was a lesson learned well, and now she stayed safe because taking chances with other people was a good way to get her life stomped on.

Fifteen minutes later the school bus stopped in front of the store, and a line of cars stacked up behind the bus. One driver seemed to think about passing, pulling into the other lane by a couple of feet, but then thought better of it. The bus doors swung open and Olivia danced down the steps. Fifteen, tall and lanky with wavy light brown hair like her father's, rest his soul, she was beautiful in a way only the very young can be. She was the light of Carol's life, and an important part of Sela's.

Olivia blew inside, her eyes wide. "Did you hear? All the teachers were going b.s. crazy. Well, some of them." Her phone signaled an incoming text, and she looked down. "What did they call it? A mass . . . something." She smiled at her phone as she read the text and then sent a quick and nimble-fingered response.

"Coronal mass ejection," Sela said.

"Solar storm, Mr. Hendricks said," Olivia said as she walked to the cooler to grab a Dr Pepper. Then she turned around and went down the center aisle. "Hey! Where are all the chips?"

"Put away," Sela said, watching the road. Traffic had definitely picked up. Most cars kept to a reasonable speed, but a few were moving way too fast in their rush to get out of Dodge—or in this case, the mountains. Making a quick decision, she took her keys off the hook and went to the door, locking it and flipping the Open sign to Closed. Why would she hang around here and let Carol prepare on her own? That didn't make sense. She had her own ice chests to fill, her own ice maker to put to work.

"Why are you closing up early?" Olivia asked. "Are you sick?"

"We have less than twenty-four hours to get ready for the CME."

Now Olivia looked confused. "Get ready how?"

Carol said briskly, "We might be without power for months. We'll need food, a way to cook it, and maybe even a way to stay warm if everything's not up and running by the time the weather turns."

Olivia didn't move for a few seconds, her eyes big and round as she pondered the impossible. Then she asked, "Are you serious? Months? Will my cell phone work?"

"Doubt it. Maybe it'll be bad," Carol said, "and maybe it won't. We won't know until about this time tomorrow. But we're going to be ready for whatever happens. The chips are already at the house, by the way, but don't get your hopes up. We're not opening a single bag until we've eaten all the fresh and frozen food. I have a cabbage I need to use before it goes bad, and the last of the tomatoes. We can't waste anything, not now."

"Unless they're wrong," Olivia said hopefully as she joined her grandmother. "I mean, this could be a false alarm, right? The mass whatever . . ."

"CME," Sela said as she joined the other women. "Just call it a CME."

"Yeah, that," Olivia said. "They could be wrong."

"Maybe," Sela said as she ushered her aunt and the teenager to the rear door, grabbing the bags she and Carol had prepped earlier in the afternoon on her way out. "But I don't think so."

Olivia, who had slung a couple of bags over her arms, was still looking at her phone. She was glued to the damn thing most of the time anyway, but surely she could understand that they were facing an enormous crisis and pay attention—

"We should unplug everything before the CME hits," Olivia said, reading from her phone. "That's what some guy at NASA is saying. It'll keep them from getting destroyed by a power surge, or something."

Olivia had been researching on her phone. Sela breathed a sigh of relief, and reminded herself not to let her anxiety get the best of her. She needed to be on her game, and Carol and Olivia were both stepping up to the challenge, too.

They'd be okay. They had to be.

CHAPTER THREE

Carol's house was a small two-story yellow clapboard with the luxury of an enclosed garage. It sat almost precisely in the middle of their small neighborhood, which consisted of Myra Road—barely wide enough for two cars to pass each other—and the three narrow, short roads that connected to it. Mature spruces and flowering shrubbery decorated the half-acre yard. In back was a small vegetable garden that Carol tended during the summer, but the plants had already ceased production and were brown and drooping.

Sela's house, tucked at the rear of the neighborhood and more private because of groups, either strategic or lucky, of spruce and fir trees that blocked most of the view of her neighbor to the left—and she had no neighbor to the right, because she was at the end of the road—was smaller and didn't have a garage. She did, however, have a much larger screened-in porch, one she used a lot, often having her breakfast out there where she could see Cove Mountain looming over the valley. With the way the road curved, her house was close to the store and in fact she sometimes walked there and back, using a path that was wide enough for an ATV, rather than driving; walking it was not quite half a mile, while driving meant turning back toward the highway, and added a couple of miles. The back way, as they called it, was a favorite cut-through of kids and grown-ups alike, bypassing the highway and offering a good place to ride bikes and generally be a kid. There were large shade trees, a lazy stream or two in which to cool off, picnic beside, or try to catch frogs and darting little fish. She loved walking the trail in winter, especially in the snow when everything was so silent and pristine, the only sound that of her boots crunching in the snow, the only movement that of the occasional bird. The back way skirted properties, dipped and curved, and gave an occasional glimpse of a house. She was more wary during the warm months because of the bears, as were all the locals. The Smokies and black bears went hand in hand.

They lived in the middle of a gorgeous, peaceful scene, which made the impending catastrophe seem like a tall tale one of the local old men might spin while sitting in one of the service stations, telling yarns with his buddies.

The three of them entered the coolness of the house and, without asking, Carol got a couple of glasses from the cabinet, put some ice in them, and poured tea from a full pitcher she took from the refrigerator. The three of them took their seats around the table in the eat-in kitchen.

Olivia fished her tablet out of her backpack and turned it on—then she turned a stricken expression on her older relatives. "Will this still work . . . you know, *after*?"

They all looked at each other. Finally Sela lifted her shoulders. "It should. I think. Except for going online. You'll be able to access anything that's already on there, as long as you don't have it plugged in when the CME hits. Make sure it's charged before then." She hoped she was right. The thing was, no one knew for sure, because a CME this powerful hadn't hit since the dawn of the electronic age.

Olivia paused, then turned off the tablet and returned it to her backpack and instead got a pad of paper and pen from the kitchen counter, where Carol kept a running grocery list. "This won't run down my battery," she said matter-of-factly.

Despite the gravity of the situation, Sela and Carol both chuckled.

A lot of people would be coming to the same conclusion very soon, if they hadn't already done so.

Olivia wrote a big "1" on the paper. "So, what should we do first?"

"Shelter and food are the most important," Sela said. "And we've got that covered, as best we can." But there wasn't enough food, not for the duration if it lasted a year or longer, and maybe not even enough to last until next summer when the gardens would be producing again. "I'll get more food if I can, though. If we have enough, we'll share with the neighbors."

"You should move in here with us," Carol said firmly. "We'll be sharing supplies anyway. That way there'll be just one house to heat."

Carol's proposal was pure common sense, but Sela's stomach tightened at the thought of moving in with them. She liked being alone, liked the quiet. She'd never been a social butterfly, but since her divorce she seemed to need even more alone time. Adam's betrayal and rejection had shredded both her courage and her self-confidence; building herself back took a lot of time and thinking, of just *being*. For a while after returning to Wears Valley to live, she'd barely been able to make herself leave the house; only the necessity of earning a living had spurred her on.

She wasn't adventurous. She didn't like putting herself forward. She'd never had the yearning to do anything risky, and her refusal to do so had eventually led to Adam feeling nothing but disgust for her. She wouldn't try strange foods, she wouldn't go snow skiing even though Adam loved it, and she didn't like for him to drive fast. She liked the *idea* of foreign travel, but when it came to actually planning a trip, she began thinking of everything that could go wrong and would eventually back out.

She didn't blame Adam for leaving her. She blamed herself for being such a nothing-burger. Right now she wanted to refuse Carol's invitation/command, but the truth was that as much as she liked being alone, she wasn't certain she could cope without electricity.

There was the sound of a car turning in the driveway, and Carol craned to the side to look out the living room window. "It's Barb."

Barb Finley was Carol's best friend and had been for years, even before they had each been widowed. Barb was a few years older, and the two women looked as if they'd have nothing in common. Where Carol was lean, Barb was fluffy. Carol had that dashing pink streak in her hair, while Barb kept her white hair severely styled. Carol was style, Barb was comfort. But the two got along like a house on fire, and spent hours cooking together and gossiping and laughing. Sometimes Sela would take Olivia for a week and the two older women would take off for the Outer Banks. Olivia had gone with them once, and after their return had whispered to Sela that *no matter what* she never wanted to do that again, so Sela earned bonus points from both Carol and Olivia for stepping up and taking Olivia while the two friends went gallivanting off on their adventures.

Carol went to the front door and opened it. "Come on in," she called. "We're making a list of what we need to do." Then she returned to the kitchen to get down another glass for iced tea.

Barb's expression was tense as she came in the door. She was limping a little, and there was an elastic bandage around her left ankle. "What happened to your ankle?" Sela asked, getting up and moving to the other side of the table so Barb could take her chair, which was closest to her.

"Turned it this morning when I was cutting the grass." She sank onto the chair and wrapped her hands around the glass of tea that Carol set in front of her, but didn't drink. She took a deep breath and her eyes filled with tears. "Is this"—she gave a distracted wave that appeared to include the universe—"*thing* really going to happen? I don't know what to do. If there's no electricity my security system won't work; anyone can break in with no warning, and I won't be able to call for help, either. Our cars will run out of gas, there won't be enough food, I don't have a fireplace for heat and can't cut firewood anyway—"

"You'll move in here," Carol promptly said, breaking into Barb's panicked litany though she darted a concerned look at Sela even as she said it. She gave Carol a small nod, telling her it was okay she'd asked Barb instead. Okay? Sela was downright relieved.

Barb's face crumpled with relief. "Really? Is there room?" She looked at Sela. "I thought you'd—"

"No, I'm staying in my house," Sela said firmly. "Carol and I are combining supplies and I'll eat here, but I'm sleeping at home."

"Won't you be safer here?" Bless her, despite her deep gratitude at being invited to stay with Carol, she was persistent in trying to take care of Sela, too.

"I'll be as safe as I've ever been, living alone," Sela said practically. She had a small portable generator, but it made more sense to move it to Carol's house since three people would be here, and she herself would mostly be here except for the nights. She would keep warm with her wood-burning fireplace for heat, backed up by her kerosene heater. She'd be stingy with the heater because she didn't have an unlimited supply of kerosene . . . and that reminded her they should get down to business. In a pinch, she could share a room with Olivia or Carol, but that would be a last resort. She needed her own space.

She tapped Olivia's sheet of paper. "Number two: we need more wood. Oh crap! I forgot about getting gas and kerosene! I'll fill a few five-gallon cans at the store, so we'll have enough on hand to run the generator until we use everything in the fridge and freezer, but we have to buy kerosene."

Olivia dutifully wrote it down, and the three older women looked at each other with worry in their eyes. Everyone else would be thinking the same thing, and the window for acquiring those supplies was rapidly closing.

"Dear God," Sela said, getting to her feet. "I need to be working on that right now."

"I'll help," Carol said, also rising. "First things first. Barb, go back to your house and get what you want, bring it back here. Olivia, go with her to help. Bring all your food, Barb, batteries, flashlights, oil lamps—"

"And ammunition and whiskey," Sela added, with a quick smile at her aunt.

"I don't have any ammunition," Barb said smartly, and smiled. "Get all the produce you can grab, and we'll work all night canning it. I have lots of jars and lids. I meant to put up a lot of food this summer but always found something more fun to do. That'll teach me."

All over the valley, Sela thought, people were probably coming to the same conclusion and hauling out their pressure cookers. She hoped they were, anyway. She'd never done any canning herself, but that was about to change.

"Chop-chop," Carol said, and they all headed out on their assigned errands.

Carol had two fuel cans at her house and got them; Sela had one at hers, which she fetched, and five new ones in the store. She stopped there, darted in to get them, then she and Carol evenly divided the cans and went their separate ways.

She half expected someone to pull up to the door, looking to clean off her shelves. But the cars that were on the road didn't even slow down. There weren't enough supplies in her little store to tempt anyone. If there was, she wouldn't be heading to town herself.

Sela could barely pay attention to her driving. Her thoughts were doing the crazed rabbit thing again. What else would they need? Duct tape. She didn't know why, but duct tape seemed important. Salt, lots of salt; sugar, flour, cornmeal, powdered eggs, powdered milk, any basic food stuff that wouldn't need refrigeration. Anything canned—literally, anything.

She imagined before this was over, people would be eating whatever they could get, even things they never would have touched before. She'd bought what seemed like a ton of stuff earlier in the day, but viewing it from the other side of the official warning, she knew they'd need more.

Town was chaos. The grocery store parking lots were full, with people driving up and down the aisles looking for parking spaces. She couldn't find a break in traffic to make the left turn, so went up to the traffic light—for some reason people were still obeying the lights—and circled around to enter the parking lot. It was a useless effort; there was literally nowhere to park. She spotted some open space on the grass in front of Taco Bell and managed to squeeze in there before someone else grabbed the slot. So what if she was on the side of the road? So what if she got a ticket? She'd never had a ticket before, but this seemed like a good time to take the risk.

Her heart beating hard with urgency, she ran across the scorching heat of the parking lot and threw herself into the blast freezer of the grocery store, headlong into what seemed like just short of a riot. The aisles were packed with people grabbing whatever they could, wheeling carts left and right with none of the usual grocery store method. Barb had said get all the produce she could, but the produce area was so crowded she couldn't squeeze in. Skirting the edges, she took whatever she could reach. Bypassing the bread aisle, she then went to the canned goods and repeated the process, spurning nothing, getting what she could. Next was the baking goods aisle for staples like flour, sugar, powdered milk, and all the salt she could grab while other shoppers were doing the same thing. She was bumped, shoved, pushed, and once knocked into the shelving; she barely kept herself from going down.

The self-checkout lanes were closed down, and she stood in line for forty minutes before she got to the counter. It helped that some people were being refused checkout because they wanted to use either credit cards or checks. Handmade "Cash Only" signs hung above every register. They left their full shopping carts where they were standing, and the people still in line raided the carts to fill their own needs.

Thank heavens she'd hit the bank earlier and had cash on her, because normally she wouldn't have had much more than twenty bucks or so. If she were forced to abandon her supplies . . . she didn't know what she would do. She was already tense with stress and anxiety, fighting the sense of impending doom.

After paying, she wheeled the cart across the parking lot, jerking it over the curb onto the grass, and reached her white Honda CR-V. After the chill of the grocery store the sunny heat felt good on her skin. She put the groceries in the back seat, because the cargo area was full of empty fuel cans, and by the time she'd finished the chill had gone and she was beginning to sweat.

Heavy traffic snaked down the highway, as well as around and around the parking lot, and she had no idea how she was going to find a way to squeeze into a lane. She saw tense, almost predatory faces turned toward her as vehicles inched past; there was no way she could return the cart to the grocery store and leave her vehicle unattended; it would be broken into and her supplies stolen within half a minute. Her heart pounded from stress. If it was this bad now, what would it be like when there actually was no power, no food to buy?

The highway was impossible, so she bumped over the curb into the Taco Bell parking lot, and managed to weave her way, through parking lots and side streets, to a gas station that sold kerosene. The gas pumps were clogged, but she didn't need gas, thank God.

She was able to park next to the Dumpster, close to the kerosene pump. A whipcord lean white-haired man wearing overalls and a stained John Deere cap was at the pump, an unreadable expression on his face as he watched the parking lot turmoil. *Local farmer,* she thought. The old-timers like him would likely be the ones who got this area through the approaching crisis, because they knew how to grow food and how to get by without all the modern conveniences.

She noted the cost per gallon of the kerosene and did some quick math: she had four five-gallon fuel cans, for a total of twenty gallons. She pulled out the appropriate cash as she darted into the station and got in line to pay. Just as she had earlier, the station manager had stopped credit card payments. People were cussing, some under their breaths and some not, as they handed over their cash and complained that now they wouldn't have the money to get something to eat on their way home. Mostly tourists, she thought, catching a variety of accents. They were rightfully in a panic to get home; some of them might live so far away they wouldn't make it.

She kept an eye on her vehicle, making sure no one approached it. The people here weren't thinking about groceries, though, they were thinking about gasoline. Turning, she looked at the rows of shelving in the store: mostly empty.

The sense of unreality was so strong she wondered if there were camera crews hidden somewhere, secretly recording everything, because she felt as if she were in the middle of a disaster movie. No buildings were falling sideways, nothing was exploding, no one was screaming or fighting each other, but the tension and barely restrained panic were pushing at everyone. Tension crawled along her veins and she tried to think what she would do if someone *did* start fighting here in this crowded store. How would she get out? Should she get behind some shelving, or duck down to the floor and try to crawl out? Would she get trampled?

But nothing happened. Despite the tension, the line to pay inched forward. When she reached the clerk, a middle-aged woman whose own face mirrored the stress Sela felt, she handed over the money and said, "Kerosene. I have four five-gallon cans."

The woman nodded, and rang up the sale. Behind Sela, someone said, "I'll give you fifty bucks for those cans."

Sela didn't dare look back. She darted out the door and over to her vehicle, where she dragged out the fuel cans, lined them up, and filled them while keeping a weather eye out for anyone approaching her from behind. She'd never fought for anything or with anyone in her life, but she'd fight for these cans of kerosene.

Finally—*finally!*—she wrestled the heavy cans back into her SUV and slammed the hatch. With her peripheral vision she saw a man heading her way and she quickly used her remote to lock the vehicle, securing everything until she could get to the driver's door. Hearing the beep of the horn that signaled the lock engaging, the man halted, and turned away. Breathing fast, Sela unlocked the door, slid in, and quickly locked the vehicle again. She started the motor and the air-conditioning blew in her face, evaporating the sweat.

Slowly she reached out and turned off the air-conditioning. Mileage mattered, now more than ever.

The highways were clogged; she could see police and deputy cars crawling from motel to motel, blasting on their bullhorns that all non-locals should check out and get to their homes while they still could. At least the off-season had begun with Labor Day; the Rod Run had provided another spurt of tourists, but the crush had dropped drastically after that—at least until October brought the tree colors and tourists returned. There wouldn't be an October crush this year, she thought. But even during the off-season there were always tourists, and the weekends were crowded. She shuddered to think what the traffic would have been like if this had happened during one of the busy times.

The only way she could get home was to wind her away around secondary streets and roads until she hit Goose Gap. Even the secondary roads were crowded, though mostly with locals who knew how to avoid the traffic on the main drag. Eventually she had to hit the highway, though, and she sat for several minutes before there was a gap big enough for her to shoot into.

Fifteen minutes later she pulled into Carol's driveway and sat there shuddering in relief. Carol was already back, as well as Barb and Olivia. Olivia came outside and down the steps, coming to help her carry in supplies, and when she looked at that innocent, pretty young face, Sela thought again that, come hell or high water, she would protect her family—no matter what it cost her.

Carol had done better at gathering produce than Sela had. "I stopped at a couple of roadside stands," she said. "I knew town would be a madhouse."

That was an understatement. Sela didn't tell her aunt that she'd actually been frightened. Nothing had happened, and the man who had been approaching her SUV might have wanted to ask her where she got the fuel cans . . . though he *had* turned around when she locked the doors.

Carol and Barb were already shucking corn, and a pressure cooker filled with jars of tomatoes was doing its thing. Olivia got some sterilized jars out of the dishwasher, put another load of jars in, and started the machine. Sela got a glass of iced tea, guzzled it, then poured another glass before she sat down at the table to join the others in food prep. Everything they could do, even if they had to stay up all night, would help see them through the crisis.

Olivia helped, too, though she kept looking things up on her phone and detailing what dedicated preppers did. Some of the tips were good, some impossible at this late date. She also made a plate of sandwiches and put it on the table, so they could eat while they worked.

Yet another pressure cooker full was cooling down, and the sun had dipped behind the mountains to finally give them some relief from the heat, when Olivia looked out the window and said, "Gran, there's some people out there."

"What people?" Carol and Sela both went to the windows to look out, and saw a knot of people out front, with some others straggling in from their houses up and down the road. Barb shoved out of her chair and peered over Olivia's shoulder.

There was nothing like an impending disaster to bring people together. Sela couldn't remember the last time so many of her neighbors had gathered together. There were at least twenty people out there, standing around looking at the sky as if they could find answers written overhead. The point of contact seemed to be the middle of the narrow asphalt road, directly in front of Carol's house. Carol had lived here her entire life, and knew everyone; Sela had lived here for years, some of them before her divorce and all of them afterward, but she wasn't much on socializing and while she *mostly* knew the names of her neighbors, at least half of them she didn't actually know as individuals.

"Wonder what this is about?" Carol mused, but it was a rhetorical question because of course they were talking about the CME, and she was already heading out the door, crossing her porch, and going down the steps, with Olivia and Barb right behind her.

Sela followed more slowly, instinctively lagging back and trying to avoid attention. The background was always more comfortable for her than being front and center.

"Whattaya think about this solar storm business?" asked Mike Kilgore; he was a stocky, capable man, a self-employed plumber.

"Cops seem to be taking it seriously," Nancy Meador replied. As if to verify that, in the distance they suddenly heard a bullhorn, a deputy slowly driving around all the rental properties and advising tourists, for their own safety and survival, to immediately pack their belongings and head for home. A significant solar event was expected to happen in less than twenty-four hours, which could result in long-term power outage.

Nancy looked at Sela with a touch of censure. "I stopped by your store to pick up a few things, but no one was there."

Sela's instinct was to mutter "sorry," even though she had nothing to be sorry about.

A little boy about six years old began to cry. His dad put a hand on the kid's shoulder and said, "We'll be okay." His mother, who was holding a toddler, also put her arm around him and tried to comfort him. Sela tried to remember their names . . . Greer, maybe? She felt ashamed for not knowing her neighbors better.

People began talking, speculating. Their opinions and attitudes varied, from calm doubt that anything would happen to conviction that the world as they knew it would end, with everything in-between also represented. As Sela listened she realized that everyone had already made some effort to prepare, no matter what they believed.

"We're canning everything we can get our hands on," Barb said, and a couple of the older women nodded in agreement, while the younger ones, who were less likely to have a pressure cooker, looked scared.

"Bring your food over, and what jars you have, and we'll help those of you who don't know how to can," Carol offered. Of course she offered, as did the other older women. They began discussing who would go to whose house, what produce they had, how many jars—though jars would be a problem, because only people who canned were likely to hold on to glass jars.

Work. They had to work, and work hard, for as long as the electricity stayed on. And they would have to be stingy with their supplies, because they didn't *know* how much would be enough, or exactly what they would need. They were as unprepared as the first settlers from Europe setting foot in the New World . . . well, maybe not. They did have the farmers and the old people, ample game for hunting, and plenty of fresh water. When she thought about it, right there where they were, in Wears Valley, they had everything they needed for survival.

The crowd shifted, from one large gathering to several smaller ones. Sela stood back and listened, picking up bits and pieces of several conversations. Several men talked about security, making plans to start a community watch. One woman said she had her dehydrator working overtime, drying the last of the summer garden veggies. Another was making soup and canning it. Eventually the last of the panic faded, at least outwardly, and was replaced by preparation. Sela could only hope it was the same everywhere, though she knew it wouldn't be.

The sound of her own name caught her attention and she snapped her head around.

Barb smiled at her, looking smug. "I nominate Sela."

She should have paid better attention to that particular conversation. "What?" No good ever came of being nominated for anything.

"We'll need someone to be in charge."

"In charge of what?" It didn't matter. Thanks, but no thanks. *Being in charge* wasn't in her DNA.

"Getting things organized," Nancy replied. "You have common sense, and your ego won't get in the way."

No, no chance of that. But the idea of being in charge of anything other than her store and herself filled her with a sense of dread. "Really, I don't think—"

Barb interrupted. "The people who don't want leadership are the ones who should have it. The ones who shouldn't be in charge are always the first to raise their hands. There are assholes everywhere." She darted a quick look in Olivia's direction to see if the teenager had been close enough to hear. She wasn't, and likely Olivia and her friends said much worse than that, but still. "Pardon my French," she added in a lowered voice.

The next thing she knew, Sela was surrounded. Not just by her aunt and friends, but by several other smaller groups. There were fifteen houses in this little neighborhood, and at quick count it appeared that every home was represented by at least one resident. And they were all looking at her.

"So?" Barb prodded. "What do we do?"

Neighbors ranging in age from five to seventy-five looked at her as if she should have all the answers. She threw a panicked look at Mike Kilgore, but he held up his hands and shook his head. "Don't look at me. I don't have the patience. Tell me what to do and I'll do it, but I know my shortcomings."

The thing was, Sela knew hers, too, and being forceful enough to lead anything wasn't in her wheelhouse.

On the other hand, what they needed at this point *was* organization more than leadership. She ran her store, kept the inventory ordered and organized. She could do that much, get them at least on the same page so things that needed to be done got done but efforts weren't duplicated.

Olivia was watching her. If she refused, what would that teach Olivia about stepping up, about being strong even against her own inclinations? She wasn't Olivia's only role model, but still—being a role model sucked.

She blew out a breath, thought a minute, then said, "We need a plan not just for this street, but for the entire community." There were about six thousand residents in Wears Valley, give or take. Thanks to the topography, they were pretty spread out. It was a rural area, an unincorporated township. They had no organized form of government. "Okay, everyone think. While we still have phones and internet, let's contact everyone we can and set up a community center." There was one logical answer. "Tomorrow afternoon, if we get hit the way they say we will, we'll meet at the school. Everyone who wants to attend can, but at the very least each neighborhood should be represented. We need a list of residents, their addresses, next . . . next of kin and how to contact them." That was hard to say, but had to be put out there. "Put the word out, try to get as many people to attend as we can. The people who can walk the distance, should, to save gas. At the very least people should share rides. Once we're there, we'll make a plan for the days to come."

Days, she said, not weeks and months. She didn't want to bring the panic back to those who had managed to dismiss it.

"We can elect a community leader at that time." So far as she knew, they didn't even have a county deputy who lived in the area, but she might be wrong about that. There was a forest ranger, she thought, but she'd heard he retired.

One thing for sure: her little neighborhood might have nominated her to get things organized, but she certainly wouldn't be voted on to lead the entire community.

One of the men who'd been talking about upping security spoke up. "Who's going to contact that Jernigan guy up on Cove Mountain? He's retired military, right? That's what I heard. He'd be an asset."

If they only knew. Sela and Carol both kept their mouths shut. No one needed to know Jernigan had given them a heads-up about the solar storm several hours before everyone else found out.

A few people nodded their heads in agreement and one asked if anyone had his phone number.

It appeared no one did, no surprise there, and eventually Mike Kilgore offered to drive up in the morning and ask Jernigan personally to join in on the community plans. The men would no doubt prefer someone like Ben to be in charge, and to be honest so would she. But she didn't think he'd agree. In fact, she was almost certain he wouldn't.

As twilight deepened, a few people still stood around talking but most began wandering back to their homes, to prepare, to wait, to call loved ones they might not be able to talk to for a while. Maybe some would cry, or try to convince themselves that despite the warnings nothing would happen. Different people coped in different ways.

Sela was exhausted. She murmured a vague excuse about going in to check on something, though there was nothing to check, and went back into Carol's house. It had been a hellish—and hellishly long—day, and she just wanted to go home. Home wasn't possible just yet, unless she was willing to leave Carol and Barb to do all the work of canning their produce, which she wasn't.

She began pulling stuff out of the refrigerator to throw together a meal. *Perishables first*, she thought. That meant the luncheon ham needed to be eaten. Okay, ham and cheese sandwiches it was.

Olivia was teary-eyed when she came inside, just ahead of Carol and Barb. "I want to talk to Josh," she said, "but he isn't answering his phone."

"He's probably on duty," Sela said practically. "Every active-duty soldier will be preparing. Send him a text, tell him to call whenever he can regardless of the time." Carol had to be as worried about her grandson as Olivia was, but she was holding it together for her granddaughter's sake.

As far as that went, Sela wanted to know that her cousin was safe, too, and maybe find out some preparations the military was making. And after that she wanted nothing more than to go home and sleep, though she doubted sleep was coming anytime soon.

First, though, there was work—a lot of work. They had to do what they could while the power was still on.

CHAPTER FOUR

Mike Kilgore was a man who kept his word; he set out the next morning for Ben Jernigan's house, high on Cove Mountain. He didn't look forward to his task, because from what he'd heard Jernigan wasn't the friendliest man in the valley, but Mike had been in the military himself and he figured that might give them some common ground . . . or not. He wouldn't know until he got there.

The morning news was not good, and already cell service was spotty, satellites were going out . . . it looked as if they'd better prepare for the worst. Mike didn't like thinking about that. He'd seen what he'd thought was the worst, in Desert Storm a quarter of a century before, then found out what was going on now was worse than his worst—and when the power grid went down, what happened in the cities would rank right up there. He felt sick to his stomach thinking about it, so instead he focused on what was right around him, on his family and neighbors, on Wears Valley. Think small; he could handle that. But the valley needed help, needed leadership who knew what the hell was what, and he figured the best man for that was Ben Jernigan.

The early-morning mist still clung to patches of ground as he navigated the turns and curves that wound around and up the looming hulk of Cove Mountain. September was a dry month, but all the vegetation produced moisture and an ecosystem that gave the mountains their descriptive name of Smoky. In a few weeks the leaves would begin turning color, but right now the heat still lingered. That was good, he thought; people wouldn't have to use resources to stay warm. Everyone would have to learn how to be stingy with what they had, to make it last through the winter.

He turned off the almost-two-lane road onto a narrow, paved one-lane, a private road meant only for the residents of the houses built along it. There was no through traffic, no side roads branching off it. If he remembered correctly, though it had been years since he'd been up here, the road grew narrower and narrower, the paving gave out and became gravel, and it was damn steep.

Up ahead on the right he could see a man pushing a lawn mower over a narrow strip of grass beside the road. Out of caution he slowed, and pulled as far to the left as he could and still stay on the pavement. The man looked up, then to Mike's mild astonishment held up his hand and stepped out into the middle of the road.

Wants to talk, ask if there's any news, Mike thought, and obligingly slowed. He didn't recognize the man, but several of the houses up here were vacation homes. Huh. If this was a vacationer, he should have gone home. Maybe he'd moved here permanently. It was impossible, even for the old-timers, to know everyone who lived in the valley.

As he rolled to a stop, he tried to keep his mouth from falling open. This guy looked like Teddy Roosevelt, complete with pith helmet and mustache. And he wore a khaki shirt and khaki shorts, with black shoes and brown socks.

He lowered the passenger-side window and leaned over. "Mornin'," he said in greeting.

Teddy Roosevelt bent over and looked in the window, a stern, disapproving expression on his face. "This is a private road," he said. "What are you doing here?"

Mike's hackles rose a little, but he kept his face pleasant. Maybe everyone should start being more cautious. "I know. I'm going to visit someone."

"Who?"

The hackles rose even more. For one thing, Mike was driving his work pickup with the magnetic sign proclaiming *Kilgore Plumbing* on both sides, along with his phone number, so it wasn't as if he would be looking for a place to ransack. Instead of answering the question he countered with one of his own: "Who're you?"

"I'm Ted Parsons. I own this house here." The man indicated the house behind him, a spacious-looking D-log cabin like tourists mostly preferred, thinking it looked mountainy.

From his accent, Mike knew the man wasn't local, at least not born-and-raised local. "Vacation house?"

The man's face went stiff. "I'll give your question back to you: Who are you?"

"Look at the sign on my truck," Mike said. "Mike Kilgore, plumber."

Teddy—Ted—glanced down at the sign. "Someone call you?"

Hell with this. Mike mentally rolled his eyes and lied. "Yes. Why?"

"Who?"

"Mister, if you can tell me why it's any of your damn business who has a leak in their bathroom, I'll give you all the information you want. But since I'm guessing you can't, I'll be on my way." He buzzed up the window and hit the gas, forcing faux-Teddy to step back or get his toes run over. God almighty. He hoped the guy didn't live here, and would soon be hightailing it for home—something he should have done yesterday. But idiots abounded in all areas, and Lord knew the valley had its share of homegrown ones. The one thing they didn't need was more.

Ben mentally ran through everything he'd done yesterday, the supplies he'd gathered, what he already had on hand, what he'd done to protect his equipment, and figured he was as ready as he was going to get.

He didn't consider himself a prepper, a survivalist, or an alarmist. He hadn't collected freeze-dried food, ammo, alternative power sources, and water storage because he expected the end of the world to be right around the corner. He was simply ready for whatever life decided to throw his way—and to minimize the necessity for contact with the rest of the population. He could easily weather the grid going down, without much change in his lifestyle other than having to preserve his gasoline, and making do when that ran out, but with his training that was no big deal. He could and did regularly hike miles through these mountains, partly to keep in shape, but also because the solitude and the ancient majesty of the mountains appealed to him.

Today was the SHTF day—when the shit hits the fan. Preppers and theorists had warned about it for a long time, and today was the day. The culprit wasn't a bad actor exploding a thermonuclear bomb in the atmosphere, it was the sun. The sun ruled everything on Earth, and they were about to be reminded of that in a big way.

Europe and most of Asia were already dark. News was scarce, because communications in those continents were down: power grids, satellites, land lines, all fried. The US military had hardened power sources and what little information was out there came from them, but they had their hands full with one crisis after another at bases and embassies around the world, and spreading the news wasn't their job. Their job was holding the line, protecting the country and its citizens, and every service member right now was focused on that. Still, there were some calls, some news leaking through on his ham radio though the atmosphere was getting screwier by the minute, and some texts.

The news wasn't good, and it wouldn't be for a long damn time.

He didn't have a television, didn't want one, didn't need one. He'd seen more than enough online. Many larger cities were already experiencing gridlock as the smart people tried to get out, and the stupid ones were trying to stock up on a couple of days of food thinking that would be enough. Some people were stuck because of their situations, maybe an ill family member they refused to leave behind, and he felt sorry for them because they were likely going to die. A big city wasn't built with long-term survival in mind. Too many people lived without having more than a couple of days' worth of food on hand. They couldn't imagine weeks or months without power, couldn't imagine not being able to stop for takeout, or at the market to pick up something to cook right then.

In some areas of the country the power was already out, or else spotty, because nuclear plants were already being shut down safely, powering down ahead of the CME. If the solar storm had come without warning, nuclear plants wouldn't have had time to do a safe, emergency power down, so they were doing it now.

And of course there were people who didn't believe anything would happen. Ben didn't know how people could ignore what was right in front of them, how they could even casually look at the news, find out Europe and Asia were dark, and still think it wouldn't happen to them. They went on about their lives as normally as they could, laughing at those who were making preparations. This wasn't Y2K. They wouldn't be laughing tomorrow.

He hoped Sela Gordon wasn't in that group. He'd done what he could, given her a heads-up. He could have—probably should have—gone to a bigger store in town for the few supplies he'd decided to add to his stash. No one there would have thought twice about his purchases, the way Sela had. Everything would've been cheaper, too. No small store could compete with a chain, pricewise.

He could've charged everything to his credit card, knowing the store wouldn't be able to collect for a long time, if ever, because all data before the coming grid crash could well be lost. Like everyone else, he wanted to conserve his cash. But when it came down to it, he didn't want to stiff Sela. She'd need cash, too, more than he would, because he was far more self-sufficient.

His errant second thoughts didn't last long. He simply hadn't been able to pass by her store without experiencing a gut-deep feeling that he should tell her what was coming. She wasn't his responsibility; no one was, but that didn't mean he was comfortable leaving her hanging. His read on her was that she was one of the gentle souls, a quiet, warm light in a world that needed all the warmth it could get. Gentle didn't mean weak, though, and he hoped she'd acted on his warning.

That single warning was where his desire to participate in life beyond his cabin ended. He expected he wouldn't see another living soul for months, maybe years, and that suited him just fine.

Don't tempt the devil.

No sooner had he had the thought than the motion alarm sounded, immediately proving him wrong. Hoping his visitor was a bear, he turned to check the video camera, and swore aloud. A middle-aged, slightly overweight man was huffing and puffing his way up the incline toward the porch, head down, steps short. His gaze narrowed, Ben took his Mossberg shotgun from its usual place by the front door and stepped outside.

He wasn't trying to be stealthy, because he wanted the visitor to realize he was there and not come any closer. At the sound of the door closing, the trespasser stopped, lifted his head, and immediately fixed his gaze on the shotgun. He lifted his right hand in a staying motion. "Mornin'. I'm Mike Kilgore, from the valley." He glanced over his shoulder. "You have a big-ass rock in your driveway. I had to park at the end of the drive and walk up."

"I know. I put it there. What can I do for you?" Ben's tone was matter-of-fact. He didn't intend to do anything, he just wanted this man gone.

Mike Kilgore took a couple of deep breaths so he could speak more easily. "We're trying to get organized, in case . . . you know. Things happen, people need to be notified. Anyway, no one had your phone number or someone would have called, so I volunteered to drive up and talk to you." He wiped the sweat off his face. The early morning was still fairly cool, but walking up the drive would wring a sweat from almost anyone. Ben could do it without effort, but he made a point of being able to do so. Graying hair stuck to Kilgore's temples, and his cheeks were unnaturally pink. "We're also putting together a list of contacts—you know, next of kin, in case something happens, to let them know after things normalize."

Ben gave a brief thought to his father, a rancher in Montana, who didn't give a shit about any of his kids. His mother was dead. His father had remarried and the other kids were Ben's half siblings, none of whom he was close to. They might be interested in knowing if he'd died, but only to find out if they'd inherited his stuff, in which case they'd be disappointed.

A good neighbor would invite the man in for a drink of water or even a cup of coffee, but Ben wasn't a good neighbor and didn't intend to be. He maintained his stance on the porch with the shotgun in his hand. If no one around had his phone number, then it should be obvious that he didn't want calls. Or visits.

But Mike Kilgore wasn't about to leave before he accomplished his mission. And now that he was closer, and Ben was seeing him in person, he altered his impression of Kilgore from "overweight" to "stocky muscular."

"Anyway," Kilgore continued, "the school will be our community meeting place. If the power does go down, that's where we'll gather this afternoon to get things organized. At times like this we need to band together, neighbor helping neighbor. We'd like to have you join us. You have some useful skills, and, hell, under some circumstances you might need us. I'm a plumber, by the way. Everyone eventually needs a plumber."

That might be a universal truth, but Ben didn't respond.

"My wife and I live on Myra Road, down the way from Sela Gordon." Kilgore swiped at his sweaty forehead. "You know Sela, right? Owns the little store on the highway? I think I've seen your truck there. Some of the women want her to be in charge, but"—he shrugged—"she isn't willing, and I'm thinking she might not be strong enough for the job, anyway. On the other hand, you'd be perfect."

"No." Ben's rejection was swift and flat. He had no desire to be in charge of anyone other than himself. He'd had enough of that in the military.

Kilgore took a step back. "Well, if you change your mind . . ."

"I won't."

He glanced at the shotgun. "Think about—"

Ben gave a deliberate, definite shake of his head.

Kilgore heaved a sigh. "Well, I tried. If you change your mind, come to the meeting at the school." He looked down Ben's driveway and scowled. "I'm going to have to back down the road a ways. There's no place to turn my truck around for at least half a mile."

"I know." Ben didn't offer assistance, or express sympathy. Kilgore would spread the word. He wouldn't be back, and neither would anyone else he talked to about Ben's lack of hospitality. And the shotgun. Perfect.

He stood on the porch and watched Kilgore leave. After the other man had trudged out of sight, Ben went back inside and stood the shotgun in its place beside the door.

He thought about Sela Gordon being in charge of the valley, and couldn't quite picture it. She was so damn quiet it was hard to tell, but he figured she was competent and probably better suited to the job than most, if she could develop a sense of command.

Ben's way of organizing would be to tell everyone they were on their own. Those who were unprepared had only themselves to blame. Those who had prepared would be okay, for the most part. People would die, and soon, but here in this part of the world, most would probably do just fine. They could hunt and forage, fish and barter with neighbors. Those who were so inclined would band together and make it work.

They didn't need him, and he sure as hell didn't need them.

Ted Parsons sat on his screened-in porch and looked out over the valley. It was always quiet here, but at the moment the silence was deeper than usual, more complete. Even the birds seemed to be hunkered down, waiting for the solar event to pass.

Most of the neighboring houses on his road had been vacated; they were rentals, though there were a few locals who lived here, like John Dabbs, the widower who lived up the hill a ways. John was a pain in the ass. Whenever Ted and his wife, Meredith, were here, John would come knocking on the door asking for something, anything, from coffee to a screwdriver or to borrow the lawn mower. John was a mooch. The fact that he hadn't been around likely meant he was visiting his daughter in Memphis. There were a couple of other full-timers, people Ted knew from the neighborhood association where they discussed things like upkeep on the road, and maybe doing some landscaping at the entrance, putting up a security light there. Ted was against both the landscaping and the security light. He didn't want to make the road look more inviting, or easier to find.

His vacation house was located in what he considered a prime spot on the side of the mountain, not so high that it was difficult to get to, but high enough that he had a nice view. He and Meredith tried to drive down from Ohio at least one long weekend a month, and they'd talked about retiring here when the time came. He considered himself as much a local as anyone else in the area. He contributed with his dollars, in taxes and purchases made in the valley and beyond. He made legitimate complaints to the agencies who managed the rental cabins on this road, when the grass grew too high or repairs needed to be made, or when renters parked on the street or worse, in Ted's own driveway. Why the hell would people think they had the right to park in someone else's driveway?

Yesterday a sheriff's deputy had knocked on his door and asked him to leave, because "tourists should go home while they could." He was still pissed about that. He wasn't a damn tourist, he owned this property, and so what if he didn't live here full-time? This was still his property and he belonged here as much as anyone else did. They should've been asking for his help, not attempting to run him out of his own house. He knew how to run things, how to take charge and give orders.

If nothing happened, he and Meredith would go home when they'd originally planned to, on Sunday. If the CME did hit and it was as bad as it had been predicted to be, then they were in a good place right here. He'd never admit it aloud, but he'd be disappointed if the scientists were wrong and when this was all over nothing changed. There were opportunities to be had in a crisis, if someone—like himself—was smart enough to seize those opportunities.

Meredith walked onto the porch, phone in hand. "My texts won't go through. It just keeps spinning and spinning!" Her voice trembled and her hands shook. He immediately got up and put his arm around her. Not being able to get in touch with the kids, or her family, would weigh on her. He didn't want her upset, not with her weak heart.

"The systems are overloaded, with everyone trying to call and text," he said soothingly. "You know everybody's okay, you talked to them yesterday." They'd been married thirty-four years, and he couldn't imagine life without her. Almost losing her to a heart attack ten years ago had shaken him to his core. Ted didn't like most people, their stupidity got on his nerves, but Meredith was his center. He'd do anything to protect her. She was soft where he was strong, but she didn't need to be strong. He was strong enough for both of them.

Like him, she was fifty-six years old, though her skin was still smooth and her expression habitually pleasant. With her light brown hair and blue eyes he'd always thought she had an angelic quality to her, and it infuriated him when people took advantage of her.

She sat down and he resumed his seat; she was clasping her phone and looking at it as if she expected it to ring at any moment. "We should have gone home," she said, not for the first time. "The gas tank is full, we would have made it."

"We're better off here."

"But—"

He shook his head. "The kids aren't there. They said they'll be fine, and they have their own families to take care of. There's nothing you can do to help them. They're too far away." Both his kids had moved out of Ohio right after college. Ted Jr. was living in Washington State with his new wife, and Kate had moved to Texas for a decent job. "They're tough. They'll be okay." Not everyone in the family was tough, but that wasn't his problem. "Your sister and your mother will just have to fend for themselves."

He waited for another "but" that didn't come. Meredith's family was a big factor in his decision not to go home. They were constantly running to her with their problems, stressing her out, expecting her to give them "loans" when they overspent—which they never repaid—complaining about the deadbeat men her sister hooked up with when she kept choosing one loser after another, and their mother always defended her sister and guilted Meredith into coughing up more money. The last thing he and Meredith needed was to have to deal with those two leeches.

He'd never say so to her, but he hoped they both died. Meredith would be upset, but she'd be better off in the long run.

Thinking about it, he decided an electromagnetic pulse would be a better disaster than a CME. If a surprise attack had taken down the power grid without warning, no one would have been able to leave. Cars would've been damaged—some of them, anyway. The chaos would've been immediate and devastating.

No one would have come around to demand that he leave his own damn house.

A man could make a name for himself in a disaster like this one. Some would survive this crisis, even thrive, but others wouldn't. He intended not only to survive but to be a leader.

There would be a meeting this afternoon at the elementary school. No one had told him about the meeting, and that stung a bit. He'd seen the news in an informational crawler on a Knoxville television station, shortly before his TV satellite had gone out, and he planned to be present. Someone had to tell these yahoos how to organize and what needed to be done. A lot of the people who lived around here had never traveled much beyond east Tennessee; their ignorance would be massive.

He scanned the valley, thinking. There would be food at the school, at the restaurants, at the convenience stores and gas stations. The liquor at the moonshine place would be as good as gold in the coming months. So would the apple butter and fudge and relishes at the country store next door to the moonshine cabin. Someone would have to take control of the available commodities.

Ted was good at taking control. He'd owned his own business for years. In the beginning he'd been at the tire store, that first location, seven days a week. He'd worked his ass off. Now he owned six stores and had competent managers in each one. It was no longer necessary that he be involved in the business, though he did like to drop into those stores unannounced and stir things up a bit to keep his managers on their toes.

His stores would suffer during this crisis, as would all commerce, but when it was over he'd rebuild. He'd get by. He was a survivor, and he'd take care of Meredith.

They had enough supplies on hand to get by for a short time. Everything else he might need was located in the valley below. All he had to do was take control of it. All he had to do was stir things up a bit.

CHAPTER FIVE

Olivia burst into the kitchen where Sela, Carol, and Barb were still preparing and canning as much food as they could. While the power was still on, the work couldn't let up. "I heard from Josh!" she said, waving her phone at them, then burst into tears.

"Oh, honey." Carol dried her hands and went to Olivia, put her arms around her. "That's such a relief. How is he? Is he still on base?"

Olivia wiped her eyes and showed the text message to Carol.

"'I'm good,'" Carol read aloud. "'We're prepared, have backup systems. I won't be able 2'—he used the number two instead of the word *to*, I taught him better than that—'get leave for a long time, so take care of yourself. Tell Gran I said hi, & love U both.'"

Carol wiped her own eyes. "What a load off my mind. I figured the military would be fine, but hearing him say it makes me feel better." She gave Olivia another squeeze, then rejoined the food prep.

Sela glanced at the clock, did some calculations. "Olivia, if you'll shell the last of those peas, we'll have time to get them in the pressure cooker before time runs out."

Olivia made a face, because she'd already discovered she hated shelling peas—and shucking corn—but she sat down without protest and picked up a pod. They didn't have a lot of peas left, maybe enough to fill five or six pints. Barb had made some fresh bread in her bread-making machine, and Sela had baked a couple of dozen corn bread muffins. They'd get stale, but they'd last longer than soft bread.

They'd done what they could. They had just a few more hours before the CME hit. Sela wished someone could tell them the exact time, but a solar storm didn't obey anyone's schedule. Nature was awe-inspiring and powerful, and nothing on Earth was more powerful than the sun.

She was so proud of Olivia, who had pitched in with the food prep but gladly escaped when she could, and they'd let her because sometimes the kitchen got too crowded with all of them working their butts off. Olivia had taken the warning about unplugging everything to heart, not only seeing to the chore in their houses, but warning neighbors. The only things plugged in now were what they were actively using, which were all in the kitchen. Olivia had continued to text her friends, but the topic of conversation seemed to be all about the CME, and texts were already sporadic. At Sela's suggestion, Olivia had also gone back and forth between Carol's house and Sela's, getting all the laundry done. Any crisis was better faced with clean clothes.

Carol's satellite TV was already out, but she had a backup antenna that picked up the local channels from Knoxville, and the small TV in the kitchen was on. Though there was some interference, the occasional static or blip or both, they were able to watch the wall-to-wall local news coverage while they worked. News anchors were trained to inject all the drama they could into any news event, but now they all looked genuinely scared. It was definitely time to worry.

Sela kept an eye on the clock, and when she judged it was time she said, "Olivia, you should go take a shower and wash your hair while we still have hot water. All of us need to do that, so wash as fast as you can."

Olivia raced up the stairs, and was back down in ten minutes with her long hair wet and slicked back. "You go next," Carol firmly told Sela. "Your hair is longer than mine and Barb's, and you'll need time to dry it. We're almost finished here, anyway."

That wasn't quite true; there was still cleaning to be done. But it was also true that Sela's hair was thick and heavy, and wouldn't dry before bedtime unless she used a blow-dryer on it. Something else to plan for, she thought as she climbed the stairs: with the power out, she'd have to wash her hair early enough in the day that it could dry. She'd seen movies and read books where the female character sat by a fire drying her hair, and never thought the practice anything more than romantic or picturesque. Suddenly she had a very different take on the situation. Every mundane thing would become more difficult, require more planning.

Like Olivia, she rushed through the showering process; she wanted to linger, to savor, knowing this might be the last hot shower she'd have in a long time, but this wasn't a time for lingering. When she was dressed again she took the blow-dryer downstairs with her, to clear the way for the next one to shower.

By the time everyone had taken their turn in the bathroom and the kitchen was cleaned up, time was getting close, and they didn't want to push their chances on destroying any of the kitchen appliances. The pressure cooker had finished with the peas, and the jars were sitting on the kitchen counter, cooling. The four of them ceremoniously unplugged everything except the little TV, which Carol had said she would sacrifice because it was old anyway and when the power came back on she'd get a new little flat screen for the kitchen.

"What do we do now?" Olivia asked, her eyes big.

Sela shrugged. "Wait." She hugged Olivia—all of them seemed to be doing that, reassuring the kid as much as possible—then took a seat at the table where she could see the TV. One by one, the others did the same. Olivia squeezed in between Carol and Sela, as if she felt safer there.

There was a scroll at the bottom of the screen that held their attention. Several communities had done what Wears Valley residents had and set up meeting places for this afternoon or tomorrow morning. Anyone in the area who hadn't been contacted might see the information on TV, if they still had access and if they were watching. At least three Knoxville radio stations had plans of their own. They'd scheduled ongoing updates at prearranged hours, though they also warned that for the first few days after the CME radio signals would be disrupted, so listeners shouldn't be alarmed if they had no reception.

Shouldn't be alarmed. Ha.

"*Radio,*" Olivia said in disbelief. "No one listens to radio."

"Sure they do," Barb countered. "And a lot more will now."

Sela's text alert sounded and they all jumped. She looked at the screen and said with relief, "It's Kristina." She'd texted her closest friends, Amy and Kristina, the night before. Amy had responded within an hour, assuring Sela that she was as prepared as she was going to get. She, her husband, Trace, and their two kids—both under five years old—had been visiting his parents when the alarm had gone out. Trace's folks lived on a farm a couple of hours away, and they had decided to stay there. Not only was the farm set up for a long period of self-sufficiency, Trace's parents were in their sixties and could use the help.

But she hadn't heard from Kristina, and she'd worried. Kristina lived in Gatlinburg, close enough that Sela could have gone there if she hadn't been so busy with all the food preparation. Kristina traveled a lot with her job, though, and when she thought about it Sela realized they hadn't been in contact for a week or so.

In Mississippi with Nathan & his family. Staying here. You okay?

She read Kristina's text aloud, then quickly tapped in a reply that they were good and Amy and Trace were with Trace's parents. Part of her wished her friends were close by, but common sense said they were better off where they were: with family. Kristina's parents had retired early and moved to Arizona, so she had no family close by. She'd been dating Nathan for about six months and things had been looking serious.

This would certainly be a compatibility test, Sela thought. They'd be living together, with Nathan's parents, whom Kristina had evidently just met, for no one knew how long.

What would it be like to face this crisis with a strong, dependable partner by your side? The errant thought blindsided her, and hard on its heels came another: *she* had always been the timid one, the one who dodged risk. Who would want to face this crisis by *her* side?

The realization was mortifying. She had to be tougher, smarter; she had to pull her weight, and more. She'd worried about Carol and Olivia stepping up, and they likely were thinking the same thing about her. Carol might have, anyway; Olivia was too young to be that analytical.

The coming crisis would test them all. She didn't want to be one of those who failed.

"I'm glad she's with Nathan and his folks," Carol said. "Being alone right now would be awful."

The three others nodded, all of them imagining how bad it would be to have no one to rely on.

"I'd feel better if I knew what to expect," Barb said, her soft face worried. "I don't mind hard work; that's how I grew up. I just need to *know*. What will work, what won't? What should we be doing, what should we forget about?"

For some reason, the others looked at Sela, as if she had the answers. She *had* spent some time reading up on CMEs, but that didn't make her an expert. How could anyone be an expert on something that hadn't happened in the modern world?

"All I can do is guess," she said slowly. "Texts should work—might work—even after the grid goes down, unless the CME fries the towers. They work on radio waves, right? The radio stations all say the waves will be wonky for a few days. After that . . . maybe. But cell phones have to be charged, and even then coverage is bound to be spotty. We have to decide if it would be worth using precious power to charge a cell."

"Yes!" Olivia said instantly.

"I don't see having a powered-up cell phone as being more important than having light," Carol said. "Especially since the odds are against anyone you'd want to talk to also having a charged cell phone, and that the networks would be operational. Not right away, anyway. Later on, maybe, because you know everyone will be working their butts off trying to get everything up and running."

"I charged my cell phone this morning," Sela said. "What about y'all?"

"I did," Olivia said. Of course.

Carol made a face. "I think it's about seventy percent."

Barb sighed. "I haven't even turned mine on today. I forgot."

"Then we're good for a while, between the four of us, if any cell service works." Another thought occurred; they'd been so busy doing all the food prep and canning that she'd forgotten about water. She had a good bit of bottled water from her store, but that wouldn't be near enough. "We should get busy, right now, filling everything we can with water. When the power goes out, it'll be a lot harder to come by."

They all got busy, filling every glass, every cup, every bowl, every pitcher and jug they could find, all while keeping an eye on the small television. Sela sent Olivia to Carol's small bathroom, which was attached to her downstairs master bedroom, to fill the tub there with water, as well.

The anchors were seriously explaining that anything that relied on satellites was already down, and there was no telling how long it would take to repair or replace them. Getting the power grid up and running would have to come first. Then they began listing places where emergency rations would be distributed, and where medical centers would be set up. Hospitals would be too difficult to manage, with dark stairs and inoperable elevators. The practice of medicine would become smaller, and more basic.

As she automatically filled containers with water, Sela wondered how long those emergency rations would last. Here in the valley, at least, starvation wasn't on the radar. Getting food would be more difficult, but there were deer and other game in the area, as well as hunters who'd be happy to provide. She'd never had squirrel stew, but there were plenty of them around and she wasn't entirely opposed to trying it if their supplies and deer ran out. Okay, she was opposed, but that would pass. She imagined a lot of food dislikes would be ignored before this was over.

The water coming from the faucet suddenly thinned to a trickle, then stopped altogether. "What on earth?" Carol said, looking at the television, which was still on.

"The water board must have turned everything off and disconnected, so the pumps won't be fried," Sela said, looking at the clock and thinking that, truly, the water board had taken a chance leaving the water on this long. She turned the faucet off and looked at their supply of water, at the kitchen counters and table covered with every kind of container they'd been able to grab. Olivia returned to the kitchen, looking to Sela and shrugging her shoulders. Still, she'd had time to fill Carol's bathtub. They'd be okay, for a while, and when they had to they'd use creek water to flush the toilets.

Everything at her own house was already unplugged, and her perishables and generator were already here at Carol's. They were as ready as they were going to get.

They all took a seat at the table, watching the little television, saying nothing. The minutes ticked by, moving closer and closer to three P.M. Then the hour hand on the battery-operated clock moved past three, and Olivia stirred restlessly. "Maybe—" she began.

The television went black.

That was it. No drama, no burst of static, just . . . gone.

Carol's house was eerily quiet, all of the normal sounds missing. There was no refrigerator hum, no central air blowing, no television. All of them sat there, scarcely breathing, because surely something so momentous should have been more . . . well—momentous. The quiet ticking of the clock, something Sela had never before noticed, was the only background noise.

And so it began, not with thunderous noise, or drama, or a cataclysmic collapse, but with . . . silence.

"It looks like *The Walking Dead*," Sela said under her breath as they joined people from all over Wears Valley in walking to the elementary school.

On the other side of her, Olivia giggled. Carol barely suppressed a snort of laughter. "Hush!" she whispered. Then she said, "Though a few people are kind of lurching around."

They looked like either zombies or lemmings, and in the end it made no difference which, because they were all going to the same place like metal shavings pulled by a powerful magnet.

The day's heat had begun to cool and the late-afternoon shadows were lengthening. Sela had brought a flashlight, in case the meeting ran until after dark. She hoped it wouldn't, but realistically she expected people to have a lot to say, whether any of it was constructive or not. Everyone was worried, including herself. Maybe someone would have some good ideas on how they could weather this.

They worked their way inside to the cafeteria; she'd never seen it so crowded. She hadn't been here in a few years, but the school hadn't changed much. The smell was the same, the tables and chairs the same. Maybe the walls had been repainted, but that was it.

Instinctively she scanned the crowd, looking for Ben Jernigan even though instinct told her he wasn't there. If he were anywhere around, there would be one of two possible reactions: he'd either be standing alone because most people would be wary of approaching him, or he'd be in the center of a bunch of men who were looking to him to be the natural leader. There was no in-between, he wouldn't be chatting with a small group of people.

Even *knowing* he wasn't there, until she had scanned the entire room, her blood was still thrumming through her veins at the mere possibility that she might be wrong.

Of course he wasn't here; no surprise there, though she really wished he was. If anyone had the skills to help them get through this disaster, it was Jernigan. She couldn't even be annoyed that he wouldn't help, because, honestly, if she had the option of hiding away until the crisis passed she'd probably take it.

She didn't have the option, so wishful thinking was a waste of time.

Every seat in the lunchroom had been taken, and many people stood along the walls and in the aisles. Almost immediately the low roar of constant chatter began to wear on her nerves. She hated crowds and the noise that came with them, hated the way it made her want to crouch down like a small animal trying to escape notice. She wished she thrived on people and experiences, instead of wanting to run.

A man noticed them and said, "Miss Carol, here," and got up to let Carol have his seat, at the end of a long table. Sela and Olivia took up positions behind her. It wasn't necessary that all three of them be here, but she and Carol had felt as if they had to be there, and Olivia was sticking close to them. Barb had stayed at Carol's house, both to rest from the hard day's work and because she said they could tell her everything she needed to know, which was true. Her ankle was already better, so she could've handled the walk. Sela suspected that Barb was hiding, in her own way, the same way Ben was hiding. Everyone handled crises differently.

In the midst of the dull roar, she caught bits and pieces of conversations:

"I don't have enough blood pressure meds."

"I really didn't think it would happen."

And so on and so on. Panic, concern, curiosity—they were all around her, and inside her, though she held her fears close because she didn't want to burden Carol and Olivia with them.

A woman at the next table toward the back was telling people that Mike Kilgore had gone to Ben Jernigan's place and been met with a shotgun. Any lingering hope she'd had, that he'd miraculously come to help, faded away.

With the electricity off and no air-conditioning, and the lunchroom crowded with people, heat was quickly building to the uncomfortable level and so was the level of irritation.

From what she could hear, a couple of men were already attempting to take the lead, but so far there was nothing resembling organization in their methods. They were at the front of the room, arguing about food, security measures, rationing gasoline and propane. More men began to join them, some adding their opinions to the argument, others just moving close enough to listen.

The noise level grew, as did the feeling of panic in the air. Carol looked around and scowled, then said to Sela, "If someone else doesn't step up, those butt-holes up there will end up running everything."

Olivia said, "Why don't you do it, Gran? You and Sela."

Carol looked startled, then she glanced up at Sela with a speculative look on her face. "You should do it," she said. "You're the one who got this meeting organized, after all."

Sela's stomach clenched at the idea of dealing with this many people; she'd have to get up and talk in front of them, persuade the ones who had other ideas, and a whole bunch of other things that made her think about running. Horrified, she protested, "I don't even know the majority of people here! Do you?"

Carol looked around, frowning. "Most of them," she admitted. "After all, I've lived here all of my life. Some of the new people who've moved here, I don't."

"I think you should do it," Olivia said to Carol. She made a face as she looked at the knot of arguing men. "They scare me. Do it, Gran, please?"

Carol said irritably, "You do know I don't have much chance of being elected, don't you?" even as she pushed her chair back and stood.

"Then why did you tell me to do it?" Sela demanded. "You know more of them than I do!"

"Don't try to trip me up with logic."

Sela followed her aunt as Carol slowly worked her way to the back of the room. It was a chore to get there. They had to ease past clusters of concerned people, muttering "excuse me" again and again as they made their way toward the men who were attempting—and failing—to lead. Everyone was watching the argument, some scowling, some looking alarmed as if they expected a fight to break out at any minute.

The air was close and hot, and evidently a lot of people hadn't thought ahead to taking a bath while they still could. Some people were trying to open windows, maybe catch a late-afternoon breeze to clear the air.

This was the way it would be for a long time, she thought. Central air and heat had spoiled them; everyone would have to get used to existing in the real-world temperature again, enduring the heat, sitting close by the fire when winter came. The electricity hadn't been off long enough yet for this to feel like anything more than an inconvenience. Reality would set in soon, as food supplies dwindled and stores didn't reopen.

Finally they reached the group of men, but before Carol could interrupt them in her usual inimitable manner, there was a shout from the other end of the room and as one they all turned to look at the red-faced, harried-looking man who was coming toward them, progressing pretty much the way she and Carol had done, weaving around, tapping people on their shoulders, repeating "excuse me" until those in the way moved to the side as much as they could. It was close quarters in the lunchroom, and getting closer as more people trickled in.

"Who's that?" she asked Carol in a low voice.

"I don't know," Carol replied, "but he evidently thinks he has something important to say."

The man finally reached the back of the room where the serving area and kitchen were, and turned to face the crowd. He was dressed in the ubiquitous Southern male uniform of khaki pants and a blue button-down shirt, and he drank from a water bottle in his left hand before he began speaking. "Let me have your attention," he said in a loud voice, repeating the phrase over and over and being roundly ignored. The noise continued unabated.

Sela didn't think she had many talents, but by God she definitely had one: she could whistle. She placed two fingers between her lips and blew, producing a shrill, loud whistle that silenced the entire room.

The sudden silence was a relief, but now everyone was looking at her. She felt her face get hot. Quickly she pointed at the man who had been trying to talk over the noise.

He gave her a grateful nod and said, "I'm Jesse Poe, with the county commission."

That prompted a rush of questions, but he shook his head and held up his hand. "I don't have answers to most of your questions. We're still working out a plan. What I'm here about today is the food here in the lunchroom. There are perishables in the coolers, and a lot of staples, and we don't want this food to go to waste."

A woman said, "How do you plan on handling it?"

Jesse Poe cleared his throat. "We propose going by the latest population numbers, figuring out the weight of the food here, and dividing the weight by the population to see how much food each person gets."

The woman stood up, a disbelieving look on her face. "The county commission doesn't have any idea how a lunchroom works, does it? The staples are in big bags. How are you going to divide that, have everyone bring a measuring cup? And what about the people who stayed here instead of going home? There's a rental cabin next door to me and those people are still here, said they didn't know anything about a solar storm. Are we supposed to include them in the food giveaway, when their tax dollars didn't buy any of it?"

"Now, wait just a minute," a man who looked alarmingly like Teddy Roosevelt said loudly, his scowling face turning red. "I don't live here, but I own a vacation house and I pay property taxes just like everyone else. Are you saying my wife and I aren't entitled to any extra food?"

The woman shrugged. "You aren't here all year paying local taxes the way we are. I'd say yeah you could have some, but not a full share."

"That's bullshit!" His head jutted forward and he advanced on her.

"Settle down, now!" Mike Kilgore appeared, pushing his way between people and getting in front of the Roosevelt look-alike. "There's no need to start acting up, this can be worked out."

"They both have legitimate points," Carol put in; Sela saw the alarmed look she cast at Olivia, and knew her aunt was trying to play peacemaker to head off any possible violence because she didn't want the girl scared. The situation was frightening enough to kids, without adding adult anger to the mix. Mike Kilgore gave her a grateful nod.

"It doesn't matter." Another woman stood up. "I work in the lunchroom, and I can tell you, Mr. Poe, dividing the food likely won't work. This other lady is right about the staples being in big bags. The meat won't keep long, and neither will the eggs. The produce, lettuce and tomatoes and such, will last longer but they need to be eaten within a week. I don't know what you think you're going to do with all that meat, either, just cut off hunks and hand them out to people who may not have a means of cooking it?"

Sela immediately imagined big hanging sides of beef, though she knew that wasn't what the lunchroom had. The lunchroom worker had a point; how did one cook that much meat, when, other than their backyard grills, most people had lost their means of cooking? Eventually people would work out systems for cooking, but the meat would spoil before then. She and Carol and Barb had canned what meat they had so it would last just fine, but what about the others?

Thinking about the large amount of meat, she saw the solution and leaned forward, murmuring to Carol, "Those big meat smokers. Right off the bat I can think of three men who have them, so there are bound to be more."

The people around them heard her and turned around to look, nodding their heads in agreement.

"How many people here have those big smokers?" Carol called out, looking around the crowded lunchroom. "Those who have generators can keep a fridge running for a while, but let's face it, we'll need those generators when the weather turns cold. What we need to do is cook this food and have us one big party, before it goes bad! Harley Johnson, I know you have one."

"I do," said a man from the side of the room. "So does Bob Terrell."

A couple of other names were added, and going by the size of the big smokers Sela had seen, they now had the combined capability of smoking a couple of thousand pounds of meat, way more than was likely in the lunchroom—which meant they could also smoke the meat that people had in their homes that they hadn't already cooked.

"That's a darn good idea," said the lunchroom lady, nodding her head emphatically. "Everyone can join in."

"The big field beside the bank would be a good place," Sela said to Carol, trying to keep her voice low enough that people wouldn't notice her. It didn't work; they were turning around again, looking at her, giving her the thumbs-up signal. Again she felt her face heating at the attention.

God, why couldn't she grow out of this awkwardness? She was fine in small groups, with people she already knew. Why couldn't that carry over when she was in a crowd?

Carol put a comforting hand on Sela's shoulder, the touch saying she understood even if she didn't quite agree, and raised her voice again. "The big field beside the bank. That's big enough to hold the smokers and all the people who want to come. We'll get tables and chairs from the churches, or everyone could just bring a blanket to sit on, or some lawn chairs, and we'll have ourselves a big picnic."

There was another chorus of agreement, a flood of suggestions, but none of them mentioned the uncooked meat people had in their freezers, meat that would go bad unless it was cooked soon. Carol was right; they'd need the generators more in a couple of months. Starting tonight, with the smokers, would be an even better idea.

Sela waited, hoping someone would think of that. Hadn't anyone else gone on those survivalist websites and gotten some ideas about how to salvage their food supply?

Evidently not.

"For crying out loud," she muttered, frustrated in her attempt to remain unnoticed. Carol turned around, eyebrows raised in question, and Sela leaned closer. "Anyone who has any uncooked meat and can't cook it at home needs to bring it so it can be smoked, too," she whispered. With all the background noise in the room, Carol couldn't hear her. She shook her head and Sela repeated the suggestion, slightly louder.

"You should be doing this," Carol muttered, then called out again, "Anyone who has any meat that needs to be cooked, bring it!"

The room buzzed as Harley Johnson and Bob Terrell got together and came up with a time to meet in the big field and get the smokers fired up. Others volunteered camp stoves and charcoal grills, so the eggs and other items could be cooked. The school sometimes offered breakfast for lunch, and because the school year had just started they had more on hand than usual. The lunchroom ladies who were in attendance began organizing how such a large amount of food would be cooked.

Jesse Poe looked relieved that the lunchroom food would be distributed, though somewhat perturbed that the county commission's plan had been so quickly discarded. He went with the flow, though. "Y'all seem to have this in hand, so I'll get back to Sevierville," he said, not that anyone paid him much attention. The county commission was giving permission for them to take the food, so they were accepting the opportunity and handling it as they saw fit. Sela wondered how the county commission could have expected anything different; country people had their own ideas about how to handle things.

"Before you go," Mike Kilgore said, "what are the plans for the sheriff's department?"

The commissioner paused. "There isn't a lot they can do. They'll patrol as long as they have gas—and the county does have some in reserve—but when that's gone . . ." He shrugged. "With the phone system down no one can call 9-1-1. When the atmosphere settles, the people with ham radios will be able to operate, if they took steps to protect their radios, and the sheriff's office is prepared for that with their own ham radio, but in reality—" He stopped again.

"In reality, we're on our own," Carol finished for him.

He heaved a sigh. "Yes, ma'am, I guess you are. I'm sorry."

"It's better to know where we stand, instead of waiting for help that can't get here," she said briskly. "It won't be easy, but we'll do okay."

He nodded and wound his way out of the crowded lunchroom, having delivered his news. People watched him go, conversation mostly suspended as they thought about what it meant to essentially have no law enforcement.

The Teddy Roosevelt guy looked around and said loudly, pitching his voice to carry, "We'll need to organize the community, set up our own protection. I'm willing to—"

Mike Kilgore interrupted. "For those of you who haven't met him, this is Ted Parsons; his house is on Cove Mountain."

Sela choked back a startled giggle. Teddy Roosevelt's name really *was* Ted. What were the odds?

"Where are you from, Mr. Parsons?" Carol asked in a neutral tone that made Sela's people-radar start beeping. Carol didn't like Mr. Parsons, because normally she was boisterous and friendly; neutral for her was just shy of downright enmity.

"Columbus, Ohio," he said, for some reason giving her a disdainful look as if she'd asked the state of his underwear. "I own six tire stores, four in Columbus and two in Dayton. I'm accustomed to managing people and resources; I could handle the organization of this little community in my sleep."

"Bless your heart," Carol said, a polite smile fixed on her face, "but the valley has about six thousand people in it, which is way more than you're used to handling—unless your little tire stores average a thousand employees each?"

Several people coughed at hearing Ted's heart being blessed, the Southern equivalent of "you're a moron." Sela ducked her head and pressed her lips hard together. Oh Lord; she might have to break up a fight any minute now, so she needed to be ready, not doubled up laughing.

Ted Parsons's face turned red at hearing his stores referred to as "little," signaling that Carol's retort had hit him square on the ego. Maybe Mike Kilgore saw the same thing because he stepped forward and clapped his hands, saying, "All right, let's hear some ideas, people, about what we want and how we want it done."

"Before anything can be done," Ted Parsons pointed out, "a leader has to be elected. As I said, I volunteer for the job."

"But you aren't from here," someone from the back of the room called out. "You don't know people."

Parsons looked annoyed at the reminder, then smoothed out his expression and shrugged. "People are people. Management is management."

"It ain't that simple," a weathered old guy in a sweat-stained John Deere cap said. "If you don't know where people live, or what they can do, or even what their names are, you can't manage squat."

Carol leaned closer to Sela and whispered, "I might have exaggerated about knowing everyone in the valley, but I damn sure know more of them than Teddy Roosevelt does."

"Anyone else volunteer?" another man said grumpily. "It's damn hot in here, let's get this voted on and get home."

There was a moment of relative silence, no one else speaking up, and Sela winced at the idea of Ted Parsons being in charge of the valley's resources. He seemed to be more ego than ideas, though she might be wrong about that. After all, he was here, and wouldn't he want things to go well because it meant his survival as well?

The same woman who had been in the disagreement with Parsons stood up and said, "I nominate Carol Allen. She's the one who had all the good ideas about how to handle the food." She gave Parsons a smug look as she sat back down.

Those standing around Sela and Carol looked around and a few muttered, "Not exactly," because they'd overheard Sela feeding the ideas to her aunt. Sela almost panicked, afraid one of them would nominate her; she ducked her head, not meeting anyone's eye.

Carol said, "I can't take credit for that, my backup here is the one with all the good ideas," and she put her hand on Sela's shoulder. "This meeting is her idea, too."

Thank God, Ted Parsons plowed right over that; Sela hadn't been nominated, Carol had, and he focused on Carol. "I think we want someone more capable than an o—" He stopped abruptly, before the word *old* came all the way out of his mouth, but it was too late.

Carol stiffened; even the pink streak in her hair seemed to stand on end. "An 'old woman,' you mean?" she snapped, glaring at him. "This old woman has been working her butt off all day canning food to get us by. What have *you* been doing, other than coming here and trying to claim the same amount of school food as the people who live and work here all year long?"

Sela didn't often get angry, but Parsons's contemptuous dismissal of her aunt had her stepping forward, her hands curling into fists, shyness forgotten. Carol grabbed her arm, pulled her back. "I can handle this," she murmured.

A groundswell of hostile muttering followed the exchange. Parsons glared right back at her. "And you yourself said I had a point."

"I was being nice—something you might not understand."

"Anyone else want to volunteer?" Mike Kilgore asked loudly, once more trying to deflect the hostility into a more productive direction. "Or nominate someone?"

Silence.

"Okay, then, let's take a vote. Everyone for Mr. Parsons say 'aye.'"

"Aye," came a chorus of voices, mostly male.

"Now Carol Allen—"

"*Aye!*" This time the voices were mostly female, and definitely louder.

"You can't go by whoever yells the loudest," Ted Parsons snapped. "You have to take a real vote. Plus not everyone's here. My wife—"

"Could your wife have come if she'd wanted to?" Carol asked, lifting her brows. Sela wondered if they were going to get through this election without fisticuffs. She'd never before seen Carol be so openly antagonistic to someone, especially on such short acquaintance.

"Of course—"

"Then whether or not she's here doesn't matter. I can't think of any election in America that has a hundred percent participation."

"But this means the decisions for *six thousand* people—according to you—will be made by the few hundred who showed up here."

"That's right. That's how it works, Mr. Parsons. The word went out; the people who didn't bother to show up opted out of the decision making."

Oh no, now they were moving into politics. Hurriedly Sela said, "Let's just line up, Carol's voters on the left, Mr. Parsons's on the right."

"Good idea," Mike said promptly, and raised his voice. "Line up, people! If you vote for Carol Allen, go to the left wall; for Mr. Parsons, go to the right wall."

"Depends on how we're facing, doesn't it?" an old geezer said, then wheezed with laughter at his own wit.

"I guess it does," Mike admitted. "Okay, this is the left wall"—he pointed to his left—"and this is the right wall"—he pointed to the right. "Anyone have any problem with that?"

"I'm good," said Carol, as she grabbed both Sela and Olivia by an arm and towed them toward "her" wall, dodging people as well as tables and chairs that had been shoved helter-skelter.

"Way to go, Gran," Olivia whispered, leaning forward to grin at Sela. Sela stifled a sigh. The little shit was actually enjoying seeing her grandmother get in someone's face.

It *was* kind of fun, she admitted, giving in to a return smile as they lined up against the wall.

"No spreading out," Mike Kilgore instructed. "Single file! Let's get this done."

It took several minutes of shuffling and jockeying and arranging, but finally the lines were mostly uniform. Sela looked around; Ted Parsons's line consisted mostly of men, though there were some women here and there. She looked at Carol's line; yep, mostly women, with a few men. No doubt about it, Ted Parsons's aggression had definitely gotten on the wrong side of most of the women present.

And the women outnumbered the men.

When everyone was lined up, the line on the left wall was a good five or six feet longer than the one on the right wall. Ted Parsons looked thunderous. "This is an ignorant way to have an election! We should have written ballots."

"Are you calling us 'ignorant,' Mr. Parsons?" Carol asked in a chilly tone.

He scowled, but was smart enough to backpedal. "I'm saying this particular process is ignorant, and the position is too important to rely on—"

"It isn't even a paying position, and no matter how you look at it, my line is bigger than yours." And Carol smirked at him, knowing he and almost everyone else in the room would catch her inference.

Mike Kilgore blew out a big breath and once again stepped into the breach. "That's it, we're calling this done. Carol Allen is the valley coordinator."

"This will be a complete mess," Parsons said in disgust. "There'll be some hard decisions to make, and does anyone really think a—" Again he stopped, baffled as to how he could call Carol an old woman without alienating even more people.

"If it comes to human sacrifice," Carol said, grinning a shark grin at him, "I think I could come up with a nominee."

People began laughing, despite the seriousness of the situation they were in, and as Parsons looked around Sela saw that he finally accepted he'd lost.

The heat was building to the stifling stage; Sela ruefully thought that her shower had been wasted, because she was now so sweaty. The election over, some people began moving toward the exit, no doubt as eager as she was to get out into the fresh air. A cacophony of chair legs being scraped against the floor as they were pushed back filled the air, adding to the overall noise.

"Hold it!" Carol hollered, and most people did hold it, stopping to look back at her.

"This is just the beginning!" she said, keeping her voice raised. "Sela and I have been talking about all that needs to be done. We need volunteers to check on people, identify the ones who are elderly or sick and can't do for themselves. We'll need wood to burn this winter, so that means trees will have to be chopped down. Everyone who wants to help, stay behind so we can get this ball rolling."

With a pang, Sela realized that she, Carol, and Olivia were on the list of people who would need help keeping a fire in the fireplace. She could pick up wood from the forest, she could even fell saplings— with a hacksaw, and a lot of sweat and determination—but she didn't even have an axe, much less a chain saw. "We'll be needing firewood ourselves," she said quietly, not expecting anyone other than Carol and maybe Olivia to hear her, because of the noise of the growing exodus. She was wrong.

"Don't worry about firewood, Miss Sela," said a man behind her. She turned and recognized one of her customers, Trey Foster. "You were good enough to give me gas and some groceries on credit when I was between jobs, so the least I can do is cut you enough wood to get you through the winter."

Tears stung her eyes at his kindness. "Thank you, Trey. You paid me every penny owed, all I did was wait a little while."

"Still. I can't tell you how much difference it made to me and my family. If you hadn't done that, I wouldn't have had gas to *get* to work when I found a job."

She didn't know what else to do but extend her hand, and solemnly they shook. Her firewood was taken care of.

Despite Carol's call for volunteers, most people were still leaving. Some of them, of course, had to begin making preparations for the huge cookout they were having the next day, and would actually get started on that night. Ted Parsons made a disgusted face at the departing crowd, scowled, then said, "I'll help do whatever you think needs doing. I don't have a chain saw or anything like that, but I'm willing to do the labor."

Sela hid her surprise. Carol said, "Thank you, Mr. Parsons, your help is appreciated." She looked around. "Does anyone have a notebook and a pen?"

No one did, at least no one among the small group of perhaps ten people who had stayed to volunteer. "Then we'll meet . . . Sela, is it okay if we meet at the store? Everyone knows where it is."

"Of course."

"Then . . . Never mind. We'll all be busy in the morning. Everyone be thinking of things that will need doing, making a list, and tomorrow at the cookout we'll start getting organized."

It was a relief leaving the overheated lunchroom, which had been getting too dark for them to accomplish much more of anything anyway. The cooling air washed over Sela's bare arms, a sensation as pleasurable as a light touch. Twilight had deepened, edging into night. Everyone called their goodbyes, then split up to walk to their various homes. Their little group, consisting of the three of them, Mike Kilgore and his wife, and a couple of other neighbors, trooped down the school road to the highway and turned left. The others walked at a faster pace and gradually the three of them fell behind.

"Let's walk in the middle of the road," Sela suggested, both because the smooth walking would be easier and because . . . well . . . they could. There was no traffic at all. Walking in the middle of the usually busy highway felt both daring and freeing, and the fact that they could was one more example of how drastically their world had changed in a single day.

"Damn it," Carol muttered when they were alone, making Sela think their leisurely speed was more by design than nature. "Why did you let me volunteer for a job like that?" she peevishly asked Sela. "Do you know what an aggravation this is going to be? How much time it's going to take up?"

"There was no stopping you, once you got the bit in your teeth about Mr. Parsons," Sela replied in amusement. She turned on her flashlight to light their way, the beam both reassuring and somehow feeble, as if it were nothing more than a whisper in the night. Normally the valley would be lit by lights in the homes, by headlights of traffic, the occasional security light, the gas station outposts of glowing light. Now there was only a growing darkness, and a silence she hadn't heard in her lifetime. Nightbirds called, insects buzzed, frogs croaked, and the trees rustled from a faint breeze, so the silence wasn't absolute, just—different.

"He made me mad, bulling toward Geneva Whitcomb the way he did."

"I'm proud of you, Gran," Olivia put in from beside Sela, who was walking in the middle because she had the flashlight.

"So am I. And you *are* a good person for the job," Sela added. "I didn't know the woman's name."

Carol sighed. "I guess. Still—I'm going to rely on you to help me think of things. You see things I don't, think things through where I'd plow ahead without seeing the pitfalls. Look how organized you were about getting us as ready as possible for this."

"We all had good ideas to contribute."

Carol patted her arm. "Sela, honey, don't sell yourself short. You bring more to the table than ninety percent of everyone else out there, me included. You just don't trust your strengths."

"That's true," Olivia chimed in.

Ruefully Sela wondered how much of a wuss she'd been that even a fifteen-year-old had noticed it. That had to change. She *would* change. She didn't want to be the breakable link in their small family chain, she wanted to be as strong and dependable as they needed. She was the one in her prime, physically stronger than Carol, more experienced than Olivia. She had to be their fulcrum, no matter how much against her nature it was.

There didn't seem to be much to add, so they continued in silence until they reached their neighborhood road and turned in. Now that true night had fallen, they could see faint, flickering lights inside each house, as either battery-powered or oil lamps took the place of electric ones. This must have been how the valley had looked a hundred and fifty years ago, when people had traveled by foot or by horse. Now that it was after sundown, the way the world had changed was striking.

They reached Carol's house and she saw them in, said goodnight to them and Barb, then continued alone down the narrow road to her own house. She walked faster, aware that the bears foraged at night, and this was the time of year when the animals were actively looking for anything they could find. She swept the flashlight beam back and forth, looking for the gleam of eyes or the black bulk of an ursine body, resisting the urge to run back to Carol's house and spend the night there.

This was how their lives were now; they couldn't rely on their cars to go everywhere, nor were there security lights chasing away the shadows.

This wouldn't be the last time she walked a night road alone.

CHAPTER SIX

She couldn't sleep.

The house was too silent, too dark; the hours crept past like cold syrup, barely moving. Normally Sela went to bed between ten-thirty and eleven, but after she'd gotten home and locked up—something she double-checked, because not having lights made her feel more vulnerable—there was nothing to do, no television to watch, and she was exhausted from almost two days of nonstop work. Going to bed seemed like the thing to do.

Sleep should have been easy. It wasn't.

She dozed, woke, tossed and turned, dozed some more, then her eyes popped open and she lay staring upward in the darkness, her mind racing with details of all they had done, all they could have done, and all they still needed to do. She went over and over the community meeting, trying to think of who should be in charge of what, but the reality was they'd have to go with the group of volunteers they had regardless of their individual skill sets. In any given community, there was a small core of people who were willing to commit their time and efforts to getting things done while others simply waited to reap the benefits. Whether or not that core of workers would be large enough remained to be seen. More "volunteers" might have to be drafted.

Too bad Ben Jernigan wasn't one of the volunteers.

Her memory flashed to his hard, scruffy face, the fierceness of his green gaze, and the reluctance with which he'd warned her about the coming disaster. Interacting with people didn't come easy to him; even she was better at it than he was, and most days she sucked ditch water when it came to socializing. But he'd made the effort, which meant he wasn't totally closed off; perhaps she could convince him to join them.

Or not.

The problem was, they needed him, but he didn't need them.

Thinking about him wasn't conducive to feeling sleepy. Suddenly she was too hot, though she had only the top sheet pulled over her; the house was too warm without air-conditioning, even with the screened windows open. She threw the sheet back and lay there in her tank top and pajama pants, hoping for a cooling night breeze, but the air didn't seem to be moving.

A red glow lit the room, then vanished.

Startled, she sat up and cocked her head, listening for unusual noises. Was there a fire? Her heart thumped, because a fire now, with the valley's resources so drastically limited, would be catastrophic for the people involved.

The red glow shimmered through her bedroom again.

She jumped out of bed and ran to the window, expecting to see a neighbor's house on fire. Instead . . .

. . . the fire was in the sky.

"Ohhh," she breathed, an unconscious tribute to the spectacle overhead. Entranced, she stared upward for a few minutes, then raced through the dark house, unlocked the front door, and stepped out onto the screened porch where she had a much broader view. She stood transfixed by the sight.

If she'd needed a reminder of the magnitude of this event, if she had not yet accepted that the CME had arrived, this was it. The sky was on fire. Not literal fire, but still . . .

A bloodred aurora danced across the sky, above and around

Cove Mountain like a gentle ribbon of crimson light twining into the darkness in all directions. It was a haunting, celestial waltz of power, and she caught herself holding her breath as she watched. She couldn't remember ever being more entranced and terrified and awestruck.

She unlatched the screen door and went down the steps to stand in the yard, turning slowly around, eyes still on the sky. The aurora danced behind her as well. She'd never before seen an aurora, much less a rare red one. They simply didn't happen this far south, until now.

Now the bloodred color, shot through with green streaks, covered the sky like a sheet, trembling back and forth, vanishing briefly, then flaring back to life and morphing into a shimmery curtain.

How many of her neighbors had had trouble sleeping, unable to turn off the worry, and now stood watching the fiery display that stood testimony to the immense solar storm? She couldn't see anyone else in their yards, though the trees blocked most of her view anyway; surely she'd have heard them talking, though. She seemed to be alone in the night, alone with this unbelievable grandeur taking place above them.

Ben had been walking for a few hours, driven by a bone-deep impulse. He was walking patrol; he knew it, but still he couldn't stop himself. He was annoyed and bitter about it, even angry. Didn't matter. He was driven to do what he'd been trained to do. This was an emergency situation and civilians were at risk; he didn't have to join their meetings or chat with them or share his supplies with them, but evidently he damn sure had to keep the boogeymen away, at least for tonight.

It was bullshit. He knew it was bullshit.

He still did it.

He'd managed to get a few hours of sleep, but once he'd awakened there was no going back to sleep. And why should he? Through his windows he could see the dancing curtains of light; why miss the celestial show? Restlessness gnawed at him, telling him he should be doing something, so he'd gotten dressed, slid his Mossberg shotgun into a scabbard across his back, and started walking the dark, narrow road down the mountain.

Silence enveloped him. Normally the night was alive with animal sounds, but not tonight. Even the insects were quiet, as if the world around them had changed and they sensed it.

As he drew closer to the valley he saw and heard—and smelled—what appeared to be a big cookout in a clearing off the main road. There were a few lights shining dimly, but not too many. He heard the hum of a generator in the distance. Whoever was manning the smokers and grills kept their voices and lights low. It was a smart move, cooking up the meat they had on hand.

He gave the area a wide berth, preferring to continue on alone and unnoticed. Soon enough they were behind him, and the silence—and dark—turned deep again.

The eerie sky glowed and danced over the dark, looming mountains. The Smokies were old mountains and had undoubtedly seen skies like this before, but he sure as hell hadn't. Holy shit, that was one heck of an aurora. It was the color of blood, immense and unnatural. The atmosphere had to be highly charged for the sky to turn that shade of red—any shade of red, come to that.

He'd seen the lights before. Auroras were supposed to be blues and purples and greens across a quiet night sky, not this ominous crimson. Still, it was damn impressive, this testament to the power of a smallish star about ninety-three million miles away. If it had been ninety-two million miles away, likely life on Earth wouldn't exist, because even at the current distance heat from the smallish star could bubble asphalt. He had to give it to nature, to the universe: it kicked ass.

If he had to spend the night walking the damn valley, at least he was getting to watch something that was damn amazing.

The valley was dark. So many nights and early mornings he'd sat on his porch and looked down at a blanket of lights; he could see the service stations, the houses with outside security lights, the lamps of night owls who were up late or very early larks who had already started their day. No matter the time, there had always been an occasional vehicle threading through the valley roads or running down the highway, headlights stabbing forward. Not now; now there was silence and darkness, no vehicles, no lamps. It was as if Earth and civilization had been turned back two hundred years—and civilization had, in most of the industrialized world.

The government bodies had contingency plans, and would function on a deeply reduced basis. The military would be as prepared as possible, and had portable nuclear reactors that would keep the bases functioning as well as likely providing the key points from which recovery would begin. Some small electrical company somewhere, maybe several of them, would have hardened its grid, taken precautions, had backups in place, and would likely come back online well before the major players. Those small bright spots would be overwhelmed with refugees, though, and might deliberately stay offline until recovery was well underway.

Regular people were pretty much fucked. They'd have to get by as best they could.

And he'd walk night patrol in his tiny corner of the world.

His well-worn boots crunched softly on gravel as he turned down one of the smaller side lanes. With the red glow above lighting the dark earth almost like a red lens on a flashlight, he could make out the name on the sign: Myra Road. That was where Mike Kilgore had said he lived—and that Sela Gordon lived on the same road. His steps slowed, and he almost turned back. He didn't want to know where she lived, what her house looked like; he didn't want to be able to imagine her going about life in her neighborhood, know the roads she would walk, speculate about which room was her bedroom. Yeah—that. Feeding his already uncomfortable interest in her wasn't smart. He should turn around, literally not go down this road.

He didn't turn around. He kept walking.

It was a nice little neighborhood. None of the houses were new, but they all looked well tended, at least by what he could see by the light of the aurora. All of the yards had neat grass, there didn't seem to be any piles of junk lying around. He could smell a few late-blooming flowers, overlying the faint but telling scent of autumn. The living would definitely be easier in summer, but summer was over.

There were a few dim lights shining. At least one house on Myra Road had a couple of solar-powered garden lamps. The lights were far from bright; he wouldn't have spotted them from his vantage point high on the mountain.

Then he spotted her vehicle, a small white SUV, in the carport of a one-story house with a screened porch across most of the front. The house was maybe forty, fifty years old, sturdy but without flash. A line of evergreen trees blocked the view of the neighbors' house. The windows in the house were dark of course, and he got the sense of stillness. Deliberately he moved his gaze forward, and in the eerie red glow saw that the road dead-ended about fifty yards ahead.

"Hey."

The single word was soft, so soft that if he wanted he could legitimately pretend he hadn't heard it. It came from the direction of the dark porch. Maybe she thought he'd seen her, and rural manners had compelled her to greet him. Maybe she didn't really want a conversation in the dark early-morning hours. He could keep going . . . but he'd already had this talk with himself, and look where he was.

He stopped in the middle of the road, turned his head toward the house. Yes, he could make her out, a pale blur barely visible in the dark protection of the porch.

"Hey," he said in return.

Sela had stood in her yard for a while, face turned skyward, then returned to the porch with the intention of going back inside to try to get some sleep. The red sky held her, though, and she remained standing at the screen door just as entranced as she had been when she first saw the glow. Then she saw Ben. She recognized him almost immediately, though she felt a split second of alarm at seeing a strange man walking down her road. The smooth, silent way he moved registered with her and with some astonishment she realized she'd watched him enough that she knew how he walked, could recognize him even in the faint, eerie red glow.

Her heart began pounding.

She started to shrink back, not say anything. She had no idea why he was walking down the middle of the road in the wee hours, but one thing she did know about him was that he didn't like interacting with others. The fact that he'd warned her about the solar storm was more astonishing than if he hadn't. At the time she hadn't fully appreciated what he'd done, but now she did; however well they survived this crisis, they would have been much worse off without his heads-up. The least she could do was say thank you.

"Hey," she said, the one word all she could manage because her heart was beating so hard and she didn't have the breath to say more. She doubted he'd be able to hear her, her voice had been so weak.

Then he stopped, looked at her, and repeated her greeting back to her. Her knees went weak, so weak she almost slumped against the screen door. Her reaction to him was so extreme she felt like a teenager; the realization was enough to strengthen her spine, her knees, and she barely trembled as she pulled open the screen door and stepped outside so he could see her, perhaps recognize her. That was as far as her determination carried her, and she sank down on the top step. She crunched her toes, the wood cool under her bare feet, and waited to see if he'd resume his walk down the road.

She expected him to; she even wanted him to. When, after a pause so long she almost stopped breathing, he turned and walked across the yard toward her, she sucked in a quick breath of . . . maybe panic, maybe excitement, likely both.

As he got closer she could make out some kind of stick across his back . . . no, a scabbard. A gunstock was protruding from it. Of course; no sane person would wander these mountains at night without the means of protecting himself from the wildlife.

He slipped the scabbard off over his head and without a word sat down on the step beside her. He kept the weapon at hand, though, right beside his leg.

She took a deep, silent breath, caught in the moment with crimson magic above her and him beside her. On a cellular level she realized she'd remember this forever, no matter where life took her or how long she existed. This, now, was ingrained in her being. Red ribbons danced overhead, fading, then pulsing with power again. The red glow bathed them, making it seem as if the heat she felt all along her left side came from the lights in the sky instead of from him. He wasn't actually touching her but he was so close there seemed to be a mild magnetic field between them, lifting the fine hairs on her arm.

Sela tilted her head and looked upward, permanently giving up the self-fiction that she was uncomfortable with him for any reason other than the power of her own reaction. She felt almost painfully alive at his nearness, her skin heated and ultrasensitive, her nipples pinched and aching. This was pure physical chemistry, lust on the most basic level. Likely it was one-sided, because he'd never looked at her with even faint interest. Her experience in dealing with something like this was basically zero, because she'd never reacted so intensely to any other man; this was outside both her experience and her comfort zone.

After about thirty seconds he still hadn't said anything. She wanted to bombard him with questions—Had he been in the military? Why had he moved here? Had he ever been married? Did he have children?—but held them all back. She might be ridiculously turned on by his nearness, but instinct told her that the best way to make him retreat was to push. Normally he avoided personal contact. Just the fact that he hadn't ignored her, that he was actually sitting beside her, was enough for now. She settled for murmuring, "Thanks for the warning. It made a difference."

She was still looking up, but by the movement beside her she could tell he turned his head toward her for a brief glance, before he, too, gazed upward. "You're welcome," he finally muttered, as if he'd had to cast around for the appropriate response.

Wow, at this rate in a year they might manage a real conversation. She wanted to laugh, but she was exasperated with herself, too, because she wasn't much better than he was. The unfolding crisis was a safe subject, though, so maybe she should stick to that.

"I keep thinking of things I should have done," she admitted. There, that hadn't been agonizing; she hadn't even really thought about what she'd say, the words had just come out.

"Such as?"

She realized she wanted his evaluation of what they'd done, his advice on what else they could do or improve on. She wanted to know if she'd done the right thing, if she should now concentrate on something else. She wanted to hear his voice, deep and slightly rough, and so masculine it gave her the shivers, wanted to keep him talking even if he didn't think she'd done the right things. Learning what not to do was important, too.

"We concentrated on food, mostly, canning as much as we could. I bought things that will keep, like canned meats, peanut butter, dried beans. I think we'll be okay there, though we'll have to cut back, and be careful not to waste anything. I have extra fuel for the generator, wood for the fireplaces, candles and oil lamps, prescription refills and first-aid supplies—but I almost forgot about water for flushing and taking a bath, so we don't have much on hand," she confessed. "Right now I have plenty of bottled water, but it won't last long. After it's gone I can handle water for drinking by boiling it, but I should have gotten a rain barrel for the rest. Making trips to and from the creek is going to get old fast. I've been trying to think what I already have that I could put under the downspouts to catch the rain, and the best I can come up with is some big plastic storage containers." She made herself stop talking, give him a chance to weigh in.

When he spoke, it wasn't about her preparations. "We?"

He'd asked a semi-personal question. She was so startled that she blinked. "My aunt Carol and her granddaughter, Olivia. They live together just up the road. The yellow two-story. You've seen Carol in the store, the one with the pink streak in her hair. She was elected valley leader at tonight's meeting."

He grunted an acknowledgment. Maybe he'd already known she and Carol were related, but likely not, because she called Carol by her name without the "Aunt" attached to the front. "You should consolidate, move in with her."

"An elderly friend already has, and taken the spare bedroom. If things get desperate I will, but—I like being alone."

He made another sound, this one not quite a grunt. She suspected he understood wanting to be alone.

Finally a light breeze began stirring through the night. It felt wonderful on her overheated skin and she sighed in relief. "Anyway, dipping buckets of water out of plastic containers will be easier than hiking to the creek and back every day." She didn't specify which creek, because it didn't matter; the valley was veined with creeks.

"That'll work," he commented.

He hadn't exactly praised the idea, but she was nevertheless pleased. She was thinking, she was identifying problems and coming up with solutions. In the coming weeks she'd be doing a lot of that, and could only pray the solutions would work.

The breeze picked up, and a faint chill ran over her bare arms. After the heat they'd been having it felt nice to actually be chilled, but soon the moving air on her bare feet was too cold and she pulled her legs up and tugged the legs of her pajama bottoms down to cover her toes. Her movement made her arm brush against his; the skin to skin contact, slight as it was, almost took her breath. He was so hot she felt almost singed where she touched him. She went motionless, still touching him because in that second she was incapable of moving away, and all she could do was wait to see if he moved away.

He didn't. Neither did he increase the pressure, or move closer himself, but he didn't move away. It was as if he hadn't noticed something that, though small, had rocked her so off-balance. Tilting his head back, he watched the red aurora that was flooding the sky and with admiration said quietly, "This is something."

The change of subject was welcome, even though it brought home to her how insignificant the moment was to him. She was overthinking . . . well, everything, rather than simply living in the moment. Realizing that gave her the inner composure she needed to pull herself out of her thoughts and back into the world. "Yes. I'm glad I couldn't sleep. I'd hate to have missed this."

More silence. She was becoming comfortable with it, and let herself enjoy simply sitting beside him in the dark. Not having to search for something to say was remarkably freeing, not to mention relaxing. If he'd been expecting to be entertained by her wit and insights she'd have been miserable, but while she didn't know much about him she did know that he liked silence better than noise, and solitude more than company. For him to be sitting there now, and showing no signs of itching to leave, was like an early Christmas gift and she accepted it for what it was, without wishing for anything more. This was enough.

Holy shit, he could see her nipples—the shape of them beneath that thin tank top, anyway. She probably thought she was safe in the darkness, but it wasn't all that dark because of the glowing aurora, and he had very good night vision anyway. Her breasts were small-ish, and her nipples were tightly puckered from the cool breeze.

After being mostly alone for so long, even by his own choice, be-ing this close to unfettered breasts felt like the erotic equivalent of a naked lap dance. Better; he was as turned on as if he were on top of her, about to slide home—which was nuts, because their only contact was a light brush of her bare arm against his, and all he could see was the outline of her nipples. Not having sex with a woman didn't mean he hadn't jerked off now and then, so it wasn't as if he hadn't come in three years. He had, just not inside a woman. Which meant he wasn't so turned on because he was sex-deprived, but because there was something about her that checked all his sexual boxes. He hadn't known he even had sexual boxes, other than he was hetero, but only a fool ignored the evidence right in front of him.

He should leave right now. He didn't like the companionable si-lence between them, or sharing the magic night sky, because this was about connecting and he didn't want to connect with her. He wanted her to stay a distant acquaintance, someone he recognized from the service station. He wanted to go back up his mountain and sit in sol-itude on his own porch, not beside her on her wooden front steps.

But . . . nipples.

It was hard for him to walk away, with *hard* being the operative word.

Which made her even more dangerous to his self-imposed semi-exile from the human race, because every time he came in contact with her he became more interested in finding out who she was, what made her tick. She was so quiet and self-contained that even years into the future she could still supply surprises, and he wasn't a "future" type of guy. He was a here-and-now, don't-let-anyone-close-enough-to-give-a-fuck-about type of guy. He shouldn't be wondering if she had a temper, how far someone would have to push her for the hot to surface, if he could make her scream in bed or if she tried to be as quiet as possible—

Shit. Just when his dick was settling down, he had to default to thinking about sex.

She said, "If you run short of food, we'll share ours. We wouldn't have what we have if it hadn't been for you."

He surprised himself by almost snorting a quick laugh, holding it back at the last second. Here he'd been torturing himself thinking about sex with her, and she'd been thinking about food. There it was in a nutshell, the difference between men and women.

His dick took that as a challenge to refocus her attention. He knew he could. He had the self-control to really make a woman happy, several times a night. Give him five minutes and she wouldn't be thinking about eating pizzas and Pop-Tarts, she'd be eating—

Fuck! Shit! He needed to get out of here. He needed to go, and go now.

Then a bright curtain of crimson waved over the sky, and he saw a black shape on the other side of the road. He was on his feet and the shotgun in his right hand, pulling her upright with his left, before his brain finished forming the word *bear*. She didn't yelp, though he knew he'd startled her. He released her to pull open the screen door, then pushed her up the step and onto the screened porch. He joined her, putting himself between her and the door and silently closing it.

He pointed toward the bear, hoping she could see his gesture in the deeper darkness of the porch. She turned her head in the direction he'd indicated, and went totally still as she spotted the problem.

The bear was rooting around on the ground, likely snuffling for fallen acorns. The breeze was in their faces so it hadn't scented them, and a bear's nose was far more acute than its eyesight. Likely they could have stayed still and remained sitting on the steps without the bear ever knowing they were there—and he had the shotgun—but he didn't want to kill it if he didn't have to, and neither did he want Sela in harm's way. They were safer on the porch, where he could quickly get her inside if the wind shifted and the bear scented them.

They stood motionless, watching the creature root around. They heard a few grunts and snuffles, then it moseyed deeper into the bushes and was soon lost from sight. Ben listened as it got farther and farther away, and the sounds faded.

He realized he was holding Sela's slim wrist, his big hand wrapped completely around it. Her skin was cool and silky smooth under his rough fingers, and the impact of willingly touching someone after years of holding himself apart was so strong that he felt as if he'd been punched in the solar plexus. He had to force himself to release her.

"I gotta go."

He pulled the screen door open. His voice sounded raw and a little strained, but at least he'd gotten himself moving in the right direction.

She didn't ask him to wait. Instead she said, "Be careful." Then she let herself into the house, leaving him there, and he heard the click of the door lock.

He blew out a gust of relief when he was once more walking the road, heading back home. He kept the shotgun in his hand because obviously the bears were active tonight . . . and she hadn't asked him to wait until the bear they'd seen was farther away. She hadn't fussed, but her quiet "be careful" carried the weight of a benediction that warmed him all the way home through the red night.

CHAPTER SEVEN

The new day dawned as hot as the one before. The valley inhabitants began gathering early in the open field beside the bank. The big smokers and grills were operating, watched over by the tired men who had been cooking all night and refused to let others take over because they suffered from the stereotypical male fixation with grills and the belief that no one else could operate one as well as they could. The delicious smell of grilled and smoked meat permeated the air, making Sela's mouth water even though she'd had breakfast, such as it was: a bowl of dry cereal, some nuts, and water. She hadn't felt like bothering with making either coffee or tea because that would mean boiling water, and now she was feeling the lack, but that would soon be remedied.

Long tables were set up and covered with plastic picnic cloths. Some of the more enterprising women had big jugs of sweetened water and tea bags basking in the sunlight to make sun tea. Of course almost no one had shown up with nothing other than meat to cook; Sela didn't know how the dishes had been prepared, but there were pots of beans, big platters of salad, mashed potatoes, and anything else the women could think of that needed to be cooked and eaten before it ruined. Sela had made a big salad, using all of her romaine lettuce before it went bad; better eaten than wasted.

There were some vehicles, pickup trucks that brought the heavy items, but for the most part people had walked to conserve their precious gasoline. Some kids had ridden their bicycles, and a few people had saddled up and ridden their horses. There were a lot of horses around, some used in tourist trail rides, some privately owned. She figured they'd see a lot of horse and bicycle traffic in the months to come.

Patio umbrellas and pavilion tents were set up for shade, folding chairs were placed around the tables, kids were running around shrieking and playing, and despite the seriousness of their circumstances the atmosphere was more like a giant picnic than a survival effort.

She and Carol and Olivia had loaded most of their stuff in Josh's old Radio Flyer wagon and pulled it to the field, where Carol commandeered the space under a pavilion tent. At Sela's suggestion, they had brought a small portable grill, charcoal, a blue enamel camp kettle, and a few bags of coffee. She and Carol swiftly got the charcoal going and the coffee brewing. Soon the smell of coffee was luring a constant stream of people to the pavilion, where they found themselves cornered into either offering ideas or volunteering to help—Sela hoped they were doing both, but one thing for sure, if they got a cup of coffee then their names were going on Carol's list.

After helping herself to a single cup of much-welcomed coffee, she murmured to Carol, "I'm going to walk around, see who all is here and what they've done."

"Take a pen and notebook, and jot down their names," Carol replied, handing both items to her.

Good idea. She roamed the big field, not only noting exactly what different people had to share but also seeing who was the most organized and prepared, because they were the people Carol would want to talk to. She kept an eye on Olivia, who had connected with some of her school friends; there was a lot of laughing and dramatic gesturing going on. And she couldn't help checking the perimeter to see if Ben would appear at a distance, watching but not joining.

He didn't, of course; he was likely grabbing some sleep, which she wished she could do. After he'd left she had gone to bed and managed a few hours' sleep, but already she could feel the lack of rest. When the cookout was over and some organization was in place, maybe she could catch a nap.

Not surprisingly, most of the talk she overheard was excited discussion of the red aurora.

"Did you see that sky last night?"

"I thought it was the end—"

"Damn it, I was so tired I went right to sleep and missed it—"

She thought the red aurora would be showing up for a while, with all the atmospheric turmoil, but didn't stop to join in the various conversations because she had nothing to share. Sitting on the steps with Ben and watching the sky was an experience she hugged to herself; she hadn't even told Carol about the awkward but strangely alluring interlude they'd shared—if sitting beside each other could be called an interlude—because it was both too intimate and too casual. Carol would make a big deal out of it, joking that Mr. Hot Body had a thing for Sela, and Sela discovered that she couldn't regard anything about Ben as a joke.

It wasn't that they'd had any deep conversation; in fact, she'd be surprised if he'd said a grand total of thirty words to her. But still— they'd communicated. They had shared a piece of magic that they'd never forget. Their bare arms had brushed. If there was any other person in the valley with whom Ben Jernigan had willingly spent that length of time, and actually touched, she didn't know who it would be. Of course, for all she knew he regularly had booty calls with any number of women, but he seemed far too solitary for that.

Abruptly she realized that she had stopped walking and was simply standing motionless in the middle of the big field, while eddies of people swirled around her. Her face heated, even though no one walking by knew she'd gotten lost simply thinking about Ben, the

mystery and appeal of him. She knew, and she was both appalled
at herself and unreasonably excited. This was how her adolescent
crushes had felt, and she had thought she'd grown beyond that.
Evidently she was wrong.

Someone behind her gripped her arm, and she turned to find Ted
Parsons standing there. If that wasn't immediate punishment for letting herself get distracted, she didn't know what was. He released her
and caught another woman's hand, tugging her to him. "Meredith,
this is—sorry, I didn't catch your name last night."

"Sela Gordon," she supplied, and held out her hand to Meredith.
"It's nice to meet you."

"Right. This is my wife, Meredith."

She'd already figured that out. Meredith Parsons appeared to be
the exact opposite of her abrasive husband. She had a kind, gentle
face, and her smile was genuine. She shook Sela's hand, then looked
around the busy field. "Isn't this something? So many people, all
helping each other and sharing."

"It's important to cook the perishable things and not let them go
to waste—" Sela began.

Ted interrupted with, "Her mother was chosen as valley leader."
He was still visibly disgruntled that not only had he not been chosen,
but a female senior citizen had been.

"My aunt," Sela corrected. "On my father's side."

The curl of Ted's lip said he didn't care on which side of Sela's
family Carol came in. "Where is she? I've come up with some ideas
about what we should be doing."

"I'm sure you have," she murmured, and turned to point across the
field. "She's set up in that pavilion tent with the red stripes. And she
has coffee brewing, if you'd like a cup. All ideas are welcome."

"Ted's really good at getting things done," Meredith said, looking up at him with a smile, one that he returned with such obvious
affection that Sela blinked in surprise. When he looked at his wife,

his expression changed completely. It was a reminder that even jerks could have a few good qualities, something she should remember. Seeing him with his wife made her feel less hostile to him, and that was a good thing considering how they would all have to work together in the coming months.

The morning wore on. She was approached by a couple who had to be in their seventies but were lean and spry, and offered their knowledge of herbs in the event of sickness. A group of women in a quilting club offered to make quilts for those who didn't have enough bedcovers for the coming winter. A few men offered to hunt for those who couldn't. Sela wrote down names and addresses, with notes about capabilities and offers. A system needed to be created to connect those in need with the people offering services, and also a means of payment by barter, though what the people in need could offer in return would be way more complicated to set up. She was mulling that over when someone over by Carol's tent rang a cowbell, calling them all to congregate.

The sun was really beating down now, so the pastor who gave the blessing was smart enough to keep it brief before Carol invited everyone to start eating. Sela had made her way to Carol's side, and winked at her aunt. "Good strategy, feeding everyone before you start roping them into work."

"I wasn't born yesterday," Carol replied, smirking. She paused. "Or in this century, come to that. And speaking of that, have you seen Olivia, who *was* born in this century?"

"She's fine. She's hanging with her friends." Sela looked around and caught sight of one of Olivia's friends, a girl who was easily spotted because of her bright red hair. A quick survey of the group let her locate Olivia. "There she is." There weren't any boys in the knot of teenagers, at least not right now.

Carol nodded, then gestured to Sela's notebook. "Did you get any good stuff?"

"I did. How about Ted Parsons? Were any of his ideas something we could use?" She actually hoped they were, because that would soothe his ego and make him less problematic to deal with . . . she hoped. Not that he was a big problem, but he was certainly going to be an irritant.

Carol rocked her hand. "Maybe, maybe not. I wrote them down. You never can tell how things will work out."

Sela filled plates for Carol and herself, got glasses of tea, then they sat with their heads together under the tent and tried to brainstorm with the information they had gathered that morning. Carol did have some volunteers, a few of whom she deemed worthless. Zoe Dietrich couldn't be trusted to check on the elderly because she would likely steal their medications. Patty Stone had good intentions, but she was one of those people who never followed through. And so on, and so on.

"We can't expect people to routinely donate their time and services," Sela said as she absently drew circles on the notepad. "In a short-term emergency people will give, but this is going to last a while."

"You're thinking a barter system?"

"There isn't anything else that will work. Well, there is right now, but what about later on when winter is here and food is getting scarce?"

"But what could people offer? If they need someone to hunt for them then they can't offer food, right? Food's what they need, not what they have a surplus of."

"Mending. Babysitting. Cooking. Knowledge. The elderly will be the most in need, but they also have the most knowledge in how to get things done without electricity. Teaching. The kids can't be left at loose ends, they still need to be in some kind of learning environment, as well as helping out with everything that needs to be done." Sela sat back, thinking of her own situation. She needed firewood and Trey Foster had offered to keep her supplied, so now she needed to come up with some way to pay him for the wood. Cutting firewood was hard work. The chain saws would work only until they ran out of fuel, then any cutting would be done by hand, with axes.

Damn, this was getting complicated. In one way everything was being stripped down to the basics, but they needed to survive as a community, which meant there were a lot of moving pieces.

Carol took a sip of tea. "I say again, you should be the one doing this. You just came up with several things that never crossed my mind."

"And I didn't know about the medication thief," Sela returned, determined not to be maneuvered into something she didn't want. "Besides, I wasn't elected; you were."

"How could you be elected when you wouldn't step forward?" Carol demanded, her tone exasperated.

"Going over ground that's already been plowed," Sela pointed out, unswayed, which earned her a rude noise from her aunt.

An uproar exploded in the direction of the big grills, and they jumped to their feet. A crowd was already gathering, but through a gap they saw two men rolling on the ground with fists flying.

"Oh shit," Carol said, and sighed. "This is never gonna work."

The big cookout was a good idea in that it took care of a lot of food that might otherwise have spoiled, but other than that not a lot was accomplished. Carol had names, they had some ideas, but there was almost no forward movement in organizing anything. The crisis was too new, and the situation wasn't critical yet. The weather was still good. People still had food. For the most part, the valley inhabitants were adjusting to life without electricity, puttering around outside, going to bed early, and solitarily tackling whatever they thought they needed to do to get ready for winter.

While part of Sela was impatient to get some organization in place, another part of her was content to do exactly as the others were doing. She managed to cut enough off her drainpipes that she could fit her big plastic container boxes beneath them to catch rainwater . . . not that there was a whole lot of rain this time of year, though if a big tropical storm swept in from the Gulf that could change. In the meantime, every afternoon she and other people in the neighborhood walked back and forth multiple times to the nearest creek, collecting water in whatever container they could carry.

Every day, Carol tried the Y2K windup radio to see if she could pick up any broadcast, but heard only static. Nevertheless, they all immediately formed the ritual of gathering around while Carol searched for a signal, and after Sela suggested they go outside so there would be less interference, the radio became sort of a neighborhood thing. People volunteered to operate the crank to charge the battery. Someone brought out a folding card table, and Carol would set the radio on it while everyone gathered around, hoping that each day would be the one where they finally heard something from outside the valley.

After four days of silence, words emerged from the static. People had been chatting but they immediately fell silent, crowding around the card table.

"—stores are empty. Communications are—" The signal was overtaken by static, obliterating what else was said, but at least there had been something. They were a good distance from Knoxville and the atmosphere was still wonky, as evidenced by the aurora that still danced overhead at night, though Sela thought the vibrancy was fading and the red was now mixed with more green.

"It'll get better," she murmured. "The reception, I mean." Though obviously the radio stations were running on reserve generator power, and who knew how long that would last. She hoped the atmosphere would settle down before transmission stopped, so they could get some useful information.

"Maybe if we move the radio to higher ground," Mike Kilgore said, looking around. "I can get a ladder and take it to the top of the house."

"We'd all have to get on top of the house to hear it," his wife, Leigh, pointed out, punching him in the arm.

"Let's just keep trying from where we are," Carol said, feathering the dial, searching for another station.

When another voice came through, this one more clearly, they all jumped.

"—operating under emergency power, and will continue to do so as long as possible. PSAs are scheduled to be aired every day at nine A.M. Please tune in tomorrow at that time. This is our last broadcast today."

The exact time had become less important since the grid died, but some people still wore wristwatches and they all automatically noted the time. "It's four-thirty," Mike noted, and everyone who wore a watch synchronized the time, to make certain their watches weren't running slow; they didn't want to miss the nine A.M. broadcast.

"I can look for another station," Carol said.

"No point. We can wait until tomorrow. At least that station was clear."

The next morning they all gathered in Carol's yard; word had spread that Carol had a hand-crank radio and it wasn't just neighborhood people gathered around to listen. Others in the area had battery operated radios, mostly old-timers, and some had actually cranked up their cars to listen to the radio. But these days most took any opportunity to be together, and this was one of those opportunities. Carol's yard was full of people milling around. At 8:59 she turned it on, and they all fell silent, waiting.

Olivia stood to the side and played with her hair, twirling a strand around one finger. It was a nervous gesture she hadn't fallen back on for years. Barb was noticeably pale, but of the four of them she'd been the most upset and nervous.

Sela moved to stand beside Olivia and hooked a companionable arm over her shoulder. An outright hug might feel too coddling to the girl, but a we're-in-this-together touch to let her know she wasn't alone was acceptable. Olivia gave her a fleeting smile—a strained one, but still a smile.

They all seemed to be holding their breaths, though Sela didn't expect to hear anything of great importance this morning. It was just that—they needed this contact, however routine it might turn out to be. They'd felt so isolated, cut off from all news, from friends and family who weren't close by. It was a subtle, ongoing strain that they had never expected to face and hadn't been able to prepare for.

The station signed on. "This is Robert Keller, reporting." Sela recognized the name. The tone of the announcer's voice was telling; he was a man who normally greeted his audience with humor and a devil-may-care attitude, but was somber as he reported. "The governor has sent couriers to report that the Tennessee National Guard is working to keep the capitol in Nashville secure, but everyone is hampered by fuel shortages. There are unconfirmed rumors of widespread looting and several shooting deaths. Emergency services are unable to respond, so everyone is urged to conserve their resources." His voice shook a little, then he cleared his throat and recovered. "Supermarkets here are empty, but Knoxville residents are so far weathering this crisis. Continue to check on your neighbors, and be careful out there. The next update will be at nine A.M. tomorrow."

Barb said, "I wonder if all the college kids were able to get home."

"I hope so," Mike replied. "I don't imagine the town could handle the care and feeding of twenty-eight thousand kids."

The brief news, while not exactly sunshine and roses or really even that informative, at least hadn't been as catastrophic as it could have been. Just hearing the broadcast was comforting. Some technology still worked, at least for now.

The next morning, the crowd in Carol's yard was even bigger.

Sela had walked over just after dawn, and she was startled when she looked out the window. "You gotta get a bigger yard," she said.

Carol looked out, too, her eyes widening at the milling crowd. "Lord have mercy. I guess we need to take this somewhere more wide-open."

The time was approaching, so she took the radio out and set it on the card table. They had cranked and cranked and cranked, to give the battery a good charge. Maybe today's broadcast would be longer, have more information.

"This is Robert Keller, reporting. There was widespread looting in several Knoxville neighborhoods last night, with reports of people coming into the city from other locales, following the interstate highways. The KPD has performed heroic work during the night, quelling the looting, and for now all is quiet. The hospitals are not accepting critical cases, as dwindling supplies have to be carefully managed so as to provide care for the maximum number of residents." He gave the locations of the shelters that were open, as well as the times and places for food and water distribution, along with the warning that "Armed police officers will be ensuring order." He signed off with a reminder of the next update.

In the small silence that fell afterward, someone said, "I'm glad we live here." While Wears Valley had come together, the larger city, if not already in a panic, was getting there fast. And it was fewer than thirty miles away.

Sela suspected there were similar reports being made around the country, in places that were lucky enough to have access to radio. Many, more rural areas, wouldn't have even that.

So far they were doing okay. The last few days had been stressful and strange, but not difficult. There was no television, no phone calls, no access to the world outside this valley. There was no reason to go to her store, so she didn't bother. At this point, anyway, there was plenty of food to go around.

The handful of gardens along the street were now being tended by more than one hand, as neighbors pitched in to help, hoping to extend the life of the vegetables. The one greenhouse in the neighborhood was being converted from . . . well, whatever, to vegetables they'd need in the coming months. They were working, and working together. Things had been peaceful, and the weather was still good. But during the coming months . . . who knew?

It was frightening to realize that the grid would be down that long, but Sela had no reason to think otherwise. The world had gone dark, and Ben had said getting the grid back up would take months, if not years. They had to face that, and prepare as best they could.

Barb had tears in her eyes, and so did Olivia. They weren't caused by sadness, Sela suspected, but were tears of absolute fear. Knoxville wasn't all that far away, and what had happened there and in other cities wasn't going to get better.

Carol clapped her hands and said, "Show's over, let's get back to work. Tomorrow I'll set this up in the big field, so more people can listen."

How different their days already were, Sela thought as she watched the crowd disperse. She, Carol, and Barb planned to spend part of the day working on quilts in preparation for winter. Olivia and a friend from down the street were helping an older couple with the last gasp of their garden. The girls were lost without their phones, and the physical activity did them good. Sela had even caught Olivia reading a time or two, and she had also joined in with the quilting—for a short while. She didn't have the patience for the craft. Sela stifled her own impatience, because the chore needed doing.

They settled into their activities, and as Sela stitched she thought of Ben. Did he have enough covers to keep him warm? As soon as the thought ran through her mind she scoffed at herself. Of course he did. Of all the people here, he would be the most prepared for whatever happened. He was fine. No looter would dare to bother him, and if they did, well, too bad for that looter. But just because he was prepared didn't mean he had everything. He had no neighbors to share or commiserate with, no fresh-tomatoes-for-recently-thawed-chicken trades to make—not that she could imagine him commiserating with anyone. Still. Being totally alone wasn't good. What if he got hurt? Living as isolated as he did, no one would know if he was injured and needed help.

Though maybe he could perform field surgery on himself.

Instead of being comforted by that idea, she suddenly felt like crying, and she ducked her head so the others wouldn't see her damp eyes.

She wished she had reached out to him before, not that he'd ever given any indication of wanting her, or anyone else, to reach out. Her retiring personality had undermined her. Why had she been so shy around him? Why hadn't she ever smiled and asked him how he was doing, those times when he'd come into her store? Likely he would have grunted a non-reply, but maybe . . . maybe he'd have talked to her a little. And maybe eventually they might have—

She was bedeviling herself with too many mights and maybes. She couldn't change the past. The future, however, was something else. Seeing these missed opportunities was giving her a lot to think about. What a time to realize that maybe there was more to life than work, her aunt, and her young cousin. She'd been marking time, playing it safe, living in a bubble of her own making.

The thing was, bubbles were made for popping.

CHAPTER EIGHT

Ben stepped out onto his porch into another fine, warm morning, but for a change there were low clouds in the sky that hinted at changing weather. The world had gone dark just over a week ago, which meant no weather predictions. September was prime hurricane month, though, so who knew what was brewing in the tropics. At any rate, rain would be welcome, because so far they'd been hot and dry for too long.

After his unplanned meeting with Sela he'd kept to the mountain, and stayed busy by chopping wood, doing some hunting and fishing so he wouldn't have to dip into his canned or dried food supplies before winter set in. His solar panels provided what light he needed at night, conserving his lamp oil and candles. The atmosphere had settled down some and he'd gotten the ham radio up and going again, but so far transmissions were spotty and limited in range. Maybe in another week he'd be able to get some worthwhile information over the airwaves.

He had his breakfast with him, some fish he'd cooked the night before, and settled down in a chair with that and his coffee to kick back to enjoy the bright morning and the simple food. The cup was almost empty and he had one strip of fish left, when in his peripheral vision he spotted movement off to the right about forty yards away, on the left side of the driveway. He turned his head a fraction of an inch, focusing on the movement. Could be deer, bear, turkey—any kind of wildlife. Turkey would be nice; he could smoke some, dry some for jerky.

But it was a dog that emerged from the underbrush and stood watching him warily. Ben held himself motionless, waiting to see what it did. It was a black and white mountain cur, a leggy youngster, maybe six or seven months old from the looks of it. It edged farther out of the brush, twisting its body, tail hesitantly wagging.

It was thin, its ribs showing. Mountain curs were great hunting dogs; Ben figured when the CME hit some shortsighted asshole had figured he wouldn't be able to feed the dog and simply abandoned it, not realizing what a great asset the dog could be once it was trained.

From its body language, the dog was friendly but unsure, wanted to approach but was afraid to. Likely it smelled the fish and hunger had compelled it to show itself.

"Hey," Ben said softly. Its ears perked up at his voice. He didn't want a dog or any other attachment, but his tours of duty had given him a deep appreciation for the war dogs, and he would never let one suffer if he could help it. The dog needed food, and he had food in his hand. If he stood and walked toward the dog, though, it would likely run.

He eased to his feet and walked slowly to the steps. Without looking directly at the dog, he broke off a piece of fish and laid it on the top step. Another piece of fish was placed halfway between there and the front door. He gradually opened the door, moved inside, and put another piece of fish on the threshold. He placed the last piece of fish three feet inside. Then he retreated all the way to the kitchen and sat down where he could see the dog, watching it through the open door.

The dog could see him, too, so he sat relaxed and motionless. He had no idea if the animal had ever been inside a house; if it hadn't, it might not venture as far as the threshold, much less enter for the last piece of fish. Still, hunger was a powerful motivator, and the young dog wouldn't be as cautious as an older one.

It crossed the yard toward him, still body-twisting and tail-wagging, its gaze darting back and forth between him and the food on the top step. It stopped a couple of times and backed up, sat down, got up again and ventured closer. When Ben didn't move and nothing bad happened, the pup reached the steps and with one fast, courageous bound went to the top where it wolfed down the fish in one swallow.

It immediately pounced on the second piece of fish, then the third piece lying on the threshold.

The pup's tail was wagging faster now, and the bright gaze fixed on Ben didn't seem nearly as wary. "Hey," he said again, keeping his tone soft and crooning the way the war dog handlers had spoken to their canine charges. "Come on in, buddy. There's plenty of food and water, and a rug to bed down on, if you need a break."

The dog eyed the last piece of fish, dashed forward to get it, then stood as if uncertain what to do next. But that tail was still wagging, even if the wagger didn't feel ready to come within Ben's reach just yet. It was wearing a bedraggled red collar, but no tag on the collar. If there had been one, it had been torn loose during the dog's journey of survival—or the former owner had removed the identifying tag. Either way, the collar was proof that the dog was accustomed to humans, and so far its behavior didn't indicate it expected mistreatment. It was just unsure of itself and the situation.

Ben looked around the kitchen. He had a lot of food, but nothing specifically for dogs. He did have jerky, though, and the pup needed some protein. He yawned and looked away—a trainer he'd deployed with had told him that a yawn told a dog there was nothing to be alarmed about—and went to the cabinet to open a pack of jerky. The pup backed up a couple of steps at his movement, but didn't bolt. When he opened the pack, the smell of the jerky riveted the animal's attention.

Ben went back to his chair, sat down, and took a piece of jerky from the pack, placed it on the floor at his feet.

The dog whined, and eased forward. Ben didn't move. It grabbed the jerky, gobbled it down, then looked expectantly at the open pack. When Ben still didn't move it looked at him, then back at the pack.

Huh. This was a smart little shit, but mountain curs were usually very intelligent dogs.

The dog butted his hand, and looked at the pack. *Give me some more food, human.*

"Pushy, aren't you?" Ben murmured, but got another stick of jerky and held it out, ready to jerk his hand back if the pup went for it too aggressively. Instead it tilted its head and gently lipped the jerky from his fingers, though all signs of gentleness vanished once the treat was in its mouth.

Ben held out the back of his hand, and the pup sniffed it, then gave him a lick.

Still moving slowly, he got up and poured some water in a bowl, set it on the floor. The pup came over without hesitation and drank thirstily, almost emptying the bowl. Then it looked back at the jerky, but Ben thought he should wait a while to see if what he'd already given the animal stayed down or would end up ralphed on his floor. He took the chance and gave the dog's shoulder a pat, and it crowded against his leg in delight.

"Okay," he told the animal. "I'll help out, you can bunk down here for a while. But fair warning: I'm not looking for company. Got it?"

Whether or not the dog got it, it knew a good thing when it saw it. Over the next several days, Ben had a constant companion. He discovered that, hunting dog or not, the pup was house-trained and at ease inside. It didn't try to get on the bed with him but did sleep on the rug beside the bed. Maybe its former owner hadn't dumped it, maybe it had wandered away and gotten lost. Ben didn't normally think the best of people—experience was a hard teacher—but for certain the dog hadn't been mistreated. It was too trusting and comfortable with him for it to have been abused.

He didn't name it, he just called it "dog" or "buddy." Naming it would imply a permanency he wasn't prepared to accept, though maybe the pup's companionship wasn't as onerous as he'd expected. Sometimes, though, even that was too much, and he'd leave the dog in the house while he took a long, solitary hike through the woods. He'd hunt, or he'd just walk, get in some PT by sprinting up the steep mountainside, leaping deadfalls, dodging boulders and trees. He had some free weights in the house but he much preferred moving, and in all his years of training he hadn't found anything that compared to mountain running.

Two weeks after the CME, he finally made some distant contact on the ham radio. The dog sat beside him, head cocked as if trying to figure out where that other voice was coming from when it couldn't smell another human anywhere nearby. The radio operator he reached was outside Memphis, about four hundred miles away.

"The city's trashed, looted clean and a lot of it burned," the disembodied voice said. "A lot of people were killed. There are some pockets where it's too dangerous to go, but for the most part a lot of people have moved on because there's nothing else here to loot. The national guard is beginning to secure some areas, but there's not much food to be had. From what I've heard, it's the same in Little Rock."

"Same for Knoxville and Nashville. How far out can you reach?"

"You're the limit, so far, but it's getting better every day. What's your power source?"

"I have solar." He had a lot more, but Ben didn't intend to let the world know the extent of his resources. That would be inviting trouble, in the form of looters who would take anything they could. "Be safe." He signed off, then tried to raise his buddy Cory Howler, without success. Cory would have taken his radio equipment with him when he bugged out, but there were some hefty mountains between them and the atmosphere wasn't letting transmissions overcome that yet . . . either that, or Cory wasn't capable of responding. Ben had seen too many of his buddies die to reject that possibility. Cory could be dead, badly injured, or his radio equipment stolen or destroyed. Anything could have happened. Eventually he would find out; he'd either make contact, or he wouldn't.

Restlessly he got to his feet and walked outside, the dog at his heels. A light rain had fallen that morning but now the sun was breaking through. So far there hadn't been a drastic change in the weather, though the September heat had broken and the nights were getting cooler. He looked out at the valley. Since the first night of the aurora, he hadn't been back down. He didn't want to walk patrol, and though he couldn't get Sela's nipples out of his mind, neither did he want to see her . . . Hell, face it, he was lying to himself. He *did* want to see her, but from a distance. His nerves had felt raw after that accidental midnight meeting, as if he'd been skinned alive. The contact had been too much, and he'd retreated to give himself the time and space to heal.

Being alone was much more comfortable. He could find peace in the silence and solitude. So why was he thinking about trekking down the mountain?

Because he was a man and she was a woman, and his dick was pointing at her like a German Shorthair pointing at a covey of quail. *Fuck!* Literally. Yeah, it was nice to know the thing was still alive, but actually getting involved and doing something about it was a step too far. Everything in him recoiled from the thought . . . everything except the part of him that kept thinking about her.

Almost before he realized he'd decided to do anything, he was kitting up with his shotgun and water, and threading a length of rope through the ring on the dog's collar. The youngster needed a good walk, but its hunting instinct was strong and it hadn't been trained; he didn't want it plunging through the woods after game and not knowing what to do when called. Instead of pulling on the makeshift leash it began bouncing around, reaffirming his belief that it had *some* training.

"All right, dog, let's go on a walk."

The farther down the mountain he got the more pissed off he was at himself, but as on the night of the red aurora, that didn't seem to matter. It wasn't even dark, and he was going down where people could see him. Finally he just thought, *To hell with it,* and concentrated on his surroundings. The mountain and the exercise always made him feel better, even if he was having to deal with a young dog who wanted to investigate every new scent it came across. The dog didn't make him laugh—he hadn't laughed in so long he couldn't remember the last time he had—but its puppy eagerness somehow lightened his mood. Okay, so he was going down the mountain. He might have to talk to people. The world wouldn't come to an end; he could always retreat to the mountain and not come back down again until he was good and ready.

No one in Wears Valley, or anywhere else, was his responsibility. He had no one to save, no one to worry about. Anything he did or didn't do now was his own choice, without any bullshit orders to follow. All of this was his choice, and he could talk to people or not.

Funny how he hadn't realized that before, that every interaction he had was under his control. He'd sat beside Sela and talked to her because he'd wanted to, not because he'd been trapped and hogtied. He could talk to her again if the mood took him, or not talk to her if he didn't want to. The same went with everyone else he might encounter.

He was the one in control. He could talk or not. The realization was freeing.

He avoided the houses down below his, leaving the road and striking through the woods whenever he neared one of them. He didn't know who his nearest neighbors were and didn't feel as if he was missing anything. That might change one day, but not right now.

Even admitting that there might come a day when he got to know his neighbors felt as if he'd turned some mental corner . . . or at least seen that there *was* a corner to be turned. He wasn't yet ready to go around it.

The uncut path he took down was rough enough that he pushed all other thoughts aside and concentrated on getting himself and the dog safely down. Acorns had fallen and crunched under his boots, and the smell was different as the green vigor of summer faded away. Ben was in his element in the wild: he liked the fresh air, cool shade, the only sound the crackle of his boots in the dirt and fallen, dried leaves and the occasional cry of a bird. To his right, leaves rustled, but it was likely a bird because the sound was small and no limbs were moving.

The day was warm enough that he soon worked up a sweat and the dog was panting. When they reached the valley floor he stopped to let the dog drink from a creek, then they cut across a fenced pasture where cows eyed them with some curiosity. He went over the fence and the dog went under, and they reached Covemont Lane.

Unbidden he remembered the elderly couple who had invited him to dinner. He hadn't wanted to go; dinner with chatty grandparent-types was his idea of a nightmare. Their intentions had been good, and they seemed to be kind, honest people. Talking to them didn't seem so nightmarish to him now, and he wondered how they were getting along since the grid went down. Did they have anyone, family or neighbors, who kept an eye on them? When food began to run short, would they be able to protect what they had?

Shit, did they have anything to protect? Maybe they hadn't done any prep at all, despite the warnings that had been broadcast. Some people just ignored warnings, and sat in their houses with hurricanes or tornadoes bearing down on them, as if they couldn't grasp that they were in danger. The warning about the CME would have been difficult for some people to process, because it was something they couldn't see or hear.

His spatial memory was excellent. When the old couple had told him where they lived, he had marked the location on his mental map of the area. He knew about where they lived—in fact they weren't far from him now—and could probably locate them without too much trouble.

Their welfare wasn't his business, but they'd been kind to him. It wouldn't hurt him to check on them, make sure they were okay.

If his memory served him, he needed to take a left on the next road. And speaking of memory, what the hell was their name? They'd introduced themselves. Richardson? Masterson?

Livingston, that was it. His first name was Jim; that was easy enough to remember. She had a very Southern double name that he just couldn't pull up. He was safe with just calling her Mrs. Livingston.

The dog was bouncing along, looking at everything as if he was having the time of his life. There were only six houses on the Livingstons' short street. Their house was easy to spot, since Jim drove a 1998 Cavalier that looked to be on its last gasp. It was parked in the driveway of the second house on the right. Not only that, their name was on the mailbox. Ben contained a growl. The days were long gone when it was safe to put your name on the mailbox. On the other hand, with no social media or internet searches, they were now perfectly safe from identity theft.

He walked up the driveway toward the faded-red Cavalier. The little house was nice and well kept, one story, traditional redbrick. There was a flower garden in the side yard. You couldn't eat flowers, at least not enough of them to live through the winter. Insects had more nutrition, and God knows he'd eaten his share.

He and the pooch went up the two steps and knocked on the front door. No answer, and he didn't hear anyone stirring inside. Maybe they had relatives who had picked them up before the CME hit, and took the old couple home with them. That would have been the perfect solution.

But the house didn't *feel* empty, and he'd cleared enough houses to have a good sense about things like that. He even reached back and touched the shotgun before he remembered he wasn't clearing the house, he was . . . fuck, he was *visiting*. How alien was that?

He walked around the house, looking in every window as he sidestepped flowers. He reached the backyard, and his hopes that someone was taking care of the Livingstons died a quick death.

Jim stood over a charcoal grill, intent on the meat cooking there. The wind was blowing away from Ben or he'd have smelled it. The pup sure smelled it now, and he began bouncing up and down in eagerness and the surety that these humans would give him some of the good-smelling meat. Double-name sat in a lounge chair just a few feet away, and she was the one who spotted him first.

He wouldn't have been surprised if she'd reacted with alarm; any woman in her right mind would be alarmed by the sudden appearance of an armed man, one she knew only slightly, in her backyard. Apparently double-name was not in her right mind. "My goodness!" she said as she stood and headed Ben's way. "What a nice surprise! I wasn't expecting visitors. We'll have supper ready in a little while and we'd love to have you join us. We don't see many people these days. And we're eating awfully early to call this supper, but without electricity we go to bed as soon as it gets dark so it all works out. How have you been? What a sweet-looking dog!"

"Ah . . . good." He reminded himself that this conversation was his choice. Being here was his choice. "I was just passing by, thought I'd check on you."

Jim smiled and nodded, but he didn't leave his station at the grill. "A neighbor brought us some venison," he said. "We ran out of meat a week or so ago. I'm doing the cooking, and a couple of other neighbors will be by shortly. We eat together a lot of times. JD is bringing some of his last tomatoes, and Janet said she'd bring some baked beans."

They should save the beans for winter was Ben's first thought, but it was too late for that advice. "Thanks, but I have somewhere else to be. I'm checking on a few other people."

Mrs. Livingston beamed at him as if he was the biggest, finest Eagle Scout on earth. Jim said, "I didn't hear your car. Things have been so quiet around here, I thought I'd hear anyone headed our way."

"The pup and I hiked down."

They both stared at him for a moment, then Mrs. Livingston said, "You *walked* down Cove Mountain?"

"Yes, ma'am." He'd walked a lot farther than that before, and in rougher conditions.

"Oh, call me Mary Alice! The mountain is so steep, I can't imagine going up and down it on foot."

Mary Alice. That was it. He committed her name to memory. "Do y'all have everything you need to get by for a while?" he asked, taking a step away. He hoped to make his escape before the rest of the neighborhood showed up.

Mary Alice shrugged. "Oh, I imagine we'll be fine. We have a few canned goods put back, and plenty of peanut butter to put on some apple slices. We didn't go to the meeting at the school right after the power went out, but JD did, and he keeps us up to date on what's going on. Carol Allen is in charge of organizing things, but I don't think this will go on much longer, do you? People always blow things like this out of proportion, they see disaster in everything."

Jim frowned and cleared his throat. "The power better come back on pretty soon. Mary Alice is going to run out of her prescription pills in a few weeks. We'll need to get a ride into town to get refills.

My old car's already out of gas. I had close to a full tank, but JD and I siphoned it to use in his generator, to keep it running a while longer. I thought the service stations would reopen, but so far they haven't."

Jesus. They were a disaster waiting to happen. "I hate to tell you, but this is going to last for months." They both looked dismayed, but they needed to be dismayed; maybe that would wake up what little survival instinct they seemed to have. This wasn't a damn picnic, and before long their little neighborly cookout was going to look like a damned feast. In spite of himself, he turned to look down at short, plump Mary Alice. Maybe it was his imagination, but she didn't look as plump as she had when she'd invited him to dinner several months ago. "What meds do you take?"

"Oh, just my blood pressure and heart pills."

He scrubbed his hand over his face. He didn't know much about medications, other than to pop an Ambien when he needed some sleep before a mission, or inject morphine in a wounded brother to ease the pain. For years he had slept on the military's schedule, which was nothing like a normal circadian rhythm. Blood pressure and "heart pills" weren't in his wheelhouse, and there was no way he could research them.

"You have to conserve them," he said firmly. "Cut them in half, if they're tablets, and take them only every other day or even more spread out than that. Make them last as long as you can. Same with food, same with everything." God, some medications weren't made to be halved, but desperate times, desperate measures.

Her eyes got wide, and he saw some dawning of comprehension that they needed to assume the worst. She slowly nodded. "I understand. There are some people here in the valley who know about herbs and things, I can probably handle my blood pressure that way."

"Good idea," he said. "I'll check back by every now and then. You folks take care. C'mon, dog." He and the pup started back the way they'd come, though the dog was reluctant to leave the smell of cooking meat. Thank God he didn't run into any of the neighbors as they walked away from the Livingstons' house. His well of social chat had just run dry.

He and the dog reached the highway and made their way down it to Sela's neighborhood. There were more people walking the highway than he'd expected, and he was taken aback when several people waved and called out hellos. He didn't recognize them, so how the hell did they think they knew him? Then again, for the past few years he'd made a practice of not looking directly at people so they wouldn't try to talk to him, but that didn't mean they hadn't been looking him over. It was something of a shock, scraping uncomfortably on his nerves, to realize that a lot of people in the valley would know him by sight.

He returned the waves, but kept walking. God save him from friendly people. What the hell was wrong with them?

When he reached Sela's side road he realized he'd assumed she'd be at her own house, but in reality she could be anywhere. The two most likely choices, though, were her house and her aunt's house. He passed the yellow two-story she'd said belonged to her aunt but didn't stop, because he didn't want to deal with any extra people; he'd had enough for the day, about all he could stand. If she wasn't at her house, he'd go back to the mountain.

But she was there; he saw her sitting on the screened porch. When she spotted him, she laid aside the book she was reading and stood. The pup barked in greeting and tried to bound forward, to be thwarted by his grip on the leash.

Walking across her yard, though, didn't fill him with dread. Somehow talking to her was different, as if the night they'd watched the aurora together had gotten him past that stage with her. Maybe seeing the outline of her breasts had something to do with it, he thought with a tinge of amusement. *Amusement.* It had been a long time since he'd been amused by anything, much less himself.

"You have a dog!" she said as she opened the screen door, smiling down at the pup.

A quick glance told him she was wearing a bra, which was both a relief and a disappointment. At least he wouldn't have to fight to keep his mind on the conversation, but damn, he missed the view. "He wandered up; he'd either gotten lost or been abandoned."

She opened the door wider. "Come on in, and bring him, too. I'll get him some water. Do you want some tea?" She gestured to the half-full glass sitting beside her open book. "I have some fresh sun tea."

He hadn't acquired the Southern taste for sweet tea, but he said, "Thanks. I'll keep him here on the porch, though. I'm not sure of his manners in a strange place." Plus going inside her house was something he was reluctant to do, though he couldn't say why.

"I'll be right back."

He watched as she went inside, and yeah, he noticed the way her jeans cupped her ass. Her dark hair was in a ponytail, and she was wearing a red T-shirt. No shoes. He'd never seen her dressed to attract attention; for the most part, she seemed to be content to be under the radar.

She came back out with a glass of tea in one hand and a bowl of water in the other. He took the glass and she set the bowl down on the porch for the dog, who began lapping as thirstily as if he hadn't had plenty to drink from the creek just an hour before. He released the leash and the dog began sniffing around, dragging the rope behind him.

"Have a seat." She gestured to the porch chair beside hers, separated by the small table on which she'd set her book and tea. She took her own seat and pulled her feet up into the chair, curling to the side toward him. "What brings you down the mountain?"

He couldn't say, exactly, but used the opening to ask, "Do you know the Livingstons, just off Covemont? Jim and Mary Alice. Old couple."

"I do, though not well. Jim stopped at my store for gas, every Saturday." She smiled. "About half the time he didn't need much, but he always topped off the tank anyway."

"They didn't make any preparations for the power to be out this long. They're low on food, though the neighbors are helping. Mary Alice takes blood pressure and heart medications, and is running short on both." With amazement, he heard the words coming out of his own mouth. He sounded like someone who was *involved*. Shit. "Do you know anyone in the valley who knows about medicines?" Mary Alice had said she knew some herbalists, but he figured having backup wasn't a bad idea.

"I do. I'll get in touch with them, have them talk to Mary Alice. We have a flowchart set up with people who volunteered to help, what they can do. I wish we had a pharmacist or a doctor, but so far we've been able to get by."

He took a slug of the tea, and was relieved it wasn't *too* sweet. Some of it he'd tried was like drinking candy. He drained most of the glass and set it down, looked for the dog. It was nosing around a potted plant and he said, "Here, dog," to call it away before it began eating the leaves. The pup trotted over to him and he rewarded it with a scratch behind the ears.

"He's well behaved," she said, leaning forward to stroke the dog's sleek head.

"Evidently you didn't notice him about to eat your plant."

She smiled, and something in him warmed, not just at her smile but knowing he'd put it there. He wasn't exactly a jokester.

"I'm glad you stopped by. I've been thinking about the gasoline in my storage tanks at the store."

That got his attention. His head snapped around. "You have gasoline?" Right now gasoline was worth more than gold.

"I turned off the pumps the day you told me what was going to happen."

"Smart thinking. Does anyone else know?" His tone was sharp, but this was serious business.

"Carol, for certain. I don't know if she's told anyone."

"Ask her. Know for sure what you're dealing with. If she hasn't told anyone else, *don't*. People will kill for gasoline right now, and the situation will get worse."

She looked uncertain, and he wished she was more street savvy. "People here in the valley won't—"

"Some of them will. Gasoline is money, and you have drug addicts here the same as everywhere else. Food doesn't matter to them as much as getting their next dose, nothing does. Are your tanks locked?"

"Yes, of course."

"Eventually gangs and looters will start working their way here. Hell, if the population in the northern half of the country has any sense, they'll be walking south right now. Wears Valley isn't on an interstate but some people will come through this area. Start hiding what you have or you'll lose it."

She slowly nodded, her gaze turning inward as she processed the realization that the valley wasn't as secure as she'd assumed.

"The gas is a problem. Ethanol gas is good for about three months, so you either use it or lose it. Pure gasoline is stable much longer, but—"

"I have a pure gasoline tank," she said. "Not a big one, but I keep it because people like pure gas for their lawn mowers and such. It's on the left side of the station, with a separate pump."

He'd seen the small pump, and assumed it was for kerosene. That was a resource he hadn't expected, and it was available because she'd had the foresight to turn off her pumps. A couple of other stations in the valley had been pumped dry, with the owners making as much money as they could while they could. Both views had merit.

"Do you have any fuel stabilizer in your store?"

"Some. Not much."

"Okay." He thought a minute. "It's a balancing act. I won't tell you to hoard the gasoline, because it'll go bad. But if you let people have access to it now, a good portion of them will use their generators *right now*, instead of waiting for colder weather. I say wait another month before you sell it, or barter with it. The weather will be colder and they can save firewood by using the generators. Use the stabilizer when you sell the ethanol blend, but keep the pure stuff for yourself."

"That's selfish." She sighed. "And pragmatic. It isn't just me, I have Carol and Olivia to think about." Her smile this time was crooked. "This survival-of-the-fittest stuff is challenging."

It never had been for him, but Sela was made of gentler stuff. He doubted she'd ever been shot at; that made a difference.

"Anyway, I wanted to ask if you knew of a way to pump the gas out of the tanks, without electricity? I intended to check online before . . . well, *before* . . . but I got busy and never did."

"A suction pump system will do, like siphoning gas from a car tank. Let me know when you're ready to let people have the gas, and I'll get something rigged up."

"Thanks. I figured you'd know."

She'd had confidence in him, even though she knew nothing about him, his background, his experience. Just like that, he absorbed a hard punch to the chest, because his squad members had had confidence in him, followed his lead, looked to him to know what to do. For the most part he'd carried out his missions and got his guys back alive, but his unit had absorbed casualties and fatalities like every other unit. The deaths added up, and one day the weights of those deaths had been too heavy for him to carry. All of it had crashed and burned for him, the dumb-ass orders, the incompetence of people in command, the cost paid by his men and others like them.

He wanted to leave. Like the night they'd sat on the steps, he'd suddenly crossed a mental line and needed to get away from everyone, be alone for a while—like a month or so. It was all he could do to remain seated, and only the fact that this was Sela kept him there. Being here was his choice. Talking to her was his choice. He made himself finish the small amount of tea left in his glass, because he didn't want to offend her by being too abrupt.

"I should get back. I just wanted to make certain someone checked on the Livingstons," he said as he stood.

She stood, too. "I'll take care of it. Thanks for letting me know." She took a step toward the screen door and the movement brought her close to him, so close her arm brushed against his abdomen. She faltered and stopped, as if the contact had rocked her. He looked down at her, noting that the top of her head didn't quite touch his chin, that her hand shook a little as she reached out to open the door. His wrists were almost twice as thick as hers.

She looked up at him, and her brown eyes were wide, both soft and a little alarmed, as if she sensed what he was thinking.

He was thinking that he'd need to be careful with her, that he wanted to feel her pussy tightening around his dick, and that he wanted to make her scream while she came. He could feel his expression changing, becoming hard and intent, knew he couldn't hide it from her.

"I need to get away from you," he said softly. "Right now."

She didn't protest as he took the dog's leash in his grip and went down the steps. He didn't look back.

CHAPTER NINE

Sela was trembling as she sat down and watched Ben until he and the young dog were out of sight. She didn't want to look away from him, to stop seeing those broad shoulders and the line of his back, the easy, fluid rhythm of his long, muscular legs. She wanted to call him back, to have him close enough to once again smell the hot maleness of his skin, to touch him.

Holy shit. She couldn't say she didn't have any idea what had almost happened because she did, she wasn't naive, but she'd never before seen that almost violently hungry expression on a man's face.

I need to get away from you.

Or . . . what?

He'd have kissed her, and she wasn't sure they'd have stopped at kissing. She didn't know if or why *she* would have put on the brakes, and how likely was it that *he* would have? Not very, and yet he'd managed to pull himself back into his shell and walk away before anything had gotten started.

Uncertainty seized her. What if he'd left because he *didn't* want to get involved with her, and he'd thought she was about to make a suggestion that he'd have to turn down? Her cheeks burned in retrospective humiliation. Maybe she'd misread his expression; not being naive didn't mean she couldn't be mistaken. She'd never before inspired savage lust in a man, so what made her think something had suddenly changed and a man like Ben Jernigan would want her?

Sex, yes; men went for casual sex. But what about wanting *her*, the person, who had nothing special about her? Had he thought she'd be needy, demanding more than he could give, and that was why he'd bolted? She'd never done casual sex, because she couldn't let herself be that vulnerable. Her instinct, always, was to protect herself and attract as little attention as possible.

She gathered both tea glasses and took them inside, washed them in the cold pan of dishwater she prepared every morning. The mundane chore gave her a little bit of distance, let her step back from what had and hadn't happened with Ben. There was nothing she could do to change it. If he was interested, he'd come back. If he wasn't interested, she'd have to accept that and move on.

The next morning Sela walked up the road to Carol's house, for the morning ritual of listening to the nine A.M. radio broadcast. Sometimes she'd go early and have breakfast with them, which these days consisted of a cup of instant coffee and whatever they'd settled on that day, maybe an apple with peanut butter. Mostly, though, she'd skip breakfast. She wasn't hungry early in the day, and she was always acutely aware that every bite they took today was a bite they wouldn't have when winter came.

As soon as Sela walked in the door, Carol looked at her, eyebrows raised, and said, "Ben Jernigan walked by yesterday afternoon. Did you see him?"

"I did." Helping herself to a cup and the instant coffee, she dipped, poured, and stirred. She still hadn't told Carol about the night of the aurora, and didn't intend to. She might have misled herself about what sitting with Ben could have indicated, but it was still a memory she cherished and didn't want to share, or listen to Carol's comments about Mr. Hot Body. "I was sitting on the porch."

"I wonder where he was going," Carol continued, her tone sly. "He came back by in just a little while."

Sela ignored Carol's insinuation that he'd been going to *her* house. Well, he had, but for a different reason. "He told me the Livingstons, the old couple over near Covemont, needed checking on. You know them, don't you?"

"Sure. Jim and Mary Alice. How does he know them? I didn't think he associated with anyone."

"I don't know. Anyway, Mary Alice is on a couple of medications and needs some help managing them and finding substitutions for when she runs out. I thought after the radio broadcast I'd go by their house and find out exactly what she's taking, then talk to the Bouldins about it." Pat and Helen Bouldin were the herbalist couple she'd met the day of the big cookout.

Carol looked disappointed that Sela didn't have anything more interesting to say about Ben, but took up her ever-present notebook and made a dated entry about the Livingstons. That way nothing was forgotten or overlooked.

Olivia came down the stairs and made a face at the breakfast offering, which today was some instant oatmeal, two packets divided between three—or four—people, and dried prunes. She didn't protest, though she took only one prune and very little oatmeal. Barb wasn't eating much either, but the uneaten oatmeal wouldn't be thrown away; they'd stir hot water into the leftovers for lunch. "We need some bread," she announced. "Toast would be great." Their ready-made bread supplies were gone, but they had the ingredients to bake bread, they just hadn't done it—again, saving supplies for harder times.

"I'll make some pan biscuits tomorrow morning," Barb promised. "It won't be long until we'll have to keep a fire going, and we'll have bread more often." She smiled, looking inward. "I remember my mama baking bread in the cast-iron skillet, in the fireplace. I've done it a time or two myself. I'm not the hand my mama was with bread, but I can get by."

"Thanks!" Olivia said fervently, and bent to kiss Barb's cheek. The older woman flushed with pleasure. Since the CME Barb sometimes seemed lonely; though she and Carol were great friends, she had no family and the crisis had uprooted her from her own home. Olivia's casual gesture meant more than she could imagine, because it made Barb feel useful and treasured.

Sela made a mental note to see if she could trade something for some butter. Some of the people who owned cows were now milking and churning, and trading the raw milk and fresh butter for other goods. She would stay busy, and not think about Ben.

Breakfast taken care of—or suffered through, in Olivia's case—they got the radio and left the house, walking up the road to the highway, then to the big field. They'd done this for the past nine mornings, to listen to the morning broadcast report. That brief contact with what she now thought of as the "outside world" was a lifeline to them, giving them hope that while modern normality was still perhaps months in the future, at least it still existed in small pockets. If it existed, it could be built on, expanded. The news was never good, but some days it was worse than others. There was nothing they could do about the problems in Knoxville and elsewhere, but it did give them a connection to the rest of the world. They needed that connection, for as long as they could maintain it.

For the first few days after they began receiving the radio reports, mostly what they'd heard had been about widespread looting, and a number of deaths due to the loss of electricity in hospitals and nursing homes. After that things had seemed to settle down, though they were still critical. Sewage and trash buildup had quickly become an issue.

She could only be thankful they were a rural community; if things were that bad in Knoxville, what was it like in the large cities, like New York and Chicago, with winter bearing down on them? The residents there couldn't hunt and fish, and the food supply had likely been used up in the first few days after the grid went down.

Yesterday's news hadn't been good at all. Even in Knoxville food was running critically short, which led to more rioting and looting, as if riots would magically make food appear from thin air. There had been several home invasions, when desperate people looking for food found undefended houses and forced their way in.

What was most frightening was the realization that most of these incidents were going unreported. The radio announcer could report only what someone told him; there were no phone calls, no internet alerts, no police blotters. The Knoxville police force had devolved to a skeleton crew, because most cops had been forced to stay at home to take care of their own families. There was no one to handle mobs, chase burglars, or investigate break-ins.

Just yesterday Robert Keller, the announcer they'd listened to since the radio waves had settled down, had been in a panic over a melee in the station parking lot. His voice cracked as he'd delivered the news he had, and he'd warned his listeners that the generators wouldn't last much longer, they were almost out of fuel. The other radio stations had already gone dark. They either hadn't enough fuel for their generators, or the operators had all fled—or the fuel had been stolen. Keller had hung on longer than the others, but he was definitely harried and getting more harried. The stress in his voice was increasing day by day.

Maybe it would be better to stop listening, Sela thought, and spare themselves the constant mental battering of bad news, but she doubted anyone else would agree with her. Everyone seemed compelled to gather around every morning and listen. What if there was information about the grid and when it might be repaired? What if something important had happened in the world, something they really should know about—though how that news would get to a Knoxville radio station, Sela didn't know.

There were plenty of other concerns. Right now the valley inhabitants were doing okay, but they were in a good time, with good weather and supplies not yet running low. They were adjusting, coping, improvising. Sela was still mentally holding her breath, because this good stretch couldn't last. Someone would get sick, someone would get hurt, people would get in fights—they were human, after all, and that's what humans did.

One of Olivia's friends called out to her and she said, "Here, Gran," and handed off the radio to Carol before darting over to join her small group. The kids wanted to hear the broadcast, but they also wanted to socialize.

At one minute till nine, Carol turned on the radio. They were all going by their wristwatches now, those who had them, but they really had no way of knowing how accurate their watches were. Carol had set hers to the radio on the second day, but allowed for error by turning on the radio early.

They listened to the static, standing around and talking quietly among themselves, waiting for the broadcast to start. A minute ticked by, then another. An alarmed murmur ran through the crowd. They began looking around and at each other. Sela met Mike Kilgore's eyes, and saw awareness in his.

There was only static.

Carol looked at the dial, adjusted the knob a little in case it had been bumped and knocked out of place, at one point or another.

Static.

People crowded around, hoping against hope. Carol scanned up and down the dial, trying to find another station they could receive, however weak the signal. Nothing.

The alarmed murmur got louder. Barb made a sound of distress, then pressed her hand to her mouth. Sela saw a girl in Olivia's group start crying, and Olivia try to comfort her though she, too, looked as if she was about to start tearing up.

Sela tried not to be too disappointed but she felt as if they'd turned a corner, and not a good one. It was inevitable that the radio station would go dark, but he'd said just yesterday that they had enough for another two or three days. Had he simply miscalculated the amount of fuel? Had the station been attacked?

Had he given up, and simply not gone to the station? They had no way of knowing.

"Well, that's that." Decisively Carol turned off the radio with a quick and final flick of a switch. "I never thought I'd actually miss hearing so much bad news. Damn, I need another cup of that weak-ass instant coffee."

Mike had moved closer, and Sela said to him, "We need to take a look at our security situation."

Carol and Barb both looked at her, and the people around them fell silent to listen. "Why?" Barb asked.

"People are leaving Knoxville," Sela replied. "Most of them will stick to the interstate going south, but some of them might come this way, and they'll be desperate." Desperate or mean, the end result didn't matter. Whoever came to the valley would be looking for food, for shelter, for weapons and supplies and anything that could be sold or traded. "We have enough to get by for a while, enough for us and our neighbors. But if we're overrun what we have won't last a week, assuming we're left with anything at all, or aren't killed outright."

"She's right," Mike said. "We should have already thought about this and got something set up."

"Who would come here?" Barb asked, alarmed. She wasn't the only one; some younger people were looking around in confusion, as if expecting to see hordes of people pouring down the highway toward them, while the people who had been in the military were nodding their heads.

"Could be anyone," Mike said. "Look how many tourists drove through this area every day. And people in the cities already know they can't stay there, so if they have any sense they won't head for another city, they'll look for small communities—like this one—that are self-sustaining. They know country folk have guns and gardens, and that's what they'll want."

Sela hadn't noticed Ted Parsons in the crowd, but now he maneuvered into the nucleus of the conversation. "Looters and gangs will be in the minority. A lot of regular people will be leaving the cities, too, and they could be a lot of help. There's safety in numbers. A gang will look for isolated people they can overwhelm, not a place where they'll be outnumbered."

"If we had unlimited resources I wouldn't disagree with you," Mike said.

"As it is, we wouldn't be able to house and feed a bunch of other people," Carol pointed out. "All the vegetable gardens have stopped producing, and we won't have a fresh supply of food or the ability to grow more until next spring . . . say, eight months until more crops are in. We can't take in more people without shortchanging the ones who are already here."

There was a rumble of agreement around her. Ted looked frustrated. "But more people are more hands to cut wood, and hunt."

"That works only if they bring their own axes and ammunition with them," Sela said quietly. "Otherwise they'd be using tools we already have. No matter how much we want to help people, if we want to make it through the winter we will already have to severely conserve what we have."

That earned her a scowl from Ted, which she wouldn't care about if he didn't have just enough argument on his side to cause serious dissent. Their resources were so thin she didn't know if they could survive a break in their united front.

She wished Ben were here, for all the good wishing did. He'd know what to do, but though he'd taken the trouble to warn her, and then flabbergasted her by checking on the Livingstons, weeks could go by without anyone seeing him. He'd already refused Mike's invitation to join them. He was in great shape up there on Cove Mountain, and didn't need them. Assuming anyone wanted his supplies, they'd have to first climb the mountain, then fight him. Even street gangs would go for easier prey, and leave him and his shotgun alone.

But he wasn't the only person around here who'd been in the military; there were several standing here around her, mostly men but a couple of women, too. They had a forest ranger, a retired cop, and a whole lot of people who had spent their whole lives hunting in these mountains. The valley people weren't helpless, or without knowledge.

Carol reached for her ever-present notebook. "Okay, people, I need some names. We're going to need people who can start riding or walking patrol. We need enough to keep an eye on the main highway approaches, and that new parkway over the mountain from Knoxville to here is going to be a pain in the butt, you just wait and see."

Sela agreed on that. The new parkway had sat unfinished for years, then the project got going again just in time to cause a problem by creating another vulnerability. Keeping an eye on it would require at least two people, each pulling twelve-hour shifts, and that wasn't going to be easy.

Trey Foster, the man who had offered to keep her supplied with firewood, spoke up. "I was in the army, I can help with patrolling. But if we're patrolling we won't be able to hunt, or chop firewood, and our families will suffer for that."

Mike said, "The sensible solution would be to pay the security team with food, everybody chipping in with a little. If someone brings down a deer, part of it goes for payment."

"Some people can't afford to give away their food!" Ted said, looking alarmed, which told Sela he and his wife hadn't gathered as much food as they could have.

"Then you should join the community patrol," Mike said, immediately coming to the same conclusion.

Ted looked startled, then said, "Well, okay." After a second, his expression morphed into one of pleasure. He was not only being included, but doing something important. Maybe that was the key to handling him: keep him busy, and stroke his ego.

Carol wrote down their names, Trey's and Ted's, and at Mike's nod added his to the list. "I'm waiting," she hollered. "Y'all step up here and help keep the valley safe, or I'll be talking to your mamas and wives, and you don't want that."

That provoked a rumble of laughter, and men began moving forward. There weren't that many of them, maybe two dozen, but there were enough to patrol the highway approaches, and eventually they would have to settle disputes, but for now—it was a start.

CHAPTER TEN

Late October was normally a time for tourists, with roads clogged with traffic and crowded restaurants. The leaves were changing—red, yellow, and orange amid the evergreens—the festivals were going on and the weather was thankfully turning cool. Previously, October and early November were among the busiest times of the year, for Sela's store and elsewhere in the valley.

Not this year. This year there was little or no traffic on the highway, because people seldom drove, using their precious gasoline only when they had to. Usually there was no place to go, anyway: no doctor or dentist appointments to keep, no eating out or going to movies. Mostly people walked or rode bicycles, though the community patrol they'd set up—which was still evolving—mostly rode horses. Not everyone was an accomplished rider, though, and they either learned or walked. For the first couple of weeks there had been a lot of sore butts and legs.

But, people being people and Southerners being generally gregarious anyway, the valley inhabitants had begun gathering in their own neighborhoods in the late afternoon, and by the end of October the gatherings were a ritual. On the nicest of days, those gatherings continued well into the evening. No one had planned them, they'd just happened organically. It had started with a few neighbors hanging out in the road at the end of a long day, and had grown from there. In a matter of a couple of weeks, there were small get-togethers all over the valley. They talked about food, power, and how damn dark it got at night. The days were getting shorter, and many had adjusted their sleep patterns to conserve batteries and candles, going to bed when it got dark and sleeping—or trying to—until the sun came up. That was going to be more and more difficult, as the nights got longer.

They also talked about kids, movies, books, and knitting. It was a search for a touch of normal in an abnormal world.

There was more to survival than food and water. People needed people, a sense of community. They'd always had that here but now it was growing stronger. Last week a kid from the far end of the road had brought his guitar out and strummed a country song or two while others gathered around and listened. He was merely competent, but competent enough that listening wasn't painful. Sela didn't exactly love country music but she was entranced anyway. It seemed as if it had been years since she'd heard music, rather than a month. They said music had the power to soothe the savage breast, and while her breast wasn't particularly savage she definitely felt soothed, and she wasn't alone. Everyone enjoyed the music.

Halloween was a particularly beautiful night, clear and mild, with bright stars overhead. A fire was going in a portable fire pit, because despite the mildness there was something comforting about a fire. People had brought folding lawn chairs or camp chairs to sit in, or put blankets on the ground. Inspired by the kid, Mike Kilgore also brought his guitar. The two amateur musicians took turns and sometimes played together, their timing a bit off but who cared? People knew the songs and sometimes sang a few lines.

This night there were close to thirty people standing or sitting in the middle of the road. Olivia and one of her friends who had walked over to spend the night were sitting on a blanket with their legs drawn up and their fascinated gazes fixed on the boy with the guitar. Sela thought the boy was perhaps a year younger than Olivia, but pickings were slim in the neighborhood and hormones were hormones.

Sela, Carol, and Barb were in camp chairs set up in the middle of the crowd. Barb felt the cold more than they did, so she was closer to the fire. Sela stretched out her legs and relished the moment of relaxation, because those moments were few and far between.

Describing the past month as stressful was a massive understatement. She'd never expected to be in this situation, and neither had anyone else in this gathering, but they were making the best of it. She no longer felt as if she was scrambling every minute, trying to stay on top of the unknown and doubting her every decision. They had done okay, she and Carol and Barb, in their marathon canning session and the extra supplies she'd gathered in her frantic shopping expedition.

The new normal was melding with the old normal. Sunday services had started up just last week, with the nearest church making it clear that everyone was welcome. The preacher had gone to great lengths to make his sermon nondenominational. "God is God," he'd said at the beginning. "Everything else is us trying to organize things to our liking. I'm going to concentrate on the God part, and y'all can argue in the parking lot."

Most people had laughed, and simply enjoyed resuming services.

For now, with everything that had happened, with all that was still to come, the music made this moment beautiful. Sela sighed as her mind eased. The music flowed over and through her, and thoughts of tomorrow faded away.

Carol suddenly grinned, slapped the arm of her chair, and jumped up. Weaving her way past the others, she reached the two musicians and leaned down to whisper to Mike. He grinned, too, whispered a reply, and with a satisfied expression Carol positioned herself between the two guitarists.

Olivia hissed, "Gran, no!" and covered her face with her hands in the teenage horror of being embarrassed by her elders. She knew what was coming. Sela did, too, but unlike Olivia she enjoyed it whenever Carol belted out a song.

Carol was no Janis Joplin, but she did have a pretty decent voice and not a shy bone in her body. "Cry Baby" was one of her favorites, and she did it justice, bending over to launch into the first notes. Mike knew the song, or at least parts of it, and the kid did his best to follow along with the guitar licks but keeping it soft so Carol's voice was in the forefront. Some of the older people laughed and began joining in.

Barb whispered to Sela, "Your aunt is such an old hippie." She said it with a smile.

"I know." She looked again at Olivia, who still had her face buried in her hands. She was mortified, though her friend was grinning and her foot was trying to keep up with the jerky rhythm of the song.

This was community, Sela thought as her aunt belted out an almost-Janis-like note, people supporting people, enjoying one another's company at the end of a long day, coming together in whatever ways they could. This was so much better than each person going into their own homes to watch TV or play video games or read a book.

Maybe stories told around the campfire would come next. She could get into that—listening, of course, not as a storyteller. The thought of performing in front of other people horrified her.

Unbidden she thought of Ben, up on the mountain all alone except for the dog he wouldn't even name. She tried *not* to think about him and how she'd embarrassed herself, but no matter how busy she was or what she was doing, she couldn't keep her thoughts under control. She hadn't seen him since he'd come to tell her about the Livingstons and she was pretty sure he was now actively avoiding her, which deepened her humiliation. Evidently that didn't matter because she was still ambushed by the errant thoughts and longing she couldn't control.

Worrying about him was pointless. Feeling her heart clench because he was alone was equally useless. He was more than capable of taking care of himself, and being alone was what he wanted. But what if he got hurt, or sick? He wasn't Superman, he wasn't invulnerable. What if—

Useless. She was wasting her time and energy. He'd made it very clear that he didn't need anyone. He definitely didn't need her.

"Cry Baby" ended, but Carol didn't return to her seat. She crooked a finger at Olivia and then at Sela. They both shook their heads, Sela even more vehemently than Olivia.

"You know what I want next," Carol said devilishly. "And God knows you both know all the words."

Olivia's friend elbowed her in the side. "Go on," the girl said. "You can sing, I've heard you!" Reluctantly Olivia got up and went to stand beside Carol. Her stomach twisting in stage fright, Sela didn't move. Olivia mouthed *Please!* at her, and the others around them began encouraging her to get up. Within seconds, her refusal was drawing more attention than singing in public ever could. She was making a spectacle of herself by digging in her heels. Reluctantly she stood and headed toward Carol and Olivia. With a giggle, Barb heaved herself up and joined them.

How many times had she sung "Mercedes Benz" in Carol's living room? When she was a kid, the song had been on a vinyl album that Carol had played on a record player, before reluctantly succumbing first to a cassette tape and finally a CD. There might even have been an eight-track tape in there, somewhere. "Mercedes Benz" was Carol's all-time favorite song, and she was ruthless in inflicting it on family and visitors alike.

At Carol's lead, the four of them launched into the song, singing a capella. By the second line, a number of the older people grouped around were enthusiastically joining in because the song was a lot easier than "Cry Baby." All the younger folks—basically anyone under thirty, with Olivia being the exception—were stumped, but entertained.

All through the crowd there was laughter, along with the voices loud and soft, talented and untalented. It seemed that everyone had allowed the power of the music to wipe away their worries, for a while. The short song was over too soon.

Sela and Olivia returned to their seats, and so did a breathless Carol.

Barb remained standing, and began singing a very different type of song. She'd never been a Joplin fan the way Carol was. She was, apparently, more into folk music. Joan Baez, maybe; Sela wasn't sure. Barb had a surprisingly good voice, and her slow, easy song grabbed everyone. A hush fell over the crowd. After the raucousness of Carol's Joplin offerings, Barb's full, warm tones wove a kind of spell that was all mixed in with the bright stars overhead and the soft night air, the crisp smell of autumn and wood fire. It was a magical moment, one Sela knew she'd remember long after the lights came back on.

As Ben neared Sela's neighborhood, he'd been surprised to hear the music. It wasn't loud enough to carry far, but in the still night it did carry. The dog's ears perked up, he even pranced a little, but he stayed close to Ben's side. They avoided the road and skirted back-yards to get where they were headed.

From one side of Sela's house large trees blocked his view, so Ben walked through the backyard until he could see what was going on in the middle of Myra Road. Thanks to the dark and the distance no one saw him, but in the light of the fire he could see them well. Was that Sela's aunt? Singing? God, what caterwauling. She screeched at the top of her tiny but apparently powerful lungs. He was about to leave, thinking he could come back another time when Sela wasn't so busy, but when Carol motioned to Olivia and Sela and they joined her . . . Well, there was no way he could leave now. He leaned against the side of the house and prepared himself for whatever might come.

None of them would ever make a professional singer, but there was joy in their stupid song, in the way they grinned at the crowd and shared smiles with each other. His eyes were drawn to and remained on Sela. She moved to the song a little. She wasn't as boisterously into it as the others, but the way her hips swayed . . . Shit, he did not need this distraction. What he had to do could wait until tomorrow. And to be honest, he didn't have to do anything at all. He shouldn't even be here.

But he didn't walk away. Even the dog, who sat at his side, seemed oddly entranced.

The song ended too soon, and Sela returned to her seat. He couldn't see her nearly well enough from this vantage point, but he wasn't willing to move from this safe spot to get a better view, though he was tempted. The older woman who had been singing with them remained standing to sing her own song, something slow and easy. She wasn't too bad on her own.

Music by firelight. He hadn't expected this.

When she was done with her easy song, someone else from the crowd took her place to sing a hymn. Several people joined in, until it seemed everyone was singing the familiar hymn. They should've sounded terrible, but they didn't. They were out of tune—with gruff and less-than-pleasant voices mingled with those more talented—but . . . not terrible.

Ben didn't leave, as he'd intended, but stood there in the deepest shadows of the night until the crowd began to disperse and Sela headed his way. She spent a lot of time with her family, but she slept here, in her own house, all alone. She thought she was safe. They all did.

No one was safe. He knew that, and surely some of them did,

too. So why were they laughing and singing? This was a crisis, not a damn picnic.

And yet . . . A part of him envied their innocence, their ability to come together and forget for a while. He wished he could let himself believe everything was going to be okay.

He didn't.

Sela, flashlight in hand and pointed to the ground, had almost reached her front door when he stepped around the corner and surprised her. He really surprised her. She damn near jumped out of her skin.

"Damn it!" she gasped, as she placed one hand over her heart. "Sorry, I didn't mean to cuss at you, but I'll die ten years sooner now." She took a breath. "How long have you been standing there?"

He didn't smile, but he wanted to. "Long enough."

He knew Sela well enough to know she had to be blushing. "Sorry. I can't sing at all."

"You did okay."

She cocked her head and looked at him hard. "You should've joined us. We can always use a baritone."

"I don't sing."

"Come on . . ."

"No way in hell."

She laughed at that and headed for her front porch. "Come on in. What can I do for you?"

She had no idea. Well, maybe she did. The attraction that was driving him nuts wasn't one-sided, he knew it wasn't. What it was, was more than he could handle.

He had no intention of sitting next to her again, of tempting himself with impossible ideas. So why was he here, unless he liked torturing himself?

Right. He actually had a reason. He swung his backpack off his shoulder and unzipped the main compartment. "I had some extra solar lights, and I thought maybe you could use them."

She turned to face him. "Extra?"

He'd noticed that she didn't have any, and he did have more than enough, and damn it, she didn't have to look at him that way. "If you don't want them—"

"I didn't say that!" she interrupted, and then she smiled and walked back toward him.

He placed his backpack on the ground and drew out not one but two powerful garden solar lights. He knew Sela well enough to know that if she had just one she'd give it to her aunt. This way they'd each have one. She pointed the beam of her flashlight down as he screwed the main unit into the stick. The lights would've been too long for his backpack if he hadn't taken them apart. "Stick them into the ground in the morning, to collect sunlight, then bring them in at night." He pointed out where the small on-off switch was located on the base.

She took the first one he handed her. It seemed they were both being extra cautious not to touch as the device changed hands. "This is fantastic," she said. "Will it work on cloudy days?"

"Some, though it won't be as bright. You should still get some use out of it." He assembled the other light and placed it to the side, leaning it against the house.

"I'll give one to Carol, if you don't mind. These will really come in handy."

He'd already assumed she'd do just that, and she did not disappoint.

There was a too-long moment of nervous silence, until the dog got involved. He danced at Sela's feet. She smiled and set her solar light aside, leaned down to give the dog a good vigorous rub behind his ears while she called him a good boy.

Lucky mutt.

He wanted those hands on him. He could be a good boy, too.

Mentally he snorted at the idea. More than wanting her to touch him, he wanted to put his hands on her. That was why he'd made this ridiculous trip, to offer her a couple of solar lights. Was he looking to impress her? To make himself useful? What a load of crock. His dick had pointed him in this direction, and he had followed.

"Dog," he called gruffly, turning away and walking away from Sela. "Let's go."

"Uh, thank you," she called in an uncertain and too-soft voice.

He muttered a gruff "Welcome," as the pup pulled up beside him, but he didn't look back.

The days slipped past and the reality of living without electricity became more routine. Sela no longer automatically flipped a light switch when she entered a room. October was always a dry month but there had been some rain, enough that she'd collected some water in her makeshift rain collectors and was able to skip a day or two of carrying buckets of water from the creek.

She loved the solar light Ben had given her, and Carol loved hers, too. Carol loved hers because it saved her precious candles, and that was a great benefit. For Sela, the simple gift was more personal, more . . . well, she didn't know what it was.

Sela thought of Ben every night, when she brought the light in. Had that been his intention when he'd given it to her? Surviving was her focus all day long, but at night, when she switched on that light, her thoughts took another turn.

Carol said a gift of solar lights qualified as true and romantic apocalyptic courting, but Sela wasn't so sure. Carol was just . . . Carol.

They were all losing weight, not necessarily because there wasn't enough food but because they were all doing more physical work and automatically eating less in order to save food for later. The occasional biscuits or pan bread that Barb made—very occasional because flour and cornmeal were precious—were a treat rather than something they took for granted.

The valley had seen a few frosty mornings in late October, and then November brought more. The smell and smoke from fireplaces wreathed the valley almost every morning, though winter approached in fits and starts and some days were warm enough for people to go about in short sleeves. Those increasingly rare, bright days always saw people out more, moving around, getting things done.

Sela was stingy with the stack of firewood Trey Foster had delivered, because she didn't want to be a burden on him. To stretch the supply she walked the woods, gathering sticks for kindling and larger pieces whenever she could find them. She carried a blue tarp with her, and loaded her find on it, dragging it behind her and sharing everything with Carol's household. Sometimes Olivia joined her because getting out of the house gave her a chance to expend energy. She and her friends got together whenever they could, but everyone had chores to do now.

"I miss school," Olivia confessed one afternoon as they gathered wood.

"I can see why." Sela paused and stretched her back. They had a good load already, and her lower back was feeling the strain of bending down so much. "Wait." She stared at Olivia, wondering why she hadn't thought of it before, why *no one* had thought of it. "If church can start back, I don't see why school can't." Hadn't that been mentioned back at the very beginning when the grid had gone down? She couldn't believe she'd forgotten!

Olivia's eyes brightened. "You mean, open the elementary school?"

"No, we couldn't heat it. It'll have to be somewhere that can be heated. I wonder how many kids we'd be talking about? Not all kids would come because of the distance involved." A hundred years ago kids had routinely walked miles to school, but that was a hundred years ago. People's outlook hadn't changed sufficiently back to those times for parents not to blink an eye at pushing their kids out the door to walk a few miles in the rain or snow. If the electricity stayed off for over a year, though, those times might return.

"Fifty, maybe?"

Sela thought that might be a good number. The elementary school had almost four times that number of students, but that included kindergarten kids and kids who weren't close enough now to attend.

"There has to be someone in the valley with teaching experience," she said, thinking. As usual, Carol would know more about that than she did. "Regardless of that, you kids have your books, right? What you need is structure and someone to go through the material with you."

Feeding that many kids would be impossible, so everyone would have to bring their lunches. Just dividing the classes, getting volunteers to teach, and heating the area selected for school would be a big job. Logistically, the best places for having classes would be private houses, one for each group, so the firewood wouldn't be used to heat entirely separate spaces. Emergency situations required emergency adjustments. Later on they'd worry about setting up a more traditional school setting.

"Thanks," Olivia said, giving her a quick hug. "I knew you'd come up with something."

They dragged the tarp-load of sticks back to Carol's house, where they unloaded and stacked half of it a few feet from the back door. They covered the stack to keep it dry, then Sela pulled the remainder to her house and repeated the process.

The chores were so simple now. She didn't have to deal with fuel deliveries, inventory, bank statements, or taxes. She had to eat, keep clean, and keep the fire going on cool days. She walked a lot, hauling water and firewood, and going about the valley. She'd met with the Bouldins and they had gone to see the Livingstons, to teach Mary Alice which particular herbs to use to keep her blood pressure under control, and how to use them. Once a week she and Carol walked to the store to meet with Mike and the rest of the community patrol, see how things were going, if any of the volunteers needed relief or had seen something Mike didn't already know about. Ted Parsons always had a lot to say, but he was taking part and she no longer thought he was as obnoxious as he'd first seemed. He and Carol would never be friends, but at least they were cordial.

They were getting by. The valley residents were pulling together, cooperating. Even the oldest people were contributing by taking in mending, making quilts, and any other way they could think of to pay the people who brought them food. The old women knew how to cook without electricity, more than heating a pan of soup on the fire. Some of them would watch younger kids while their parents did other chores. The barter system was very informal, everyone sort of made their own bargains except for what was needed for the community patrol, but it was working. So far they hadn't had any trouble, except for one guy on the Townsend end of the valley who had somehow gotten his hands on some meth and trashed his house and slapped his wife around, before shooting at the neighbor's house. The community patrol, two former military guys, had taken it on themselves to kick the guy's ass and tie him up in a barn until he settled down. Other than that there was nothing they could do, they had no jail and no one wanted to take on the care and feeding of a prisoner anyway.

Sela had the uneasy feeling that if he made a practice of taking drugs—and God only knew where he'd gotten the meth—and slapping his wife around, he'd end up with a bullet in his head in a hunting "accident." She didn't want anyone in their small community to have to kill someone, but everyone who attended the weekly patrol meetings knew that anything was a possibility. All they could do was hope things stayed as relatively peaceful as they had been so far.

The very next morning, the mini-disaster she'd been waiting for happened. She hadn't known who, what, or when, but eventually something had to happen to someone. She just hadn't expected it to be *her* family.

"Sela! *Sela!*"

She was standing in the road talking to Mike. They'd been checking on the elderly couple who lived at the beginning of Myra Road, and discussing recruiting another volunteer for patrol so Trey Foster could cut more firewood, not just for his own family but for others who weren't able to cut it themselves. At Olivia's high, wailing cry, they both turned.

Something was wrong.

Olivia sprinted down the middle of the road toward them, her ponytail whipping behind her. Sela ran toward her, and when Olivia was close enough, Sela saw the tears on her face.

Carol. It had to be Carol. Nothing else would upset Olivia so much.

"Gran fell," Olivia panted as she skidded to a stop. Each word was an effort, each breath ragged.

"Fell?" Sela's heart skipped a beat. At Carol's age a fall could be disastrous—especially now, when there was no 9-1-1 to call, no EMTs, no hospital.

"Down the stairs." Olivia bent over and took a couple of deep breaths. It wasn't the short run that doubled her over, it was the thought of losing her Gran. The kid had lost too much in her short life. She choked on a sob. "Barb said she's broken her leg."

Sela took off at a run, Mike beside her. As she ran she tried to control her emotions. *Better a leg than a hip.* Maybe it wasn't a break. Maybe it was just a bad sprain, and Barb, who tended toward the emotional rather than the logical, had overreacted.

Please let it be a sprain. Please let it be a sprain. Not that a sprain wouldn't be bad enough, in these circumstances; some sprains could take longer to heal than a broken bone.

She ran up the steps and through the front door, with Mike right behind her and Olivia coming in a close third. Her heart almost stopped at the sight of Carol lying in an awkward position at the bottom of the stairs, her eyes closed and her face pale. Barb knelt beside her. Sela hurried forward and as she did, Carol pressed a hand to her side and moaned. Then she said, "Shit!" That one curse word sent a wave of relief through Sela; not only was Carol conscious, she was angry, and that was a very good thing.

Barb looked up, surprisingly calm for someone who normally didn't handle any crisis well. "Thank heavens you're here, Mike; we'll need some help moving her."

"What happened?" Sela asked as she dropped down. "How bad is it?" And was it safe to move Carol? It had to be; what choice did they have? Leave her lying there until her leg healed?

Carol opened her eyes and looked at Sela. Pain was clear in her gaze, her expression, and the way she pressed her lips together. "I lost my balance at the top of the stairs. I went up to get a box of winter clothes out of the closet to air them out, because we're going to need them. It'll probably snow soon, and I want to be prepared." She wasn't quite rambling, but close. "Damn it! I'm disgusted with myself, falling like an old—" She grimaced in pain. "Damn near seventy years old and I've never broken a bone before now. Spectacular timing, wouldn't you say?"

"What do we do?" Olivia asked, dread in her voice. "Oh my God, oh my *God*!"

Mike knelt on the other side of Carol and said to Olivia, "She'll be okay, honey. From what I can see, if her leg's broken, it's a simple fracture. I'll get a medic over here to check, but I'm pretty sure."

Sela danced on the edge of her own hysteria, but she couldn't give in. She was still dealing with what could have happened, not what actually had. She tamped down her sense of dread. Yes, it was likely Carol's leg was broken, but it wasn't a compound fracture. It was a warm enough early November day, and Carol wore capris instead of jeans or sweatpants. If bone had been sticking out, if the skin had been broken, then she wouldn't have been able to stop the panic because she knew enough about compound fractures to know that without expert medical care they could be deadly.

Someone had to handle this crisis. That someone was her.

"Let's get her to the couch. Mike, what do you think would be the best way to lift her? On a quilt, maybe, like a sling?"

"I don't think we'll need that," he said, slipping an arm behind Carol's shoulders and lifting her to a sitting position. Barb hurried to spread a blanket on the couch and fetch a pillow; with Sela and Mike on each side and Olivia gripping Carol's clothes from behind, they got her to a standing position.

Once Carol was upright she put her weight on the left foot, but kept her right foot lifted. Already her lower leg was swelling and bruising some. That wasn't a good sign. Together they lurched and hobbled their way to the sofa and lowered the injured woman there as gently as they could. Later, and with more help, they'd move Carol to her bedroom, but for now this would do and make it easier for any immediate care.

Carol groaned as they positioned her on the couch. She closed her eyes again.

Barb put the pillow behind Carol's head, and another underneath her right knee. "We need to immobilize and elevate the leg."

"You've done this before?" Sela asked.

Barb sighed as she took another pillow and put it under Carol's right foot. "Yes, Harold broke his leg on a camping trip once. It was horrible, really traumatic for both of us, but everything turned out okay. I wish we had some ice. That would help with the swelling."

Might as well wish for a healing fairy; they didn't have any ice, not a single cube. They did have cold water, though, because the water they dipped from the creek was icy. "Olivia, get some towels and wet them, the cold water will help. What else, Barb?"

"A splint, to keep the leg immobile. She'll have to stay off it for at least a couple of months."

Carol's eyes popped open and she tried to come up, but she didn't make it far. She winced and fell back, resting a hand over her rib cage. Were her ribs broken? That was something else to worry about. "A couple of months? Are you kidding me?" She closed her eyes. "My leg hurts like hell. Everything hurts, but the leg is the worst." She lifted a hand to the side of her head, sucking in her breath sharply. "Damn it, I hit my head, too. Is it bleeding?" She turned her head so they could all see.

"No blood," Olivia said. "That's good, right?" She still sounded tearful.

Sela turned to her cousin. Carol was settled, for now, and Olivia needed reassurance, she needed her own kind of care. "Honey, your gran is going to be fine. She's ornery as ever, and that's definitely a good sign."

"Don't talk about me like I'm not here."

Barb placed a hand on Sela's arm. "I have some pain pills left over from my surgery last year." She hurried away, but when she reached the stairway she slowed her pace, taking the stairs up to her room with extra caution.

Olivia dropped down and very gently rested her head on Carol's stomach. "You'd better be okay," she whispered.

Carol stroked Olivia's head, and that was when Sela saw the scrape on her forearm. It was a minor injury, but another one that needed to be tended. Carol had taken quite a fall, and if the broken leg was her only serious injury they should count themselves lucky.

Mike said, "I'll go fetch Terry." Terry Morris was a medic with the volunteer fire department. "Be back as soon as I can," he said as he went out the door.

"I'll definitely be okay, sweetie." The bite was gone from Carol's voice as she continued to stroke Olivia's hair. "I'm just pissed that I fell."

And still not herself, if she'd use the word *pissed* in front of Olivia.

Barb returned, still taking extra care on the stairway. They all needed to be extra careful, now that medical care wasn't readily available. She detoured to the kitchen to get a cup of water, then handed a single pill to Carol, who raised herself enough to toss it back and chase it with water.

Sela said, "Olivia, get that wet towel, and a dry one to put under her leg so we don't get the blanket wet." This time, Olivia darted off to get the requested items.

Sela focused on what needed to be done next. What could they use for a splint? Someone in the neighborhood would have crutches, and she was pretty sure Mrs. Armstrong had had one of those portable toilets when her mother had lived with her. Maybe it was still around. Prosaic matters, but the prosaic had to be handled, too.

All this, and more, was whirling through her head when Carol said, "You'll have to take over."

"Take over what?" Did Carol want her to move in? It would probably be a good idea, at least for a few days, so she could help Barb and Olivia take care of the patient while she was in the most pain.

"Everything," Carol said in a weak voice. "I know, I was the one elected, and you were just supposed to help, but let's face it, I'm not going to be able to make the meeting tomorrow, or the one next week."

Before Sela could voice her instinctive protest Carol added, "My leg really does hurt like hell. I didn't want Olivia to see, but I ex- pect I'll be taking Barb's pain pills for a while, so I won't be in my right mind." Gingerly she touched the sore spot on her head. "I don't know how bad the head injury might be, but the fall knocked me out. It's probably not smart for me to make any decisions for a while."

Instinctively Sela began, "Someone else can—" then stopped herself, bracing for the inevitable.

"You want Teddy in charge of Wears Valley?" Carol snapped.

No. No she didn't.

"You know damn well he'll take any opportunity to bully his way into a position of power."

That was assuming there was any power involved in the position, but it was the idea of being "in charge." Yes, he would. "Just for now," Sela finally conceded. "I expect you'll be back before you know it."

"Oh, honey, I don't think so." Carol grimaced and closed her eyes and hissed a low and angry "Shit!" right before Olivia returned with the cold wet towel.

Terry Morris came, carefully felt Carol's leg, and said it was likely both of the lower leg bones were broken, but the good news was they were simple fractures and the bones weren't out of place. The leg needed to be immobilized, though. Terry used two short pieces of plank for the splint, and Olivia sacrificed several old T-shirts that he cut up and used to tie the splints in place. Carol cursed, mostly to herself, as she was moved from the couch to her bed. She usually watched her language around Olivia, trying to be a good role model and all, but she was in a lot of pain and muzzling herself was something she thought of only *after* she'd said something she shouldn't—not that she'd said, or muttered, anything Olivia hadn't heard before. The young girl just hadn't heard it from *her*.

Once she was settled, Sela went outside to talk with Mike and Terry, maybe tell them she was stepping into Carol's position for now.

The pain pill Barb had given her had already kicked in, thank the Lord, but though she was fuzzy she still had most of her faculties. After Carol heard the front door close behind Sela, she took first Olivia's hand and then Barb's.

"I don't want you two to worry too much. This is annoying, I *am* in a lot of pain and will be for a while, I won't lie about that, but I'll be fine." Her mind began to swim a little, like it did when she'd had too much wine, which didn't happen often enough these days. She was kind of a lightweight in the alcohol department and she had Olivia to think of, so she was extra careful when it came to booze of any kind.

"But Gran—"

She squeezed Olivia's hand and forced a smile. "I promise you, honey, I'm going to be okay."

Carol glanced at Barb, then, and caught her friend's eye. "Here's the thing, y'all. Sela should've been in charge of the community organization from the beginning. I'm too old, and too cranky, and let's face it, all the good ideas were hers. She just needs a little push. If I exaggerate my disability while Sela is around, don't be concerned."

"Gran!" Olivia's mouth fell open. "You want us to lie to Sela?"

"Not lie, exactly. *Exaggerate*," Carol said again.

"You fell down the stairs, and your first thought is to use the accident to force Sela to do something she doesn't want to do?" Barb asked.

"Of course not. It was my second or third thought." One thing this crisis had taught her was to make the best of a bad situation, and that's what she was doing now. "Maybe the fourth."

"Your little bird needs to be pushed out of the nest." Barb got it. She even smiled, her eyes crinkling.

The pain pill was really kicking in now. Carol closed her eyes. The entire world spun and swam. Maybe next time she'd take half a pill. That should be plenty, and they'd last longer that way.

"Sela is stronger than she knows, and yes, she needs a little push."

Carol realized she'd be walking a fine line for the next few weeks, pretending to be more feeble than she was without causing Sela to worry too much. If Sela didn't step up, as Carol was sure she would, then when the break healed she'd get back to it.

But if Sela proved to herself and everyone else that she was capable—well. That would be the best outcome, and almost worth a broken leg.

CHAPTER ELEVEN

Jim Livingston had spent another restless night, sleeping in fits and starts. Not being able to sleep annoyed him but out of habit he rolled over easy, hoping not to wake Mary Alice. He'd had trouble sleeping since the sun storm had knocked out the power, but she hadn't missed even one night's sleep. She'd always been that way, sleeping through thunderstorms and worrisome times of their lives. The only time he'd known her to lose sleep was after their son Danny had died. That had led to sleepless nights, and a lot of heartbreak, for both of them. He'd gone off by himself to cry so he wouldn't upset Mary Alice, but she always seemed to know anyway, and would hug him extra hard when he returned.

That was what kids did: they took a piece of your heart when they were born, and you never got it back. Even now, thirty-odd years after Danny died, Jim still missed him and mourned him. From time to time he grieved that Danny had never married, never had kids of his own, but then he'd been just in his twenties when he died. Jim and Mary Alice were alone, no daughter-in-law and grandchildren to love and spoil and protect, almost all of their families already gone and the ones who weren't so distant that he didn't know their names and wouldn't recognize them if they came knocking. A lot of their old friends had already passed, too. Mary Alice keenly felt the lack of people who belonged to her through kin or friendship.

He'd thought a time or two that Danny was the reason Mary

Alice had been so drawn to Ben Jernigan. Danny had been in the army, too. Not that Danny and Jernigan looked anything alike, and though no one seemed to know anything for certain about Jernigan it was obvious that he was a military man through and through. It was in his walk, those long ground-eating strides, the way he carried himself, and the "don't fuck with me" look in his eyes. Both he and Danny had willingly joined the military, were willing to sacrifice their safety and comfort for others. Danny had made the ultimate sacrifice. Jernigan had survived, but carried ghosts around with him.

But Mary Alice hadn't seen any of that, other than maybe sensing that he had a military past. She'd cottoned to him immediately, like the way she'd invited him to dinner, when they first met. Now, Mary Alice was friendly to a fault, but that was fast even for her. Look how she'd lit up when he'd stopped by. He suspected if she had her way, she'd have Jernigan moving in with them. Good thing Jernigan wasn't likely to want to move in with two old people.

Restlessly Jim changed positions again, his thoughts moving on to what Janet had told them about Carol Allen breaking her leg yesterday. That was bad, not just that Carol was injured, but she'd been elected community leader and she had a way of getting people moving. Basically, she bulldozed them. He wondered who'd take her place. Her niece, Sela, was a sweet thing but never put herself forward; maybe the new leader would be someone else—

Creak.

Jim froze, his thoughts suddenly focused, every muscle tense. If he'd been asleep, he wouldn't have heard the unusual noise. If the power had been on—with the heat or air running, the refrigerator humming and occasionally making that noise that Mary Alice had told him for months needed to be fixed but he'd never gotten around to doing—he wouldn't have heard it. But the power wasn't on, no sound, no light, and he'd definitely heard something. His heart was suddenly pounding as he went on alert.

Moving cautiously, he eased from the bed and reached into the bedside drawer for his pistol and a small flashlight. He crept around the bed to the bedroom door, turned on the flashlight and pointed the beam down, blocking most of the light with his fingers. If the house hadn't been so dark he wouldn't have needed the light at all, but even so he had an advantage over any possible intruder, because he'd lived here for over forty years and knew this house like the back of his hand.

As dim as the light was, as quiet as he was being, Mary Alice still woke up and stirred. He immediately said, "Shhh," hoping she heard the soft hissing sound and recognized him, hoping whoever was in the house *hadn't* heard it and realized they were awake.

He held up his hand toward her, signaling her to stay put, then put his finger to his lips.

She'd never listened all that well, but then, after all these years had he really expected her to do what he said? Hah. She was quiet, but she slipped out of the bed and positioned herself behind him. When they heard another sound, a creak from down the hall, she placed her hand gently against his back.

Their bedroom door was open; they lived alone, no reason to close it. In normal times, before the power went off, he'd have dialed 9-1-1, then closed and locked the door and taken Mary Alice into the bathroom and locked that door, too, to shelter until the cops arrived. He was eighty years old, and while he owned a pistol he hadn't shot it more than a handful of times. He was glad to have it for protection, but—shooting someone? He'd never seriously thought he might have to.

Another sound, a soft click as if a drawer had been eased shut. From the direction of the sound the intruder was in the kitchen. What food they had was there, of course. He didn't want to shoot someone who was driven by hunger, but—they didn't have much, and they needed what they had. If their food was stolen, they'd have to rely on friends and neighbors, none of whom had a whole lot themselves. Down the road, any loss could mean the difference between surviving or not.

He'd scare them off, that's all he'd do. When they realized the house wasn't empty and that he was armed, they'd run.

His bare feet soundless on the cold tile, he slipped down the short hall, Mary Alice close behind him. Another sound in the kitchen, like another drawer being opened and closed. Jim thought about calling out, trying to scare away the looter, but what if whoever that was already had a bag packed and took it with him? What if he came into the narrow hallway with a weapon of his own? They'd be sitting ducks. So Jim waited until they were in the kitchen doorway before he barked, "Stop right there!" as he raised the flashlight and shined the beam full into the face of the surprised intruder.

He got the fast, blurred impression of a middle-aged man, no one he knew. He expected a look of shock, expected the guy to bolt for the back door. Instead the looter spun toward them, reaching down to jerk a pistol from his waistband. But Jim's pistol was already in his hand, and Mary Alice was standing right behind him. Knowing he had to protect her wasn't really a thought, it was something much faster and more basic than that, something that had him pulling the trigger almost before he saw the pistol in the intruder's hand.

The intruder fired, but he hadn't brought his hand all the way up and around, and the bullet hit the wall to the left. Mary Alice screamed, and Jim fired again.

The intruder fell, overturning one of the kitchen chairs, knocking over the trash can.

Mary Alice kept screaming, though she slapped both hands over her mouth. Jim turned and put his arms around her. To his surprise he was shaking like a leaf, worse even than she was, and carefully he reached out to place the pistol on the countertop before he dropped it. Then he held on to his wife, and they shook together.

Sela had spent the night at Carol's house, to help take care of her. Barb didn't need to be going up and down the stairs at all hours of the night to check on Carol, and if Carol decided to do something stupid—like try to get up by herself—Olivia wouldn't be able to stop her. That left Sela to sleep on a pallet on the floor in Carol's bedroom.

Not that Carol didn't protest; she did, vociferously and often. Sela said, "If it were me lying there with a broken leg, where would you be?"

Carol scowled at her. The expression was kind of funny, because Carol was loopy on pain medication and instead of a real scowl she looked more as if she had just bitten into a crab apple. Sela swallowed a laugh as she turned out the light and tried to make herself comfortable on the pallet. Her makeshift bed wasn't terrible; she'd put Carol's yoga pad down, then a sleeping bag, then a quilt folded in half lengthwise. She had her pillow. The door was open so the heat from the fireplace could come through. No, it wouldn't be a restful night, but she'd get *some* sleep.

She turned on her side and got comfortable; she was even beginning to doze off when Carol started up again. "I'm perfectly all right by myself. I know I can't get up and go to the bathroom. There's no way you'll be able to sleep on the floor—"

"I was almost asleep when you started talking again," Sela said, and followed that with a firm *"Hush."*

There was a muted grumble from the bed. Sela listened, and in a few minutes Carol's breathing had slowed and deepened. Tired from the stressful day, Sela dozed off. She didn't get any deep sleep, of course, and three times during the night she got up to put wood on the fire. Once she had to help Carol to the portable chair toilet they'd placed by her bed. The patient's restlessness told her the pain medication was wearing off, so she gave her another pill.

Because she didn't sleep well, she was up well before dawn, and put the kettle on the fire to make coffee. She got dressed as quietly as possible, then sat at the table and made notes about getting classes organized for the kids. It occurred to her that, when Carol could get around better and wasn't in so much pain, in a few weeks, one of the classes could be held here. Having something to do would keep her aunt out of trouble, and the kids could help her. It was a win-win.

She had drunk half of her instant coffee when heavy footsteps pounded up the steps. Her heart leaped and she jumped for the door, before whoever was out there could pound on the door and wake Carol. "Who is it?" she demanded, leaning close to the door and cupping her hands around her mouth to contain the noise.

"Mike."

Quickly she unlocked the door and let him in. His face was stark, and his clothes were slightly askew as if he'd put them on in a hurry.

She held up a finger, went to Carol's bedroom door and closed it so the noise wouldn't disturb her. "What happened?" Something had, obviously, something bad.

"Someone broke into the Livingstons' house a couple of hours ago. Jim shot and killed him."

"Oh my God." Shock didn't hold her still. Carol obviously couldn't go, which meant she had to. Because Mike looked as if he needed it, she quickly made him a cup of the instant coffee—which he gratefully took—then she went up the stairs to wake Olivia.

"There's been an emergency and I'm going with Mike," she quietly told the sleepy girl. "Get dressed and come downstairs so you can hear your gran if she needs something. You can grab a nap on my pallet if you want."

"Okay." Olivia yawned and stumbled out of bed. Sela hurried

back downstairs. Mike was standing with his back to the fire, warming that side of him while he sipped the hot coffee.

"Were the Livingstons hurt?" she asked as she pulled on her shoes and a coat.

"No, but they're pretty shook up."

"Who was it?"

"Man named Phil Millard, Milford, something like that. From Nashville. He had a driver's license on him."

Nashville was over two hundred miles away; as alarming as the break-in was, just as alarming was that the intruder had traveled that far to the valley, rather than moving straight south down the interstate. Why come here? What had been the lure? They'd never know now, but it was worrisome.

Olivia came down the stairs, still yawning, with a jacket over her pajamas. Sela said, "I don't know when I'll be back. I gave her a pain pill about three hours ago, so she'll sleep for a while yet."

"Okay." Olivia was slipping through Carol's bedroom door as Sela and Mike went out the front. She was glad that Olivia was still too groggy to ask questions, because she herself had more questions than answers and she didn't want to alarm the others when she couldn't tell them anything beyond the bare bones that Mike had told her.

The predawn air was cold, and their breath fogged in the air; she and Mike walked fast, lighting their way with flashlights. "Jim took Mary Alice next door and woke his neighbor, who went to get the community patrol," Mike said. "I guess one of us could make it to Sevierville and see if anyone is at the sheriff's department."

"If there was, I doubt they'd come out." It had been weeks since they'd seen a county patrol car, and before that only rarely.

"We should probably take the body in . . ." Mike's voice trailed off as he realized how futile that would be. There was nothing the sheriff's department could do that they themselves couldn't do right here.

There was literally no working law enforcement, no way to investigate anything. They couldn't even notify his family, if he had any.

"We'll keep his ID, take a picture, write down what happened, and bury him here," Sela said, feeling helpless. There was nothing else they *could* do, except say a prayer for the man.

Mike nodded, and she had the abrupt, discomforting realization that he was taking her opinion as a directive, as if he'd assumed without question that she'd be taking over Carol's role. He hadn't been there yesterday when Carol had told her she'd have to handle things now, and she was staggered that he'd so easily come to that conclusion. Evidently the people around her had more faith in her than she had in herself.

That was something worth thinking about—later. Right now there was a serious situation that had to be dealt with.

There were a lot of flashlights bobbing around the Livingston house and the neighbor's house, with some hunting lanterns providing additional illumination. A lot of people milled around in the yards, the street; probably almost everyone who lived anywhere in the neighborhood was out there, as well as several members of the community patrol.

"Might as well get it over with," Sela murmured to Mike, gathered her nerve, and entered the Livingston house. There were more people inside, some of them in the living room but most of them in the kitchen.

"In there," someone said, indicating the kitchen, so she and Mike joined the crowd grouped along the cabinets and around the small eat-in table. The dead man lay awkwardly on his side in the middle of the floor, facing away from her. A chair and trash can had been knocked over, and no one had picked them up. The air was ripe with the odors of death and Sela gulped, then tried to breathe only through her mouth.

Trey Foster was propped against the sink; when he saw Sela he straightened and said, "We haven't moved anything. The guy's pistol is lying right there, no one has touched it. He got off a shot, the bullet went through the wall."

They had all watched so many police procedural shows on television that, overall accuracy aside, none of them were about to touch a weapon that had been used in a crime. In other circumstances, Sela would have smiled. Instead she tried not to look at the body, and focused on the people standing around who were all watching her, waiting for guidance.

"There isn't a lot we can do," she said. "Does anyone here have their cell phone with them? No? Then someone find one, and take the man's picture. Also get a picture of the bullet hole in the wall. Better yet, see if you can find a regular camera. I'll talk to Jim and Mary Alice, and write down their account of what happened." She paused, trying to think of what else might be done, wishing someone else would step up and take charge. No one did. "Is there any way we can take the guy's fingerprints? I don't know what good it will do, but it seems sensible."

A few people shrugged. A man who had been a park ranger before retiring several years back said, "Maybe an index card and some graphite scraped from a pencil. Or ink, if we can find some."

A woman said, "Mary Alice has one of those rolling things that she used to black out her address and info on papers she was throwing away. I'll go ask her where she keeps it." She slipped away through the crowd.

"Is there anything else, other than burying him?" Sela asked, looking around.

"Not that I can think of," Mike said. "You have it covered."

Trey looked down at the body. "I hate to waste good wood building a coffin for someone who would rob old people and try to kill them, but it don't seem right to just dump him in a hole so I'll get it done. I can't waterproof it, so we'll need to bury him somewhere he doesn't pollute the water supply."

Sela blinked at the pragmatic outlook. But pragmatism was what they needed to get through this crisis, both the immediate one and the ongoing one of having no electricity.

"If y'all can handle the pictures and the fingerprinting, I'll go talk to Jim and Mary Alice." She looked at Mike and he nodded, indicating they'd get it done.

She went next door to find Jim and Mary Alice huddled in the neighbor's living room, a single quilt wrapped around both of them because they were both barefoot and in their nightclothes, Jim in pajamas and Mary Alice in a nightgown. The house didn't have a fireplace, and Sela wondered how the people who lived here were keeping warm. She made a mental note to ask, once this crisis was taken care of.

Quietly she asked if anyone had a pen and paper, and when that was in hand she sat down beside the old couple.

"Am I going to jail?" Jim asked, his thin voice quivering.

"Lord, no!" Sela's response was automatic. "You did exactly what you had to do, to protect yourself and Mary Alice." In other times and other places his worry would have been justified, but not here, and not now.

Mary Alice burst into tears and fiercely hugged Jim. "Thank God, thank God," she said over and over.

Something else occurred to Sela, and she hoped this was the last "something else." Getting up, she went over to a group of women standing in the kitchen, where a coffeepot was heating over a camp stove. In a low voice she said, "Once the men get the body moved out of the house, is anyone willing to go over and clean up the kitchen? Mary Alice shouldn't have to deal with that."

"I will," a woman said. "I'm Janet Seahorn, I live here. I'll do anything I can for them, they're such nice people."

Okay, while the opportunity had presented itself . . . "Nice to meet you, Janet. Tell me, how are you heating your house?"

Janet grimaced. "We aren't. We have friends down the street who told us we could go over there when winter really hits. They have a gas stove, and a fireplace, but they also have family staying with them already so it'll be a crush. So far we've made do with wearing lots of clothes and staying covered up, when we're inside. I don't want to put them out before we have to."

"That's a plan." It was also only one household. There were a lot of houses in the valley that didn't have fireplaces. Maybe . . . braziers? She'd seen them mentioned in books. Grills were basically braziers, but they burned charcoal and that wasn't safe inside. But as long as there was a fireproof container and a rack, wood could be burned, too. That was something the whole community needed to work on.

In the meantime, she had an upset elderly couple and a dead man to deal with. She returned to Jim and Mary Alice, sitting beside them and writing down everything they said, asking a few questions but mostly just letting them talk. She wasn't a law officer, she didn't know the questions to ask, and they needed to get this talked through to help them process it and deal with the emotional upheaval. "I never in my lifetime thought I'd kill anyone," Jim said, staring into space. "Never. Our boy Danny was in the army—he's passed—and when he went in I worried about him maybe having to pull a trigger on someone. I talked to him once about it and he just said, Pop, you do what you gotta do."

"That's what you did," Sela said, putting her hand over his and feeling the frailty of it. Once that hand had been big and strong but now it was thin, each bone clearly felt. "What you had to do. You protected Mary Alice."

Mary Alice laid her head against his shoulder. "He did."

When she thought she'd done all she could do there, Sela crossed back over to the Livingstons' house. The sun had come up now, and frost glittered on the browning grass. Mike reported that Trey had handled the fingerprinting, though he didn't know how good of a job they'd done, and the dead man had been taken away. A small crew of women were at work in the kitchen, cleaning with bleach, setting things to rights. Neither of the Livingstons would feel easy about being there for a while, they could stay with friends or neighbors for as long as they needed to, but this was their home.

They didn't have a fireplace, either.

"We've done what we can," she said. "The neighbors will help them through today."

The crisis had brought something else to the top of her mental list of things that needed to be done, and that was dispensing the gasoline. Maybe there was a potter here in the valley, and the gasoline could be used to fire a kiln to make clay braziers. If not, they'd make do somehow, but people needed to have heat. But first and foremost, the gas needed to be used before it went bad, in vehicles for stepped-up patrolling given that outsiders were now making their way to the valley. They couldn't afford to assume the dead man was the only one, and that no one else would come looking to loot, maybe kill.

Some of the community patrol members were there, because that was their shift, but others were just now starting their day and likely hadn't yet heard what had happened to the Livingstons; otherwise they'd have already arrived. "There's not a lot of time, I know, but spread the word that everyone who works patrol needs to be at the meeting today," she said. "We'll hold a special session after we finish with normal business. It's important."

Mike nodded, then asked, "What's on your mind?"

"I don't want word to get out too soon, so I'll wait until we have everyone together." He nodded again, accepting her statement, and once again she marveled that no one seemed to be questioning her as leader. She started to tell Mike to have everyone drive, so their tanks could be topped off, but she didn't have a suction pump in place for getting the gasoline out of the storage tanks and making two trips would be wasteful. Once they had a way of getting the gasoline out, then they could drive to the station. One step at a time, she reminded herself. One step at a time. That way, maybe she wouldn't fall on her face.

CHAPTER TWELVE

Ben got up at first light, took the dog out, then back in where he made his coffee and fed both of them, human and dog. The morning sky was cloudless, and the air was chillier than it had been for the past few days. Frost glistened on the ground, on the bushes, and on the fallen leaves.

He had a specific mission for the day.

Yesterday afternoon he'd examined his woodpile and decided that, while he almost assuredly had enough wood to last him through the winter, having some surplus would be a good idea and cutting the wood now would give it a chance to dry out in case winter hung on longer than usual. *Almost* wasn't good enough. He wasn't assuming the power would come on within the next few months, or even in the next year. It would come on when it came on, and until that moment he'd keep preparing as if it never would. Cutting firewood was going to be a constant.

He put some of his supply of gasoline into his chain saw, and kitted up with a jacket, gloves, safety glasses, chaps, and boots. He never took chances while cutting wood, but shit happened even to careful people. Living alone meant he had to be extra alert and careful, because if he slipped up and got hurt, getting medical help was a roll of the dice—and that was before the grid went down. Now there was no medical help to get.

In particular, he wanted a hickory tree for his additional firewood, for the density and extended burn; the density was why hickories were more difficult to cut and split. Maple and oak were his go-to varieties, with hickory added in for when he wanted to grill or smoke some meat. Nothing beat slow-smoldering hickory chips for adding flavor to meat.

Finding a hickory wasn't hard; finding a hickory that was the right size and was in a good location to cut took some walking. He didn't want the felled tree getting hung up in another tree when it went down, because that was an accident waiting to happen. After almost half a mile he found what he was looking for, a good-sized tree that wasn't too big for his chain saw, and with a clear fall line with the correct cuts.

Before he started cutting he took off the jacket and tossed it aside, because loose clothing and chain saws didn't play well together. He made his guiding cut, then the notch, then moved around to the other side to make the felling cut.

He was almost ready to stop cutting when the universal law of "shit happens" kicked in.

For whatever reason, the tree began toppling before he was ready for it to, twisting as it went down, and the broken base of the trunk kicked out toward him. His reflexes saved him. He threw the chain saw in one direction and he went in the other, twisting so the tree caught him a glancing blow on the back of his shoulder instead of hitting the center of his chest and perhaps crushing his sternum. The chain saw brakes engaged as soon as he released it, of course, but he still didn't want to fall on the jagged teeth. Instead he crashed on the forest floor and rolled a few yards downslope, until he fetched up against a good-sized rock.

"Son of a fucking bitch!" he ground out as he climbed to his feet, shaking off the leaves and sticks and dirt that had stuck to his clothes and skin. He moved and rotated, checking that all his parts were in working order. They were, though the back of his shoulder felt as if he'd been kicked by a mule. That still wasn't as bad as taking a round to the chest while wearing ballistic plates, but bad enough. He went over to the chain saw and picked it up, checked it. It had landed half-propped against a bush; he didn't have to clean dirt out of the chain. When he pulled the starter cord, it roared to life.

He turned it off, and assessed the situation. The tree might have kicked the shit out of him, but at least the son of a bitch had fallen clean and he could get back to work. He could feel a hot trickle down his back where the tree had broken skin when it hit him; nothing bad, though. He'd kept going in combat with worse injuries. Besides, he was pissed, both at the tree and at himself. If he'd done something wrong he wanted to know what it was, so he didn't do it again. Mentally reviewing every step, though, he couldn't see a damn thing he should have done differently.

He began methodically removing the limbs—limbing—and worked steadily through the morning. His shoulder ached, and blood made his shirt stick to his back. He ignored both. When he was finished with the limbs his stomach told him it was time to put some food in it, and his head told him he needed to let the dog out. Maybe he'd come back later this afternoon to begin cutting up the trunk.

When he got back to the house he let the dog out to do its business, which it did, then came running back to the house and barked to be let in. Hunting dog or not, the pup liked being inside, liked company. Ben ate some stew, then stripped off to take a shower. Not only was he sweaty from the morning's work, but his back was still leaking red. Standing with his back turned to the bathroom mirror, he looked over his shoulder at the injury.

It was hard to tell with all the blood smeared around, but he thought the injury looked more as if the impact had broken the skin open, rather than an actual cut. For sure the area was swollen and bruised, and still trickling blood. Maybe it needed a stitch or two but he didn't think so, and in any event he wasn't going to hike around the valley looking for someone willing to sew him up. It might heal ugly on its own, but it *would* heal.

He showered, keeping it brief but enjoying the warm water. The bleeding got worse, of course. He got some gauze out of the bathroom cabinet and folded a thick pad, put some antibiotic salve on it, and with several tries managed to get it placed just right over the wound. Then he leaned his back against the door frame to put pressure on the pad until it stuck. There. Good. First aid taken care of. Now he wouldn't drip blood all through the house.

He put on a flannel shirt and some clean jeans, put his bloody clothes in the bathtub and ran cold water for them to soak. Then he made some coffee and sat down for a while to read, pleased with the morning's work despite the injury.

Sela took a deep breath; there were sixty or seventy people gathered in her store—some she knew, some she didn't—and from what she could tell all of the community patrol was there, which was good. She'd never been good at public speaking; school presentations had been agony for her. But this wasn't performance, it wasn't showing her stuff, it was communication. People needed to know what was going on.

"Some of you may already know, but Carol fell down the stairs and broke her leg yesterday, and I'm in her place until she can get on her feet—"

"Wait a minute." Predictably, it was Ted who interrupted. "You weren't elected. You weren't even in the running. Why are you taking her place instead of someone who *was* interested in doing the job?"

"For crying out loud, Teddy, give it a rest," Trey muttered, earning himself a glare from Ted and a titter from a few others, because the Teddy Roosevelt look hadn't gone unnoticed.

"*Ted,*" Ted snapped.

Her heart started pounding hard and her cheeks burned. Sela wanted to just walk out and leave them to it, but she mentally bolstered herself and said, "Because Carol asked me to. And because I talk to her several times a day, every day."

"That still doesn't make you the logical—"

"It does to me." Mike frowned at Ted. "Maybe you weren't standing close enough to hear that night at the school, but most of the ideas Carol presented were ones Sela whispered to her. Sela was the one who handled things early this morning when the Livingstons had that break-in."

There was an immediate buzz of comments from people asking what had happened, exactly, how were the Livingstons, had the sheriff been contacted, etc., which set Ted off in another direction. "I didn't hear about the Livingstons until just before I got here. Why didn't someone make the effort to notify me last night?"

"Maybe because no one wanted to walk halfway up Cove Mountain," Mike said irritably. "For God's sake, Ted, we didn't roust out everyone on community patrol. We let people get their sleep. There was nothing you could have done."

A flurry of comments and questions, about both Carol and the Livingstons, drowned out and deflected anything else Ted might have said. He subsided, but he looked sulky about it.

Sela held up her hand, and wonder of wonders, the noise subsided. "Carol will be fine, it was a simple break, but she has to stay off her feet for about eight weeks. The Livingstons aren't hurt. We have no way of notifying the sheriff, so we did what we could. It looks like a clear case of self-defense. The intruder was armed and shot at them, and Jim was a better shot. The intruder was from the Nashville area. We have his driver's license, he was photographed and fingerprinted, and Jim gave a signed statement. The man has been buried. That's the best we can do."

There was another half hour of basically the same questions asked over and over, just framed slightly differently, and a couple of people who for some reason fixated on minor details that they wanted explained, such as what Jim heard that woke him up.

She caught Mike's eye, gave him a look that combined "help me" and exasperation, to which he responded with a small smile and a thumbs-up, which wasn't at all helpful.

As firmly as she could, she said, "Moving on, I have a couple of other things on the list. First, is there a potter in the valley? And a kiln, too. I know there's a pottery over Townsend way, but I'd prefer one that's more convenient. There are a lot of people here in the valley who don't have fireplaces, and they need a heat source. A clay brazier with an oven rack over it would provide both heat and a way to cook."

That provoked some thought, scratched jaws, and conversation as they worked through the problem set before them. A woman said, "I'll go talk to Mona Clausen, over close to Dogwood. I think she used to do some pottery, or maybe that was her mother. Either way, she might know something about a kiln."

"Thank you. Anyone else know anyone who can throw pots? They don't have to look pretty, they just have to function."

"My kids did, in vacation bible school."

There was a round of laughter, but Sela pointed at the man who had spoken and said, "Good, we may need your kids." She was only half joking.

A few people brought up things that Sela jotted down in her notebook to check out and get back to them. The meetings had taken on a routine. They talked about what would be needed in the immediate future, what had happened in their respective neighborhoods, and some of what they'd need long term, though discussions of the last sort were scary and short, because no matter how they tried to prepare, the truth was they had no idea what might happen. Day to day was easier; they could manage that. Wondering what January would be like scared the stew out of all of them.

She'd talk to Carol about everything mentioned, though she was fairly sure she knew what Carol would say. That way Carol wouldn't feel left out, because despite her protestations, she had always loved making a show of things—hence the pink streak in her hair, which was growing out. Sela made another note: find a hairdresser who could freshen the pink streak, if possible. That would keep her aunt in good spirits.

Finally people began filing out of the cold store. Without a heat source the inside always felt as if it were twenty degrees colder than it was outside, where the sun had heated the day to around sixty. By the end of the month it would be unbearably cold. Sighing, Sela made another note. Find another kerosene heater, or else tote the one they had—the one they'd been saving for when it would really be needed—to the store for each meeting. Or maybe they'd luck out and find someone who really could make braziers. It was either that or find another place to meet.

Through the windows she saw knots of the others still standing around outside, talking. In the almost two months since the power went out she had met and recognized many more of the valley residents than she had before, but every week she saw new faces after the meetings, people who didn't necessarily want to attend a meeting but who wanted to talk to the ones who had. They were usually people who lived in Wears Valley but well beyond the heart of the community, and who had to travel several miles to get here. Most of them just wanted to make sure that their neighborhoods weren't forgotten, and to be included in any food distribution—as if that ship hadn't sailed back at the very beginning. What people had now was what they had either put back, or hunted, fished, or bartered for.

As she had requested beforehand, the members of the community patrol remained behind, and gathered closer around now that the majority of people had gone outside. "What's up?" Mike asked.

"Do we need to step up patrols, after what happened with the Livingstons?" Ted suggested, which wasn't a bad idea.

"Probably," she replied, nodding at him. Being a pain in the ass didn't mean all of his suggestions were bad—it just meant he was a pain in the ass. He looked somewhat gratified, and smug, that she hadn't shot him down again. "But that's up to y'all, because you know what you can do. This is something else entirely." She blew out a breath. "When the announcement came that the solar storm was coming, I shut down my gas pumps."

There was silence, realization dawning across their faces. "Holy shit," Trey said. "You're sitting on gold."

"Not really. It's gold with a time limit. It's ethanol gasoline so it'll go bad if I keep it much longer. We need to dispense it, get it out into the community where it can be put to use. Likely January and February would be times when it'll be more needed, but who knows if it'll be any good by then? We'd be gambling big. By now the octane level has degraded but it's still usable."

She took a breath, organized her thoughts. "We can fill up your vehicles, run some generators, chain saws to cut more wood. People can get warm, take hot showers, do some emergency cooking. If we can find a kiln anywhere near and use the gasoline to fire it up, to make braziers, then we'll have heat sources for people who don't have fireplaces. Those are my suggestions. If anyone has more, or different uses, that's up to them. I'm not about to try overseeing all that."

Predictably, Ted burst out with anger. "You've been sitting on tanks of gasoline all this time—"

"Saving it for when we'd need it more. Yes." Her tone didn't quite have an edge to it, but she was getting there. It took a lot to get her angry . . . but she was definitely getting there. If the chore of "community leader" actually *paid* anything, or had prestige, his resentful attitude would make more sense—but it didn't, and mostly it was endless lists, a pain in the butt, and listening to people bitch. And damn if she'd apologize to Ted for how she managed *her* resources.

"The first freeze can come anytime," Mike said. "I'm surprised it's held off this long. I'd say you have good timing."

"I have tanks for ten thousand gallons each of 87 and 91 octane, and would get a delivery every four days during the tourist off-season, every three days during peak. It had been two days since my last delivery, so I have roughly five thousand gallons of each, ten thousand total. What I don't have is a way of getting it out of the tanks. Does anyone know how to rig a suction pump?" She'd asked Ben about rigging a pump, but he wasn't here at the moment so she might as well see if anyone else could handle it.

"I've siphoned gas out of a car, but never anything that big," Trey said. "Most of us have done that. Still, I guess the principle's the same. I think I could have something rigged up by tomorrow."

Someone else said, "Some people have propane generators, so there's no help for them, but just as many have gasoline powered."

"Get the word out," she said. "Hoarding it won't do any good, because it'll go bad. What they get, they need to use. Everyone who can needs to come tomorrow to fill their tanks or gas cans."

"Another suggestion," Trey said. "It's up to you, because it's your gas. But you paid for that gas, and if we take it without paying *you*, you're going to be left holding the short end of the stick when the power comes back on."

"People don't have money—"

Ted. Of course. For a surprisingly potent moment she thought about shooting him the finger, something she'd never done to any-one's face before. The urge was so strong she had to clench her hands. One day, though . . . well, maybe. She'd need to work on that. The unrelenting stress was either wearing her down or building her up, and she wasn't sure which.

Trey held up his hand. "I know that. Hear me out. We should pump it out in five-gallon cans so we can write down who gets how much, and the price gas cost when the grid went down. When everything gets back to normal, people should pay you for the gas. That's only right. You can't afford to just give away thousands of dollars of gasoline."

He was right, and she hadn't thought that far. Her mind had been more on using the gas before it went bad, and helping people survive the winter, than it had been on profit and loss. She *had* kept the much smaller tank, the one with hundred percent gasoline in it, for herself and emergencies and she felt guilty doing even that, but she had three other people to think of and take care of.

She looked around at her empty store—and it was completely empty. The shelves and refrigeration spaces were bare, not a cracker left, not a can of Spam, literally nothing other than some oil and fuel additives. She'd have to completely restock, and wouldn't be able to do it all at once because goods would only gradually become available again. Who knew when the pipelines would start moving oil to the refineries again? Just *living* was going to be a struggle, at least until spring.

"That's all I have to say. Y'all get the word out about the gasoline. I'm not going to play favorites, not going to pick and choose who gets it—except for maybe someone with a gas-fired kiln, but that will benefit all of us and could save some lives this winter. Starting at nine o'clock tomorrow, if Trey has a suction pump going, we'll start emptying the tanks. I suggest y'all drive here and have your vehicles first in line, because Ted was right about stepping up the patrols. We might have more people who are up to no good coming into the valley."

Almost everyone filed out; Mike was the only one who stayed behind. "That was a smart thing, shutting down the pumps."

"I didn't feel smart, I felt scared."

"Right along with everyone else. You still did the smart thing." Crossing his arms and tucking his hands into his armpits to keep them warm, he stared out the window at the people still standing around in the parking lot. The patrol members were moving through the crowd, spreading the news about the gasoline. She watched them, saw excitement dawning at the prospect of a small taste of luxury, because that's what the gasoline represented: heat, cleanliness, mobility, a brief respite from making do, and a means of swiftly increasing their woodpiles. Fire meant life.

"Bill Haney from over near the Cades Cove shortcut almost cut his finger off this morning, chopping wood. One of his neighbors is a retired veterinarian and he sewed it back as best he could; Bill should be all right, except for a stiff finger. A couple of cases of what might be flu are over on Little Round Top."

They had no medical team. So far, medical care had been catch-as-catch-can, with the herbalists doing what they could, the fire department medic helping, as well as a couple of nurses. No one was organized, and she didn't know if organization was needed.

"Flu? This early in the year?" That didn't seem likely. If anything, they should be safer from flu this year. They'd had almost no contact with anyone from outside the valley, no one was touching contaminated cart handles in Walmart or Kroger.

Mike shrugged. "That's what I heard. I kind of doubt it. Colds, yeah, but I'm not going over there to check." He frowned as he looked out the window, and Sela turned to see what had caused the frown.

"What?"

"Ted's talking to Lawrence Dietrich. I know you said don't pick and choose, but I hate to see good gasoline going to a piece of trash like him. Still, he's got a couple of kids, so that's that."

Sela watched the two men, who had stepped away from the others. Ted's body language was saying he was large and in charge, or at least he thought he was. Lawrence Dietrich looked vaguely familiar, or maybe it was his name she'd heard before. He was a young man, and good-looking in a lean, wolfish away. Maybe he'd bought gas here before. She was tired and didn't much care. She wanted a nap, but that wasn't going to happen. There was too much to do, and she felt as if the avalanche of responsibilities was about to smash her flat.

Ted might not like Sela Gordon hiding the fact that she had thousands of gallons of gasoline hoarded, but he did like telling people about it, seeing how excited they got and being able to answer their questions. It was as if they thought *he* was doing them a favor. He was slapped down so often in this community, for a change it was nice to be looked up to.

For once he agreed with her that the community patrol should be first in line; he'd fill up his car, and if Meredith wanted to go anywhere he'd be able to take her. Too much walking wasn't good for her. She was losing weight—not a lot, and really everyone was, but it worried him. If anything happened to her, he wanted to be able to get her down the mountain to the medic. He couldn't stop himself from worrying about her, even though she insisted she was fine.

"Hey, Ted."

He jumped a little, because he'd gotten distracted, and looked at the young man he'd been talking to a minute ago. The man inclined his head. "Let's step over here, away from the others, so we can talk."

Ted started to decline, but maybe there was something interesting he needed to know. Together they walked to the edge of the parking lot, where they couldn't be overheard.

"Sorry, I don't know your name."

"Lawrence." The man put out his hand for a quick shake. "Lawrence Dietrich."

Dietrich had a hard look to him. He was lean to the point of thinness, and he needed both a shave and a haircut, but these days who didn't—except for himself, of course. He made an effort to stay well groomed, partly for Meredith, and partly because when he was at his tire stores it was important to look professional. In his opinion, it was a good habit to have.

"Do your friends call you Larry?"

That earned him a hard stare. "Do yours call you Teddy?"

Point taken. Dietrich had been inside the store and had heard that sharp little exchange with the Foster guy. "What can I do for you, Lawrence?"

"I have a few thoughts about this community patrol."

"Then you should have spoken up at the meeting."

Dietrich made a sharp, dismissive motion. "Like that would work. That Gordon woman and her smart-mouthed aunt, they think they're better than everyone else, that they know best how things around here should be run."

He was right about that. He'd thought that Carol Allen was so full of herself it was a wonder she could eat, while the niece had stayed in the background, but now he knew that one was just as bossy as the other.

"What's your idea?"

"My idea is that the community patrol is a waste of time, the way they've got it set up. Me and my cousin, we volunteered at the beginning. Most of the stumblebums involved don't know their ass from a hole in the ground. They just walk around and look important. Did they do anything to stop old man Livingston from being broke in on? No, he took care of it himself. I think we need our own community patrol—patrol 2.0, you might call it. I don't have the smarts to lead an effort like that, but I think you do. I think you'd be good at putting together an army of sorts, taking control of this valley, making people do what they should."

Ted hesitated. He was already *in* the community patrol, and Lawrence Dietrich looked like the type of person he'd always avoided. On the other hand, no one else in the valley had sought him out, asked his opinion on anything, or made use of his expertise in management and organization. Sela Gordon was going about everything all wrong, waiting for people to step up and volunteer, waiting for them to donate their goods and time and services. People would hold back for themselves, instead of pooling their resources so everyone was taken care of.

"I don't see any harm in discussing options," he finally said.

"Good. Maybe tomorrow afternoon you can meet with me and a few of my friends. At your house?"

Ted's first instinct was to keep this far away from Meredith. "No, no sense in everyone walking that far, I'll come down. Beside the bank, after lunch. Maybe around two?"

Lawrence nodded, said, "See you there," and with a quick wave of his hand walked away.

An army . . . of sorts. Ted couldn't stop the thrill that ran through him at the thought. And they wanted him to be in charge. They would take over this valley, and do things right.

CHAPTER THIRTEEN

Sela was still mentally worrying at the puzzle of Lawrence Dietrich and where she'd either met him or heard his name when she left the store. Mike waved and headed off, and she turned to lock the door—not that there was anything to steal inside, but she still didn't want the building vandalized by kids, strangers passing through, or . . . or anyone. People were people, they did crappy things, and the times were stressful.

She hadn't gone ten steps before a hefty woman with blond hair and three-inch-long dark roots charged up to her and snapped, "So you've been sitting on this gasoline for two months when people could have used it?"

What?

She didn't know the woman; she took a step back because the blonde looked ready to swing and she didn't want to get into a brawl, especially since she was pretty sure this woman could kick her butt. "I thought it would be more useful now, when the weather is getting cold," she said as evenly as possible, trying to hide how alarmed she was. And, yes, getting angry, too.

"Who gave you the right to decide what people need?"

Sela felt her fingertips begin to throb, and the skin of her face felt tight. Slowly she took the pen out of her pocket, opened up her notebook. "I'm sorry, I don't know your name."

"Carlette Broward," the woman answered, suspicion mixing with the aggression in her expression as she looked at the notebook. "Why?"

Sela made a show of flipping back through the notebook, though she already knew for certain she'd never seen the name before. Nope, no mention of Carlette Broward, or indeed any Broward, anywhere in the book. She went back to the original page and wrote Carlette's name down. "Just checking."

"Checking on what? And what does that have to do with you hogging the gas?"

Other people were looking their way, edging closer. Sela would have been humiliated, if she hadn't been fed up. Fed. Up. And she was. To the gills. "I was looking to see if you were on any of the lists of volunteers."

Her jibe hit its target and the woman flushed. "I got two little kids," she said resentfully. "I can't just walk away and leave them alone, to do good deeds."

"You could bring them with you. Or send word of something you could do."

"I got all I can handle, you snide bitch, and what does that have to do with the gasoline? Answer me that!"

A hot surge of anger left her almost breathless. She was so seldom angry that she didn't know what to do but her brain kind of disconnected and her body reacted. Sela took a step forward, erasing the distance she'd put between them, and lowered her chin to stare at the woman. "You mean *my* gasoline, the gasoline I paid for, and you haven't? That gasoline? The gasoline I could have sold when we got the warning about the solar storm, but didn't because I thought the people in this valley would need it to help survive the winter?"

Someone in the crowd muttered, "You go, girl."

Sela didn't think she had a choice about going on, because she'd never felt this angry, this outraged. Surrendering to the moment she stepped even closer, so close she could smell the sourness of the woman's skin, the stench of dirty clothes. Every muscle in her body was trembling, but it wasn't from fear, or stress, it was from the effort of holding herself in check. She wanted to shriek at the woman. She wanted to *punch her in the face*, she, who had never struck another person in her life. "Are you planning on being in line tomorrow morning to get *my* gas, after insulting me today?"

To her surprise, Carlette Broward stepped back. "I deserve it as much as anyone else," she muttered resentfully.

"Really?" Sela moved forward again, all but spitting the words out. "Do you deserve it as much as the people who've been working their *asses* off cutting wood for others? Staying awake at night, patrolling, trying to keep everyone safe? Feeding old people who don't have enough food? What have you contributed to the community? Anything? Bitching doesn't count."

A couple of snorts of laughter made Carlette turn red. "I don't have to take this shit," she snarled, taking two steps back this time.

"That's right, you don't. You don't have to take my gasoline, either. Feel free to leave at any time."

"Don't think I'll forget this, you snotty bitch!" Carlette threw over her shoulder as she stomped away.

"Thanks for the warning!" Breathing hard, Sela stared after her, then growled a bit and said, "Shit!" under her breath. Before Carlette got out of hearing she called out, "Carlette!"

The woman whirled. "Fuck you!"

Sela ground her teeth together again, reaching for her thin store of patience. "Bring your car tomorrow. And bring your kids. I won't stop you from getting gas." Not if she did have two little kids, that is. No kids, no gas.

Carlette paused, still looking violently resentful and sulky. Then she said, "What about filling a gas can?"

"That, too, if you have one."

With a jerky nod, the woman walked away.

"Oh, jear Desus," Sela said, and closed her eyes. She was trembling and breathing hard and for some reason felt torn between wanting to cry and wanting to hop up and down and scream as loud as she could. She didn't do confrontations, didn't know how to fight, but she'd been ready to get into a face-slapping, hair-pulling battle with a woman who outweighed her by a good forty or fifty pounds.

Nancy Meador, one of her neighbors, came and put an arm around her. "You did good, hon," she said, giving Sela a hug and a smile. "Gave me a smile today."

Sela was astonished. "You like seeing fights?" Violence had always made her a little sick to her stomach.

"Well, the TV's out, so we have to do something for entertainment," Nancy said, throwing back her head on a laugh. Several other people around them laughed and nodded.

"Besides, you have to stand up to bullies or they just get worse." Nancy squeezed her shoulders. "You should go take a nap, you look worn out. I bet you stayed up with Carol last night, didn't you?"

Sela nodded. "And I need to get back to check on her. Not that Barb and Olivia aren't there, but—"

"I know. Carol can be a handful. Tell you what—I'll come stay with her tonight, let you get some rest. How does that sound?"

She opened her mouth to tell Nancy she could handle it, then paused. Neighbors helped neighbors, and truth to tell she could use more sleep than she'd gotten the night before, or she wouldn't be any use to Carol or anyone else. "That sounds wonderful," she said truthfully.

"Good deal. I'll come over tonight after I get the supper dishes washed and everything squared away. See you then."

Other people wanted to give her encouraging words or pats and she worked her way through them, wanting nothing more than to be alone so she could scream, or cry, or jump up and down in a hissy fit. She didn't know which. Maybe all three. "I'm not good at this crap," she muttered under her breath as she walked home. "I'm so not good at this crap."

She walked past Carol's house, though she knew they'd be waiting to hear the details of everything that had happened; she didn't feel like rehashing it all, and more than anything she wanted to go to bed, pull the covers over her head, and take a long nap. She wouldn't do that, but she desperately needed to be alone and get her emotional bearings again.

Dead leaves crunched under her feet as she walked. Now that there was no vehicular traffic to blow them off, leaves accumulated on the roads, and had almost completely covered the paved surfaces in her neighborhood. When the CME hit, civilization had slipped backward about two hundred years; she had coped, she had thought and planned and tried to organize, and though she'd accomplished some things at the end of the day she was acutely aware of how much she fell short.

Mike Kilgore was a rock, but he wasn't a leader. He would back her up any way she needed, when what she needed was someone who could help her decide which way to go. Same with Trey Foster: capable, but not a leader. Carol had taken the job, but she didn't want it any more than Sela did, and now she was injured and *couldn't* help.

She let herself into her house, put some wood on the low-burning fire, then wrapped herself in a quilt and plopped down on the sofa, her tired mind spinning.

The house was chilly and quiet; she'd gotten accustomed to the silence and the darkness of night, but even though the sun was shining outside she felt as if the dark and the quiet had isolated her as if she was deep in a cave.

What had happened at the Livingstons wouldn't be an isolated case. More outsiders would be coming through; some would be friendly, some not—and it was the "not" that scared her to death. She'd been naive to think she could handle this, even temporarily.

Actually she hadn't thought it at all; Carol had. And Carol likely wouldn't know what to do, either, because this was as far outside her experience as it was Sela's. She couldn't even ask her aunt about this new development, not now. Carol needed to rest, to recover, not to mention that any advice she gave while she was taking pain pills might not be well thought out.

Carol. Jim Livingston. Ted's hostility. Being accosted by Carlette Broward. It was too much, too much all at once.

In all her life, she'd never asked for help, at least not in anything big. Never. Maybe she was too quiet, maybe she was painfully shy, but she took care of her own problems. Adam. The business. Even Carol didn't know that early on Sela had had to take out a loan, after a few bad months at the store. She'd paid the loan back, had scraped and done without until she'd managed to pay it off early. There hadn't been any financial troubles since then, but no one else knew how she'd initially struggled.

No one else realized how deeply the divorce had hurt her. No one saw how she continued to carry that pain. Given the chance, she wouldn't take Adam back—no way, that ship had most definitely sailed—but that didn't change the fact that failing at her marriage had hurt. It had hurt that she hadn't been enough for Adam, that he'd seen her as weak, as *less*.

She'd never gone for counseling, never poured out her heart to Carol or to her friends. She'd borne her hurts, her fears, in silence, rather than burden others with what she considered her failings.

But this was something she couldn't handle, and others would suffer if she did it wrong. This time, she had to ask for help. And she knew only one person who had the experience to help her with the outside threat that had come to the valley.

CHAPTER FOURTEEN

She couldn't drive by Carol's house without stopping to let them know where she was going. Any vehicle on the road now attracted notice. To her relief Carol was napping, and Barb and Olivia didn't ask many questions.

She wasn't about to walk up Cove Mountain. Ben might be willing and able to make that hike—he'd done it at least three times since the CME that she knew of, and likely more times than that—but she wasn't. It was afternoon already, and she wanted to get up there and back before dark.

Her heart thumped hard at the prospect of seeing Ben. It had been a month since he'd sat on her porch and drank tea with her, and looked at her as if . . . well, she still wasn't certain how he'd looked at her. At the time she'd thought he looked aroused. Then she'd thought maybe he'd been alarmed that she might make a pass at him, because how could he know she'd never made a pass at any-one in her life? And what did it say about her that she couldn't tell the difference between arousal and alarm?

It had been weeks since he'd gifted her with not one but two solar lights . . . and then stalked away as if he didn't even want to look at her. Was she entirely wrong about the way he'd looked at her? She didn't think so, but then again, maybe it was just wishful thinking.

She was so fiercely attracted to him she almost couldn't make her-self go to his house. Being that attracted meant she was vulnerable, that she was exposing herself to the pain of rejection, even if that rejection wasn't personal. Her instinct for self-protection shrieked at her to turn around.

Duty kept her going.

She needed him, needed his help. Everyone in Wears Valley needed him. They needed his experience, his brain, his tactical thinking and expertise.

If Ted would listen to anyone, it was Ben. There was something about Ben that said "dangerous" to anyone with a lick of sense about them, or at least "this man can kick my ass seven ways from Sunday." And even if Ted, or anyone else, didn't *want* to listen they'd do so anyway, precisely because of that aura of danger.

She remembered about the big rock Mike had said was in the middle of Ben's driveway, so she stopped short, well down the hill where there was a bit of a shoulder she could use to turn around. Doing so left her with a longer hike, but that was better than trying to drive in reverse down the narrow, winding private road.

Big, tall trees loomed around her on both sides, blocking out the sunlight and making it seem as if sundown was near. Living in the Great Smoky region she was always aware of the old, mysterious mountains, but actually being up in the mountains was always a different experience. She felt their age, the isolation, the sense that here humans were at the mercy of nature.

When she got out of her Honda the difference in temperature struck her, too; there was a good fifteen, maybe twenty degree difference between here under the big trees and down in the sunny valley. Cautiously she looked around, and listened for the sound of anything moving in the brush, but there was nothing alarming.

Even though there was no one around, no sign that a human other than Ben was anywhere near, she locked her car and stuck the keys in her pocket, and started up the steep road, which narrowed more and more and finally transitioned from asphalt to two parallel paths of gravel divided by weeds, testimony that even before the CME no one had come up here very often, if at all, and Ben had seldom driven down.

The way was steep, so steep that within fifty yards she was huffing and puffing, her legs aching. To ease the strain on her muscles she changed tactics and instead of tackling the mountain head-on she zigzagged her way up, like a boat tacking into the wind. Wind sighed through the big trees, the tops gently swaying, and the rich smell of the forest wrapped around her.

She stopped and just stood there for a minute, something in her connecting to the vibrant power of the mountains. She wished for more time. She wished for a camera, to record what her eyes were seeing, but what she felt wasn't something that could be caught in a photograph.

Another hundred yards and she rounded a curve, came to the big rock Mike had mentioned. It was an effective security measure, one positioned exactly where no car could go around it on either side, and only a truck riding on a frame as high as Ben's could clear it. The rock was mute testimony that she wasn't making a mistake coming here. Ben would know what to do, how to give them a tactical advantage.

Finally she puffed around another curve and abruptly there was the house, sitting on a miraculously flat piece of ground, with Ben's truck parked there on the side. The mountain continued rising on the left; on the right, the valley spread out before her. She slowed to a stop, her eyes wide and her lips slightly parted as she stared in awe. A wide porch encircled the house, and she could see a rocking chair on the end of the house looking out over the valley. The view was breathtaking. He would sit there, she imagined, watching the world below him and not participating, alone in this aerie.

The house was one story, dark brown planks or siding running horizontally; from the valley it would be impossible to pick out, especially in the summer with the trees in full leaf. It wasn't in the cabin style at all, but had a kind of . . . nautical style to it, because there was a round porthole window. Country midcentury nautical, maybe, which meant there was no real style to it. It was a functional house, period, and that fit Ben Jernigan more than any certain design.

A thin haze of smoke rose from the chimney, meaning he was at home. She would have hated to waste all this momentum and energy for him to not be here, because she wasn't sure she'd be able to work up the nerve again. Abruptly she realized that he might not be home anyway, despite the presence of his truck and the woodsmoke. He could be out hunting. He could—

The door opened, and he stepped out on the porch.

He was wearing jeans, boots, and an untucked flannel shirt with the sleeves rolled up over his muscled forearms, a couple of days' stubble darkening his jaw. The sight of him twisted her insides in knots, started her heart BOOM-BOOM-BOOMing. The dog darted past him and leaped off the porch to race toward her, barking as it ran around and around her in a paroxysm of joy. Ben watched the dog with an impassive expression, and gave a shake of his head. "Dumbass dog." But there was no irritation in his tone, just an acceptance of the young dog's exuberance.

Giving herself time to school her expression, Sela bent down to stroke the animal's head. He twisted against her legs in joy.

At least Ben wasn't carrying the shotgun with which he'd greeted Mike, so he didn't intend to shoot her for intruding on his privacy. That was a promising detail, though he didn't exactly look welcoming. Still, he'd been on her private property twice, he'd drank her tea, so maybe they were past the shoot-on-sight stage. She wished she felt welcome here, but right now she'd settle for "tolerated." He stood there, big and intimidating, his hard face as unreadable as stone; maybe tolerance was an optimistic expectation.

"What's wrong?" he asked bluntly.

Because of course something had to be wrong or she wouldn't be here—and what *wasn't* wrong? Pretty much everything was wrong. She was in over her head and overwhelmed. Where to begin?

She took a deep breath and walked up to the steps, which was as close as she dared to get before she lost momentum. Her voice wouldn't quite work, with her heart pounding so hard and her stomach tied in knots. She stood there staring up at him, wondering if he could see the desperation crawling under her skin.

Then he stepped aside and said, "Come on in."

She wanted to go in, and she didn't want to. She wanted to say what she'd come here to say, and leave before she embarrassed herself by breaking down. Yes, she was curious about his house, how he lived, but at the same time that old sense of caution and self-preservation was yelling at her to keep her distance, that distance equaled safety, and safety equaled . . . what? Never living?

She went up the steps. Maybe no one other than her would ever know what an emotional effort that took, but *she* did. The dog scampered past her, darted inside, and before she reached the door was standing there with a shoe in his mouth, tail wagging.

Despite her attack of nerves, the idea of the dog chewing one of Ben's shoes made her smile. "You gave him your shoe?"

"It wasn't exactly giving it to him as much as it was he appropriated it. It was an old pair anyway. Move, dog."

The dog moved. Ben put his hand on her lower back and ushered her inside, a light touch that nevertheless burned through layers of clothing and left her scorched. She almost faltered to a stop but managed to keep her feet moving—for a few feet, at least, when astonishment brought her to a halt.

The interior wasn't anything like what she'd expected. For some reason she'd expected at least a little shabbiness. It wasn't. It was utilitarian, almost Spartan, but there was nothing shabby about it. The big open room was kitchen, dining, and living space all together, wide plank flooring, with a flat-weave rug under the eating table and another defining the living area, which contained a leather couch, two leather recliners, a coffee table, end tables, and a couple of lamps. She had expected pine walls, and instead found drywall painted a no-nonsense beige. No knickknacks, of course; she couldn't imagine Ben Jernigan owning even one decorative piece, much less several. No art on the walls. If a gun rack filled with multiple weapons could be considered decoration, then that was his effort at it. The room was comfortably warm—warmer than her house, anyway—thanks to the wood-burning stove.

There were a couple of oil lamps sitting around, and heavy curtains that were pulled open to let in the sunshine. She suspected those heavy curtains did a lot at night to help hold the heat inside.

"Want some coffee?" he asked.

She didn't normally drink coffee this late in the day, but the warmth would be welcome, as well as something to occupy her hands. "Yes, thank you," she said, and took the chair at the table that he indicated.

"How do you drink it?"

"Ah . . . black." She did now, anyway.

He made two mugs of instant and brought them to the table, setting one in front of her and choosing the chair across from her for himself. Then he waited. He'd already asked once what was wrong, and evidently saw no need to repeat himself.

She took a deep breath. There was so much weighing on her, and maybe she'd be more coherent if she laid things out chronologically.

"One: Carol fell down the stairs yesterday and broke her leg. She's out of action for a couple of months, and evidently I'm heir to be community leader, because no one else wants to do the job other than Ted Parsons, and no one wants him to do it, so I'm the patsy.

"Two: about three this morning, someone broke into the Livingstons' house. Jim and Mary Alice heard him, got up, and"—she swallowed—"he shot at them, and Jim shot him, twice, and killed him. Jim and Mary Alice are okay, just upset. The man was from the Nashville area, according to his driver's license. We recorded what happened and his identity as best we could, and buried him."

At that news, Ben straightened, his green eyes turning almost feral, but he relaxed some once she said the Livingstons weren't hurt.

"Finally, at the meeting today, I told everyone about the gasoline in my tanks. Trey Foster is going to rig a suction pump and we'll start distributing it tomorrow morning at nine. If you need to fill up, tomorrow's the day."

He nodded.

She left out the part about Carlette Broward because, while it had been upsetting, in the long run that wasn't important.

"I'm afraid the man from Nashville is just the beginning. If he could find his way here, others can. I don't know what to do, and no one else seems willing to make any decisions. We have the community patrol, but slipping past them wouldn't be hard at all."

He nodded again and said impassively, "You should expect trouble, from here on out."

She already did, and that was why she was here. "I don't know how many people are on the move—"

"A lot. Pretty much everyone in the cities who survived the first month. I get news over my radio system, and now that the atmosphere has settled down I'm hearing transmissions from coast to coast."

She didn't know whether to be happy that people were getting news out, because that was a tiny bit of civilization returning, or alarmed by the phrase "survived the first month."

"How bad is it?"

"In the big cities, it's total disaster. The smart ones were the ones who got out right away." He regarded her for a moment, his eyes grim. "You don't want to know the details."

No, she probably didn't. If Ben said it was bad, it was bad on a level she didn't want to know. "If a lot of people are moving out of the snowbelt . . . Ted Parsons, the one who wants to be community leader, thinks we should let them in, that there's safety in numbers—"

His eyebrows went up. "Stupid." The succinct answer echoed her own gut instinct, that letting in people they didn't know was risky, and would strain their resources to the point that everyone suffered. She wanted to be humanitarian, but she also wanted to survive. This first winter would be the hardest. If the power was still out next winter, at least they would have had the summer to plant and harvest, and they'd be better prepared.

"What should we do?"

"Shoot first, ask questions later. That's what I plan to do."

The simple, brutal advice left her breathless. Despite the violence at the Livingston house, part of her hadn't quite accepted that things would come to that.

"You *do* have a weapon, don't you?" he asked, his eyebrows going up again as if he couldn't conceive of not being armed.

"Yes. Carol and I both have .22 rifles. She calls them our varmint guns."

He didn't look impressed, but then she hadn't expected him to be, not by something used for squirrel hunting. "There are a lot of hunters here in the valley; they'll have more suitable rifles for self-defense."

She mentally worried at the situation. Obviously the dilemma was ammunition; they had to have enough ammunition to hunt, but if they didn't defend the valley, hunting wouldn't matter because they'd be dead. And if they defended the valley but then weren't able to hunt and feed their families . . . If there was a solution, she didn't know it. Ben would. She clasped her hands around the warmth of the mug and went for it. "If you could come down to the valley for a couple of hours, meet with some of the community leaders and give us some tips, maybe talk to this one guy—"

"No." He didn't let her finish, and she couldn't see even a flicker of interest in his eyes. Despite living here the past few years he had no sense of community, no ties to the people in the valley. The only interactions he'd had, that she knew of, were with the Livingstons and herself—that and giving Mike Kilgore the same answer he'd just given her: No.

Until that moment she hadn't realized how acutely she'd wanted him to say yes. She was holding herself together, barely, but scratch the surface and she was terrified that she'd do something wrong, not think of something crucial and get someone hurt or even killed. She *needed* his help . . . but what did *he* need? Nothing. He had everything here to make it through the crisis. All she could do was plead with him, because she had nothing to offer in barter.

An idea, a realization, blasted through her like an explosion. She had nothing he needed, but what about *want*?

Did she dare? She, who had never dared anything?

She was too self-aware to fool herself into thinking she could do this as a personal sacrifice for the good of the valley. The unvarnished truth was that she wanted Ben, sexually, in a way she'd never imagined she could want a man. She had never taken chances; her life was built around making the safest choice, not pushing, not demanding, not attracting attention. She *thought* he might be interested, but she'd never really gambled in the man/woman sweepstakes so she had no practical experience to guide her.

She knew she wasn't a beauty queen but she was attractive enough, unless he required a woman with a voluptuous figure, which for sure wasn't her. Carol said that deep down men weren't picky, but Adam had somewhat disproved that theory because Sela knew he'd never been completely satisfied with her.

But that was Adam. This was Ben. And they were so far apart in terms of masculinity they might as well have belonged to different species. If Ben said *yes*, she would get what she wanted, which was him—and the valley would get his military expertise.

She could *ask* . . . or she could duck her head and quietly leave, backing away from challenge and risk the way she always had before. She had never reached out to take what she wanted.

She had never *tried*.

Her lips were numb. Her ears were buzzing. The challenge to be more than what she'd been, to risk not just something but her very self, was so overwhelming she thought her bones might buckle under the pressure. And yet she couldn't just do nothing, not and live with herself. This wasn't chickening out on a ski trip, this was a chance to have something with *Ben*. No matter what, she wanted that chance.

As if from a distance she heard her own voice, low and only a little shaky: "I'll sleep with you if you'll help us."

His expression didn't flicker. The words lay between them . . . or did they? Had she actually spoken? Was the offer only in her imagination?

Then he said, "I don't know who that insults the most, you or me." He paused. "No."

That was it, just one word, and it was devastating.

It wasn't only her lips that were numb now, she'd lost feeling in her entire body. The heavens didn't blast apart, the floor didn't open to swallow her up, no matter how much she wished it would. She had to sit there, exposed and humiliated, fighting to breathe through the crush of pain, of rejection.

If her heart was beating, she couldn't feel it.

Slowly she managed to push to her feet, though she didn't know how. She would also somehow manage to go down the steps, walk down the steep driveway. She told herself she'd do that, no matter what. Where she would find the strength was something else entirely, but that, too, she would manage.

Except she couldn't, not like that. She couldn't leave things un-said, because that would bring even deeper regrets that she had left with him thinking she was willing to trade herself to anyone. Dredg-ing up the last tattered remnants of her pride, she said, "It isn't just the valley. I wouldn't have made that . . . offer . . . to anyone else. Only you. Because . . . because I thought, I felt . . ." She stumbled to a halt, gathered herself. "I felt . . . attraction." She was done. She couldn't take any more. She said "I'm sorry" in a thin, stifled tone and turned to leave.

She hadn't taken a single step before his hard hand closed around her arm and pulled her to a stop. Everything in her rejected being halted; she needed to get away, get out of his sight, before she broke down completely. She didn't want him to see, to know. Helplessly she tugged on her arm, knowing she would break free only if he let her, but trying anyway because she couldn't *not* try.

"Well, now." His voice was low, almost a growl; she hadn't heard him move but he was standing right behind her, and the timbre of his words was a stroke along her exposed nerve endings. "That changes things."

Blindly she shook her head. Anything he said now would seem like pity, and she couldn't bear that. "No. It doesn't." She pulled on her arm again.

"Sure it does. Let me show you."

He released her arm but closed both of his hands around her waist, turning her around to face him. She didn't want him to see her face, to know how devastated she was; quickly she ducked her head, and found herself with her forehead resting on his chest. He smelled of soap, of man, of heated skin. She could hear the beat of his heart, muted but strong and steady, luring her to nestle her cheek against him so she could feel as well as hear. She resisted the lure, too shat-tered to do anything other than endure.

Slowly, almost cautiously, he eased her body against him.

She felt more of that heat. She felt his chest and abdomen, like ridged iron covered with warm flesh. She felt the grip of his big hands, sliding down to her hips. She felt the long, muscled thighs. And she felt the thick ridge pressed against her stomach, felt him move her hips and rock her back and forth against that thick ridge.

Whiplashed first by rejection and now this, strung out on nerves, she shook her head. "I—no. I don't understand."

His left hand stroked from her hip up her back, fisted in the hair at the back of her head and tugged, tilting her head back. The expression in those sharp green eyes mesmerized her, like a rabbit being frozen by the predatory gaze of the wolf creeping up on it.

"Understand this." He kissed her—and nothing about it was anything like how she'd been kissed before. He kissed her as if he wanted to devour her, possess her, wipe the memory of every other kiss out of her mind forever. The kiss was hard, almost bruising; his lips were firm, his tongue in her mouth before she had quite realized what he was doing. He ate at her mouth, holding her head back to give him complete access. He kissed her as if he was about to strip her clothes off, pick her up, and put her against the wall.

The taste of him . . . oh, the taste of him.

A small part of her wanted to push him away and yell at him. He'd said no, and the single word had gutted her. Now he was kissing her as if he intended to never let her go. She wasn't good at this man/woman stuff and being jerked back and forth like this was so upsetting she wanted to *punch* him.

Instead she put her arms around him and clenched her fists in his shirt, returned the kiss with her own hunger and fervor, reveling in the strength she could feel under her hands, against her body. That wasn't enough; she released the fabric, dug her fingers into his back, tried to squirm closer because the only thing that would be *enough* was being naked with him, under him, having him inside her where she ached with emptiness.

Her hand was wet. And sticky.

The discordant sensation took a while to sink into her consciousness, to register as being not right. He finally lifted his head and she caught her breath, staring up at him. Absently she rubbed her thumb against her forefinger. He was bending his head down for more when her brows drew together in a puzzled frown and she said, "Wait."

He went still, sensing that something had fractured her attention. He cocked his head, listening, alert for an unusual sound. The dog lay panting contentedly under the table, though, not showing any sign of alarm. Ben looked back to her. "What? Did you hear something?"

"No." She withdrew her arms from around him, stared in puzzlement at the red stain on her hand. "What *is* that?"

He glanced at her hand and his expression cleared. "Blood. Mine, to be specific. Nothing serious, just a little cut, but it must have started bleeding again."

Her mouth fell open. "You're kidding."

"About what?"

"It's started bleeding *again*, but it's nothing serious? Turn around, let me see."

He got that impassive look, the one that said he wasn't going along with whatever other people wanted him to do. Sela got that, understood that he didn't want to be fussed over, but . . . but she was shaky inside after what had just passed between them and she needed something else to focus on, and checking on his wound was that something.

"You kissed me," she said fiercely. "That gives me rights, and sorry if you don't like it. Now turn around."

The impassive look morphed into something close to amusement. "A kiss gives you rights?"

"That one did." She'd never been kissed like that before, but on a cellular level she knew that something was happening between her and Ben that went beyond anything she'd imagined. She'd never been so pushy before, either, but she'd had twenty-four very rough hours and she seemed to be making a habit of doing things she'd never done before. Knowing she was so far out of her comfort zone, and was still functioning, made her both giddy and terrified. What the heck, she might as well keep going. "Pull your shirt off and—" She made a circle with her finger. Then she waited, barely breathing, to see what he did.

CHAPTER FIFTEEN

Those black eyebrows went up, but he began unbuttoning his shirt. With every button that was opened she saw more and more of his chest, his stomach, and she went breathless again. A diamond of hair centered his chest, then more lightly spread across his muscled pectorals and in a narrow line down the ridges of his abdomen. She wanted to put her hands on him, stroke him, but his eyes were still a bit feral with arousal and she knew if she did the cut on his back wouldn't get taken care of.

He tossed the flannel shirt across the back of a chair, and turned so she could examine his back. She caught a soft breath. At least he'd put a gauze pad over the wound, though it had bled through. The pad was small, about three by three inches; discolored skin surrounded it. The cut itself might be small, but the impact hadn't been. She reached up and gently tugged at the pad, but though the edges were free the center of it was stuck.

"What happened?" She continued lifting the edges of the gauze, leaning close in an effort to see the actual wound.

"I was cutting firewood and a tree kicked out, knocked me down. It isn't much, nothing that even needs a stitch."

"But it's still bleeding."

"I can't reach it to put clotting powder on it."

"Well, the gauze is soaked through, and it's stuck to the wound. I need to soak it off with warm water. Where are your first-aid supplies?" Yes, she agreed with him that the wound obviously wasn't serious, or he wouldn't be moving as easily as he was, but his shoulder still needed to be properly bandaged.

"The bathroom," he replied, after a long pause that told her he was teetering on the edge of telling her to back off, that kiss notwithstanding. Sela began working up her determination, because damned if she was going to leave here without first taking care of him.

"Lead the way," she said, and held her breath.

For a few seconds he didn't move, then she could see him mentally tell himself "What the hell," and led her through his bedroom to the bath. She stayed right on his heels, not taking the time to stop and look around because a delay might prod him to change his mind. His well of patience with people was woefully shallow. She did get a quick look around; her impression of his bedroom was the same as his living quarters: spare, functional. Even the area rug was more for function than decoration, helping keep the cold from his feet. His bed was covered with a dark green blanket, no bedspread. There was one pillow.

The bathroom was more of the same, larger than she'd expected, double sinks, both a tub and a separate shower with a glass door. It smelled of soap and felt somewhat humid. It had been so long since she'd encountered that combination that she skidded to a stop, her brow knitting in puzzlement. The shower door was open, and she noticed that the floor of the shower was damp. Not only that, the towel hanging on the rack looked recently used.

"You . . . your shower still works?" And though the wood-burning stove was in the living area, the bedroom and bath were warmer than she'd have expected, certainly warmer than hers was.

"Gravity system, and solar panels for heating the water."

Hot water. She swallowed a moan. She missed television, she missed being able to go to the grocery store and buy whatever she wanted, she missed central air and heat, but most of all she missed being able to take a hot shower.

He got out an impressive first-aid kit and placed it on the vanity, then lowered the lid on the toilet and straddled it backward. "Just put some clotting powder on it and I'll be fine."

Sela unzipped the sturdy black kit and spread it open, looked through it to see what was there. She took out antiseptic wipes, antibiotic salve, the envelope of blood-clotting powder, some adhesive bandages, looked for some disposable gloves but didn't see any and mentally shrugged. Somewhat hesitantly she turned on the hot-water faucet, because despite what she was seeing, believing verged on a miracle. The water began flowing.

"Oh my Lord," she said softly as she picked up the soap and began washing her hands.

"What?"

"Running water." Her hands were clean. She didn't bother drying them, just took two pads of gauze, held one under the water, and then plopped it over the bloody one on his back. The other pad of gauze she pressed against his skin below, to catch the red rivulets. When the bandage was soaked, she gently peeled at it again. The stuck part released a little, but more blood began welling up.

"Just pull it off, get it done," he said, glancing over his bare shoulder at her.

Maybe that was the best way, because it was going to bleed regardless. The pad was soaked, she couldn't get it any wetter. Wincing a little, she caught hold of the upper edge of the pad and gave it a firm pull. It came free, and she immediately slapped it back over the wound and put as much pressure as she could on it.

"Use the clotting powder."

"Just dust it on?"

"It takes more than that." He leaned forward some. "Pour it on and pat it in with your fingers."

She tore open the envelope and poured some of the white granules on the bloody wound, then used her finger to wipe most of it into a pile where the bleeding was worse, where she then patted it in as he'd instructed. After a few seconds the clotting began, and in less than half a minute the bleeding had stopped.

In silence she began cleaning around the wound, then, when the bleeding didn't resume, she gently blotted away the stained granules. The skin was broken in a jagged pattern, rather than a cut. The area around it was swollen and bruised. "Too bad we don't have ice," she murmured, then paused. "Or do you?"

"Not at the moment."

Indicating he could have ice if he wanted it bad enough. "What *don't* you have?"

"No satellite television, air conditioner, or internet."

"I miss all three of those," she admitted softly, blotting the wound with an antiseptic pad. "Not as much as running water, though." She examined the jagged edges. "I think you do need a stitch or two."

"Not bad enough for me to go hunting someone to sew me up, unless you're volunteering. There are sutures in the kit."

"I'll try if you want me to." Dubiously she eyed the wound. "I've never done anything like that before, though." She didn't know how she would stomach sticking a needle through his skin, but come to that, just three months ago she wouldn't have thought she could handle any of the things that defined her life now. She had, and if Ben needed stitches she would manage that, too.

"Just stick some butterfly bandages on it, that's all it needs."

She didn't quite agree with that, but used more antiseptic pads to make certain the wound was clean, then applied antibiotic salve. As she worked she became aware that this certainly wasn't the first time he'd been hurt. A puckered scar formed a white star close to his waistline on the left. A long, narrow ridge bisected his back from the left shoulder across his spine to wrap around his rib cage on the right. The pad of his right shoulder, right above the current wound, bore a small, thick scar as if the muscle had been gouged.

This would be yet another scar, given the unevenness of the break in the skin.

She didn't know much about the military but she did know he'd been in service and his was a warrior's body, a living testimony to pain, sacrifice, and a spirit of steel. With these scars he'd either seen combat or maybe had a hell of a vehicle accident. She put her money on combat. Perhaps he'd always been a solitary person, but she thought his withdrawal from people had more to do with his experiences than his personality. Her heart swelled with pain for him. She would have stroked those scars, but sensed that he wouldn't welcome it. However he had gotten them was his past to share or not.

As gently as possible she pulled the ragged edges together and positioned several butterfly bandages over the wound, then covered *that* with a thick gauze pad that she taped into place. "I'm not a doctor, but I've seen plenty on television, and I doctored plenty of Olivia's boo-boos. Don't chop any wood for a week, and don't get this wet."

He glanced over his shoulder and this time she definitely saw amusement. "How am I supposed to shower?"

"Ah . . . okay, don't shower for two days. If you're not doing hard manual labor, you won't be getting all that dirty and sweaty, right?" She began putting the first-aid kit to rights. "But keep an eye on it. If it shows signs of infection, don't ignore that. Come down to the valley and I'll do something. We have a couple of herbalists who can make a good poultice."

"Yes, ma'am." He got to his feet and turned to face her, and wow, his chest. Sela quickly looked away before she embarrassed herself again. She had regained her equilibrium thanks to the way he'd kissed her, but that didn't mean she'd lost her memory of how he'd so easily said "no" to her offer.

He put his hands on her waist just as he had before, his thumbs rubbing on each side of her navel in a subtle but potent caress that made her nipples and vagina tighten in response, made her want to flow toward him until their bodies were touching. Part of her was still astonished that he was touching her, and that astonishment kept her in place though she couldn't stop herself from putting her own hands on his muscled forearms. "I'll be there tomorrow morning, and I'll talk to the valley people," he muttered, his sharp green gaze on her mouth, then moving down to her breasts. "When we have sex, it won't be because of any negotiation or part of any deal. It'll be because we want it. Are you clear on that?"

Mutely she nodded. *When* they had sex. Like it was inevitable.

It was.

She accepted that. Wanted that. The only question was the one he'd pointed out: *When?*

"I have to get back," she said, wishing the when was now even though she knew it wasn't. She needed to check on Carol, see about supper. Thank goodness Nancy had volunteered to stay with Carol tonight, because Sela was fast running out of steam. She wanted to curl up under a quilt on her couch, in front of a fire, and catch up on the sleep she hadn't gotten the night before.

He tilted his head toward the shower. "Want a shower before you go?"

She stared up at him, her lips parting. He couldn't have offered her a new car and tempted her more. A shower! For two months she'd been washing off with water carried from the creek and heated in a kettle in the fireplace, which wasn't very efficient. Washing her hair was a big deal and required waiting until she had the time to sit beside the fire to dry it. She worked hard at basic cleanliness, and now hot running water was the ultimate in luxury to her.

He almost smiled—not quite, but almost. "If you could see your face. I take that as a yes. Towels and washcloths are there." He indicated the linen closet. "I don't have any fancy-smelling soap or shampoo—"

"I don't care!" she said hurriedly, already reaching for the buttons on her shirt. She stopped, blushed, and dropped her hands before she found herself stripping in front of him.

"Take as long as you want." He went out and closed the door.

Sela peeled off her clothes so fast she almost tore them. A shower! She was going to have a wonderful hot shower!

Ben threw on his shirt, then took the dog and went outside. He didn't quite trust himself to be in the house, knowing he had a naked woman in his shower—and not just any woman. Sela. Quiet, gentle Sela, who kissed him back with a fire that still had his balls aching. It wasn't just the way she'd responded, but the concern she'd shown over the annoying but definitely not serious cut on his shoulder, and the gentleness of her touch as she tended to him. All his prior wounds had been treated either in the field—not gentle—or in a military hospital—still not gentle. She hadn't been treating a wound, she'd been taking care of *him*. He couldn't remember the last time, if ever, he'd been taken care of as himself rather than as a soldier, part of a fighting force.

Talk about a surprising turn of events. From the second he'd seen her walking up the driveway, things had happened fast.

Shit. Sela had balls. Not actual balls, which he intended to eventually prove for himself, but when she wanted something she was apparently willing to do anything to get it. She hadn't even been asking for herself, but for the people around her, who would never know what she'd offered and perhaps didn't deserve that kind of sacrifice.

Sacrifice? He'd make damn sure it was neither a sacrifice nor a payment. He'd do what she wanted, no strings attached. Whatever happened afterward would happen because they both wanted it.

He didn't want to deal with the townsfolk, community folk, whatever the fuck they were. Wears Valley wasn't a town. Whatever it was or wasn't, he still didn't want to deal with them, but he was committed now and obviously they needed the help. Despite himself he was concerned about the old couple, the Livingstons. They'd have a tough time emotionally dealing with what had happened, and would need help getting past it and feeling secure in their home again.

He looked at the dog, bounding around and sniffing at everything. He hadn't wanted the responsibility or the company of the dog, but he'd gotten used to both. He patted his thigh and the gangly pup bounded over to him, body wiggling with delight. Ben crouched down, scratching behind both ears. "I'll miss you, boy," he murmured, "but there's a couple of old people who need you more than I do." There was a concept; he hadn't realized he needed the dog at all. "Reckon you could be happy being spoiled rotten? I don't think you'll get in much hunting, but you'll have all the attention you could want." Maybe the Livingstons wouldn't want a dog to take care of, though having a mountain cur in the house keeping guard might be just what they needed to make them feel safe again. All he could do was ask.

And, fuck, that meant he'd have to do some hunting for them, to help them keep the dog fed. That was what was wrong with getting to know people. It was like getting caught in a damned spiderweb, with more and more strands getting wrapped around him.

One of those strands was in his shower right now. He kept stroking the dog, but his thoughts had zeroed back in on Sela. When he'd mentioned the shower . . . the expression on her face had been priceless—and arousing. He'd seen joy, wonder, and desire, her soft dark eyes filled with longing. For a shower.

He had a hard-on. Again. Gingerly he straightened to give his dick room to stretch out, and realized that he wouldn't be able to walk away again. He wanted her to look at him that way. Admit it, own it, act on it.

He looked at the house, every hunter's instinct in him on alert. There was a naked woman in his shower, and he wanted to be in there with her.

CHAPTER SIXTEEN

Ben and the dog walked Sela down the steep driveway to where she'd parked her SUV. He carried his shotgun, his gaze alert and his head on a swivel, constantly looking around him. He was far more alert than she'd been on the walk up, she realized, and he was armed. She had simply walked up without taking much notice of her surroundings. The community patrol would learn from him but she should, too. It was everyone's responsibility to help keep the valley safe.

She felt wonderful. It wasn't as if she hadn't washed every night with soap, but there was something about standing under warm flowing water that was downright miraculous. She smelled like his soap and shampoo, both of which were plain Jane without any perfumes added, and that was pretty great, too. She had sat in front of the fire and finger-combed her hair while it partially dried; she could have stayed indefinitely, but knowing her responsibilities waited for her made her antsy.

When they reached her SUV she took the remote from her pocket and unlocked the doors. She gave him a slightly guilty look. "I used your toilet, too," she confessed, her tone a little shy but jubilant, too. "And flushed."

"I know. I heard. I'd have been surprised if you hadn't." He slanted a look at her and this time she definitely saw amusement. "Flushed, that is."

Before she knew it she'd lightly punched him on the arm, then realized what she'd done and clapped her hand over her mouth. She could feel her face heating. "I'm so sorry," she mumbled behind her hand. "I didn't mean— I don't . . ." she trailed off, because it was ludicrous to say I don't hit people when she had just now hit him.

"Give people love taps?" he asked. He looked down at her and hooked his arm around her waist, pulled her against him. "It wasn't even much of a tap, I barely felt it. That said, my feelings are hurt and you have to make it up to me."

His . . . feelings were hurt? She was momentarily bewildered, then like the rising of the sun she realized he was flirting with her. Flirting! Ben Jernigan! Warmth flooded through her and a smile bloomed across her face. Rising on her toes, she wound her arms around his neck and brushed a light kiss across his mouth. "Does this make you feel better?" she asked, giving him another kiss. Even as she did she was astonished all over again that he was holding her, that she was kissing him. So much had changed today, things she hadn't imagined would ever happen no matter where her imagination had taken her.

"Getting there," he replied, and took over.

It had been so long since she'd felt attractive to a man, since she'd known passion. Ben made her feel as if she could light him up with the slightest touch, underscored by the thick ridge in his jeans. Looking back, considering how he'd sought her out, however reluctantly, she thought he must have been as attracted to her as she had been to him. The knowledge thrilled her, excited her. She'd be having sex with him soon—maybe not in the next week or so, because of Carol needing care, but soon. She hadn't had sex since Adam had divorced her. Her confidence had been so thoroughly destroyed that she'd shied away from even dating, but soon she would be sleeping with a man who made Adam look like a Ken doll, and not even an anatomically correct Ken, at that.

He turned her and lifted her onto the hood of the Honda, stepping between her legs as naturally as if they had been having make-out sessions for months instead of . . . an hour? Sela's breath went ragged as he settled that hard ridge right against her clitoris and rubbed it back and forth. "Oh," she said in a soft, breathless tone, her fingers digging into the back of his neck.

He made a raw sound deep in his throat and eased away from her. Disappointment shot through her until she saw his face, and was transfixed by the glorious realization that the carnal caress, even through their clothes, had almost sent him over the edge. She liked knowing he was that turned on. She bent her head to let it rest on his left shoulder, her face turned into his throat. The hot man-smell of him filled her with both excitement and joy.

"You should leave now," he said, his voice low and rough.

"Yes." She had things to do, and even more to think about. On the trip up she'd felt as if she was approaching doom, but what had actually happened between them now made her as exhilarated as if she'd successfully been playing hooky. She was going to have sex with Ben Jernigan, someday soon. The situation in the valley was still fraught with tension, difficulty, and possible danger, but that was balanced by the amazing fact that people kept on being people, doing what they had done for eons. Sexual attraction, getting drunk on hormones and pheromones . . . she had to say it was an excellent counterbalance to everything else.

He lifted her down from the hood and opened the driver's-side door for her. "I'll be at the store early. You said you'd start at nine, but people will be lining up by daylight."

"I hope I have enough gas for everyone."

"Anything is better than nothing. Ration it, so everyone gets some."

Reluctant to leave him, she told him about her idea of making braziers to heat and cook, for the households that didn't have fireplaces, if they could find a potter and a kiln for firing the clay. He nodded. "Good idea. There should be a potter in the valley, with all the crafts going on around here. If there is, there'll need to be fireproof brick, or slate, or an indoor sand pit to put under the braziers so they won't burn the floor."

"Another thing to think about," she said, sighing. "Every solution comes with its own problem, doesn't it?"

"Way of the world." He leaned down and kissed her again, as if, now that he'd started, he intended to seize every opportunity to do so. She didn't mind at all.

As she turned the SUV around and drove down the mountain, she began mentally worrying at the complications that could develop. She hoped the woman who knew a woman who had thrown pots had some good news. So much had happened today that she couldn't remember the possible-potter's name, but she did know who had said she'd check. Finding that out came before everything.

Sela thought about stopping at Carol's when she drove by, but her hair was still damp and even though she was alone she could feel herself blushing. No, she didn't want to explain why her hair was wet; not only did she not want anyone knowing she'd taken a shower in Ben's house, but Ben might not want anyone knowing that he had a working shower with beautiful hot water. Instead she went to her own home and built up the fire, then sat in front of the flames combing her hair until it was dry. Oh, it felt so wonderful, to be clean from head to toe—such a little thing, but a huge boost to her sense of well-being. When her hair was dry she pulled it back and secured it with a clasp at the back of her head, the way she usually wore it these days.

Then she walked back to Carol's house, and let herself in. "How's the patient?" she asked Barb.

"I can hear you!" Carol yelled from the bedroom, answering that question, because she sounded cranky and impatient.

"The whole county can hear you," Sela countered, going into the bedroom because obviously Carol was awake.

"Ha ha." Carol shifted uncomfortably on the bed. She didn't look feverish, which was great, but neither did she look well. Now that twenty-four hours had passed, her bruises were blooming, including one on her jaw that had been nothing more than a red spot last night. "My leg hurts, my ribs hurt, and my head hurts. I'm tired of this. I'm bored. I want to move to the living room."

"Sorry. You can move to the portable toilet for right now, but that's it. How about a book to read?"

Carol glared at her. "I have a book, thank you, and you've turned into a tyrant. Power has gone to your head."

Sela burst out laughing, and bent to kiss Carol's forehead. "You wanted me in charge, so if I'm a tyrant it's your fault."

She might be in pain, on drugs, and irritable, but nothing was wrong with Carol's powers of observation. She narrowed her eyes at Sela. "You look different. Like you're high on something. Have you been smoking dope?"

"It's been quite a day," Sela replied. "A couple of times I wished I had some dope to smoke, and that I knew how to smoke. Has Barb or Olivia filled you in on what happened at the Livingstons' house?"

"Barb said someone broke in on them, but both Jim and Mary Alice are all right." Again the narrowed eyes. "Is that wrong? Is one of them hurt?"

Sela pulled the bedside chair around so she was facing Carol, and sat down. "As far as that goes, they're all right. But the man had a gun, and Jim shot and killed him."

Carol sucked in a breath. "Shit. Shit shit shit."

"We did the best we could." She detailed how they had handled the situation, with the photographs and Trey's efforts at fingerprints, the statement she'd written up and had Jim sign. "If there's anything else we could have done, other than sending someone to Sevierville to fetch the sheriff—assuming anyone is even in the sheriff's office these days—I can't think what. We also have another problem. A lot of people in the valley don't have fireplaces.

Some are probably getting by with kerosene heaters, but they're going to run out of kerosene eventually, when the weather gets cold and stays cold."

"Which could be any day."

"Yes. A possible solution is clay braziers, if we can find a kiln here in the valley. Someone is checking with another woman who maybe used to do pottery—"

"Mona Clausen used to do some pottery, if I remember right."

"That's the name! I've been trying to remember. Someone else mentioned her and was going to check."

"She used to have a small kiln, too. She and her mother made pottery to sell in the souvenir stores."

"Then pray she still has the kiln or knows someone local who does. I also told the community patrol about the gasoline in my tanks. Trey Foster is going to rig up a suction pump, and we're going to start dispensing it in five-gallon increments tomorrow morning at nine." She paused. "I didn't tell them about the small tank. Am I wrong?"

"I wouldn't have told them either, so if you're wrong, I'd be wrong right along with you." Once again Carol shifted her weight, winced as her ribs protested.

"I still feel guilty, but then I think about you and Olivia, and—"

"And family is family."

"The patrol is telling people as they go around the valley." She sighed. "I tried not to let Ted Parsons get to me, but he questioned everything I said. If it hadn't been for Mike and Trey, I probably would have walked out."

"No, you'd have wanted to, but you'd have stayed." Carol patted her hand. "I know that, even if you don't."

"I think Ted wants to feel important. He was the boss in his tire stores, but he's an outsider here and we don't listen to him so much. He was talking to some guy Mike said was a Dietrich—I don't think

I know them—and Ted was all puffed up, telling people about the gas as if it was his."

"The only Dietrichs I know live on the Townsend end of the valley. Lawrence and Zoe. Both of them are heavy into meth. I wouldn't trust them as far as I could throw them."

That was where she'd heard the name, Sela realized, when Carol had said back when they were first getting organized not to let Zoe Dietrich go into old people's homes to help them because she'd steal their medications. Without doubt the Dietrichs would show up to get gasoline, and she hoped they used it to leave, to go where they were more likely to find a thriving drug trade. Knoxville wasn't that far; they could make it on a couple of gallons of gas.

The thing was, she wouldn't be the only station owner who had cut off their pumps to save the gasoline. It was more likely that all over the country people would be getting into the gas reserves for exactly the same reason she was, to use it before the octane degraded too much to be usable. Did that mean that, for a certain stretch of time, groups of people who had been in one spot would start moving around? It wasn't just that smart people would know the rural areas would be surviving better than the urban ones, but that they'd have more to steal.

"I'm worried about strangers coming into the valley," she confided. "If one made it this far, others can. With gasoline in their vehicles the patrol can cover more ground, for a little while at least, but other than that I don't know what to do." She was silent a moment. "I went to see Ben Jernigan."

Even hurt and drugged, Carol perked up at that news. Her eyes sparkled. "You did? What happened? Anything juicy?"

"He didn't shoot me, if that's what you mean. He listened." By sheer force of will, Sela kept herself focused on what she was telling Carol, so she wouldn't blush. "He seems to have a soft spot for Jim and Mary Alice, and I thought if he knew what happened to them he might be more interested in helping us. He said he'd come down tomorrow morning when everyone lines up to get gas, to talk to the patrol members, so that's something. Oh—I also got in an argument with Carlette Broward." She couldn't control a little smile, really more of a smirk, but one full of triumph. "I won. I think I did, anyway. She started in on me about hogging the gas for myself and after putting up with Ted and all his crap I was fed up."

"I don't know Carlette Broward, I don't think, but yay anyway. Did you bitch-slap her?"

"Good God, no. From the looks of her she could stomp me into a greasy smear on the road."

"Oh! I think I know who you mean. Did you see a tattoo on her neck? Yeah, she could take you."

For all Carol had been so vocal about wanting Sela to be in charge of organization, she did love having her finger in all pies and knowing exactly what was going on, even if she hadn't been bored. Sela sat and chatted until Carol drifted off to sleep, then quietly stood and tiptoed out.

Sundown came early these days and it was already dark outside. Barb and Olivia were heating vegetable soup over the fire. Barb had made some skillet bread the day before and she was toasting the last of it to eat with the soup. The smell of the toasting bread made Sela's mouth water, and she went through the simple meal as if she were a starving plow-hand, though she did occasionally pause between bites to bring Barb and Olivia up to speed on the day's events, and to tell them that Nancy Meador was staying with Carol that night.

"I can do that," Barb protested. "We can swap nights and do just fine."

"You have day duty," Sela pointed out. Barb was now doing all of the cooking. Olivia helped, but Barb was the one in charge. "I wouldn't have a problem handling nights, normally, but today has been a challenge and it started early."

"I doubt tomorrow will be any less busy, so if Nancy or anyone else offers to stay, take them up on it." Barb dipped up a bowl of soup for Carol, added the toasted bread to the platter. "This stage won't last long, when her ribs are less sore she'll be able to get around on her own here in the house, and won't need any more pain pills. I'm guessing a week."

"I can help, too. What difference does it make if I sleep upstairs, or down here in Gran's room?" Olivia pointed out.

"Well, that's true." All of Sela's reasons for staying with Carol last night suddenly seemed less valid. Olivia wasn't experienced taking care of people, but she was a smart kid, loved Carol, and doing the basic things that needed to be done wasn't a complicated task. Delegate, delegate, delegate. Sela reminded herself to ask for help when she needed it. She'd forced herself to ask for help from Ben and look how that had turned out. She felt her face, her entire body, getting hot, and not from embarrassment. *When we have sex* . . . She felt breathless, her attention instantly fractured.

She was profoundly grateful to Nancy for staying with Carol tonight, so she could be alone and fantasize about everything that had happened today with Ben, and everything that could happen in the future. The near future, she hoped. While she understood why he was taking the very possibility of negotiation out of the situation between them, she wouldn't have minded if they hadn't waited at all.

Still, waiting was for the best. She was innately cautious when it came to relationships, and even though being with Ben was something she wanted with all her heart, she needed to mentally prepare for being intimate with a man again after so long. Basically, she would fret. Half of her was so filled with longing and excitement she wasn't certain she could contain herself, but the other half of her was uncertain. What if he didn't like her body? She had all the basic female parts, but not a single one was extraordinary. Maybe he liked adventurous sex. Maybe he was into some kink. She didn't think she could do adventurous or kink, which meant that if he did, in short order he'd be bored with her just like Adam had been.

On the other hand, just kissing him had carried her higher than making love with Adam ever had, so she could be short-selling herself as to what she could or couldn't do. With Ben, she didn't know if she had any boundaries.

"You look funny," Olivia said, staring at her.

Sela jerked herself back to the present and managed to say, "Like I'm crazy? Because that's how I feel, as if I have twenty balls in the air but only know how to juggle one."

"One ball isn't juggling. It's tossing a ball back and forth."

"My point exactly. I don't know how to juggle." She blew out a breath. "I'm going home, and going to sleep."

She did exactly that, not even bothering with bed and instead wrapping herself in a blanket and curling up on the couch where she could watch the fire. Funny how she had seldom had a fire going before, and now it was one of the most comforting things she could imagine . . .

She slept so soundly that she woke feeling as if she'd slept for hours, but the fire still had small flames licking upward so she knew she hadn't. Sleepily she got up and replenished the fire, checked the battery-operated clock—10:24—and went back to the couch. Instead of going back to sleep, though, she lay there staring at the fire while she mentally ran through everything that had happened during the long, eventful day. She wanted to think about Ben, relive those intense, exciting kisses and the promise of more; instead she mentally worried over everything else.

A sense of unease gnawed at her, but she couldn't isolate the reason for it. There were a lot of things about the day to worry about, things that had already happened and couldn't be changed. Upcoming was dispensing the gasoline, but she'd have plenty of help for that, and Ben had promised to come down and get them better organized as far as security.

But . . . what if there was trouble over the gasoline? If demand outstripped supply, those left out were going to be angry. She couldn't think of any way to avoid that; she couldn't manufacture gasoline and put more in the tanks. They could dole it out in five-gallon increments—after the community patrol had filled their tanks—and there would either be enough for everyone to get some, or not. She also had to find out about the kiln that Mona Clausen might or might not have, preferably before they pumped the tanks dry.

Those were things to do, not things to be uneasy about. Short term, life in the valley was going to be easier, because of the gasoline supply she'd protected.

Liquid gold.

The supply of gasoline was priceless, the way things were now. People would do everything they could to get it, for use or trade. It was better than money, because you couldn't eat money, or stay warm with it.

In her mind's eye she suddenly saw Ted talking to Lawrence Dietrich—Dietrich, who, according to Carol, was involved in meth. Making it, selling it, or taking it, she didn't know, but meth was death. A meth addict would steal anything to feed the habit—

And she had gasoline.

If not Lawrence Dietrich then others like him—and meth was an ongoing problem in the area—would know that come morning she'd be emptying the tanks. People had been deliberately spreading the news, just as she'd asked them to do. If anyone intended to steal the gas for themselves, they had to get it tonight, before people started lining up tomorrow. She expected people would start showing up well before dawn, and once they did, the opportunity for theft was gone. The best time to steal the gasoline was . . . now.

She threw off the blanket and surged to her feet. No one was stealing her gasoline.

Quickly she banked the fire, and threw on as many clothes as she could wear. She grabbed what she thought she'd need: a bottle of water, a probably stale granola bar, her .22 rifle, and a box of shells that she shoved into her coat pocket. She also got a couple of hand warmers from the camping supplies she'd bought that first day, along with her most powerful flashlight, and headed out. She was twenty yards down the road when she stopped.

What the heck was she doing?

The thought resonated. Her steps slowed, and she turned back. Why walk when she could drive? Seeing her SUV parked at the store should be a deterrent to anyone who was thinking about stealing the gas.

She might be inventing drama, seeing threat where none existed. She wasn't a gutsy heroine who would face down the bad guys with moxie, wit, and incredible courage. On the other hand, she would do her best to protect her family and the people in the valley who were expecting her to make decisions and look out for their common interests.

If that meant spending an uncomfortable night in a cold store, so be it. With luck, that was all that would happen. She had always erred on the side of caution, anyway. By some twisted logic she was putting herself in potential danger by being extra cautious. Rock, meet hard place.

She thought about stopping by Mike Kilgore's house and telling him what she was doing. He could help watch . . . but Mike and the others in the community patrol were already putting in long hours, and given that he'd been the one to fetch her early this morning he'd had even less sleep than she had. If she knew there was a threat to the gas supply of course she'd wake him, and anyone else who could help her, but she was guessing.

Guessing or not, she'd have to be a fool to go there and not let anyone else know.

Almost everyone in the valley had gotten in the habit of going to bed early, to save batteries and lamp oil. Carol's house was dark, too, when she pulled into the driveway, but she figured Nancy Meador at least would be easily roused.

Sure enough, when Sela knocked on the door, only a minute passed before Nancy said, "Who is it?"

"Sela."

Nancy quickly opened the door, looked out at Sela's SUV. "Has something else happened?"

"No, everything's okay. I'm spending the night at the store and I just wanted someone to know."

Nancy peered at her in sleepy confusion. "Why're you doing that?"

"Because if anyone wants to steal the gasoline, they'll have to do it tonight because tomorrow will be too late."

"But—you can't do that by yourself! It's too dangerous!"

"I'm probably overreacting, and just parking my car there should be enough to keep anyone from trying anything."

"Or," Nancy said shrewdly, "you're right on the money in your thinking and anyone who wants to steal the gas might not balk at hurting anyone who gets in his way."

Hearing it put like that, Sela wavered. Then she sucked it up and said, "I have my .22. I should be okay."

Nancy regarded her silently for a minute, then patted her arm. "You be careful."

"I will."

She drove to the store and slowly circled it, searching with her headlights to see if anyone was parked in the shadows. She didn't see anything, thank goodness. She started to park by the door then had a second thought and parked on top of the access to the tanks. If anyone wanted to get to those tanks they'd have to push her vehicle out of the way first.

Letting herself into the empty store was always a little bit of a shock to her system, no matter how many times she'd done it. This store had been her livelihood, and now it was barren. When the power came back on . . . what then? The world wouldn't immediately snap back to normal. Improvements would come in fits and starts as manufacturing slowly geared up, as food production got started again. Likely it would be a year after the power came back on before supplies began trickling in. How would banks work? Credit? She had her supply of cash—thanks to Ben's warning—but what would she be able to buy?

For the foreseeable future, likely the store wasn't going to be her livelihood. Come spring, everyone would plant gardens. Instead of people buying potato chips, they'd be growing and preserving their own food. If she sold anything, it would be gasoline and a few staples like flour, salt and pepper, sugar, and some spices if she could get them.

Sighing, she used the flashlight to check the store, looking in the storage area, the coolers, the bathrooms. Empty. She didn't lock the door behind her. She needed to be able to get out quickly, without fiddling with the lock. In the deep silence the sound of the lock turning was loud, and would alert anyone who might be in the parking lot.

Surprise was her friend.

She placed the rifle on the counter, the box of shells beside it, then turned the flashlight off and settled in the chair behind the counter. From there she could see almost the entire parking lot, and certainly anyone who approached by road. The moon was almost full, and provided enough light that she thought she'd be able to spot any trouble.

The interior of the store was icy cold, but with the multiple layers of clothes she was wearing, the extra socks and down coat, she was, if not comfortable, at least not miserable. She figured that would change, as the hours wore on. Maybe people would start lining up early, really early, which would nullify anyone's idea of stealing the gasoline, and all of them could build a fire outside, away from the tanks, and stand around talking for the rest of the night.

She wished Ben were there with her. The conditions weren't favorable for making out, but just having him beside her would make her happy. They might not talk much, but sit beside each other the way they had the night of the red aurora. She smiled in the dark, then thought of how he tasted and felt and the smile turned into a soft sigh of longing.

Her gaze was drawn from the empty parking lot to Cove Mountain, looming dark and silent in front of her. She couldn't pinpoint where Ben's house was because there were no lights, but she could get close. He was up there right now with his shower and his dog, with his solar panels and his wood-burning stove and goodness only knows what else. If he couldn't be here with her, she wished she was there with him. Lord knows they'd both be more comfortable.

What time was it? She knew she hadn't taken more than half an hour—more like twenty minutes—to get dressed, stop by Carol's, and get here. Likely it was no later than eleven; that meant she had about seven more long hours of darkness to get through. Sitting here in the cold and the dark was boring, but boring was good. Boring meant nothing was happening.

When we have sex . . .

Their conversation kept running through her mind, along with her acute memory of his arms, and his fine ass in those jeans he always wore, and his face, which was masculine and well proportioned and all-in-all drool worthy. She didn't fantasize about men, not movie stars or musicians or men she knew. Her brain didn't work that way. But here she sat, definitely fantasizing about Ben Jernigan and getting herself worked up. At least thinking about him kept her from feeling so cold, and definitely kept her awake.

Movement and a flicker of light at the left corner front window caught her eye. Sela stood quickly, lifting her rifle, not pointing the weapon but wanting it in her hand. Someone was approaching the store.

A split second later, thanks to the full moon, she recognized the form headed her way.

Olivia opened the door and stepped inside, the weak beam from her flashlight pointed to the floor.

"What are you thinking?" Sela snapped as she set the rifle aside. She seldom got sharp with anyone, but Olivia had just scared the crap out of her. What if she hadn't recognized the girl? What if she'd panicked and shot without thinking? She wasn't the type to panic, but Olivia was dear to her and her imagination threw up too many what-if situations that could have happened.

Olivia had dressed much like Sela had, with boots and a heavy coat. Carol's .22 was slung over the teenager's shoulder, along with two small tote bags.

"I was thinking you shouldn't be here on your own," Olivia said calmly, in answer to Sela's question.

"I can't believe Nancy would let you—"

"She doesn't know. I slipped out the back door, but I did leave a note on my bed so they'll know where I am. I heard you drive up and listened to what you said. I went back to bed, but then got worried about you being here by yourself, so I got up, got dressed, and here I am."

"You need to go back home."

"I will when you will." Stubbornness laced Olivia's tone. She went to the back of the store to grab her own chair, which she placed beside Sela's. She put the rifle on the counter and the bags on the floor at her side. She turned off her flashlight, saving the already-weakened batteries.

Sela battled with herself. How did she scold Olivia—who was young but had grown up a lot over the past couple of months—for doing exactly what she herself was doing? Finally she said, "I don't want anything to happen to you."

"I don't want anything to happen to you," Olivia returned, to which there was no argument.

They sat in silence for a while. Then Olivia reached into her left coat pocket and pulled out something that rustled as she extended her hand toward Sela. The moonlight lit the store interior enough that Sela was able to make out what Olivia was holding: two Reese's Peanut Butter Cups, her favorite candy. She offered one to Sela.

"I hid these," Olivia explained. "For an emergency."

"A candy emergency."

"I think this qualifies."

Sela laughed and took the offered candy, unwrapped it, and drew the familiar patty closer to her nose to savor the aroma for a couple of seconds before she took a small bite.

"Better than tuna, wouldn't you say?" Olivia asked, a smile in her voice.

They both took their time, nibbling at the candy, savoring every bite. "I wish I could have made some hot chocolate," Olivia said wistfully. "But Nancy would have heard. I brought water, though."

"So did I."

It could be worse, Sela thought. At least Olivia knew how to handle the rifle, though she wasn't any more expert than Sela was. Carol had taught her the basics, because if there was going to be a firearm in the house then she wanted her granddaughter to know how to safely handle it.

They sipped some water, sat in more silence. So far, all was quiet. If they were lucky it would be this way all night. Maybe having Olivia here was a good thing; after the long day she'd had, she'd have a hard time staying awake. Chatting with Olivia would help with that. Carol would be furious when she found out, but probably secretly proud of the girl, too.

After a while Sela asked, "Do you have any more candy hidden away?"

Olivia sighed. "No, that was it. There might be a bag of barbecue chips squirreled away in the garage, though."

Sela laughed, and it felt good after the stressful day to realize that laughter was still possible. Olivia reminded her of the reasons why she was willing to step up and do what needed to be done, of why she'd put herself front and center, why she'd sit in her store all night to make sure no one stole the gasoline her family and friends and neighbors needed to get by. "Thanks for sharing with me."

"You're welcome. You've definitely earned a peanut butter cup after all you've been through. I wish I had more."

"Me too."

For a while they talked, about Carol and her fall, about Barb and the way she'd stepped up since. If Olivia was older, Sela would be tempted to tell her all about Ben, and the shower, and the tantalizing *When we have sex* comment, but rifle aside, Olivia was still a kid. And Sela had never been keen on sharing details of her sex life—or lack thereof—even with her close friends. She was a private person. Shy, yes, but also private. She held some things, some thoughts, very close. They were for her and for her alone.

Sela almost dozed off. Her eyes drifted closed; her head nodded. Olivia did doze, though she woke at regular intervals because sleeping soundly upright in a chair wasn't something that was going to happen. Now and then they tried to keep one another alert with conversation about the weather and the future and their neighbors, but there were long periods of silence where neither of them had anything to say.

Her hands and feet got cold. She got out the hand warmer packs and squeezed to activate them, put one in each pocket and gave the others to Olivia who silently did the same. She took off her gloves so she could better feel the heat from the packs. As small as the heat source was, having warm hands was blissful and made her feel warmer all over. She began getting sleepy.

In an effort to wake herself up, she drank more water, got up and walked around. Olivia scooted her chair closer to the counter, crossed her arms on it, and rested her head on her arms. While she slept, Sela stood at the windows with her hands in her coat pockets and watched the cold, still night.

It was the reflection of moonlight on glass, a quick, subtle flash, that first caught her attention. She cocked her head, staring down the road. Then she heard the sound of engines, once commonplace but now so rare that adrenaline sent an electric charge through her body.

"Olivia!" she said urgently, because someone driving down the highway with their lights off couldn't be good news.

"Hmm?" Olivia mumbled.

"Someone's coming."

Hurriedly she went to the counter and picked up the rifle, went back to stand beside the door and look out the windows. Olivia came to stand beside her, holding Carol's .22 with the barrel pointing down and away from Sela. "I don't see anything," she whispered.

"Listen."

The sound of engines was louder—not just one engine, but several. Again, not good.

"Oh no." Olivia sounded dismayed. Sela felt as dismayed as Olivia sounded. She had come here because she knew there was a possibility someone would try to steal the gasoline, but faced with the reality of multiple people driving toward her with their headlights out— sneaking—her stomach tied itself in knots. First and foremost was a sharp terror that something would happen to Olivia.

"Get behind the counter," she ordered.

"No." Olivia's tone wavered, but she stood her ground. "I'm with you."

Sela pushed the door open, secured it so it stayed open. Maybe that was the wrong move but she didn't know defensive strategies and she did know she didn't want to shoot through glass. Her SUV was here; that and the open door might convince whoever was coming to keep on going.

"It could be people coming to get in line," Olivia offered, hope in her voice.

"With their headlights off?"

"I guess not."

Five vehicles, three pickups and two older-model cars, came into view, moving slow. They drew even with the store and stopped.

CHAPTER SEVENTEEN

Ben had slept some after supper, sprawled on the couch with the dog on the rug beside him, but after he woke up from the nap he was restless and couldn't settle down. His shoulder was just sore enough to be annoying, but what made him more uncomfortable was thinking about Sela's gentle hands on his bare skin. It had been a long time since he'd been focused on a woman, period, and never to the extent Sela grabbed his attention. He could have had her this afternoon, and his dick was telling him that he'd lost his fucking mind because he'd refused. He was beginning to agree with his dick.

Except—he didn't want her under him as payment for anything. He kept coming back to that. He wanted her there for no reason other than the two of them wanted it. His instant decision had been the right one; knowing that didn't stop him from regretting it.

He lit a lamp, kicked back, and read for a while, but he was wide-awake, uneasy, and didn't see the point in going to bed. After a while the dog raised his head and whined, so Ben took him out to let him mark his territory again. Then the dog went back to sleep; Ben didn't. He made some coffee—to hell with sleeping, it wasn't happening anyway so he might as well have some—and walked out on the porch to stare down at the dark valley. The moon was bright, the air cold but not freezing. His breath fogged in front of him.

There was enough light he could make out portions of the silver ribbons of roads into and out of the valley, including the bypass from Knoxville. He began thinking about strategy, how people would try to move in and how best to energetically discourage them from it. Not everyone would be automatically turned away; those who could contribute would be welcome. They didn't need a constantly moving patrol as much as they needed strategic sentry posts, clearly understood signals, and organization. They would be more efficient with a clear progression of authority rather than different people making decisions on the fly—in effect, more military in structure.

He didn't want to be actively involved; he'd get them set up the way he'd promised Sela, then let them handle it.

Sure.

He growled a bit under his breath as he gave up that fiction; come morning, he'd be stepping into quicksand and he'd likely never pull himself out. The idea of helping the community with their self-defense was tantalizing. As disgusted and emotionally exhausted as he'd become with political decisions that had cost the lives of his friends, his men, at his core he was military and part of him felt as if he was going home. This wasn't just in his wheelhouse, it *was* his wheelhouse. Even when he'd devoted himself to being as solitary as possible, he'd used military applications for self-defense.

Not only that, he had to accept that Sela *wasn't* solitary. She came with people she cared about, not just her relatives but her neighbors, her community. He couldn't isolate her up here with him, despite his instincts to do just that. For as long as this reluctant fascination with her held, she would link him to those people. Exactly how long that would be, who knew—

The sharp, light crack of rifle fire echoed across the valley.

Years of training kicked in and he was moving before he had consciously identified the sound as that of a .22 rifle. The mountains could mess with sound and a lot of people around here had .22s, but his instinct told him it was coming from in front and to the right, which would roughly be where Sela's store was.

Alarmed, the dog stood up and barked when Ben erupted into the house. He grabbed his hunting rifle from the rack, a box of cartridges, the Mossberg in its scabbard, and his truck keys. He was out the door again seven seconds after he entered, leaped off the porch, and was in the truck at ten seconds, accelerating down the rough driveway in twelve seconds.

In the three seconds between porch and truck he heard more gunfire, the distinctive sound of more .22 shots, and the deeper bellow of higher caliber rifles.

"Fuck!" he ground out.

This was his fault. He should have been thinking strategically, from the second he agreed to get involved, instead of letting himself stay secure behind his emotional walls for one more night, as if that meant anything. He'd told Sela himself that the gasoline was beyond valuable, and he knew she'd spread the word for people to come first thing in the morning to begin getting it. Logic dictated, then, that if anyone wanted to get all the gas for themselves, they had to do it tonight before all the valley inhabitants showed up in the morning for a share.

He'd bet his ass that the .22 fire was coming from Sela's rifle, which meant she'd been way ahead of him in planning, and was guarding the gasoline supply.

Dear God, let her not be by herself.

The small caravan slowly rolled forward. If she could see them, then obviously whoever was in the vehicles could see her SUV parked there. They might or might not be able to also tell that the store door was open. Sela held her breath as a dark-colored pickup truck slowly crunched its way over the gravel at the edge of the parking lot, facing toward the store. She couldn't tell how many people were in the truck, but she thought she saw someone in the bed. The truck stopped, and a dark figure hopped out of the truck bed. All the vehicles came to a stop; the drivers exited and reached into truck beds and back seats for gas cans. They were all men, going by their build, but with their winter coats and ball caps, or hoods pulled up, she couldn't recognize anyone.

She might have missed someone but she counted six men—at least. There could be more.

She heard muffled voices. They seemed to be looking at her SUV. Beside her, Olivia was sucking in quick, shallow breaths. Sela reached out and gave her a comforting touch on her arm. With luck, the group would decide that since she had blocked access to the tanks, they might as well leave . . . unless they thought they could move her Honda.

Three of the men started toward the SUV.

Dear God, was she doing the right thing? She didn't know. But decision was better than indecision, and Sela made her decision. She raised the rifle, aimed high so she wouldn't accidentally shoot someone, and fired over their heads.

Everyone dove for the ground, a confusion of movement in the night, people going in different directions, rolling, searching for cover.

Her wild hope was that the single shot would be enough to scare them off, that they'd leave when they realized there was an armed guard at the store. Right now the dark was her friend. They'd have no idea how many people were in here, only that their surprise raid hadn't worked.

Then another shot boomed out, and the window shattered beside her.

Panic filled her like a huge inkblot, spreading through her entire body. Olivia squeaked; Sela turned and dropped down, expecting to see Olivia lying bleeding at her feet. Instead the girl crouched by the door, staring up at her, her face a white blob in the darkness. "Back!" she yelled, ordering Olivia to retreat to the rear of the store. More shots. More glass shattered and rained on and around them. Sela felt several stings on her face, her hands. Instead of obeying Olivia moved forward, not back, raising her rifle and taking aim. She fired, then fired again.

Shit! *Shit!* They were so vulnerable here, with nothing to hide behind that would stop a bullet, and Olivia shooting back instead of taking cover. They had to get out, they had to get out now. "The back door!" Sela said insistently. They wouldn't be able to get the Honda, but they could escape down the path. She grabbed Olivia by the collar of her coat and hauled the girl backward.

This time, thank goodness, Olivia cooperated by scooting back, crawling with the rifle in her hand. Sela did the same; as she did so she saw two dark figures darting past, skirting along the sides of the store. It was already too late to run, they'd be caught as soon as they went out the back door—but at least that door was locked with a heavy-duty dead bolt, and they only had to worry about people coming through the front.

"Too late," she panted, and fired through the door to hold off any who thought they might rush through it.

More shots. The plate-glass windows were completely gone, the glass door nothing more than an empty steel frame.

Her only advantage was that in the colorless moonlight she could at least see them outside, whereas she and Olivia were swallowed up by the darkness of the store's interior. Terror almost swamped her, but for Olivia, not herself. She would shoot as long as she was able to keep Olivia safe. How could she ever have let Olivia stay? She should have insisted on taking the girl home. If anything happened to her, Carol would be devastated.

"Get behind the counter!" It wouldn't provide much shelter at all, being made of wood instead of heavy metal, but it was better than nothing. She kept herself between Olivia and the front of the store as they crawled across the glass-studded floor.

Someone would hear, someone *had* to hear. Even though it was the middle of the night, the sound of gunfire would wake people up, people who were on edge after what had happened at the Livingstons' house the night before. Someone would come. *Let it be soon!* she thought frantically.

She saw the moon glint on a rifle barrel resting on the side of a pickup truck bed, near the left edge of the parking lot. Quickly she aimed and pulled the trigger, then ducked as answering fire splintered the counter to her left. Olivia popped up like a jack-in-the-box and shot, then dropped back down. "I think I got him," she said, her voice so high it sounded as if she was on the verge of shrieking.

"Good girl!" Later she would think about what it meant that she had praised Olivia for possibly shooting someone. Later she would likely fall apart herself. For now she was too busy trying to stay alive to do more than have the fleeting thought.

"Get in the cooler!"

At least it was metal. It couldn't be locked from the inside, but it was more protection, more—

Then she caught sight of movement to the side, and saw a couple of dark figures pushing at her Honda. The shooter at the pickup truck on the left had been drawing their attention away from what the others were doing. Fiercely she swung the barrel around and fired again.

The morons! Didn't they know the entire valley would soon be awake, and heading this way? Their only chance for success had been to get in and out without anyone noticing, and that opportunity was gone.

They were *not* getting her gasoline, not a single ounce of it.

She fired again, shattering what was left of a window. Oh no! What if she hit her own vehicle? She paused a split second, then mentally shrugged and pulled the trigger one more time. If she didn't hold these *raiders* off, would they overwhelm her and Olivia, kill them so there were no witnesses? Even if she ended up riddling the Honda with holes, she couldn't let the men gain access to the underground tanks.

In the darkness behind the ring of vehicles, she saw a flash of light, there and gone in a split second. Then another. More vehicles? Or was it a trick of the moonlight, combined with wishful thinking?

She didn't have time to decide. In her peripheral vision she caught movement on the left. Olivia must have seen the same thing, because they both fired.

Outside, someone shouted, the sound urgent but she couldn't make out the words over the ringing in her ears. The indistinct figures began running in several directions; numbly she watched them opening doors and diving into the vehicles, then the cars and trucks all seemed to be moving at once as they scattered like jackrabbits being chased by hounds. In less than half a minute, the parking lot was empty.

"They left," she said blankly, her voice loud.

"What?" Olivia asked just as loudly.

"They *left*!"

Side by side, they stood looking through the shattered windows. The pale, colorless moonlight glittered on the broken glass as if on water. And here and there the darkness was punctured by headlights heading their way; finally, finally, people were coming to help—or at least to see what was happening, and that amounted to the same thing.

Carefully she laid her rifle on the counter, then took Olivia's rifle and placed it beside hers. She wrapped her arms around the girl and held her tight, felt her shaking but that was okay because Sela was shaking just as hard.

"Are you hurt?" she asked, still talking too loudly.

"No. You?"

"I don't think so. No." She continued to hold on tight. Maybe she had a few minor cuts, but her thick winter coat had protected her from a lot. Cuts didn't seem important when compared to expecting to be shot.

"We did it," Olivia said, her voice thin but touched with pride. "We scared them off."

"We did." Technically the approaching vehicles had done the scaring, but Sela wasn't in the mood to be technical.

"Girls rule, boys drool," Olivia said, and then she burst into tears.

Sela comforted her as best she could while getting them both outside. She yawned, trying to ease the ringing in her ears, and released Olivia long enough to press hard on both her ears, which seemed to help some. The .22s hadn't been that loud, but the other rifles had been a different matter. The cold air was sharp with the smell of burnt gunpowder, and a light haze of smoke seemed to hang in the air.

A vehicle was coming down the road toward them, and Sela stepped forward so she could be seen in the sweep of the headlights, waving her arms. The truck stopped and Mike Kilgore ran forward. "I heard shooting," he said urgently.

"Some men tried to steal the gas." Sela sucked in a breath, because everything that had happened during the past . . . fifteen minutes— maybe?—seemed so unreal she could barely put it into words. "Olivia and I were keeping watch, in the store. We have our .22s."

Gaping, he stared at the damage he could see behind her, and Olivia fiercely wiping her eyes.

"They *shot* at you?"

Considering the store had every window shot out, Sela thought the question was unnecessary. She didn't answer, because more vehicles were coming toward them. One, bigger than the others, was driving on the wrong side of the road and passing everyone else, not that it mattered which lane anyone was in because they were all heading in the same direction—at least ten vehicles, speeding their way. She moved toward Olivia, warily herding the girl back toward the store. The last thing she wanted was for them to get run over now, after surviving a gunfight.

A *gunfight*!

The sense of unreality was overwhelming. She didn't know whether to join Olivia in crying, or . . . sit down. Yes. She desperately needed to sit down.

Why not? "My legs are shaky," she told Olivia. "Let's sit down."

"Here?" Olivia blinked owlishly at her, and swiped her hand under her nose.

"Why not?"

They both sank down on the cold, dirty pavement, littered with grit, pieces of trash, and dead leaves that had blown across the parking lot. Here and there spent brass casings shone dully in Mike's headlights. Olivia leaned against her shoulder, burrowing in like a child; Sela hugged her tight, thankful beyond words that they'd come through unscathed, though she couldn't say the same about her store.

The racing cavalcade of vehicles reached them and the big truck in the lead slid to a stop with screeching tires and Ben jumped out before it had rocked back on its suspension. He held a big rifle in his hand, and he looked big and mean as he zeroed in on her, sitting there on the ground. Backlit by the harsh light of all the headlights, he strode across the parking lot toward her, his gaze so focused and intent that everyone else might as well have been invisible.

Energy shot through her and instantly she scrambled to her feet, momentarily unable to see anything other than him. Beside her Olivia also stood, perhaps wondering at their jack-in-the-box movements, but she, too, stared at Ben, her eyes big.

He reached them, not touching her but standing so close that even on this cold night she could feel the blast field of his heat—though perhaps that was her own reaction to his nearness, her body heating and responding. She couldn't see the color of his eyes but she could definitely see the savage fire in their expression. "You're bleeding," he said flatly.

"I am?" she asked, her tone bewildered.

Very lightly he touched a fingertip to her face, then dropped his hand as if the slight contact stung him.

"From the glass," Olivia said helpfully. "When they shot out the windows."

Ben said only one word: "Who?"

Sela swallowed. In that instant she knew beyond any doubt that if she could put a name to any of the men who had attacked them, Ben would hunt them down and deal out his own version of due process. "I don't know. There were six of them, as far as I could tell, but no one I could recognize. They wore hoods pulled up, baseball caps . . . and it's dark. Everything happened fast."

It hadn't felt fast at the time. Every second had felt as if it were mired in molasses.

Beside her, Olivia shook her head. "I didn't recognize anyone, either." She turned to watch all the other belated rescuers arrive, vehicle after vehicle pulling into the parking lot or onto the side of the road, while a few simply parked in the road where they were; it wasn't as if they had to worry about any through traffic.

"I'm thinking it was likely some of the meth heads from over Townsend way," Mike said, joining them. "The word will have spread that you have gas."

With an effort Sela wrenched her attention away from Ben. "That's what I thought," she said. "That's why I was here, in case anyone tried anything. Not that it had to be meth heads. I imagine there are a lot of regular people who'd like to have as much gas as they could get."

Ben made a noise, rumbling low in his throat, that sounded suspiciously like a growl. She'd never before been around anyone who she thought might be growling. Rather than be alarmed, she began getting warm again. It took all of her concentration to remain standing where she was, rather than taking a step forward and simply resting against him, her head on his chest, her arms around him.

More than anything, that was what she wanted to do.

"I have a first-aid kit in the truck," he said, wheeling away to stride to his vehicle, and breaking the connective circle that had surrounded them and kept everyone else at a distance. Mike watched him for a minute, his eyebrows lifted, then turned back to Sela.

"Damn, I wish I'd gotten here sooner," he said, abashed. "I'm sorry. And what the he—heck is Ben Jernigan doing here?" Nimbly he changed *hell* to *heck* in deference to Olivia's tender ears, completely ignoring the fact that a lot of teenagers swore like sailors and Sela was sure Olivia did her share of swearing when she was with her friends. Nevertheless, Mike was an old-fashioned Southern guy, and he held to his mode of behavior.

"I don't know why he's here right *now*," Sela replied, "but I went to his house yesterday and asked him to give us some pointers on what the patrol should be doing, and he agreed to come down this morning . . . is it morning yet?" She felt as if so many hours had passed, first in boredom and then in terror, that it had to be close to dawn.

"Getting close to one o'clock," Mike answered.

Was that *all*? She was aghast. Dawn was still hours away.

"Eastern standard, or daylight saving?" Olivia piped up, looking puzzled.

Mike stared at her, his mouth falling open. He gave Sela a helpless look. "I don't know. What date is it? When does the time change?"

The conversation was surreal. Sela felt as if the world had slid a little bit out of whack, or maybe this was just their reaction to shock. "I don't know." And did it matter? They had nowhere to go, no planes to catch, no appointments to keep.

"It's zero five forty-seven Zulu," Ben said, returning in time to hear their exchange. He set down the tackle box he was carrying, and flipped open the latches.

Mike nodded. "That's twelve forty-seven to us," he told Olivia, who nodded. She was staring big-eyed at Ben as he tore open a pack and extracted an antiseptic wipe, then positioned himself so the headlights were shining on Sela's face and began carefully cleaning away the blood.

Sela glanced up at him. Fewer than twelve hours ago she'd been doing basically the same thing to him, though admittedly the cut on his back was much worse than anything she had sustained from the flying glass. Her face was stinging a bit, but that was all. If she'd been judging her condition by Ben's expression she'd have thought she was dying, because he looked savage—controlled, but savage. She could have cleaned her own face much faster because Ben was taking care not to hurt her; she wouldn't have been as gentle with herself.

Trey Foster, Harley Johnson, Bob Terrell, and about ten other men were grouped around, anger in their voices as they talked quietly among themselves, glaring at the damage done to the store, to her. It didn't matter that the store was currently empty and useless; one of their own had been attacked, and they took it personally. Likely they were feeling guilty because they hadn't thought ahead and Sela and Olivia—a *kid!*—had literally been put in the line of fire. Mike went over to join them, leaving Ben and Sela relatively isolated, with Olivia watching.

"You're hurt because of me," Ben said under his breath. "Damn it all, I should have thought it through. Of course the bastards were going to come after the gas, knowing this was their only chance."

"I didn't think anyone would really try it," she murmured, letting him tilt her face up to better examine a tiny cut on her cheek. "Especially since I parked on top of the access to the tanks. I thought that would be enough to signal people that someone was here."

"Gasoline is worth the risk," he said briefly.

He touched a place on her cheekbone that had her jerking away with a surprised "Ouch!"

"Still some glass in there. Hold still." He bent and extracted a pair of long tweezers from the tackle box, then matter-of-factly seized the sliver of glass and pulled it out. She felt a fresh trickle of hot blood down her face, which he swabbed away before applying pressure to her cheekbone.

In a night of unbelievable happenings, perhaps the most unbelievable was that his touch soothed her ragged nerves to the point she stopped shaking, stopped feeling as if her next breath would be accompanied by a panic attack. The strangest thing was that while he was blaming himself because she was hurt he wasn't acting as if she'd been out of her depth.

She would have said without hesitation that she'd been out of her depth and she never wanted to do anything like that again, but she'd managed. She hadn't panicked, and her worst fears had been for Olivia. One thing for certain, she'd learned from the encounter. If she ever thought she might face armed men again, she would make sure she had a bigger rifle and better cover. So perhaps she'd been deeper than she liked, but she'd still managed to stay afloat.

Lord, she hoped she never had to do anything like that again.

He put small adhesive bandages over a couple of the worst cuts, the ones that wanted to keep bleeding. "Anywhere else?"

"Just my hand, but I can take care of that."

"Let me see."

He held her right hand in his left one, gently cleaned the small cuts there, wiped away the blood. The cuts were minor, and had already stopped bleeding.

"Will she be okay?" Olivia asked in a small voice, hovering anxiously nearby.

"She's fine," Ben said, hunkering down to put the first-aid tackle box in order and secure the latches. "Just some little cuts." He glanced up at her. "How about you?"

"I'm good. Sela was between me and the window." Olivia edged closer to them, her worried gaze skating over Sela's features as if assuring herself once again that they were both, indeed, all in one piece. "Gran's going to have a shit hemorrhage," she informed them.

Ben's mouth twitched. He didn't laugh, didn't even smile, but she saw the slight crinkling at the corners of his eyes. Sela opened her mouth to scold Olivia over her language, then shut it. After a fifteen-year-old girl stood side by side with her shooting at a group of men who were trying to kill them, she wasn't going to fuss at the kid about her language. "I imagine so," she said instead.

Now that Ben had taken care of first aid, the others moved closer and surrounded them.

"Did you get a look at any of the cars?" Trey asked her.

"I couldn't tell you colors, or anything like that. There were two cars, three pickups. I might've missed someone, in the dark, but I counted six men. When they saw all of the headlights heading this way, they scattered. None of them had their own headlights on."

"Do you think you hit anyone?" Ben's voice had gone into that dark place again. "Or any of the vehicles?"

"It's likely we hit a truck or two," Sela replied. "As for people . . . I don't know."

"I think I did," Olivia said. "I think I shot someone." The last two words wavered, and she gulped back tears.

"Sometimes you gotta," Ben said, so calmly accepting that Olivia straightened. He turned to the group surrounding them. "How about some of you get your flashlights and look for blood on the ground? Sela, about where were the vehicles positioned?"

"All around the parking lot," she replied, indicating the area with a sweep of her hand.

Several men went to their trucks to get their flashlights, and in the case of a couple of them, handheld spotlights. Others got in their vehicles and moved them back, out of the designated area. Ben watched for a silent half minute, then turned back. "I didn't pass anyone driving without lights."

"They'd have taken the side roads, stayed off the highway," Harley Johnson said. "And if they knew the side roads, that means they're local."

"Found some blood," Trey sang out. He was standing at the edge of the parking lot directly in front of the store, looking down. Ben and the others strode over; Sela and Olivia stayed where they were. She took Olivia's hand. Just an hour ago she'd have been deeply upset at the possibility she had shot and wounded someone, but she and Olivia had been on the receiving end of *their* shots, and she found it difficult to care. Considering how fast all of the attackers had been moving, she doubted any of their wounds were fatal. Pity.

Evidently she had a small wellspring of savage in her, after all.

Ben and the others returned. He stood in the center and looked around at all of them, effortlessly assuming the role of authority. They were tough men, men who were used to hard work, to hunting for food to feed their families, to putting themselves on the line, but they all looked to him without hesitation. He had been the one that from the beginning they'd all wanted involved, and now that he was here they'd have to be fools to not listen to him.

"We need to look at every vehicle. Like Sela said, the odds are more than one of them took a bullet. We also know at least one person was wounded. Talk to people, find out who got hurt tonight, supposedly while hunting or something like that." Ben looked around at all the men, his gaze hard. "Pay attention to everything. There'll be threats from the outside, but right now the biggest danger is from people right here in the valley."

CHAPTER EIGHTEEN

None of them went home. While everyone was there, Trey brought out his jerry-rigged suction pump to be tried out. It didn't work.

"I've got some parts at home," Ben said, looking at the contraption. "I'll be right back."

He returned in about forty-five minutes with the required bits and pieces, and the dog, which jumped out of the truck to a chorus of "Good-looking dog" from the hunters in the group, and "Oh! A dog!" from Olivia, who sat down on the concrete curb around the pumps and entertained the energetic animal with lots of petting and ear scratches.

"Where'd you get him?" Trey asked Ben. In some dim recess of memory, Sela recalled that Trey used hunting dogs.

"He wandered up several weeks ago, hungry and lost. I thought I'd give him to the Livingstons, so they won't be scared about staying by themselves after what happened yesterday."

Yesterday? Had it just been yesterday that Jim had shot the home invader? She looked at the dog and fought against a surprising welling of tears. Ben had stubbornly not named the dog, but she'd seen him with it and knew he'd become reluctantly attached to it. For him to give it to the Livingstons said something about him, because instinct told her he was a man who had lost too much to easily give up now what was his. Giving away the dog would cost him, emotionally, though she thought he'd rather eat ground glass than let people know.

He gave her a quick glance, as if keeping track of her location, then he and Trey began working on the suction pump. She knew nothing about mechanics and probably the best thing for her to do was stay out of the way. If she was less tired she'd have gotten the broom and started sweeping all the broken glass out of the store, but when the flood of adrenaline had drained away it left her feeling almost comatose. Olivia had to be feeling the same way. Sela sat down beside her and played with the dog for a while, then worked up the energy to offer, "Do you want me to take you home?"

"Not yet," Olivia replied, after giving it some thought. "I'd rather wait until you can go in with me."

Sela softly laughed. "Coward. I understand completely."

After what seemed like a couple of hours of tinkering, Ben asked her to move her Honda away from the tank access ports. The request made her realize she hadn't once checked to see if the Honda was damaged, but then she'd been sitting beside Olivia in something of a stupor. Getting up, she trudged over to her vehicle.

Amazingly, it seemed to be okay. She started the engine and pulled forward without closing the door, stopping when Ben barked, "Right there," though she'd moved no more than ten feet.

"What's wrong?" she asked, leaning out to look at him.

"It's your gas. You get first go."

She'd had pretty much the same thought but was so tired she'd forgotten about it. Then she looked at her gas gauge and shook her head. "I filled up right before the CME, and I still have a full tank." She had started the SUV a few times to keep the battery charged and the fluids moving, but until she'd driven it up Cove Mountain the day before to see Ben, it hadn't been moved at all in about two months. Not only that, she still had the small tank of untapped hundred percent gasoline to fall back on, but she'd save that news for later.

"All right." He waved her on, and she pulled forward out of the way. As it happened, almost everyone there had also filled up before-hand, but had brought five-gallon cans to get extra. Ben and Trey opened the access to the largest tank and in short order had gasoline flowing. Mike wrote down who got how much, for Sela's records.

Generators would be running tonight, she thought, glad for every-one in the valley. Those who had their own wells would have running water, and be taking hot showers—and likely letting their neighbors who were on a water system and thus had no water, because there was no power to pump it from the reservoir tanks, use their showers, in exchange for whatever they had to barter. She thought about making sure portable generators were taken around to warm the houses of those who didn't have fireplaces, which reminded her of the possibility of making braziers. There was so much to remember, and she was so tired . . .

"Someone's coming," Olivia said, rousing to look down the road. Her voice sounded half-drugged. She had been half-asleep, too, leaning against Sela's shoulder.

"A whole bunch of someones are coming," Sela observed. The headlights Olivia had seen were closest, but others had had the same idea and a steady stream of headlights was snaking toward them. Others were arriving on foot, plastic gas cans in hand. So much for waiting until about nine. On the other hand, with everything that had been going on, no one was getting any sleep so they might as well start pumping gas.

Ted Parsons and a couple of other members of the community patrol were the first few drivers to arrive. Ted got out of his car and stood looking around, his mouth open in astonishment. To save fuel everyone had turned off their vehicles, but there were plenty of spot-lights and flashlights at hand and the scene was lit well enough to see that something had happened. Ted had his own flashlight, and he shined it at the large open spaces of the store, where the windows had been.

"What the hell? What's going on?"

"Someone tried to steal the gas," Mike told him. "Sela and Olivia were standing guard and kept it from happening, but the store took some damage."

Ted turned to look at Sela and Olivia, sitting huddled by the gas pumps. "When did this happen?"

"Just guessing, but four, maybe five hours ago. What time is it now?"

Ted didn't reply. He shook his head, looked around, looked back at Sela and Olivia. He opened his mouth a couple of times, shut it, then turned to Mike. "Why are all of you here? How did you find out it happened?"

"I heard the shots," Mike said.

"So did I," Trey added.

"What woke me was someone driving by my house," Harley Johnson said. "That's a sound you don't hear very often now. I got up and went outside to listen, and was about to go back to bed when I heard the shots. I threw on some clothes and hightailed it in this direction."

Watching from her safe distance, Sela could see Ted's jaw clench. She imagined he was turning red, though that was impossible to tell in the beams of flashlights.

"Do you people not *want* me in the patrol?" he bellowed. "This is the second time no one has come to notify me when something *important* is going on!"

"You live kind of out of the way," Mike pointed out, though it was obvious he was struggling to be reasonable. "And I didn't know what was going on until I got here. We don't have phones, remember, and everyone who is here is someone who *heard* the gunfire and came to check. No one notified anyone, we didn't single you out. Besides, by the time we got here, it was all over and whoever was trying to steal the gas had left."

"But you're still here, keeping watch. Someone could have come to my house."

"That's true, though we aren't exactly keeping watch." Mike sighed, and glanced toward Sela in an obvious plea for reinforcements.

She sighed, too, and got to her feet. She was the acting community leader, so she had to act. She went over to them. "While everyone was here—"

"Everyone *wasn't* here, is my point!" Ted barked.

"It's a figure of speech." She paused and reached for patience, which wasn't as accessible as it usually was. "While we were here, Trey decided to see if the suction pump would work. It didn't. Ben went back to his house to get some parts, came back, and they got it working." Hoping he could be redirected, she said, "Why don't you pull your car up to the tank and get some gas now, there's no point in waiting."

He paused, and for a few seconds she hoped the redirection had worked. Then he looked around and said, "What about everyone else? I'm not the first in line."

"Almost everyone here already had a full tank, me included."

"Almost?"

"A few have topped off their tanks, and filled some fuel cans."

She might as well have said they'd handed out hundred-dollar bills, and all he was going to get was a couple of ones. "Thanks for waiting for me," he said sarcastically.

"Ted. We've pumped out a small fraction of what's in the tanks. The community patrol gets it first. You're in the community patrol. Some members were ahead of you, some will get gasoline after you." She could hear her voice getting tight, her words clipped, but *damn* this had been a tough night, a tough *two* nights with a stressful day sandwiched between them, and normally she didn't even think this way but stroking his ego was way down on her list of things to give a shit about.

"Only because I set my alarm," he said, still seething at the perceived disrespect. "Otherwise I'm sure you'd be glad to see me sitting at the end of the line and hoping you run out of gas before my turn."

"Don't judge everyone by yourself."

"Who are you to tell me how to think? I know how I've been treated by the people here, all of you have made it plain I'm not welcome."

"That isn't true. Your help is welcome."

"Of course it is." The sarcasm was back, heavier than before. "That's why you insist on trying to do this job even though you're clearly in over your head, even when it's obvious anyone else here could do it better. A *smart* person would have set up a way to contact people, a *smart* person would have asked for advice and listened—"

Over Ted's shoulder, Sela saw Ben's head turn at the raised voices, saw his eyes narrow. In almost the same instant he had assessed the situation and was coming toward them, his gaze focused on Ted, his chin lowered and every line of his body saying that he was about to kick ass.

Her own chin lifted. She might have needed help when a bunch of people were shooting at her, but she didn't need help handling Ted Parsons. Once again, she'd had enough. A faint red mist was forming in her vision, and she found herself visualizing punching Ted in the mouth, and relishing the idea. Instead, in a voice that seemed to come from outside herself, she said, "You know what, Ted? You're welcome to the gas, but as for the rest of it—" She stopped, and shot her middle finger at him, so close to his eyes they crossed a little as he focused on it.

His mouth opened, closed, opened again. He sucked in an outraged breath. Then, evidently realizing he couldn't do anything he wanted to do or say because everyone else there would turn on him, he wheeled around and stomped away.

She'd never given anyone the middle finger before, not even when she was driving.

She turned around and saw Olivia gaping at her. Then the girl began grinning, and gave Sela an enthusiastic thumbs-up.

Strange how two digits on one hand could have such completely different meanings. Aghast at herself, she pressed her hands over her face. Twice now in twenty-four hours she'd lost her temper and been rude to people.

Then Ben reached her, and stopped less than a foot away. "Say the word, and I'll hurt him for you." As always, his nearness seemed to create a force field around them that made everyone else dim in her perception. It felt as if the two of them were insulated in a bubble. Perhaps he didn't feel it, perhaps this was an effect of the strength of her attraction to him, but having him close by made everything feel . . . right.

"Thank you, but that isn't necessary." She sighed. "I kind of feel sorry for him, because he's such a butt and doesn't know why people don't like him. His wife is nice, though."

He looked down at her, that raptor gaze roaming over her face, touching briefly on the small bandages covering the cuts. "You look like you're almost too tired to move. Why don't you go home and get some sleep? We've got things covered here. After the gasoline is taken care of, I'll go over security organization with the patrol, then come tell you about it." He glanced around and located the dog, curled up by Olivia. "After I take the dog to the old couple."

She started to refuse, because she kind of felt as if it was her duty to stay, but then she saw how exhausted Olivia looked and knew she probably looked as bad, if not worse. She put her hand on his arm, loving the steeliness of him under her fingers even through the layers of his shirt and thick coat. "Are you certain about the dog? We can find another one for the Livingstons."

Ben looked at the dog again, and a brief flicker of regret might—
might—have passed over his expression before being banished.
"Yeah, I'm sure. All of the attention will be good for him, and he'll
be good for them. It isn't as if I won't be seeing him, because I'll have
to do some extra hunting and take food down for them. They sure
can't feed a growing dog without help."

And he was accustomed to being alone; that went without saying.
Correction: he'd *been* accustomed to being alone, but that had
changed. Even though he was taking the dog to Jim and Mary Alice,
he'd still be checking on the Livingstons and on the dog. However
unwillingly, he'd also forged a connection with *her*, and she'd discovered she could fight for what was important to her. Ben was important, more than she'd ever anticipated.

Not only that, without effort the valley men had opened ranks and
accepted him into their company, and the only way he could extricate
himself now would be to move completely out of the county. Given
the circumstances and how difficult travel was, that wasn't going to
happen. He was a natural at thinking strategically, in seeing what
was an urgent source of danger and what wasn't.

She looked down the road at the long line of headlights, duty
making her waffle about going home. Ben saw the indecision on her
face. "We've got this," he said, putting his hand on the side of her
waist. Even as tired as she was, she was aware that he'd made a very
public declaration by touching her that way. No one seeing the gesture would think, "Oh, they're just friends."

But she wanted to be his friend, as well as his lover. Friendship was
more difficult, more emotionally intimate and they hadn't achieved
either step yet. She looked up at him with a wan smile and nodded. "I
know you do. I just feel guilty leaving. But I need to get Olivia home,
and I think I'll fire up the generator so we can all have a nice hot bath."
Though she'd had a shower at his place, now she felt grimy with gun

smoke, and her hair and clothes smelled like burnt gunpowder. After the stress of the night, she wanted the comfort of modern conveniences. They had carefully hoarded their cans of gas for colder times and emergencies, but she thought this qualified as an emergency.

She dared to give his arm a gentle squeeze, then dragged herself into the store to get their rifles before going to Olivia. Fatigue made her feel as if she had weights tied to her legs, and her eyes were gritty. "Let's go home," she said. "And fire up the generator so we can have hot water for showers. We'll have to start the pump for the well, too." Before they'd switched over to the county water system, all of the houses had had wells, and water pumps. Without electricity they'd been pulling buckets of water from the wells or hauling it from the creeks.

Olivia's eyes lit up. "Hot water! OMG, that's worth being shot at!"

Sela gave a reluctant laugh. She wouldn't go that far, but Olivia's enthusiasm meant she'd make herself keep going long enough to get everything done.

Thank goodness she didn't have far to drive, because she kept blinking to keep her eyes open. In the passenger seat, Olivia huddled down into her coat. "I'm so cold."

"I am, too." The drive didn't last long enough for the Honda to get warm. She pulled into the driveway and saw lamplight shining in the window, which meant someone was already awake. It was nearing dawn, she thought, seeing the sky lightening in the east.

Before she and Olivia made it up the steps the door opened and Barb and Nancy both crowded out. "We've been so worried! Are you two all right? I can't believe you did such a foolhardy thing!" Barb cried, tears in her voice, then she held her palm up to Olivia for a high five. "I'm so proud of you both, and don't ever do anything like that again!" After Olivia, Barb high-fived Sela, too.

"We didn't plan on doing it to begin with," Sela murmured as they entered the warm house.

Nancy said, "What happened to your face?"

"Broken glass. It's nothing, just a few little nicks."

She and Olivia shed their coats, then both went to stand in front of the fire. Sela had just had the thought that she was glad Carol had evidently slept through the crisis, when her aunt called from the other room, "Sela! Olivia! You two get in here!"

Barb rolled her eyes. "She's been fit to be tied, since we found out what happened."

"How *did* you find out?"

"Leigh Kilgore said Mike tore out of the house when he heard shooting, and she followed on foot because he forgot his gloves. She tracked the noise and lights to the store. After she gave Mike his gloves she stopped by back here and let us know what was going on."

She hadn't even seen Leigh at the store, but then she'd been a little distracted.

"Sela!" Carol bellowed again.

"I hear you!" Sela bellowed back, because it had been that kind of night.

A shocked silence came from the bedroom, and Olivia rolled her eyes. "You've done it now," she said in a stage whisper as she headed toward Carol's bedroom. Sela trudged after her, knowing Carol had to be soothed before they could do the necessary chores to get the water heater working, but she was almost at the end of her tether.

"We didn't know anything was going to happen," she growled as she entered the bedroom.

Carol's eyes widened at Sela's appearance, and perhaps also at her uncharacteristic surliness. "You're hurt," she whispered, her hand going to her mouth.

"It's just a couple of little nicks, I promise. The store doesn't have a window left, though."

"Sela gave Mr. Parsons the finger," Olivia announced.

Sela's face got hot, though she was grateful to Olivia for deflecting Carol's attention away from the danger they'd been in; she just wished it wasn't her own bad behavior that had been brought to the forefront. "I was stressed," she muttered.

Olivia curled up beside Carol on the bed, rested her head against Carol's shoulder. "I'm not sorry I sneaked out, Gran. If I hadn't, Sela might be dead. She needed me, and y'all wouldn't have let me go if I'd asked."

Carol opened her mouth, then shut it. Perhaps she was trying to think what she could do beyond scolding them both, but she also had to admit that, faced with a difficult decision, they'd done the best they could and had succeeded in keeping the gas safe.

"You'd have been there with us if you'd been able," Sela pointed out.

"That's true," Barb said, coming into the room with Nancy, who was putting on her coat. "Don't even try to say you wouldn't."

"I have to get home and feed my bunch," Nancy said, "but I want to put in my two cents' worth before I leave. I'm proud of you, Sela, and you, too, Olivia. The two of you saved the gasoline for us. I'm grateful neither of you were hurt—or at least not hurt very much— and anytime you need backup you just let me know."

Nancy left, and Barb said, "I don't know about all of you, but I could use a cup of coffee and more breakfast than usual. Worrying burns up calories, you know."

Sela remembered everything she had to do before she could crash. "I'm going to start the generator and the well pump, if I can figure out how, and get the water heater going. I think we all deserve a nice hot shower."

"Fine for you to say, at least you can get in the shower," Carol grumbled, looking at her splinted and elevated leg.

"If you want one, we can put a chair in the shower and get you in and out," Barb said stoutly. "As for turning on the well pump, I can help with that, too. We old people used to have to do stuff like that all the time. We were constantly having trouble with our pump. Likely we'll have to have a couple of buckets of water to prime it and get it going."

Sela almost cried in gratitude that someone knew what to do. She'd been expecting to go the trial-and-error route, which would take time she so desperately needed for rest.

However long Carol had intended to scold them, those plans went by the wayside when faced with Sela's cut face, Olivia's statement of why she'd sneaked out, and the prospect of a hot shower. There was also the matter of flipping Ted Parsons the bird, which Sela suspected would be brought up later, amid a lot of teasing.

Barb insisted they would all feel better after they'd had something to eat, and she was right; the food and a cup of coffee didn't exactly energize her, but with Barb's help Sela was able to do what needed to be done to get water running. Then she turned on the water heater, and listened to the satisfying snaps and pops as the heating unit began heating water. Olivia stood next to a lamp and turned it on, staring in pleasure at the glow of the electric light. "Can we do this once a month?" she asked wistfully.

"Maybe. No promises, though." Once a month would be heavenly, but who knew what the future held? "I'll be back in a couple of hours. I have to get some sleep or fall on my face."

"I know," Olivia said, and yawned.

Sela stumbled as she went into her own house a few minutes later. The house was cold; the fire had died down, though some hot embers remained. She carefully added a few sticks of kindling and closed her eyes while she waited for the fire to catch. She dozed, sitting there, and came awake to see the kindling had almost burned up. She added more, and this time stayed awake to add wood. When the fire was blazing, she went to the couch, wrapped up in a blanket, and was asleep almost before her head hit the cushion.

The day just wouldn't fucking end.

There was the gasoline to give out, plans to be made with the community patrol—and Ted Parsons was there, still sullen, but there. Showing up counted for something, though he kept an eye on the man. Resentment could fester in unexpected ways, and have ugly consequences. After he laid out the plans to systematically search every valley residence for vehicles with bullet holes in them, as well as someone who was wounded, he watched as the patrol members loaded up and headed out. Parsons was approached by a lean, young-ish man with a feral expression, and the two stood and talked for a few minutes. Ben studied the young man, committing his face, build, and movements to memory.

"Who's Parsons talking to?" he asked Harley Johnson, who turned to squint in Parsons's direction.

"Hmm. Not sure. I think it might be the Dietrich boy, but I wouldn't swear to it."

"I don't like the looks of him." Ben didn't mind making snap judgments, because doing so had kept him alive several times. The man gave the impression of meanness, with the hollow cheeks and eye sockets that he associated with drug use. Not only that, his body language said that he considered himself in charge of whatever he was talking to Ted about.

"If it is Dietrich, I'd say you're right to feel that way." Harley frowned. "I don't like Ted talking to him. The Dietrichs are heavy into drugs, from what I hear."

"Then that moves him to the top of the list of who might have tried to steal the gasoline."

At Ben's flat statement, Harley gave Ted and Dietrich a wary look. "You're not wrong."

"That also moves his place to the first one that gets checked. Now might be a good time."

Harley nodded, understanding completely, and moved away to talk quietly to Mike and Trey, both of whom carefully didn't look toward Ted but split up and moved to their own vehicles.

People were still coming and going, getting gasoline and leaving, making it easy for their activity not to attract attention.

Ben watched until Ted moved on; the Dietrich man got back into his car and stayed in line to get gasoline, which, if he *had* been one of the bunch who had attacked the store, was damn ballsy of him—but then, people on drugs would do literally anything to get more drugs. Ben looked down the road; the line of vehicles was non-ending; people would get their allotted five gallons, go to the back of the line, and get in line again for more. At five gallons a time, pumping out thousands of gallons took time, but this was the fairest way to spread it out over the valley inhabitants.

When Dietrich was almost at the head of the line, Ben moved away to let someone else handle things, so he could concentrate on watching. Briefly he considered simply overpowering Dietrich and taking him somewhere private to persuade him to talk, but hell, if he was going to live with these people he had to act as if he was halfway civilized, which he was no longer certain he was. If he *knew* this man had been among those who shot at Sela, it would be game over—but he didn't know, he only suspected.

Sometimes shit-heads put on an act of friendliness, as if they needed to convince others they weren't truly shit-heads, but they usually went overboard in their act, talking too loudly, laughing too much. Dietrich—and it *was* Lawrence Dietrich, because Ben heard the name he gave whoever was now keeping track of who got the gasoline—was smarter than that. He kept his voice down and didn't say much, other than "Thank you," when he'd gotten his five gallons. Ben saw the quick, furtive look he cast around the store and parking lot, perhaps double-checking that nothing identifiable had been dropped and was lying around unnoticed, or maybe making plans to come back.

Ben walked over to the woman who was keeping tally and casually asked how many gallons had been pumped.

"I haven't added it up," she replied, but flipped back over several pages of entries. "It looks like a lot, though; I'm already seeing people who have already been through the line once."

"Good. We'll keep going until the tanks are empty," Ben said, noting that Dietrich was listening. That *was* their intention, and he wanted to make damn sure Dietrich knew it, knew there was nothing to come back for. As a precaution, after Sela had gone home, Ben had pulled his truck over the access to the small tank of pure gasoline, and also blocked sight of the pump he'd assumed was for kerosene before Sela had told him different. Maybe they needed to remove the pump, so no one got suspicious and started poking around.

Dietrich left, probably to go to the back of the line again, and Ben took one more look down the highway. Yep, this was going to take all day.

CHAPTER NINETEEN

The men who had gathered in the bank parking lot looked as crude as their friend Lawrence. They all looked to be between the ages of twenty and forty, though it was hard to tell when personal hygiene wasn't high on anyone's list. Ted did his best to ignore their rough appearance. They might've looked just this way before the CME, but then again, they might've been clean-cut upstanding young men before the shit hit the fan.

No, not that much time had passed. This was a tough and not-very-upstanding crowd, he admitted it to himself. Still, in times of crisis . . .

The events of the morning still stung, more than a little. He kept seeing Sela Gordon's middle finger thrust into his face. How dare she? And people around them had laughed! Not at her, of course not, but at him. That hurt as much as anything else. He wasn't accustomed to being humiliated, and he damn well didn't like it.

Ted shook off the annoyance and tried to focus on the future. Maybe Sela and her pals didn't appreciate him, but this bunch did—or would. Sela could keep her damn patrol. He could bring these men in line, the same way he had with the employees at his tire stores. Some of them had started off pretty rough, too, but his guidance had brought them around. Sometimes. Some people were lost causes.

Lawrence introduced Ted to the others. The men who wanted to join them in this new organization were a cousin, friends, a brother, a neighbor. Unsavory appearances aside, they were friendly enough, and seemed to look up to Ted. They saw him as a leader, they needed him.

His pride swelled. Here he was appreciated.

One of the younger men, Lawrence's cousin Patrick, took a step forward and winced as he almost stumbled. It was only then that Ted noticed that the jeans high on one thigh fit tighter than at the other. A thick bandage underneath, perhaps? That, and the wince, and the paleness around the man's eyes . . . he'd been hurt.

Patrick could've injured himself any number of ways. For a second, maybe two, Ted considered ways in which the young man might've hurt himself—but, damn, he couldn't fool himself for long because he wasn't an idiot. Ted's heart crawled into his throat. These were the men who had tried to rob the gas station, who had shot at Sela and the young girl, Olivia. These men had shot up Sela's store.

Ted didn't ask Patrick if he was okay; instead he concentrated on not revealing anything he'd just figured out. He kept his expression interested, not suspicious. He looked them in the eyes when they spoke. As the men discussed plans for organization, Ted casually wandered closer to their vehicles. There were some small holes, maybe bullet holes, in the bumper of one truck but again he did his best to make it look as if he *hadn't* noticed them.

At quick glance he noted that all six of the men were armed. He wanted to believe that they were here because they were willing to see that order prevailed in their community, that they felt unappreciated, as Ted himself did, but his gut said that they were dangerous and not well-meaning.

They all appeared to be flattering him, asking for his opinions, and for the first time he asked himself the obvious question: What did they want from him? He wouldn't have gone along with them stealing the gas, shooting at women, and they had to know that.

As he talked to them he tried to memorize every name. As he mingled he sized each man up. It was easy enough to tell which ones were leaders, and which were followers. A couple of them were high on some kind of drug, he could see it in their eyes. One man, a neighbor of Lawrence's named Wesley, was drunk.

Ted's thoughts whirled. Instead of planning how he'd form his own organization to help them all survive this crisis, now he tried to think how he could maneuver himself out of this mess. He had no intention of joining this crew, not that he was dumb enough to say that aloud and think they'd let him walk away. Maybe they would—but maybe they wouldn't.

What was he supposed to do with the information he possessed? He needed to think.

"We need a place to meet," Lawrence said. "A kind of headquarters." Now that keeping in touch by phone wasn't possible, they had to physically meet. In different circumstances, with a different group of men, Ted would've suggested his own house so he could be in the thick of things, but thank goodness he'd figured out what was going on before he'd taken that step, and also that he hadn't agreed to let them meet at his house today! He didn't want these men within a mile of Meredith, much less in her home.

It did make sense to suggest that they should meet at a place more convenient for the volunteers, something central, perhaps near the school. He nodded; he wanted it to look as if he was participating.

As they were discussing the matter, Wesley the drunk spoke up in a voice so loud it might have carried across half the county. "I've got a friend whose mom owns that crafty shop up by the pizza place. I'll talk her into letting us use it. It's just sitting there, empty."

A few of the volunteers nodded in agreement, and once more Ted joined in. He didn't care where they met so long as it was far from Meredith.

They set a time to meet at their new headquarters—the day after tomorrow, which would give Wesley a chance to gain permission and a key, and perhaps to sober up—and it was done.

As the others wandered off, again in small groups, Lawrence placed a hand on Ted's shoulder. It took everything Ted had not to shake that hand off. "You might be tempted to quit the community patrol and tell Sela Gordon and her folks to stuff it, and I sure wouldn't blame you, but don't do that just yet."

Here it was, Ted thought, the reason he was here.

"You see, they don't trust me, they don't trust any of us. But you, Ted, they trust you just fine."

"I don't know about that," Ted replied, letting his resentment toward Sela show. Likely Lawrence had heard about the confrontation at the store, and he'd be suspicious if Ted pretended all was well. "That bitch—well, never mind."

"Just keep it cool, man. We'll need you to let us know what's what. Food's going to get more and more scarce. Ammo too. Meds are already running really low, and I figure you can find out who's got what and where it's all stored."

It seemed right to show at least a touch of indignation. "You want me to spy."

Lawrence smiled. "We want you to gather and share important information. You can call it spying, if you want to, but I see it as another step in ensuring our survival. Survival of the fittest, and all that. We also need more men to join us. You appeal to a different element of our fine community, you can convince others to be a part of our efforts."

Ted nodded, but didn't smile. He shoved his hands in his pockets. "Half that bunch acts as if they'd rather I dropped out, anyway. Let me think about it. I don't think they're telling me everything, so I don't know how much use I'd be." Yes, that sounded about right, to keep Lawrence from getting suspicious.

"Don't think too long, Ted. We need you."

Ted turned away and headed for home. The walk up the hill to his house was becoming less and less arduous, as he built up the muscles in his legs. He no longer gave the effort much thought at all. Besides, he had other things to think about this afternoon. It didn't take a rocket scientist to figure out what Lawrence wanted, and why. People would be hurt. The men he had just left wouldn't mind that at all. They might even enjoy it.

He needed to take this information to . . . someone. Mike Kilgore, maybe, even though they hadn't gotten off to the best start. It would be a little humiliating, but Mike would know what to do. But not now, not today. He suspected Lawrence or one of his cronies was watching right now, waiting to see how he would respond to their request. The best thing he could do was go home and not do anything unusual.

They didn't want a leader, they wanted a patsy. They wanted a traitor. If he turned back now, if he showed any indication that he intended to share what he knew of their plans, he'd be in serious and immediate danger.

He hated Sela Gordon—truly hated her, especially now. But he didn't want her dead, he wouldn't have been a party to robbing and shooting at her, and if Lawrence had his way there would be more of the same coming.

Ben let the dog out of the truck at the Livingstons' house, and the animal began running around sniffing at everything as he reacquainted himself with the area. Jim and Mary Alice came out of the house next door. They both looked more worn and defeated than he'd expected. The dog dashed over to Mary Alice and she crouched down to give it some loving and croon to it in the way women naturally did with babies and animals.

"Came by to see how you're doing," Ben said unnecessarily,

because obviously he was here, but it was an opening for them to talk about what was bothering them.

"Can't complain," Jim said, though his gaze slid to his own house, a sorrowful expression crossing his face. Behind them, the neighbors came out of the house, too; the woman coming to stand beside Mary Alice and lightly rub her shoulder. "We're alive."

"I can't bring myself to go back in there." Mary Alice kept her head down, looking at the dog as she continued to stroke him. "I keep seeing . . ."

"Honey, it's cleaned up," the neighbor woman said. "If you'd just take a look—"

"No, I can't. I'm sorry. Not yet. I don't want to impose on you, we'll go somewhere else—"

"Mary Alice Livingston, you know that isn't it at all! I just want you to feel okay."

Ben decided to head that off, because he didn't want to get embroiled in conversations about feelings. "How about I take the dog in, look around? You know about Sela Gordon distributing her stores of gas from the underground tanks, right? I brought extra storage cans full, and a portable generator. If you two men will help me get the generator hooked up and fueled, we'll turn on the heat and get your house warm."

Immediately they both looked distracted by the different subjects he'd thrown at them. He knew from his own experiences that having something else to think about was a relief. Logically taking the dog in to look around wouldn't change a damn thing, but the Livingstons were too emotional right now to think logically.

Mary Alice brightened. "Yes, let the dog look around. What's his name?"

"I haven't named him. I thought I'd let you do it." That was a giant distraction.

Her eyes widened and she looked at the dog with something approaching joy. "I get to name him? Oh my! That's a big responsibility, isn't it, boy? That's a good boy, yes you are." She punctuated her words with scratches behind the dog's ears, who was properly ecstatic.

Ben whistled the dog over. "Is the house unlocked?" he asked.

Both of the Livingstons looked taken aback, because obviously that hadn't occurred to them. "It is," their neighbor affirmed, and went inside with Ben and the dog.

Ben didn't do anything specific, just let the dog run around inside and sniff at everything, let it get accustomed, and also to get his own scent in the house so the dog wouldn't feel abandoned. He looked in the kitchen where the shooting had happened, and while they were waiting for the dog to explore, he and the neighbor talked about what had happened at Sela's store, about the gas—the neighbor had filled his car and also a couple of storage cans—about how hard Mary Alice had been taking everything. She didn't feel her home was safe any longer; she'd lost her place of refuge.

Ben had thought of a lot of things when he'd gone back to his place hours ago to get the dog and the parts to get the suction pump going. He hadn't known Mary Alice and Jim hadn't been able to go back into their house, but he knew how people reacted to trauma, and he knew to change the environment. That's what he himself had done, an insight that struck him only now, for the first time. He'd come to these mountains, isolated himself after living for years as part of a team, and set about making himself as self-sufficient, and self-contained, as possible. Mountain living was different. The effort required to *become* self-sufficient had been the means he'd used to distract himself, to get him to the point where he could . . . where he could begin healing.

He hadn't thought of himself as wounded. He'd thought of himself as fed up. It wasn't until he became able to tolerate more contact with people that he could begin to see where he'd been and how far he'd come.

Sela. She'd been the lure that had brought him out of the cave, the same way he was using the dog to bring the Livingstons out of their cave. The comparison amused him, though he didn't know if he'd tell her that. Her gentleness was what he'd noticed first about her, and he'd wanted to protect that, keep it untarnished; telling her something that might embarrass her wasn't the way to do that, though he suspected she might think it was funny. Maybe one day in the future he'd tell her.

"Whaddaya think?" the neighbor asked, jerking him out of his thoughts.

He had no idea what the guy had said, so he shrugged. "I think we need to get the generator out of the truck and fired up, get these folks some heat. They can't live in a house this cold."

"They're welcome to stay with us, but they want their own space and at the same time Mary Alice has been afraid to come back. How you gonna work this?"

"The dog," Ben replied, and went back outside with the dog following on his heels.

"Have you thought of a name yet?" he asked Mary Alice as they pulled the generator out of the back of the truck.

Of course the dog had dashed back over to her for more ear scratching and belly rubs, and it was rubbing against her legs in a frenzy of affection. She actually blushed. "I think Sajack," she said. "I like— I used to like watching *Wheel of Fortune*."

"Sajack's a good name," Ben said. "Listen. Do you think you could take care of him? I'm out away from the house a lot, and the boy needs more company than I can give him. With him in the house, no one else would be able to sneak in, and mountain curs are quiet and protective dogs."

Her face lit up. Watching his wife, Jim seemed to catch on. "I'd like having a dog around," he said slowly. "I've missed having one. But how will we feed him? We're having trouble feeding ourselves."

"I'll hunt for you." Ben made the offer with a sense of resignation, because he'd already known he'd have to do it. "I brought some food, his blanket and bowls, and the rope I use for his leash. His collar is pretty ratty, sorry."

"I can make a collar for him from one of my old belts," Jim said, beginning to smile himself as he looked at the dog. He squatted down and patted his thigh. "C'mon, Sajack, come let Pops pet on you."

Obligingly the dog bounded toward the obvious invitation, and Mary Alice came with him.

While the old couple was bonding with the dog, Ben and the neighbor took the generator to the house and got the electric heat pump running. That done, Ben retrieved the food and the dog's things—which included his old shoe—and took them in. Seeing the shoe, the dog raced after him into the house, wanting his toy. Jim followed, and, somewhat reluctantly, so did Mary Alice. Ben saw the alarmed look she cast toward the kitchen, then the dog pounced on the shoe and began shaking it from side to side and a smile wreathed her face as she watched him.

Making another trip to the truck, Ben brought in a kerosene heater and an extra can of kerosene. "After the generator gets the house warm, use the heater to keep it that way, at least until Sela can get some braziers made." He had no doubt she'd manage it, somehow, if there was a kiln anywhere in walking distance. He looked around. "I think that's it. I have another stop to make, so I'll be going."

Jim approached with his hand held out. "Son, I can't thank you enough for what you've done for us." He nodded toward Mary Alice. "This makes all the difference."

Ben shook the gnarled, bony hand, still vaguely surprised to be *touching* someone voluntarily.

The sun was getting low, the long day almost gone. He was hungry and tired, and that was the least of it. Part of him, if he lived to be a hundred, would never recover from how he'd felt when he'd been racing down the mountain in the dark, terrified that he'd find Sela dead in that store over some fucking *gas* and knowing he'd never forgive himself for not thinking ahead and knowing there was a slim window of opportunity for stealing it.

Talk about a moment of clarification. He'd known then that if she was just okay, dear God please let her be okay, he'd be rethinking what he'd planned for the rest of his life. In those plans, he'd been alone. For the first time in what felt like forever, he hoped he wasn't alone, hoped he could handle the transition.

He was also inordinately proud of how she'd handled herself— with nothing more than a tin can plinker to hold off the thieves— but she'd probably never see herself as anything special. She would prefer working behind the scenes rather than putting herself out there, but when the occasion called for drastic measures she did what she had to do. *He* saw her as special, though, and that was what counted.

He never wanted to spend another ten terrible minutes wondering if she was dead. Everything had crystallized inside him during that short time, letting him see clearly what was important and what he could put aside.

All he wanted now was to see her.

Well, that wasn't *all* he wanted, but just seeing her would make him feel better.

He began driving to her house, but when he passed her aunt's yellow house he saw her white Honda there and whipped his truck into the driveway. He knew he'd be walking into a house full of women and he might feel trapped, but he'd have to tough it out. Before he got out of the truck he picked up a can of the food he'd had the foresight to bring with him, and put it in his coat pocket.

As he got out of the truck he looked around, paying attention to the sky, which had been sunny earlier but in the last hour a low, lead-colored cloud cover had moved in, and the temperature had taken a decided dip. *Snow*, he thought. Maybe not much, given it was still early in the season, but the weather had to turn sometime and he was betting on tonight.

He went up on the porch and knocked. In a few short seconds Sela's face appeared in one of the panes in the door, and she opened it. "How did it go today?" Guilt crossed her face. "I meant to get back over there but I slept too long, and when I did go, everyone was gone. Who boarded up the windows? Thank you."

She stepped back to let him enter, and closed the door behind him. He'd been right: he *did* feel better just seeing her, being with her. He liked how she'd immediately jumped to the conclusion that he'd been the one who boarded up the windows. "Some guy named Bob Terrell had some plywood to donate. He and Trey Foster helped. I didn't expect you to come back over there anyway, you were wiped out." The warmth of the house, and the smell of food cooking, enveloped him like a hug. How could he have forgotten? There was something about women, the way they took a space and without thinking made it into something softer and more comfortable.

Olivia sat on the couch, her eyes big with curiosity as she watched them, and a short, white-haired woman was stirring something in a pot set over the fire in the fireplace. Sela said, "You know Olivia. Barb, this is Ben Jernigan. Ben, our friend Barb Finley. She's living here for the duration."

"Who's there?" someone called from another room.

Sela paused, gave a subtle cast of her eyes heavenward, and called, "Ben Jernigan." Then she closed her eyes and seemed to be waiting for something.

"*What?* Stud Muffin Hardbody is here?"

"She's on pain pills," she murmured to him, her cheeks heating. "We got her in the shower today, and had to give her an extra dose afterward to knock down the pain. Since she broke her leg she's had two moods: inappropriate and cantankerous. You can guess which one she's in now."

Olivia was giggling on the couch, and she called, "Gran, behave!"

"I am behaving! What I want to do is throw something because I'm stuck in this damn bedroom by myself. Olivia, you didn't hear that."

"Yes I did."

"And . . . the mood just flipped to cantankerous." Sela gave him a small smile. "You may want to run."

He'd faced worse things than a pill-fueled granny . . . maybe.

"You have to stay for supper," said Barb, turning to smile at him. "It isn't anything fancy, just beef stew and corn bread, but there's plenty of it."

His first reaction was to refuse; habit was habit. His second reaction was to remember the woman standing right there beside him, and he said, "Thanks, I'd like that." Then he reached into his coat pocket and pulled out the can he'd put there. "I brought this. Figured you could use some bacon."

Sela went still, staring at the can in his hand. Barb wheeled away from the fire, the forgotten spoon in her hand dripping liquid on the floor. Olivia bolted off the couch. "Bacon," she said in a reverent tone as she came to stand beside him, then in astonishment added, "Bacon in a can?"

"Yeah. It's all I use." He held out the can of Yoder's to Sela and she took it as carefully as if it was made of the finest crystal.

"Well, my goodness. I've never seen bacon in a can before." Barb came over and peered at it. "How do you cook it?"

"It's already cooked, but you can crisp it up the normal way."

"What's going on out there?" Carol hollered.

"He brought bacon!" Barb yelled back.

"Bacon! Damn it! I'm stuck in here and y'all are out there with bacon—"

Ben sighed. Obviously the only way to settle down the granny was with bold action. He wanted to spend time with Sela and he couldn't with her aunt constantly yelling from the next room. "Is she decent?" he asked Sela.

"She has clothes on, if that's what you're asking. I wouldn't go any further than that." A tiny smile twitched at the corners of her mouth.

In battle Ben had learned that action, even if it was the wrong action, was better than inaction. Silently he strode in the direction of the uproar, which broke off as soon as he walked through the bedroom door. The woman in the bed gaped at him, her eyes and mouth wide. Yeah, he recognized her, knew the improbable—now fading—pink streak in her hair. She was covered with a sheet and a blanket, her splinted leg propped on a couple of pillows. Silently he went to the side of the bed, bent, and scooped her up, covers and all. Carrying her out, he asked, "Where do I put her?"

"Right here," Sela said swiftly, pulling out a chair at the table and turning it to the side, then pulling out another one on which her aunt's broken leg could be propped. "If she's going to be in here, she might as well eat at the table with us." Ben deposited the woman in the chair and carefully supported the broken leg until Sela had the other chair and some cushions arranged. "Is that comfortable?" she asked her aunt, leaning forward to straighten and tuck the covers around her. Ben watched her long dark hair slide over her shoulder, and thought about it sliding over his pillow. Instantly he pulled himself away from that topic, otherwise he'd be standing there with an obvious erection.

"I guess," the woman said, still staring at Ben. She held out her hand. "I'm Carol Allen."

"Glad to meet you." He took her hand. "I'm Stud Muffin Hard-body."

She didn't blink. Instead she said, "Oh honey, if you only knew the other names I've called you."

"You don't want to know," Sela said to him.

He took her word for it. He looked around, feeling a little awkward, but she indicated another chair at the table and he settled into it. In short order an iron skillet of corn bread was set on a pot holder on the table, and cut into squares. Following that was a big pot of beef stew. While Barb was getting that on the table, Sela and Olivia were doing a sort of dance around the table that resulted in bowls and spoons and napkins being put in place in front of five of the six chairs. Glasses of water were distributed.

It was a simple meal; Carol said a very brief grace over the food, then the bread and stew were passed around so people could get as much as they wanted. Sela had seated herself beside him, and he noticed that she took the smallest portion of any of them, and made a guess that she was doing without to make sure the others had enough to eat.

That couldn't continue. He'd make sure *she* had enough to eat.

He didn't remember the last time he'd had conversation with a meal—likely when he was still in the military. But then, this was the first meal he'd eaten with anyone else since he'd mustered out. When Sela asked, "Did everything go okay with the gas today?" it took a moment for him to realize she was talking to him.

"Okay enough." Some people had gotten testy about being limited to five gallons until everyone who had been in line had gotten a share, until he'd told the complainers he didn't mind if they went on home so there'd be more for the others. He'd given the same reply to the ones who had complained about a record being made of how much they got, and that they'd have to reimburse the store once the power came back on and they got back to work. He was big enough that not many people came back at him, plus he'd spent the day with the Mossberg strapped to his back. There was just something about a shotgun.

An added bonus was that the shotgun scabbard had rubbed against the cut on his shoulder, making him more visibly irritable. Sometimes things worked out for the best.

Sela was looking at him as if she expected more in the way of information. "*Let's go get naked*" didn't seem like something she'd want to talk about in front of her relatives and friend, so he settled for a safer subject. "Jim and Mary Alice loved the dog. Mary Alice hadn't been able to go back into the house, but with the dog there she felt better. She named him Sajack."

"After Pat Sajack," Barb said, smiling. "She does love her *Wheel of Fortune*."

Ben had never seen the show, but he'd take their word for it.

Olivia gave him a perturbed look. "I can't believe you gave the dog away."

"Yeah." Again, expectant looks that asked for more. "They can give him more attention than I can, and they need a dog there to look after them. I'll do some extra hunting to keep them all fed." He glanced at Sela. "Any progress on those braziers? I loaned them one of my kerosene heaters, but that's a temporary fix because they'll run out of kerosene."

"There is." This time it was Carol who answered. She shifted her leg uncomfortably, but focused on the subject. "Mona Clausen walked over to talk about it, while you were asleep. She does still have the kiln. It's not a big one, and it's electric so she'd need a generator and fuel to fire it up. She said the design of a brazier was simple, it's basically a grill pan, but she could do one medium-size at a time, or two smaller ones at once. How many do you think we'll need?"

"I have no idea," Sela said. "Plus people will need charcoal for them."

"Charcoal can be made, just burn the wood down to that point," Ben pointed out. "I'll set up the generator so she can get started. Even one brazier will mean a lot to people who don't have any heat or any way of cooking."

God. He'd talked to more people today than he had in the past three years, total. He could feel the discomfort gnawing at him, the need to withdraw to the top of the mountain where there was nothing but trees and earth, wind and sky. That was no longer an option, unless Sela was there with him. The compassion that was a part of her, the care she showed for others, had become something he wouldn't willingly do without.

"I'm thinking hundreds of braziers," she admitted, rubbing her eyes as if overwhelmed.

"A lot of people have grills," Olivia piped up. "I know there has to be good ventilation and all that, but they could be used and if people are too stupid to open a window a little bit, that only improves the gene pool, right?"

"While I might agree with you in theory, in practice we don't want to kill anyone," Sela pointed out, though she smiled a little. "The same precaution goes for the braziers, because like you said, they're basically grills."

She brought out a notebook and began ticking off things she'd thought about. Evidently they were in the process of getting some sort of schooling organized for the kids. Everyone—literally everyone—would need to plant vegetable gardens in the spring—and she had a list of who would need help plowing up a plot and sowing the seed. She had a list that made his head hurt, people who had medical conditions that the herbalists or medic needed to see, places where herbs could be gathered and squads of gatherers organized. A bigger drying shed would be needed. They needed a place to cure meat. They needed springhouses to keep butter and milk cold.

This was going to kill him. There was no way she'd give up trying to make her world livable, trying to get her friends and neighbors through the crisis. He was in up to his neck.

"We still have to deal with security problems." He was very aware of the word *we*. "The people who tried to kill you have to be found and dealt with, because they're an ongoing problem until then. The community patrol is looking at vehicles as they patrol, asking if anyone has been hurt. Until they're found, everyone in the valley is in danger."

"But they failed. The gasoline is out of the tanks now."

"So they start attacking and stealing from individuals. That's the next step."

He saw her flinch at the realization that by fighting off the thieves at the store, she had inadvertently made individuals the next targets. He wanted to tell her that it didn't matter, that after the asshole punks had used the gasoline they'd have moved on to smaller targets anyway, but the conversation had already skipped to another topic.

Eating had slowed and then stopped. Sela and Barb got to their feet and began cleaning off the table, while Carol looked pleased to be sitting where she could talk to them while they worked. Ben figured he was more in the way than anything else, so he went to put another log on the fireplace and stand with his back to the fire, enjoying the warmth.

After a little while, Olivia hesitantly approached, and stood beside him in an unconscious mirror of his posture. She was silent for a minute, then asked, "Were you in the army?"

"Marines."

"Oh." Another silence. "My brother's in the army. He's at Fort Stewart."

"Close to Savannah."

She nodded.

"He'll be okay, then. The military bases will have power, and they're secure."

She shifted uneasily. "Do you think he's ever shot at anybody?"

Shooting someone was bothering her. Ben wondered how in the hell he was supposed to reassure a teenage girl about doing something violent. The last time he'd interacted with a teenage girl for anything longer than ordering fast food, he'd been a teenager himself. Now they were like an alien species to him.

"Unless he's been deployed to a combat zone, no."

"He hasn't." She paused again. "Have you?"

"Been deployed? Yes."

"To a combat zone?"

"More than once."

"So you've shot at people."

"Yes."

"And hit them?"

"I was good at my job." Let her infer from that what she would. She was a kid, so he wasn't going to spell things out in detail for her. He glanced over at Sela, wondering when it would occur to her to rescue him. Even normal people had problems dealing with teenagers, and he hadn't been normal for a while now.

"I think I shot someone," she confided.

"I hope so. A bullet wound would make it easier to identify the gang."

"You don't think I killed him?"

"With a .22? Not likely. Possible, but not likely."

Then she went off on a tangent he hadn't anticipated. "So you think I should get a bigger gun?"

He sent another look at Sela, and a mental message: *Rescue me! Now!*

He sucked at mental messages, because she kept chatting with the other two as they washed and dried the dishes. "What I think is that I wish I'd been there instead of you two. Whether or not you're armed and how you're armed is a personal decision for you and your grandmother." And in a perfect world, there wouldn't be war, and a teenage girl wouldn't be asking him about weapons. The world wasn't perfect and never would be, but knowing that didn't make him less uncomfortable.

"I wish you'd been there, too," she said, and thank God that seemed to end the conversation because she had nothing else to offer, and neither did he.

Sela looked over at him and smiled, a soft smile that went all the way through him.

CHAPTER TWENTY

Ben carried Carol back to her bed, over her protests, then he and Sela said goodnight to the others. She put on her coat and gloves and they walked out to their vehicles. "I'll follow you home," he said.

She gave a start of surprise, but then since yesterday afternoon he'd been doing things that surprised her. She started to say she'd be okay, then realized that though she didn't know who had tried to steal the gasoline, they certainly knew who *she* was, and might have vengeance on their minds. She might not be okay, going home alone. Think strategically, she reminded herself.

The short distance to her house took only a minute. Ben pulled into the driveway behind her; as they walked up to the porch, a speck of white drifted in front of her face, then another. She stopped and looked up at the delicate flakes floating down from the darkness. "It's snowing," she said with mild surprise. With everything that had happened during the past couple of days, she hadn't thought of the possibility of snow.

Snow in November wasn't unusual, just a signal that though it was technically still autumn, winter didn't necessarily agree. There would still be good days, mild and sunny, even in January and February, but by and large people should be getting ready. In normal times that meant wrapping the outside faucets to protect against freezing. This year, things were both more simple and more complicated.

Still . . . the first snow of the season was always a little magical, no matter how light. This wasn't a storm, it was a silent downward spiral of flakes, peaceful in the still night. She stood there for a moment, her face upturned, a smile curving her lips. She wasn't a nature fanatic but she did enjoy the seasons, and this moment in particular. Without thinking she reached for his hand; it wasn't until the pause before he carefully folded his fingers around hers that she realized anew how wary he still was with people.

But he *was* holding her hand, the heat of his palm burning through her gloves. Though he might not feel the same as she did about the first snow, he was willing to stand there with her while she enjoyed it.

"Isn't this great?" she asked, and felt the glance he arrowed down at her.

"You like the snow?"

"I like the *first* snow," she said, smiling. "It's new and special, and listen to how quiet everything is. But if it's still here tomorrow morning, it'll be a pain in the rear end."

She couldn't be sure, in the darkness, but the flashlight cast enough light that she thought he might be smiling a little. However small a smile she could get from him, she'd take it.

"That's true. If we hadn't given out the gasoline today, everyone would be walking and there wouldn't be a problem. But if people get out on the road tomorrow—"

"Ouch." She winced, thinking that her timing sucked. In normal times the roads would be plowed and treated with salt brine, but "normal" had changed, and no snowplows would be running.

"It is what it is. Everyone here has driven on snow before."

He hadn't pulled his hand away, but she thought she'd held on to him long enough and let her hand drop; it was better to break the contact herself than to push him out of his comfort zone.

He opened the screen door and they went up on the porch, his hand on the small of her back, then he held the flashlight while she unlocked the door. Seizing her courage, she asked, "Would you like to come in?" All he could do was tell her no, and though she would be disappointed she wouldn't die from it. After the way he'd kissed her she *knew* he was attracted to her, and at the same time she also knew he'd likely had his fill of people today.

"Yes."

She was a little startled and a lot happy. They would talk and likely make out some, the thought of which sizzled through her veins. That was what she was thinking, but when she started to go inside, he stopped her with a touch on her arm. "If this is too soon, say so." His voice was rough, strained, as if he thought she might send him away.

Sela's heart gave a giant leap, then everything in her paused, as if her body waited on her decision. *That? Now?* She knew what he was saying, and wondered why she hadn't already realized it. Why else would he have come to Carol's house—bearing a gift of bacon—and actually sat down to eat with them? Taking care of security was one thing, but socializing was a giant step for him to take.

Her heart was booming in her chest. What was "too soon"? She'd been attracted to him for years. They hadn't dated, hadn't done any of the traditional romantic things, but in the world they found themselves in now perhaps a can of bacon meant more than any box of chocolates or an expensive dinner. A hot shower outweighed a movie, and tending wounds was priceless. Not only that, in this new world life was more precarious than it had been before, and tomorrow was only a possibility, not the given most people had considered it.

"No," she said quietly, and leaned her head against his arm. "It isn't too soon." If she didn't seize life, it could slip away from her. Today she could have died without ever knowing what it was like to be with him, and she wouldn't take that chance again. He had offered, and she accepted.

They went inside and she made sure the door was locked behind them. He paused a moment to look around and check his surroundings like a wary animal, then shed his coat, hung it on the coatrack beside the door, and went to the fireplace where he crouched down to build up the fire because once again it had burned down. The open space of great room, kitchen, and breakfast nook was chilly. It wasn't a *huge* space, but being so open made it more difficult to heat. She lit two oil lamps, illuminating the cozy surroundings with mellow light and adding a bit more heat.

This was her home, as familiar to her as her own face, but what did he see when he looked around? His house was bigger, and more bare. Nothing here was luxurious but her furniture was comfortable, she had nice rugs on the floor, pretty lamps that were useless for now, photos and books and a few pretty knickknacks. It was a woman's home, and to him it might feel fussy and stifling.

He straightened from the fireplace; he made everything feel small, dwarfing it with his height and the breadth of his shoulders. She went breathless just looking at him, absorbing the impact of his size and strength, but after a few seconds she managed to follow his lead and take off her coat, hang it beside his. That mundane action somehow felt piercingly intimate, seeing their coats hanging there side by side.
Breathe.

Doing so was more difficult than she'd expected. She was so overwhelmed by the look of him and the prospect of what they were going to do that she was in a daze. She hadn't been intimate with anyone since her divorce, too traumatized and insecure to even try to meet someone else. Now, suddenly, there was Ben, who was like no other man she'd ever known.

She would be naked in front of him . . . but he would be naked in front of her, too, and the thought of that was far more riveting than the vulnerabilities she felt.

He was still standing there looking into the fire. Sela regrouped, reining in her nerves and wondering if he was nervous, too—not because of the prospect of sex, but because of the prospect of emotional connection. The set of his shoulders looked tense. Instinctively she reacted, searching for something that would relieve that tension, or at least give him time to deal with it. "Would you like something to drink?" Lord, that was the wrong thing to ask; her available offerings were slim. "Mostly I eat at Carol's, but I keep a little coffee here, and some mix for hot chocolate."

He turned, his head cocked a little, interest in his eyes. "How much coffee?"

"Not much," she confessed. "Enough for a few cups."

"Then we'll have hot chocolate now, and save the coffee for to-morrow morning."

She processed that, reading between the lines and . . . he intended to spend the night here. Every muscle in her began quivering in anticipation.

"Unless you want me to leave. Afterward."

Had he read her mind, or just her face? It couldn't be her face, because she felt as if she was blazing with joy, in which case he wouldn't have asked that question. "No," she managed to say. "I don't want you to leave."

She went to the kitchen and poured some of her water supply into a small cast-iron pot, then took the pot to the fireplace to begin heating it. He took the pot from her, bent to nestle it in the coals and put the lid on it so ash couldn't fly into the water. "Do you have a generator? I could turn it on, get the house warm."

"I do, but I took it to Carol's before the CME hit. I thought she and Olivia would need it more. I sleep here, but that's about it." And retreat here, when she needed some alone time. Besides, this was her home, and she was emotionally more comfortable here even without electricity than she was at Carol's. "It was great today, running the generator and the water heater. Barb helped me get the well pump going. All of us had nice hot showers." She smiled at him. "I've had a shower two days in a row. I feel pampered."

"You mean aside from being shot at?" he asked, moving his hand to her waist and urging her closer to him. She went willingly, and nestled against his side. This was so new, such an unexpected fulfillment of her silent yearning, that she was caught in a vague sense of astonishment. Why would someone like Ben be attracted to someone like *her*? On the other hand, she was just as astonished that she was so attracted to him. She felt as if he was her polar opposite—but skin chemistry overruled a lot of things, and she wanted him to touch her, wanted to touch him in return.

"That doesn't feel real." She gave voice to her thoughts. Talking was easier like this, not facing each other but watching the flames lick at the wood. "The unusual never does, does it? It's the normal little things that anchor us."

"It was real." His tone was grim, and his hand tightened on her waist. "After a while you get used to it, to looking at everyone to see if they have a weapon, then not being in combat is what feels weird as hell." He fell silent, as if he'd revealed more than he meant to, or perhaps his own words had taken him back.

What he'd said had skimmed the surface of what he'd seen and done, of what he'd lived through. She couldn't imagine combat— and then realized that yes, after today, she certainly did have an idea of it.

They stood there in silence for several minutes, each of them lost in the overlap of their shared moment and their private thoughts, watching the fire, nestling together.

"Where's your bedroom?" he asked.

She jerked in his grip, electrified by the words. "Back there," she said, indicating the short hallway to the left, past the kitchen. "At the end of the hallway, on the right."

"I'll be right back."

Taking the flashlight, he disappeared down the hall. Sela stood there by the fireplace, flabbergasted. Why would he not want her to go with him? Curiosity got the better of her and she started to follow, only to have him exit her bedroom by the time she reached the hall. He was carrying her mattress, covers and all. She could barely flip the thing, and while he wrestled with the size of the mattress, maneuvering it out the bedroom door and through the hall, the weight didn't seem to bother him.

Automatically she took the flashlight from him so he had both hands free. "What—?"

"It's warmer in here than it is back there."

That was the truth. As the weather had turned colder, she'd begun warming a towel in front of the fireplace, then hurrying to bed and wrapping it around her feet before it cooled. She imagined as winter came on the towel alone wouldn't be enough, and she'd turn to the old-time method of heating a rock in the fireplace and wrapping the towel around the rock, then putting it under the covers at the foot of the bed. The alternative was sleeping on the couch, closer to the fireplace.

"Push the coffee table back," he said as he carried the mattress past her.

Or to stay warm she could move the bed into the great room, she thought, and almost laughed at his practical solution to the problem. She dragged the coffee table to the side, shoved the couch back a couple of feet. He positioned the mattress on the floor in front of the fireplace, and she retrieved the pillows from where he'd left them in the bedroom. When she returned he'd repositioned the couch so it was flush with the mattress. To lean back against, she thought, recognizing immediately what he was doing.

They both removed their boots and sat down on the mattress with their backs against the couch, using the pillows for support. Either it was surprisingly comfortable, or just being with him made everything feel better. He put his arm around her shoulders and she leaned against him, her head on his shoulder, her hand on his chest where she could feel the strong, steady beat of his heart.

She was filled with wonder that she felt so easy with him. When she'd been dating Adam, she'd been uncertain and self-conscious for months, wondering if she was doing or saying things that would turn him off. With Ben, the excitement and sheer pleasure of touching him, and being touched by him, seemed to override her insecurities. Once he'd kissed her, things had changed. It wasn't just that his arousal had been so evident, but that the power of his hunger had been, too. He wanted her, the woman, but he also wanted *her*, the person, and that made all the difference in the world.

He rubbed his chin against her hair. "I've never been married."

Interesting. His masculinity was such a magnet to women, she was surprised he was a bachelor. She hadn't thought he'd always been such a loner, but perhaps he had been. She tilted her head against his shoulder to look up at him, to marvel at the way the firelight played across the hard planes of his face. "Why not? Carol doesn't call you Hot Buns for no reason."

He made a sound that was half snort, half laugh, and it warmed her all the way through. "I thought I was Stud Muffin."

"She has a whole list of names. I think she has some cougar in her."

"Yeah, I should probably check for claw marks." A flicker of amusement crossed his face, then was gone. "I was in the military—I was a Marine, and I deployed overseas on several tours. When I was stateside things just never worked out. A lot of women like dating the uniform, but the reality of having a relationship with someone who's on the other side of the world half the time—it's more than they wanted to deal with. I didn't mind. There wasn't anyone I particularly cared about."

"What about after you left the military?"

He didn't move, but she felt the inner withdrawal and knew she'd bumped against his emotional wall. "No one?" she prompted, not willing to let him stall with his thoughts.

"No." A few beats later he glanced at her. "At all." He cleared his throat. "I should probably apologize in advance, because—I'd intended to take some pressure off before we got in bed together, but things happened and I don't want to wait any longer."

She'd been so focused on keeping him talking that it took a few seconds for his meaning to sink in. Her reaction pinged in several directions at once: astonishment, laughter, profound gratitude that he'd even thought of such a thing. Warmth flooded her and she turned into him, lifting her arm to wrap it around his neck and hug him closer. "I—well. It's been a while for me, too. Since my divorce, almost five years ago."

She felt him tilt his head to look down at her. "Why'd you dump him?"

"I didn't," she admitted, kind of amazed that he'd immediately come to the opposite conclusion. "He dumped me."

He drew back, frowned at her. "What is he, brain-damaged?"

Part of her wanted to put the most flattering spin on it, say that she and Adam had wanted different things—which they had—but the past couple of days had been kind of a trial by fire, and if Ben wanted to leave because she wasn't what he wanted then better she learned that now. "I haven't seen or heard from him since the divorce was final so he might be by now, but no, when we divorced he had full brain function. I was never *enough* for him." There. It was said, and she didn't feel mortified. If anything, she . . . yes, she felt a little angry—not a lot, because Adam didn't really matter any longer. "He wanted to do exciting things, interesting things, and I was always too chicken."

"These exciting things—what were they?"

"Not all that exciting. Snow skiing. Travel to Africa, South America. Parasailing, scuba diving. I know they don't sound that dangerous, but it all made me so uneasy I just couldn't do it." She sighed.

"You didn't trust him."

"I—what?" Confused, she tilted her head back to look up at him, her brows knitted.

"I've done a lot of stuff, shit that can get you killed. It's either desperation that gets you through because your life is in danger, or it's trust in your team to have your back. You didn't trust him to look after you the way you'd look after him. What was this shit's name, anyway?"

"Adam." She'd never thought of Adam as a shit. On the other hand, she'd also never looked at their relationship from the viewpoint of whether or not he'd have her back if she was in danger. If she'd gone scuba diving and something happened to her air tanks, would Adam have shared his air with her if he'd noticed she was having problems? The last was a big "if," because he'd never been sensitive to her wants or needs, if she felt ill, if she was tired. She hoped he'd have shared his air, but that was a hope, not a certainty.

"Adam Gordon?"

"No, I took back my maiden name." She could hear the water boiling in the pot, and got up to remove it from the fireplace, using the poker to drag it out. The next few minutes were taken up with making the hot chocolate, then settling back with the warm cups in their hands. As always, it was deeply satisfying to be drinking hot chocolate while the snow was falling, as if some primal need was being met. Sitting so close beside him, in front of the fire, satisfied another deep need. Sexual anticipation sizzled on the back burner, waiting to be brought to a full boil, but for now this slow approach suited her. As much as she wanted him, she also wanted to *talk* to him, learn the details of what made him unique.

"I've always felt like such a coward." She sipped her hot chocolate and stared at the fire. "Some people charge at life, but I guess I'm a background sort of person."

He snorted. "Yeah, the background sort of person who offered to sleep with me to get what she wanted, and who held off a group of men shooting at her."

She was glad the firelight wouldn't show her face getting red, but she kind of gave it away by hiding her face against his shoulder. The getting shot at—as she'd said, that was unreal, and already at a distance. Offering to sleep with him was much more immediate and personal.

He set his hot chocolate down and stroked his hand up and down her back. "About that. Make sure this is what you want, that you *know* I don't look at it as a deal. We can still wait, but—damn it all to fucking hell and back, you *got yourself shot at*." His tone turned savage. "You don't ever do that again, you hear? I aged twenty years getting down that damn mountain."

Something had to be wrong with her, because she didn't think anyone had ever said anything sweeter to her. She cuddled closer. "I promise I'll try to never get shot at again."

He put his other hand on her throat, used his thumb to tilt her chin up, and pressed a warm kiss on her mouth. The kiss quickly turned hot and deep, his tongue moving against hers, his hand sliding from her throat back to clench in her hair. Her fingers slipped on the cup of hot chocolate and hastily she steadied the cup. With a low, rough chuckle he lifted his mouth. "Don't spill it."

"Then don't kiss me." She loved hearing him laugh; it wasn't a real laugh, it was more a ragged sound in his throat, but it was accompanied by crinkling eyes and an upward curve of his mouth, so it counted. Every moment with him counted.

The hot chocolate was delicious, but it was in the way. Rather than waste it she quickly drained the cup and set it aside. "There. Problem solved."

He reached for his own cup and killed the chocolate as if it were a shot of whiskey.

Now.

"I want to see you naked."

The rawness of his tone thrilled her, made her shake. The desire was mutual. She wanted to see him naked, so much that she couldn't decide if she should undress herself, or him.

Actually, who cared? All that mattered was that they got out of their clothes. She maneuvered astride his thighs and looped both arms around his neck, kissing him with all the fire she felt, and that was the only encouragement he needed.

Dizzy under his fierce kisses, she felt his hands moving everywhere, over her breasts, unfastening her jeans, delving into her underwear and between her legs. She gasped as a big finger pushed into her, whimpered when he added a second one. She rose to her knees, driven by the penetration, lashed by the surge and shock of pleasure. Oh God, oh God, it had been so long and never like this before anyway. She'd never before felt so exquisitely, painfully aroused as if she might come before he was even inside her. She didn't want that, she wanted the whole experience, she wanted his weight on her and his thrusts and . . . everything. She wanted everything.

She sat back and pulled at the buttons on his shirt; he tugged hers over her head. They rolled over on the mattress; she pushed her jeans down, then found herself flat on her back before she could get them off. He leaned over her, his bare shoulders gleaming in the firelight. "I have nine condoms," he said, his tone rough. "Total. After they're gone, you have a decision to make."

Send him away, he meant, or risk pregnancy. Her heart leaped at the idea of having his baby. No, she didn't have a decision to make; she knew what she wanted but perhaps now wasn't the time to tell him. Just because she wanted something didn't mean she should have it. There were two of them who had to make that decision. For now, she had this, and for now this was enough. She stroked her hands over his chest and shoulders, up to cup his jaw and rub her thumb over his lips, then stretched up to kiss him.

He didn't wait to have a discussion about the matter; he'd stated a fact, and that was that. He stripped off the rest of his clothes and hers, took a condom from his coat pocket and rolled it on, then pushed her legs apart and moved over her.

Sela caught her breath, glorying in his heavy weight, the hardness of his body pressing down on her. His breathing was ragged, but he held himself still on top of her. "I'm going too fast," he muttered. "You aren't ready—"

Her breath sighed out of her. "Yes, I am," she whispered. "Hurry." She gripped his hips with her thighs, lifted herself up to him. She clung to him as he reached between them and opened the folds between her legs, pushed his thick penis at her, and slowly sank inside.

She caught her breath as a multitude of sensations overwhelmed her. There was his taste in her mouth, the rough texture of his hairy chest on her breasts, his hips on the inside of her thighs, the sharp sting of being stretched, the pressure inside as he moved deep. She was drowned in him, taken even as she took. She gasped again, her own hips instinctively lifting to take more of him in, and her gasp became a thin, breathless cry. She wanted to feel his balls; she reached down, managed to palm them, then stroked her finger around the base of his penis. He grunted and gave a short, hard shove, another, and another. Her hand was in the way and she released him, dug her fingers into his ribs as she held on and ground herself against him.

The act was breathtakingly carnal. *He* was carnal, and for the first time in her life she felt carnal, sexual, basic, and free. He drew back and looked down at her, their gazes meeting. Looking into his eyes while their bodies were joined was the most sensual, overwhelming moment of her life. Sharp waves of sensation tightened her inner muscles, strengthened, centered. A cry, female and primal, broke free. She began coming, legs and arms locked around him, her back arched, head tilted back and more of those wild cries filling the dark, quiet room.

He held himself high and deep, rocking against her; a raw, harsh sound burst from his throat and he bowed in her arms, every muscle in his body tensing, helpless to stop thrusting. She didn't want him to stop, she wanted him to feel what she was feeling. He ground into her, shuddered, bucked, went deeper.

Slowly the tension in his body oozed away and he eased his weight down on her, his movements jerky and lacking his usual powerful grace. He was breathing hard, but so was she, and sweat sheened their naked bodies. Her heart slammed against her rib cage. If the house collapsed around them right then, she didn't know if she'd have the energy to get up and put on her clothes. All she wanted to do was lie right where she was, under him, holding him.

After a while he laboriously rolled off her and got up to dispose of the condom. Without his body heat she felt chilly, despite the proximity of the fireplace, and pulled the blankets over herself. When he returned she simply lifted the blanket and he slid under them next to her, pulled her close so her head was on his shoulder. "Your feet are cold," he muttered sleepily. "Put them on me."

Sela didn't know how any part of her could be cold after what they'd done but her feet were definitely chilly. She curled into him, her arm around his neck, and tucked her feet against his legs. Utterly satisfied, utterly content, she slept.

Sometime later he got up and added more wood to the fire. When he lay back down, he rolled onto his back and pulled her on top of him.

Two condoms down.

By morning there were four left.

CHAPTER TWENTY-ONE

"I need a bigger gun."

The comment came out of nowhere. Ben's eyes popped open. The gray light of dawn pushed at the windows but he'd been awake for a while, content to hold her, in no hurry to get up. He wasn't someone who lay around in bed, he got up and began doing something . . . until now. This was different. Lying in bed with Sela was the best use of his time he could think of.

In the firelight he could see her staring at the ceiling, her mouth pooched out as she considered whatever she was considering, which in light of her comment didn't seem to be world peace. An unfamiliar sensation rose in his chest, his throat, and suddenly he was laughing, truly laughing. He couldn't remember the last time that had happened. "That's what Olivia said, too." And he was just as startled now as he'd been then.

"I'd already thought about it, then forgot, but—we were lucky, because we were way outgunned. I don't want that to happen again. Even after you find whoever was trying to steal the gas, there'll still be times in the future when we'll have trouble. Not constantly, but other people will try to come in, try to take what we have. So I need a bigger gun." She wiggled her pursed lips from side to side. "I bet I can trade something for one."

"Don't forget ammo. A more powerful weapon is useless unless you have the ammunition for it." Her head was lying on his arm and he crooked his elbow, bringing her closer so he could kiss her hair. "But don't worry about it, I have you covered." He had a hidden arsenal at his house, weapons he wouldn't be bringing out short of outright war. He hadn't exactly come by them legally, which was why they were hidden. Sela didn't need a grenade launcher, though; she needed a deer rifle—and practice. Lots of practice. If he'd been the one doing the shooting at the store, there wouldn't have been any "maybe" about wounding someone, there would have been bodies all over the parking lot.

He rubbed his hand over her bare stomach, silently marveling that he had the freedom to touch her in that manner, and more intimately if he wanted. Three days ago he'd still been firm—mostly—in his policy of isolation, but then Sela had come up the mountain to his place and all of that had turned on a dime. Now they were lying naked together, watching the room get lighter as the sun rose and neither of them willing to get up and get busy because they didn't want this time to end, even temporarily.

Then she stretched and yawned—an action that for some reason made his hand slide up to her breasts—and said, "Bacon."

"Uh . . . all right."

"Barb's probably started cooking by now; they have breakfast fairly early. She's going to cook pancakes today, she said so last night while we were cleaning up. Pancakes and bacon." She sighed, the sound blissful with anticipation. Then she gave him a look as serious as any he'd ever seen. "I *need* bacon."

Mentally he slapped himself upside the head. "I brought a can of bacon for you, too; I forgot about it and left it in the truck."

She sat up in the blankets, her expression excited. "You did? We can have bacon here?"

He kissed goodbye to his fantasy of lying there in the warm blankets for an unspecified length of time, though the blankets were now pooled around her waist and her pretty breasts were exposed, her nipples tight from the cold. His fantasy also included getting back on top of her, something else that wasn't going to happen right away. He got up and began putting on his clothes. "I'll get it." And if he hadn't forgotten the night before, he would still be lying there beside her, which proved the point that forgotten details could come back to bite you in the ass.

Unfortunately, she got up and began dressing, too, signaling an end to the naked lazy-day cuddling. He hadn't known he liked naked lazy-day cuddling until now. Sela was making him rethink a lot of things, making him consider details he'd never considered before.

One of those details had him pausing at the door, assessing all of the variables of their relationship. What he was assuming and what she was thinking might not be the same thing. The valley people weren't prudes and wouldn't shun her for letting him spend the night, but they *would* talk, and that might embarrass her. Cautiously, not certain at all how she'd reply, he asked, "Do you want me to start my truck and let the windows defrost, so it won't look as if I've been here all night?"

She'd been in the process of making coffee and she stopped cold, her mouth falling open as she stared at him. His gaze was steady, though he unconsciously braced for her answer. If she wanted to keep their relationship on the down low, that wouldn't mean anything more than that she was cautious. That was what he tried to think, but his gut was tight as he waited.

"That depends," she finally said, her tone careful, and his gut tightened even more. "Is this just a booty call for you?"

That answer was easy. "No. Not even close."

A slow, radiant smile curved her mouth. "It isn't for me, either. Don't bother with the windows." She turned back to the task of measuring coffee into the percolator.

His muscles relaxed, and the weight of dread lifted off his shoulders. Ben found he was smiling as he went out to the truck. The thin layer of snow crunched under his boots and an icy wind cut through his clothes, but he could see breaks in the clouds that promised the snow was over. He looked around, by habit checking for movement, but the early morning was still except for a few birds. The smell of woodsmoke was familiar and cozy, resonating with some cellular memory. Humans had huddled around a wood fire for thousands of years more than they had an air vent.

He unlocked his truck and retrieved the can of bacon. They might have nothing but bacon and coffee for breakfast, but he was good with that.

But breakfast was more than he'd expected. She unearthed some pancake mix that required only water, and though she didn't have butter, she did have a half-empty bottle of butter-flavored pancake syrup in her cabinets. Soon the bacon was being crisped up in a heavy-ass cast-iron frying pan, then while he wrestled the mattress back into the bedroom to clear the space, she knelt in front of the fireplace and carefully made the pancakes, one at a time.

They ate sitting on the floor in front of the fire, though there was a perfectly good table with four chairs, as well as the couch. But the rug was fine, and it kept the percolator within reach. For some reason sitting on the floor felt more intimate, and that made him happier than it should. He was a little amused and bemused at himself, turning into such a sap.

Afterward she heated some water to clean the dishes, then more water for them to wash off. She removed the bandage on his shoulder, cleaned the wound, rebandaged it. "It looks okay," she said. "No red streaks or anything."

He'd known it was okay, because the wound was sore, but not throbbing. What was better than okay was the way Sela fussed over him. He was naturally a loner and generally he'd taken care of himself, yet having her take care of him was a surprisingly touching novelty. He frowned, thinking about it. As he pulled on his shirt he studied her—no makeup, hair simply brushed and pulled back, wearing jeans and thick socks and a sweatshirt. He'd never wanted a woman more, never felt more satisfied by the having of her. The first time had been fast and hard, the times after that less urgent so he could take his time and enjoy the process, pay attention to what she liked, savor the slow push and pull. After five times he didn't think he could come again if his life depended on it—and he still wanted to be on top of her, inside her.

Everything had changed. Because of her, he wasn't alone, didn't want to be alone. And he wasn't even panicking over it. Damn.

She noticed him watching her; he could see her face turning pink. "What?" she asked, unconsciously tugging at the hem of her sweatshirt as if he hadn't spent all night naked with her and had already seen every single inch.

He wasn't a poet. He'd never in his life said anything remotely graceful. The closest he could come now was a somber, "You're sweet."

"I—what?" Now she pushed at her hair, turned even pinker.

"Sweet. You're a sweet person. You took your generator to your aunt's house. You don't eat much so they'll have more. You put bandages on me." Yeah, that was poetic. Uncomfortably he shifted his weight. "I don't know sweet, don't know what to do other than eat—" He paused, and a slow, purely male smile curved his mouth. "Okay, maybe I do know what to do."

Now the pink in her face turned to red and she clapped her hands to her cheeks, which made him think maybe her dickhead of an ex-husband had never done that for her, to her, with her. If he hadn't, tough shit for him, because Ben didn't intend to make that mistake.

He went to her and put his hands on her waist, pulled her close. Immediately she nestled against him as if there was no place on earth where she wanted to be more than right there, her head resting on his shoulder, her arms around his neck. Perfect. Maybe they couldn't spend all day together here, maybe there were things that needed doing, but right now there was nothing that couldn't be put off for a couple of hours.

Right now, they needed only this.

"Look, Ted. It snowed during the night." Meredith was in the kitchen putting together breakfast—it wasn't eggs and waffles, but so far they were still doing okay on food. Ted kept an eye on their food supplies. He wasn't a hunter, so he couldn't provide for Meredith that way. He'd thought about trying his hand at fishing, but he didn't know a lot about that, either. One of the reasons he'd joined the community patrol was because the members got a portion of food to pay them for their time. She'd stopped her food preparations, opened the curtains, and was looking out the kitchen window.

He looked out the living room window, then stepped out on the porch to get a better look. It was cold, but nothing like winter could be in Ohio. There looked to be two or three inches on the ground here, less down in the valley. He and Meredith had come here fairly often during the winters and overall found them mild—but that was when they'd had electricity, a warm cabin, and could go to Sevierville, Pigeon Forge, or Gatlinburg to any of the thousand and one restaurants that served the tourist trade, when they could stop at any of the grocery stores, when they could fill their gas tank and go home if they wanted. This winter would be a different experience.

He'd brooded until he was tired of brooding, but he couldn't put yesterday out of his mind. He was torn in opposite directions—no, not torn, because he knew what he had to do. That wasn't up in the air. What bothered him as much as Lawrence and his gang of thugs was how the valley people obviously thought of him. He could deal with not being liked; that wasn't important to him. But being disrespected, shut out, *taunted*—

Sela Gordon—he still burned over what she'd done, in front of everyone. She'd embarrassed him, but even worse, the rude gesture had belittled him.

"It's ready," Meredith called, making him realize he'd spent more than a few minutes on the porch. And though Tennessee's winters were nothing like Ohio's, he was cold, because he'd come out without a coat.

She made a soft, exasperated, wifely sound when she saw him shivering, and handed him a cup of steaming hot tea, which both of them liked okay. They had some coffee left, but she alternated what she prepared, so they wouldn't get bored. Some days she heated apple cider; that wasn't his favorite, but he never said that to her. Today she'd made some flatbread and toasted it, and there was peanut butter and jelly to spread on it.

He patted her hand as he sat down at the table. "Looks good," he said, as he always did. Meredith was a darn good cook, but even if she hadn't been he'd still have complimented what she worked to prepare for him. She smiled at him, and the first thing he thought was how pretty she looked, then he suddenly noticed that she had on some makeup, and she'd put her hair up. She looked as if she was going to work.

After her heart attack years ago she'd necessarily cut back on the hours she worked as a physical therapy assistant, then over Ted's objections gradually increased them again. A couple of years ago, though, she'd begun lightening the load again. They were getting older, closer to retirement age, and they liked to travel, liked their vacation time spent here. He'd been looking forward to spending some leisurely time with her, then that damn CME happened and here they were. He said, "You look pretty," and wiggled his finger at his head and eyes to indicate both the hairdo and makeup. "What's the occasion?"

"It's been a few days now since Carol Allen broke her leg, so it's time she started some gentle therapy. You know where she lives, don't you?"

He did, because of the community patrols, but that didn't mean he wanted Meredith associating with those ill-tempered, ungrateful *bitches*. "She has plenty of people to take care of her," he said, not answering Meredith's question and trying to deflect her.

"Are any of them a trained PTA?"

Frustration began rising in him, because he could see in Meredith's clear gaze that she'd made up her mind and likely nothing he could say would change it. He hadn't told her about Sela Gordon giving him the finger in front of the whole community, because he didn't want Meredith to know how embarrassed he'd been, how the community at large seemed to think so little of him.

"I don't know," he finally muttered.

"Well, we know that *I* am," Meredith said, patting his hand and leaning over to kiss his cheek. "Would you like another cup of tea? The water's still hot."

The change of subject told him that he might as well save his breath. Meredith wanted to contribute, not just to their neighbors but to their own welfare. She knew that her expertise could be traded for food and goods, that she'd return from Carol Allen's house with something for them to eat, whether it was a few fresh eggs or some milk, maybe a can of soup. Who knew? But barter was the way things in the valley were working now.

Like it or not, he was taking Meredith with him and dropping her off at the Allen house when he went down to see Mike Kilgore.

From a seated position in the bed she was so damn tired of living in, Carol glared at her leg, the damn traitorous lump under the covers.

She needed to stop cussing so much, Olivia was getting way too much enjoyment from it, but . . . *damn!*

She was bored out of her skull. The pain had faded quite a bit in the last three days, thank goodness, but she was still stuck in the bed. Part of it was her own fault—okay, most of it was her own fault—because she was the one who'd come up with that idea of acting worse than she was so Sela would stay in charge of the community. Sela not only had settled in, she seemed to have forgotten how hard she'd fought *not* to be in charge. Maybe having Hottie McHotHot involved made a difference to her; if not, then something was seriously wrong with the girl's hormones, which she didn't think was the case.

The good news was Carol didn't feel bad, all things considered, as long as she didn't move. Her ribs were still sore, and if it hadn't been for them she'd likely have already been up trying out those crutches, at least when Sela was nowhere around. But they were, and she hadn't. Unless Hottie carried her to the living room, she was pretty much stuck. Though . . . honestly, having him carry her back and forth wasn't a hardship. She was old, not dead.

Sela hadn't come for breakfast this morning; she usually did, but not always. Carol smiled at the thought. She wasn't blind; she'd seen the way the big guy had been looking at her niece—and he'd brought bacon. These days, that was practically a marriage proposal, and she couldn't be happier for Sela, who had never said anything but anyone with half a brain could tell that the divorce from Adam had devastated her to the point she simply hadn't *tried* again. Having someone like Ben Jernigan so focused on her could only be a good thing. Ben left Adam in the dust.

Carol sighed. She was happy to leave the community leadership to Sela, but her own home needed tending. There were preparations to be made for the coming winter. Food would be a consideration until things returned to normal, if they ever did. She'd been thinking about setting up a cold frame in the backyard. Maybe she could grow lettuce and broccoli there, long before spring arrived. She wanted to help with gathering herbs and learn what each plant was and what it was good for—besides a salad of wild plants. There was wood to . . . well, she wasn't going to chop wood, but she could stack the logs where she wanted them, nearby but not too near because she didn't want the bugs in the wood getting into the house. The simple fact was, she couldn't afford to lie here and let the people she was supposed to be taking care of take care of her instead. It was just wrong.

She had painted herself into a corner, and had no one but herself to blame.

She'd played up the pain and confusion when Sela was around, and would for a while longer. Why abandon a dumb-ass strategy now? At least it was somewhat working; as she'd expected, Sela was handling her new responsibilities well, so well that even the Cove Mountain Hottie was now involved.

She should probably start calling Buns of Steel by his name, because she thought he might soon become, not just a customer, not just a neighbor who was helping out during a crisis, but family. Imagine that! She might be counting her chickens before they hatched, but she didn't think so.

Carol had no idea what Ben Jernigan was thinking, but she'd bet her ass he was focused in and moving fast to secure what he wanted. He was no fool; he knew the treasure he'd be getting in Sela.

The evidence of his interest was obvious. Not only was he now involved with the community patrol, there were the solar lights, then he'd shown up here last night and eaten supper with them. And he'd brought bacon! That must be love.

They were both definitely interested, but would either of them actually do anything about it? What could she do to help things along?

Nothing. This was no time to play matchmaker, not that she knew how or likely even needed to. Nature would take its course. It always did.

She heard the front door open and close, and immediately dropped her head back and half closed her eyes. Best to look as feeble as possible, in case that was Sela, who stopped by several times a day, as if she didn't have anything better to do. But a moment later Carol heard Barb's voice, followed by one she didn't recognize.

Bored, after days in bed, Carol was tempted to make the effort to stand and take a quick peek around the corner. She could get out of the bed, and had done so several times to make short trips to the portable toilet just a few feet away. There were crutches in reach, in case she needed them—which she did, since she wasn't supposed to put any weight on her bad leg. She didn't make a move. One thing she wasn't, and wouldn't be for quite a while, was quick.

Barb stuck her head in the bedroom door and called out softly, "Carol? Are you up for a visitor?"

Not knowing who the visitor was, Carol managed a low groan. She'd stopped taking Barb's pain pills yesterday, because even though there was pain that came and went, those pills needed to be saved for a potential emergency down the road. That didn't mean she couldn't still pretend to be out of it. "Visitor? For me? How sweet . . ." She broke off, seeing a strange woman standing behind Barb. Well, crap. Who was this? The face was kind of familiar, but—

Barb stepped to the side of the bed; the strange woman followed close behind. She was in her mid-fifties, Carol guessed. Attractive, in an average way, taller than Barb but not by much. Her light brown hair, shot with just a bit of gray, was pulled back into a neat bun. The bun and ponytail had become the go-to hairstyles of the apocalypse.

"Carol, this is Meredith Parsons."

Parsons? As in Teddy? *Heaven save us.* That's where she'd seen the woman before, at the community barbecue—not that Teddy had bothered to actually introduce his wife to the woman who had swooped in and taken the job he considered himself perfect for. Ha.

"She used to be a physical therapist, and—"

"PTA," Meredith corrected, smiling at them both. "The *A* is for *assistant*. I never got the extra training to be a PT, but maybe I'm better than nothing."

Carol's eyes widened. Had Ted sent his wife to incapacitate her? Well, incapacitate her more than she already was.

"I'm fine," Carol said. "Barb and Olivia have been taking good care of me."

"I'm sure they have," Meredith said in a gentle voice, "but it won't hurt to let me have a look."

Wouldn't it? Did that sweet voice and those kind blue eyes disguise ill intentions?

Meredith pulled the coverlet down to expose Carol's leg. For comfort and ease, Carol wore loose, knee-length pajama bottoms. She'd chosen these pajamas for the softness of the material, not for the bright yellow ducks. The ducks were a little embarrassing, but were the least of her problems at the moment.

Both legs, the good one and the bad, were exposed. The splint, such as it was, consisted of two narrow and smooth planks of wood tied to the leg with long strips of what had once been Olivia's too-small T-shirts. The setup was crude, maybe, but it had done the trick.

"Barb told me it was a clean break, and I have to say, it looks pretty good. No redness, not much swelling. It looks as though you're doing well, though before I leave we'll want to elevate the leg just a bit more." Meredith looked at Barb. "Do you have any free weights? No more than five pounds. We'll want to start upper body strength exercises right away."

"The problem is my leg, not my flabby arms," Carol said sullenly. She wasn't in the mood to be polite.

Meredith wasn't insulted; she didn't seem to care at all that her patient was being obstinate. "We want to keep your arms and shoulders as fit as possible, even work on your core, when we can. It's too easy to lose muscle tone when you're forced to stay in bed for days at a time. When you move to the crutches, you'll need your strength."

Damn it, the woman had a point. "My hand weights are in the garage," Carol said, shooting Barb a look that she hoped said *help me*. "Behind the dusty treadmill." That treadmill had been dusty long before the CME had hit. So had the weights.

Barb nodded, grinned as if she was enjoying herself—which she probably was—and left the room, leaving Carol alone with the enemy.

Carol steeled herself for whatever pain might come, now that there were no witnesses. Instead Meredith remained pleasant and easygoing, as she moved to the foot of the bed and showed Carol how to do what she called ankle pumps. Up and down, up and down, with her feet.

Barb returned with the hand weights, five pounders, then said goodbye and slipped out of the room, closing the bedroom door behind her.

Now the real torture would begin . . .

But there was no torture. Meredith was all business, walking Carol through more ankle exercises, as well as simple moves with the weights. She worked with Carol on getting out of bed without putting any weight on the broken leg, and walking properly with the borrowed crutches, though until Carol's sore ribs were better, using the crutches was limited. She was pleased to see the portable toilet, though goodness knows Carol was not pleased at all that she needed the damn thing.

By the time Carol returned to bed, she was exhausted. Whoever thought rehab was easy work had never been through it. After placing more pillows under the bad leg, Meredith pulled a chair to the side of the bed and sat.

"You're very lucky the break is no worse than it is."

"Don't I know it," Carol mumbled. She was a little breathless, and that in itself was alarming. Here she'd been playing up the injury so Sela would take over, and it appeared she didn't need to fake anything at all.

"It's scary, isn't it? How what would've been a minor incident a couple of months ago can now be life-threatening. Scary, too, how people change, when things go bad." There remained a kind of sweetness, a patience, in Meredith's eyes, which was surprising given who she was married to.

"I can't argue with that," Carol said. She leaned back and relaxed. It was early in the day, but damn it, she could use a nap!

Meredith relaxed in her chair. "Ted didn't want me to come here today."

No shit.

"If I'd heard about your fall sooner, I would've come right away." She smiled. "If Ted knew that, he never would've mentioned your accident to me."

Against her best instincts, Carol liked Ted Parsons's wife. She never would've thought that possible. "He and I didn't get off to the best start," she admitted. "I imagine he's happy to see me suffer."

"Oh, it's not that," Meredith said sharply, firing up in her husband's defense. "Ted can be difficult, I know, and he always thinks his way is the best way because he's had to fight for what he has. But he would never purposely harm a soul. He doesn't like seeing you, or anyone else, in pain."

Carol wasn't so sure about that.

"I wish he and your niece could get along. He was so upset yesterday after that business over the gas. I don't think he slept a wink last night."

Carol didn't say anything. This woman knew Ted and his faults as well as anyone, she imagined.

Meredith sighed. "He can be difficult, I admit it. It's— He needs to feel important. It's the way he grew up, in foster care. He never felt as if he mattered to anyone. He had to fight for everything he got, and to this day he can be downright unpleasant to people who he thinks are belittling him. He's very protective of me. Always has been, but especially since my heart attack ten years ago."

Carol sat up a little. "You had a heart attack?"

Meredith waved off Carol's concern. "Yes, but it's no big deal."

"A heart attack most definitely is a big deal."

"My doctors say I'm fit as a fiddle. I recovered nicely, but Ted has never believed it. I think he's always watching me, waiting for the next one to hit without warning. As I said, he's very protective, much more so than is necessary. If he had his way I'd stay inside until things are back to normal. He tried to talk me out of coming here today, though of course he knew he was going to lose that argument." She laughed a little. "The secret is in spoiling him a little, then he gives in. When I let him know I wasn't changing my mind, he drove me down. He was coming down anyway, to see someone. Mike somebody, I think?"

"Mike Kilgore?"

"Yes, that's it. Usually Ted walks into the valley, but he drove to-day because he won't let me make the trip on foot." She laughed. "I could make it down the mountain, but I'm not so sure about making it back up, so he was right about that part."

Huh. Teddy had a good quality that Carol hadn't expected. He loved his wife.

"Are you still taking pain medication?" Meredith asked, chang-ing the subject abruptly. "Barb told me you were taking some of her leftover pills."

"I quit taking them yesterday."

Meredith nodded. "Good. Next time I come down I'll bring a bottle of wine, and we'll break it open after your session." Her eyes sparkled, and she gave a mischievous grin.

Wine. Oh, that would be better than the pain pills! She wasn't much of a drinker, so they didn't have a single bottle in the house, but right about now . . .

She leaned back against the pillows and grinned. "Meredith, I believe you and I are going to be great friends."

CHAPTER TWENTY-TWO

After Ted dropped Meredith at Carol Allen's house—he *knew* he was going to regret giving in, but Meredith's good heart was one of the reasons he loved her—he drove slowly down Myra Road. He wasn't in a hurry to get where he was going, and the patches of snow gave him a reason to creep along. He dreaded what he had to do. He didn't have a choice, but still, basically admitting to Kilgore that he'd been a fool wasn't going to be easy.

Finding the Kilgore house was easy: Mike's truck with *Kilgore Plumbing* on the side, the one he'd been driving the day Ted had stopped him on the road, was parked in the driveway.

Ted pulled to the curb, turned off the engine, and sat for a moment, looking around and postponing the inevitable. The Kilgore house was small but neat, a simply designed blue-gray ranch-style with a decent-sized front porch. There were two rocking chairs on that porch, arranged on either side of a small table with a clay pot and a dead plant sitting on it. In better times, that plant would be well tended. There might be cups of coffee or iced tea, maybe a beer or two, sitting on that table. These were not better times.

The dusting of snow on the ground kind of made him homesick for Ohio, though he was glad he was here and not there. There wasn't enough snow for snowmen, but likely more than a few snowballs would be thrown. The little bit of snow that had fallen was pretty, though. He always looked forward to coming here in the winter, and often hoped to be snowed in.

It snowed plenty in Ohio, but it was never as pretty as it was here, in the mountains and in the valley.

He knew what he had to do, but that didn't make it any less embarrassing. Maybe in the past couple of months he'd pushed too hard, at times—in the name of survival, in an effort to make sure he and Meredith made it through this crisis. His frustration had gotten the best of him more than once, but his intentions had always been good.

The road to hell . . . Yeah. Exactly.

Ted took a deep breath and opened the car door. This wasn't going to get any easier while he sat, so he might as well get it over with. Damn it, not everything he'd done had been wrong! Still, the mistake he'd made—trusting someone like Lawrence—was a doozy.

Mike opened his front door and came out on the porch when Ted was halfway across the yard. The expression on the plumber's face was one of thinly veiled annoyance, likely because of the altercation with Sela Gordon yesterday. Ted imagined she'd have to commit murder or something like that before any of the valley people would take his side over hers. Mike likely expected him to raise hell and cause trouble—and trouble was exactly what Ted was bringing, just not the way Mike expected.

"Kilgore," Ted said in way of greeting, as he walked up the porch steps.

"Parsons," Mike responded.

Ted stopped a couple of feet from the door, planting his feet and steeling his resolve. He didn't much like the taste of crow. "I have some important information, and I wasn't sure who to take it to."

Mike's eyebrows lifted slightly. "And I won?"

It was tempting to give up here and now, to turn around and walk away. He and Meredith could hole up in their house for a while, if they had to. He didn't have to participate in the community patrol or in Lawrence's less-than-legal attempts at forming an alternate organization. Alternate, hell, make that *criminal* organization. There were lots of folks in the area, and elsewhere, who kept to themselves and focused on one thing: getting by. He could do the same.

But it was too late for that. If Lawrence and his gang of meth heads had their way, no one in Wears Valley would be safe.

Ted sighed and met Mike's gaze. "We have a problem."

It was midmorning, and Ben was still there. Sela was beginning to feel guilty for not getting *something* done, but just sitting in front of the fire with him and talking was so deeply satisfying she couldn't make herself call a halt to it. Not that he was a chatterbox—anything he said was said with a purpose, and he was as efficient in his use of words as if he had a set allotment for each day and didn't want to use them all up. She didn't care. She was a quiet person herself, so she was comfortable with not talking. He could be completely silent if he wanted, and she'd still be happy simply being with him.

Reality said they would soon have to leave the house, though; Barb and Olivia could probably use a break from Carol duty, and Ben would have things to do with the community patrol—and he had his own place to see to, his own chores. She didn't ask, but she imagined he might go by the Livingstons' to take them more food and check on the dog.

To hang on to the last minute, though, she made more hot chocolate for them and they settled at her table with their mugs. As she sipped she had the sudden odd feeling that she might never sit here again, that she was a stranger in her own home. Her life had changed, shifted; she didn't know what was coming, only that things were different now. *She* had changed. More than anything she hoped that Ben would be a part of that difference—

Her thoughts were interrupted by footsteps on the back deck. The curtains had all been pulled closed to help keep out the cold, so she couldn't see who the visitor was. Ben was on his feet and her .22 rifle, which she had stood in a corner, was in his hand before she could push back her chair.

There was a knock on the French door and a woman's voice called, "Sela!"

Sela pushed the edge of the curtain aside and peeked out. "It's Mike's wife," she said to Ben, and opened the door. "Leigh! Is anything wrong?" She and Leigh were friendly but not close, ruling out a neighborly visit.

Leigh took a half step inside, spotted Ben with the rifle in his hand. She halted, surprise widening her eyes. "Ah . . . yes, but no one's sick or hurt. Ted Parsons showed up a few minutes ago and Mike wants you to come hear what he has to say. It's important, he said. I can't tell you more, because I was busy in the back and didn't hear what they were talking about."

Sela bit back a groan. She didn't want to deal with Ted, particularly now. She wanted to be alone with Ben, to explore this thing between them; she was happy and content, in a world that was increasingly dangerous and happiness could be precarious and rare. Just thinking about Ted could ruin her mood. The worst of it was, she felt guilty for giving him the finger.

Likely he'd gone to Mike to complain about her behavior. Maybe he was trying to file an official complaint, though the idea of anything "official" these days was ludicrous. What sort of violation would he be thinking of? "Conduct unbecoming," she supposed, and at this point, she could only hope that she'd be found guilty and forcibly removed from her volunteer position. There was always so much to be done, and now she had Ben and while she didn't know for sure where this was going he would definitely require some time and commitment, which she was more than happy to give. She was not only willing but anxious to step aside.

If, that is, there was someone competent to step into her shoes. That wasn't Ted Parsons, and Carol was far from ready to jump back in.

She supposed she'd have to face the music, and stand her ground, and any other cliché she could think of.

"Let's go," Ben said, reaching for their coats. She noticed that he kept the rifle in his hand. "We'll take my truck."

"Through the back is quicker," Sela said, and they went out the deck door with Leigh. The route took them through the backyards of their neighbors, none of whom seemed to be watching because no one hailed them as they walked past. When they reached the Kilgore house they went up the steps of a deck Mike had built himself just last year, to the Kilgore back door, similar to the way Sela's back deck was situated. Ben held her rifle in one hand and her arm with the other, making sure she didn't slip on the thin layer of snow, which was melting and turning slick. She loved the feel of that big rough hand, the strength with which he safeguarded her. Glancing quickly at his expression, which was set and cold, she realized that he, too, expected trouble from Ted, and from the way he looked he was ready to handle it so she wouldn't have to.

If Ted had any sense, he'd take one look at Ben and keep his mouth shut.

Leigh opened the door and led them inside. The situation Sela had been imagining wasn't anything like what they found. Instead of an angry Ted, an exasperated and annoyed Mike, what she saw when they walked into the kitchen was the two men sitting at the table over cups of what looked to be weak coffee. Like Leigh, they were surprised to see Ben with her, but that didn't last long. They had other things on their minds.

"Ted has some important information," Mike said, indicating they take the empty chairs. The table sat six, so there was room for Leigh, too. She took the seat next to Ted, while Sela and Ben sat on the other side of the table facing them.

"What is it?" she asked Ted, her concern evident. Whatever had happened, this wasn't about yesterday. As much as he disliked them, it had to be serious for him to come to them like this.

Ted didn't look at her. He shook his head a little, then looked at Mike. "You tell them."

"All right. Seems as if Lawrence Dietrich went to Ted with a cockamamie story about setting up an alternate community patrol because they didn't like the way things are being done. I guess that's to be expected, nothing is ever going to make everybody happy. But they met yesterday, and Ted noticed some things."

Mike ran through it all, the guy who seemed to be wounded and was limping, what might have been a bullet hole in a bumper, the fact that none of them seemed to be upstanding citizens, and—most important—what Dietrich seemed to want most of all was for Ted to spy on the community patrol and keep him informed of what was going on.

Ben's expression went even colder at Ted's assessment that one of the men had been wounded. "Do you have names?" he asked Ted in a soft tone that raised the hairs on the back of Sela's neck.

Ted still didn't look at them, but he efficiently recited six names. She had never seen him less bellicose. If anything, he seemed embarrassed, though she couldn't think why. Because he'd been interested in an alternate community patrol? She'd have been surprised if he hadn't been.

Six names. That couldn't be a coincidence, that six men had tried to steal the gas and shot at her and Olivia, and now six wanted Ted to spy for them.

"Harley and Trey checked out Lawrence's neighborhood yesterday afternoon and didn't find any damaged vehicles," Ben said, "and Darren and Cam checked out a nearby neighborhood where Patrick lives. They were both at the top of the list of likely suspects, but I expect even tweakers are smart enough to hide any vehicles with bullet holes in them. If you hadn't been alert, we still wouldn't know. What was your assessment, Ted?"

He'd read Ted the same way she had, Sela realized, but he'd led men before and knew the approach to take to help Ted through any awkwardness he felt. They needed to work together now.

Until yesterday, Ben hadn't known any of the community patrol volunteers, but he'd quickly judged those he deemed most competent, as well as those who could be labeled as little more than warm bodies. This was his military experience, allowing him to size people up and make the most of what they could offer. Sure enough, Ted straightened, and for the first time looked at them.

"Wesley didn't seem too smart," he said. "And he was at least halfway drunk, even that early in the day. What I saw was a small bullet hole, low on the bumper. He might not have noticed, or thought it wouldn't matter since it was just his friends at the meeting. If I hadn't been looking for evidence by that point I likely wouldn't have noticed, either."

Sela silently thanked God that Ben was here, because she wouldn't have known how to handle Ted. Just then, beneath the table, his hand settled on her thigh. The touch, the gesture, told her without words that for the first time in a very long time, she wasn't alone. They were a couple, something bigger and greater than any one person could ever be. The sex was great, but this was more than sex. It was connection on a soul deep level, a link she had never expected to understand, much less experience.

She didn't have to handle the worst of this crisis on her own. She wasn't alone anymore, and neither was Ben.

There was a lot of bad blood between her and Ted, but this was too important to be affected by her personal dislike. He'd obviously come to the same conclusion. He didn't have to be here, didn't have to share what he knew, and that meant he was a bigger, better person than she'd expected.

"Thank you," she said quietly. "I know you didn't have to come to us."

Ted still didn't look directly at her, but he nodded in acknowledgment. "They've planned a meeting for tomorrow afternoon, at a vacant building that used to be a craft store of some kind. Near the pizza place. Do I go? Do I stay away?" He shook his head. "I don't know what to do."

"That's all right," Ben said, his gaze going savage. "I do."

They sat around the table with sheets of paper and a couple of pencils. Between Sela, Leigh, and Mike, they could locate the homes of each of the six men, which were spread out but tended to be on the Townsend side of the valley. They drew rudimentary maps, listed the family members they knew of—Mike and Leigh were more useful for that than Sela was, because her natural shyness had kept her from getting to know as many people as they did. Ted was a help; he'd learned a lot on the community patrols. Ben had a natural aptitude for learning his environment and studying it strategically; before the solar storm he'd driven and hiked a large portion of the valley. He didn't know people, but he knew the territory.

"We can't hit their houses," he said, sitting back and tapping a pencil on a page. "We don't know how many kids are in each house, or where they'd be." These men had no care for life and would fight back, regardless of their families being present. Ben didn't want anyone shooting into houses where kids were; he didn't have qualms about the adults, but these kids already had hard lives because of who and what their parents were. Meth addicts—and Mike was certain all of these men were tied to the meth trade—lived for nothing but their next hit, and nothing meant anything to them beyond that next hit. If other people died because of their addiction, they didn't care.

Mike and Ted both nodded in agreement.

"If they all show up for the meeting at the craft store, that'll be our best chance, and will minimize any collateral damage."

"They should be there," Ted said. "According to Lawrence's plan, anyway."

Ben gave a brief nod. "A central meet is more efficient than someone going from house to house, telling everyone what's going on."

Mike and Ted were relatively clueless on the craft store, other than knowing kind of where it was, but Leigh had often bought things there and was able to sketch the floor layout, doors, windows, parking lot, and any buildings or tree stands nearby.

Ben's plan was simple, and even then he expected things to go sideways; they almost always did when guns and people were involved. Mike and Leigh were tasked with visiting chosen patrol members and reading them in on the plan. Ted was to stay far away from any of the other patrol members, so they wouldn't be suspicious of him. Myra Road was out of the way, a small neighborhood with hills and curves, and limited sight lines; the chances were small that he'd have been spotted unless someone had followed him, and he'd have noticed another vehicle on the road behind him because there was no traffic. Despite people having some gasoline now they were still in conservation mode, and driving around wasn't nearly as important as having fuel for generators.

With the plan in place, Ben and Sela walked back to her house. The day had warmed to the point that only thin patches of snow were left, and by afternoon there would be none. "I need to go to my house, get some things," he said. "Want to come along?"

"Yes," she replied, no hesitation. Wherever he was, she wanted to be. "I need to check on Carol, though."

"We can stop on the way." He glanced down at her. "Think I should put on body armor?"

"A chastity belt might keep her from grabbing your goodies." She smiled, because she loved Carol's boisterous personality. There was no telling what name she'd come up with for Ben today, but he hadn't blinked at Stud Muffin so she thought he could handle any other name thrown his way.

"I'll keep you between us. You can be my guard." He patted her butt as they went up the steps to her deck, and the familiar gesture didn't just warm her heart, it melted her insides.

Surprisingly, Carol was on good behavior. She beamed at them. Barb told them about Meredith Parsons being a PTA, and helping Carol with some exercises. Carol also winked at Ben and gave him two thumbs-up, and left them to wonder exactly what she was approving of: the physical therapy, his buns, or the fact that he was with Sela.

Ben's big pickup handled the narrow mountain road without any problem, and the high suspension allowed him to drive right over the big rock in the middle of the driveway that stopped most people. She was astonished that it had been just two days since she'd walked up this steep drive, both terrified and determined.

The house was cold when they went in, but of course he hadn't been here in about thirty-six hours so the fire had gone out. He stopped just inside the door and looked around; intuitively she knew he was thinking about the dog, missing its presence. He'd done a good thing for the Livingstons, giving the dog to them, but at a cost to himself. He didn't say anything about it, though, just efficiently got a fire going in the woodstove. His house wasn't as cold as hers would have been after that length of time without a fire, making her think he'd added to the insulation.

There was a small fireplace in his bedroom, and she wouldn't be surprised if the other bedrooms also had fireplaces. If she remembered correctly, Carol had once mentioned that this house had been a small bed-and-breakfast, which meant bedroom fireplaces were likely. He lit the fire in his bedroom, and also lit a kerosene heater to help warm the house faster.

He didn't wait until the house was warm, though, to start stripping off his clothes. "I need a shower." He looked at her and one of those slow smiles curved his mouth. "Want to help?"

She did, and half an hour later he had just three condoms left.

Of course the bandage on his shoulder got wet so she rebandaged that, this time with more of the butterfly bandages though the wound was closing nicely. She brushed her hair dry, bent over in front of the fireplace, and had just finished when the ham radio set in the bedroom crackled to life and a man's voice recited a series of letters and numbers.

Ben was at the radio almost before she had isolated the direction of the sound, sitting down and grabbing a microphone, reciting his own series of letters and numbers. Then he said, "Good to hear from you, bro."

"You too. How are things there in the wilderness?"

"Stable. People are coping. We've had some trouble, but it's being handled. How about you?"

"We're safe. We settled near a military base. Gen had to stop and go to ground, wait for me to catch up to her, but I managed to get to her before the grid went down. Travel was a clusterfuck. Some bad actors were already doing shit."

Sela moved closer, fascinated by news from the outside. Since the last radio station in Knoxville had stopped transmitting, she had felt isolated here in the valley. Ben reached out an arm and pulled her down onto his knee, and she leaned against him.

"Any good news, or is it all bad?"

"The military is good. They had hardened security, and SMRs. The government is functioning on a very limited basis, and only because the Pentagon was smarter than the bureaucracy assholes. Nothing is online, but the military bases are starting points and work is being done."

"How about Europe? The Far East?"

"Europe is a shit can. Their politicians were worse than ours. Japan, Korea, China—they're getting it together, but it's a long, slow haul. Russia is back in medieval times, and may stay there for a hundred years. There are a few very small electrical companies here in the States that had good foresight and they're functioning, but the people who live in those areas are having to fight for their lives because of all the fuckers moving in and trying to take what they have."

"Are any cities livable?"

"None of the big ones above the Mason-Dixon, that's for sure. Forget all the big cities in California, except San Diego fared better than most. Atlanta, no. Nashville, Memphis, St. Louis, no. I'm not sure anyone in New Orleans noticed the power went off, so I can't say about it. Omaha is better than you'd expect. Denver is trash, Colorado Springs isn't. Makes sense, doesn't it?"

Not to Sela, but she didn't ask.

"What about the weather?"

"Nasty, even this early in the year. It looks bad, especially in the Midwest. I expect a lot of that cold air will come our way, so be ready."

"Casualties?"

"Early estimates . . . most of Europe. Maybe two hundred million are still alive, a fourth of the population. Asia has lost at least a billion, some analysts think more. Africa and South America are doing okay, because of their warm weather, but the big cities were hard hit. Australia, New Zealand are in their warm season now, from what I hear they're growing all the food they can. Here . . . North America has lost between a fourth and a third of the population. That's just since September, a little over two months. It remains to be seen how many people survive the winter, and not just because of the weather."

Sela leaned her head against Ben's shoulder, stricken by what this man was saying. Here in the valley they'd worked hard, they'd done without, but in comparison to what she was hearing they were among the very luckiest.

"You and Gen and the ankle-biters are welcome here, you know."

"We'll come visit when things are better. I'm guessing a year, but it's just a guess based on what I see happening on the military side. Even then, it'll take years for manufacturing to recover, for jobs to come back, fuel pipelines to be functional. Save the seeds from your garden, bro, you're going to be growing your own food for quite a while."

CHAPTER TWENTY-THREE

After she and Ben went back down into the valley, the universe seemed to take pleasure in running her ragged, which Sela supposed was punishment for the lazy morning. She didn't care; she'd gladly work her butt off in exchange for those hours with him.

He'd brought down an impressive collection of weapons with him, and after dropping her off at Carol's, he left to make contact with others in the patrol unit.

As soon as she walked into the house, she was bombarded. Carol wanted her to come into the bedroom to keep her company, which Sela interpreted as meaning she wanted the skinny on what had or had not happened with Ben. Olivia was bored, and Sela's arrival freed her to make the longish walk to a friend's house. Barb was trying to cook, clean, and take care of Carol, which even with Olivia's help was a lot on her plate. And laundry needed to be done.

Oh hell. Of all the things that being without electricity had made daily life more physically difficult, laundry was at the top of the list.

"It's a trade-off," she said to Barb. "We can run the generator long enough to wash the clothes, then hang them to dry. Using the generator means that down the road we'll have less fuel for hot showers. What do we choose?"

"Washing ourselves is easier than washing clothes," Barb said with impeccable logic.

"Done."

They started the generator and Sela began doing the laundry. Funny—the washing machine felt like such a luxury now that she actually enjoyed using it. When she stepped back into the living area, Barb said, "Breakfast was really good this morning. That bacon was excellent, the best I've ever had." She winked at Sela. "Too bad you missed it."

Sela felt her face heating up, but she smiled and said, "I didn't miss it. We had bacon, too." *We.* How extraordinary, and how wonderful, that she and Ben were now *we.*

"*What?*" Carol bellowed from her bedroom.

Sela rolled her eyes at Barb. "How on earth did she hear that from her bedroom?"

"Superpower," Barb replied, grinning. She turned back to the supper she was cooking. After her initial shock at the crisis, and fear of the unknown, Barb had settled in; cooking was *her* superpower, and Sela had the thought that without her they wouldn't be eating nearly as well as they were.

"Sela Gordon! You come give me the skinny about him right now, or I swear I'll crawl out of this bed and come in there!"

She would, too; a determined Carol Allen was a force to be reckoned with. But Sela was chuckling as she went into Carol's bedroom, because it wasn't as if she intended to keep her relationship with Ben a secret. She'd barely settled in and started answering Carol's barrage of questions when someone knocked on the door, then Barb and Nancy appeared in the doorway.

"We need to run something by you," Nancy said to Sela.

And that was the real start of the busy day. Nancy, bless her, had taken it on herself to get with Mona Clausen and design the braziers, based on an entry they'd looked up in an ancient set of *World Book Encyclopedias.* That was one less thing Sela had to do, but they wanted her approval. By the time that was finished and Nancy was gone, the washer was finished with its cycle and she took the clothes outside to hang them on the clothesline to dry.

While she was doing that, a kindergarten teacher who Carol had contacted walked up and wanted to begin organizing the curriculum for the school-in-planning. She helped Sela finish hanging the clothes, then they went inside for a four-way confab with Carol and Barb.

Next one of the community pastors came knocking. Brother Ames was in his seventies, looked kind of like a skinny Santa Claus now that he was growing out a white beard, and he had a lot on his mind.

"People are going to want to get married, but there aren't any marriage licenses now. Babies will need to be recorded, but we don't have birth certificates—and, mark my words, starting in about seven months we're going to have a population boom here in the valley. When the lights go out and the television goes off, people find other ways to entertain themselves. How do you want to handle these issues?"

Sela gaped at him. Somehow she didn't think "community leader" was intended to be in charge of things like this. Marriages, divorces, and births were legal issues, state issues . . . and there were no functioning local governments now. Holy crap.

It wasn't just Brother Ames who would be asking; there were other churches in the valley, other pastors. Someone needed to make a decision. Sela wanted to take him into Carol's bedroom and turn him over to her aunt, but Carol was taking a nap.

There was something really serious that would be going down tomorrow, she felt as if she should be concentrating on that, but she couldn't breathe a word about it to anyone—and even in the middle of big drama, the small dramas of life went on. People would be born, and people would die. There would be marriages and divorces—

well, maybe not divorces, though people could break up and stop living together—regardless of whether or not there was a functioning government, and everything needed to be recorded.

"Get a notebook," she said. "Or one of those big scrapbooks. It doesn't matter what you use, but records have to be kept. We'll do what people did when all of this was the business of the churches, before politicians stuck their noses in. You perform marriage ceremonies, and you record them. Same with births: they need to be written down, baptize the babies if the parents want."

Brother Ames looked massively relieved. "I was hoping you'd say that. We've been talking about this—the other pastors and I—and that was the only way to handle the situation that we could think of, but we wanted some guidelines we could all follow, so we're on the same page."

She wondered why, in that case, they hadn't drawn up their own guidelines, but people had gotten accustomed to government making those decisions for them. She sincerely doubted the state would have her arrested for "authorizing" a system, so she might as well be the one to give the go-ahead. "When everything is up and running again, and that may be years, I doubt the state will take the position that all the marriages made during that time are illicit. That would be a really stupid, unpopular position to take. So treat everything as seriously as you would before. I can guarantee you that, as far as the people here in the valley are concerned, any marriage ceremony you perform is just as legal without electricity as it was with it."

"Bless you," said Brother Ames.

Then another neighbor showed up asking about the physical therapist who had been working with Carol, because her dad was down in his back again. Barb came to her rescue and told her about Meredith Parsons.

And so it went, for the rest of the day. Perhaps people just wanted to touch base after the traumatic events at the store, maybe they hoped for some gossip, but every visit ate up time and, for someone like Sela who found socializing exhausting, was very wearing. Carol woke up and wanted answers to her questions. Olivia returned, more cheerful after the time spent with her friend.

Darkness came, Barb put supper on the table, and Ben still hadn't returned. Sela took a meal tray in to Carol, who scowled at her. "Where's Ben? I want to eat at the table."

"He had a lot to do," Sela said, trying not to act worried, but she knew what was going on and she couldn't help fretting. What if Lawrence Dietrich got wind, somehow, that Ted had come to Mike? The sound of gunfire carried a long way and she thought she'd have heard any shots, but that didn't stop her from continually checking out the window, looking for headlights coming down the lane. She wanted him here. She wanted to be with him.

And then he was there. She saw the reflection of headlights on the window, the sound of the big truck pulling into the driveway. She was on the porch before he could reach it. He came up the steps and headed off any questions with a murmured, "I'll fill you in later," then pulled her close with a steely arm around her waist for a hard, hungry kiss.

Barb was already setting a place at the table for him when they went inside. From her bedroom Carol called, "Ben? I need help!"

Ben looked at Sela and cocked an eyebrow. "She called me by my name. What's up with that?"

"She wants something from you."

"I heard that!"

"You hear everything," Sela countered. Ben went into the bedroom and came out with Carol in his arms, and her carefully balancing her dinner tray. He set her down at the table and took his place, eating quickly and efficiently while they chatted around him. Things proceeded pretty much the same as they had the night before, as if a routine had been immediately established. While Sela and Barb cleaned up after supper, he brought in enough firewood to get them through the night, and even collected the still-damp clothes from the clothesline. He and Olivia hung the clothes where she directed, on an old folding clothes rack that Barb had dug out of storage at her house. They tried not to use it because it took up so much room in the living room, but sometimes it was necessary.

As he scooped Carol up to take her back into the bedroom, Sela thought of something and said, "Let me get some coffee to take home with me."

"I brought some from my house," Ben said over his shoulder as he maneuvered Carol through the doorway.

"That's good," they heard Carol say. "I like a man who's prepared." There was a pause, then she continued, "What else are you prepared for?"

"Everything, ma'am. I was a Marine. I'm prepared for everything."

Sela buried her face in her hands, torn between groaning and laughing. She didn't dare look at Olivia, though there was no escaping Barb's playful elbow jab.

"That, Sweet Buns, is the best answer you could have given."

When he exited the bedroom he wasn't smiling, but his eyes were crinkled with amusement.

Sela was so tired her feet were dragging, but she forgot about that as they said their goodbyes and went out to the truck. "How did your day go?" he asked as he opened the passenger door and lifted her bodily onto the seat.

"Busy."

He went around and got in the driver's seat, and she outlined her day just as if they'd been a couple forever. She quickly told him about Brother Ames, and the only solution she'd been able to think of for the marriage problem, the long parade of people who'd needed/

wanted to talk to her, but she wasn't interested in her day. As they pulled into her driveway she asked about the Dietrich situation.

He outlined the plan as he got two big duffle bags from the back of the truck. He, Trey, Mike, and Cam would be hidden in position an hour before the scheduled meeting at the old crafts store. With luck, they'd capture all six without bloodshed. Without luck, there would be bloodshed. Before she could latch on to the possibility of bloodshed he told her about stopping by the Livingston place to see the dog, and take them some more food.

"He—Sajack—seemed happy. He ran to me and acted like he wanted to leave when I did, but Mary Alice patted her lap and called him and he went right back to her. You can tell she already dotes on him."

And he missed the dog. He didn't have to say it. She gave him a quick hug before they went inside.

The night proceeded much like the one before it had, with him building up the fire and moving the mattress into the living area. He unpacked the duffle bags, laying out an impressive array of weapons, which he inspected by lamplight though she knew, since the weapons belonged to him, that they were already in excellent condition. But he was thorough, and he knew what he was doing.

She was so tired, and content to sit and read while he worked. She glanced at the clock once and saw that it was barely eight-thirty. Both the book and her eyelids got heavy, and with a sigh she rested her head against the back of the couch and closed her eyes, just for a minute. The next thing she knew he was lifting her in his arms, and when she looked again at the clock it was after nine.

"I didn't mean to doze off," she murmured.

"If you're too tired we can—"

She interrupted him. "You're kidding, right?"

"Most definitely." He gave her that small, delicious smile of his and her heart lurched wildly. They undressed each other—not as frantically as they had the night before, but their pace wasn't leisurely, either.

Foreplay was limited to the fierce caresses they shared before lying down; he rolled onto his back, pulled her on top of him, and without hesitation she gripped his penis and guided him inside her. She felt as if her entire body tightened around him, so intense was the feel of him, big and hot, deep inside. She groaned aloud as she leaned back, intensifying the contact. His big hands closed over her breasts, rough thumbs rubbing over her nipples, then he moved his grip to her hips and rocked her back and forth.

Her climax hit so fast and hard that it took her by surprise. Dimly, from the depths of wrenching pleasure, she heard her own high, soaring cries and was astonished at herself. She'd never been a yeller . . . until Ben. Everything about him pulled her out of herself, took her to new places even though those places were all in her head.

When she collapsed limply on his chest he rolled with her, tucked her under him, and stroked deep into her. He had enough control to hold on until she came again, then with a low, harsh sound he let himself go.

Lying together in front of the fire, nested in the blankets, was one of the best things she'd ever known in her life. His hand moved slowly up and down her bare back, gently massaging her vertebrae, stroking over her butt. She rested her head on his chest and listened to his heartbeat, acutely aware of both his strength and the fragility of life.

"Stop worrying," he said, pulling her closer and kissing her temple.

"I didn't say a word," she protested, tilting her head back to look at him.

"You didn't have to."

She didn't argue, because what was the use? Instead she concentrated on this moment, the *now*. They were naked beneath the covers, wonderfully warm on a cold night, skin to skin, legs tangled. The fire had died down to a quiet crackle of low flames, just warm enough. In the now, she couldn't have asked for anything more.

All it had taken to get her here was the end of the world as she knew it.

After a while he said, "What you told that preacher . . ."

"Common sense."

"It was." He paused. "We'll be out of condoms soon. And I don't want to stop . . . this." His hand moved along her hip, her thigh.

Her breath sighed out of her. "I don't, either."

"We should get married." His voice was rough. "Don't say anything yet. Think about it, and think hard. I'm not— I'll try to change, but I'm not an easy person to live with. There are days when I just want to be left alone."

Electricity ran through Sela and she rose up on one elbow, her eyes huge as she stared at him in the firelight. He'd asked her to marry him. He'd *proposed*. Her heart pounded and her lips parted, but he put a finger across them. "I meant it. Don't say anything yet. This is serious business, and you need to think about it."

She buried her face against his shoulder to stifle the giggles that rose in her throat. So the worst he could think of was that some days he wanted to be left alone? So did she. They each needed to be alone for different reasons, but she imagined that need for quiet would give them a peaceful life together. But if he wanted to wait for an answer, she would wait. Perhaps he needed the time to accustom himself to the idea, even though he was the one who had broached the subject.

Marriage. To him. Yes, please. Oh hell yes. Yes to the nth degree. Yes yes yes.

They lay quietly together. When she glanced up at him he was staring into the fire, his gaze distant. Proposing marriage was serious business, but she strongly suspected his thoughts had already moved on to the possible firefight looming tomorrow. People could get killed. He knew more about that, probably, than anyone else in the valley. Whatever battles he'd been in, he still carried them with him.

She could lose him tomorrow.

It was a special kind of hell, loving someone who was on the front line. Pride mingled with quiet terror, knowing that their second night together could be their last night together. Her hands tightened on him, her fingers digging into the hard muscles of his back.

His hand moved between her legs, rough fingers probing. "I can distract you for a while."

Sela closed her eyes, sighed out a soft breath. "Yes, you can."

Then he was inside her, moving, making her forget the world beyond this bed. His growling voice murmured against her ear, "I can't get enough of you."

Her orgasm rocked her to her core, and Ben was right behind her.

CHAPTER TWENTY-FOUR

An hour before Lawrence's scheduled meeting, Ben, Mike, Trey, and Cam were in place around the deserted crafts building, which was literally no more than a mile, as the crow flies, from Sela's house. The curvy, hilly roads made it seem farther than it was. The layout of the surroundings was just as Leigh Kilgore had described it, providing them with adequate cover. He had weighed the anonymity of walking in, using the terrain as cover, against the benefit of having vehicles nearby in case they needed to get somewhere fast. He'd opted for driving to a barn about half a mile away and concealing their vehicles there.

He could've used more men, definitely, but the more who knew about the plan the more likely it was someone would say the wrong thing to the wrong person, deliberately or by accident, it didn't matter. Not only that, concealment for more than four would have gotten exponentially more difficult. Four men were enough, in Ben's opinion, and he instinctively trusted the other three, as well as the two guarding Carol's house and the women in it.

Harley and Darren were guarding Carol's house, where the women waited. Ben didn't expect trouble, but damned if he wouldn't plan for it. These fuckers had nearly killed Sela once, and once was enough.

There was no cover at the front of the building, a single-story dark-wood box that looked very much like a cheaply built mountain house. There was a faded sign near the road, advertising arts and crafts, as well as homemade jam. He didn't know how long the business had been closed, but it had been long enough for bushes to grow up to the windows on the side, and for that sign to weather so much you had to be right up on it to read the words. Ben and the men he had chosen to be here were situated at the back and to both sides. Those who were positioned on the side could see most of the entrance, the front steps and most of the wide, rustic porch. The parking lot was in full view.

Ten minutes before the scheduled meet, Wesley and a second man arrived, went into the store. Ben couldn't connect all the names with the faces, but Mike could. That didn't do him any good, since Mike was on the other side of the building. They had walkies, but they were for emergency only; in such close proximity, no sense in taking a chance that someone would hear.

A few minutes later two others arrived, and one of them had a pronounced limp. That had to be Patrick, the man Olivia—or Sela—had wounded during the attack on her store.

The time to meet came and went, and no Lawrence. There was one other man other than Lawrence who hadn't arrived, but Ben didn't know which one that might be. By process of elimination, he guessed it was Lawrence's brother, Jeremy, who was also absent.

He didn't like it. He began to get an uneasy feeling, because the man who had called the meeting wasn't there. This wasn't good.

Ted pulled into the gravel lot, parked crookedly, and sat in his car for a moment before he opened the door and got out. The man would make a lousy spy. He was pale, and even from here Ben could tell he was jittery.

Ted's job was to get the group outside, all together, either by calling an end to the meeting or taking it to the front porch. In the open, Ben and the members of the community patrol who surrounded the building would surround and capture the group. There was some debate about what to do with them afterward. To kill them would be murder, under the existing—if currently unavailable—law. If they arrested the men, where would they be housed? Not only did Wears Valley not have a jail, but detaining them would make the community responsible for feeding them and keeping them warm for however long was necessary, likely at least a year and probably longer, until they could be turned over to whatever kind of law enforcement resumed activities first.

As far as Ben was concerned, there were two options: execution, or banishment. These men were a menace, but so far they hadn't done anything that warranted a death sentence. The best solution he could come up with was to split the group and drive them in several different directions, drop them off with no weapons and a day's worth of food, and be done with them. They'd end up being trouble for someone else, but he couldn't worry about that. He had to concentrate on keeping his own little corner of the world safe.

They'd shot at Sela and Olivia. They had to go, one way or another.

A few more minutes ticked past, and still no Lawrence or Jeremy. Had they smelled something wrong? Or were they just delayed, for one reason or another? For that matter, they were meth addicts; God only knows what could have sidetracked them.

The waiting was eating at him. He'd sat for days in ambush with more patience than he had as he waited to get his hands on Lawrence Dietrich.

Gunfire reverberated inside the building, shattering the quiet. Ben leaped to his feet and charged toward the building, the four of them converging on it, two toward the front door, two at the back.

Ben went in first, with Mike right behind him. From the rear of the building came the sound of splintering wood as Cam and Trey began breaking through the locked back door.

Four of the men, all gathered in the main room near what had once been a checkout counter, were caught by surprise. All four were armed, one with a rifle, the other three with handguns. Ted was on his back, on the floor, writhing and screaming, "Wait! No!" He was bleeding heavily from a wound high on his chest, and Ben knew immediately his situation wasn't good. Patrick had his rifle aimed at Ted's head, about to finish the job.

Patrick swung his rifle toward Ben and Mike, and Ben fired the shotgun. The heavy slug would drop a deer, and it knocked Patrick back several feet before he crashed into an empty display rack, then collapsed to the floor. The other three men scattered like cockroaches, not knowing where to go with men coming in both the front and back doors. But they didn't go down easy, they were shooting as they scattered. Ben was faster than any of them, his reactions pure instinct honed by years of training. Wesley fired and missed, then Ben shot him between the eyes. He sprawled backward, dead before he hit the floor. Mike's aim wasn't as good as Ben's, but he got one man in the arm. The guy screamed and spun to the side, dropped down, raised his pistol again.

Cam shot but his aim was high and wide. Trey went down on one knee and coolly took down the wounded man armed with the pistol, but not before the man got off a shot at Mike. Mike stumbled and went down. Cam kicked the wounded man's arm, sent the pistol flying.

Ears ringing, nose and eyes stinging from the smoke, Ben swiftly knelt beside Mike and checked how bad he was wounded. The wound was in the fleshy part of the chest just under his arm, likely not life-threatening as long as there wasn't infection, but painful as hell.

"How you doing?" he asked casually, pulling his knife from his pocket and slicing off the bottom of Mike's shirt to make a cloth pad. Taking a pack of blood-clotting powder from the cargo pocket in his pants, he sprinkled some over the wound then covered it with the cloth pad and pressed hard.

"Pretty shitty," Mike answered, his voice raspy.

"Look out!" Ted half shouted, half groaned. Ben spun on his knee; Patrick had struggled to a partial sitting position, despite the massive wound to his chest, and was struggling to steady his rifle. Ben rolled into the clear, and fired again. Patrick shuddered and lay still, the rifle falling from his limp hand. This time the fucker was dead, but Ben cursed at himself for not checking to make sure the first time. This time, he went over and picked up the rifle, though he was damn sure Patrick was dead now.

Three men dead, and three injured.

Swiftly Ben checked Ted, who had gone still. He was unconscious now, which was probably for the best. Ben tore open his shirt, and cussed under his breath. Ted's wound was much worse than Mike's; in different times, with a hospital nearby, he'd have about a 50/50 chance. With only rudimentary medical care available, Ben didn't think he'd make it. Nevertheless he swiftly did what he could with the same rough first aid he'd used on Mike. Frothy air bubbles in the wound told him Ted's lung had been hit.

"How is he?" Mike asked, panting as he tried to struggle to his feet.

Ben silently shook his head and took Mike's arm on his uninjured side, heaved him upright.

Urgency was still gnawing at him. He went over to where Trey was holding a weapon on the other wounded man, and dropped to his haunches beside him. "Where's Lawrence?"

The man just laughed. That short laugh was followed by a raspy cough, a groan. He didn't look good, and Ben wasn't going to waste any clotting powder or sympathy on him.

Mike edged closer, hunched over against the pain. "Come on, Kyle. No point in being loyal to Dietrich, he'd throw you to the wolves without thinking twice. What the hell are you doing here anyway?"

Kyle grimaced. "I always liked you, Mike, but this mess . . . I don't want to die. I don't want to starve to death, and I sure as fuck don't want to sit back and let folks who don't give a shit about me and mine tell me what to do. Lawrence's plan seemed like a good one. No point in letting someone else have it all."

Mike shook his head. "You didn't want to have to do without your drugs, and you saw this as a way to make sure you didn't have to. I knew your mama. She'd be ashamed."

Kyle sneered. If he'd cared what his mama thought, he wouldn't have gotten in with Dietrich. He cast a glance at Ted, then back up at Ben. "Lawrence thought Parsons there might go soft on us, so we've been watching him for the past couple of days. You think you've won, but just you wait. Lawrence and Jeremy are taking care of those women." He laughed again, choked hard, and then he stopped breathing.

Ben surged to his feet, hell burning in his eyes. He hit the door at a run, cursing every second it would take him to get to his truck.

Sela.

Sela paced in Carol's living room. This had been the longest afternoon of her life. She hated waiting, and she hated worrying even more.

Ben was in harm's way, and the knowledge filled her with cold dread. He could handle himself better than anyone she knew or had ever known, and still she worried about him. She always would. That was what loving someone meant, and she had chosen to love someone who wouldn't hesitate when the hard things had to be done. Had anyone ever worried about him before today? He gave the impression that no worry was necessary. He was tough as nails, capable of handling any crisis, he needed nothing and no one.

But everyone needed someone to worry about them. She was Ben's someone, would always be his someone.

If all went well, this would be over quickly. If all didn't go well, she was prepared—not to lose Ben, but to protect her family as best she could. Nerve-ridden, she'd brought her .22 rifle with her, not wanting to be helpless. She wasn't walking around with it in her hand but it was close by. She didn't think she'd need it, prayed she wouldn't need it, but she'd brought it in case she did.

Meredith, Carol, and Barb were in Carol's bedroom, Carol propped up in bed, Meredith and Barb in the dining chairs they'd dragged in there so they could sit beside her. They were drinking wine out of tiny paper cups, sipping, savoring, being careful not to consume too much. Carol insisted they had to be clearheaded, in case things went south . . . like those three would be so much help if there was trouble. Carol had just that morning used the crutches to get herself to the portable potty by herself, but the effort had been very awkward and painful.

Now and then Sela heard them laughing. Well, why not? They were drinking wine, tiny cups notwithstanding. They were talking about how things had changed and what other changes could be coming their way. Barb had been giving Meredith tips about cooking in the fireplace, a skill everyone was developing and expanding on.

There were two members of the community patrol stationed to stand guard outside the house. Harley was at the front, Darren had been posted at the back door. Ben was experienced enough in combat to know things never went the way they'd been planned, and you never knew which way a rat would run. In the way of losers, Lawrence likely blamed Sela for what had happened at the store, therefore in his mind she was the enemy. However the confrontation at the craft store went, Lawrence would blame Sela, and if he somehow escaped . . .

Olivia sat on the couch. Right after Ben and the others had left, Olivia had walked around with Carol's .22 in her hands, looking almost comically determined. Like Sela, she had eventually relaxed and set the weapon aside, in a corner near the stairway. What did it say about their world now that Olivia was just fifteen, but this wasn't her first rodeo. She'd already proven that she could handle herself in a crisis.

All was quiet. Maybe nothing had happened yet. Maybe everything had gone so smoothly not a single shot had been fired. If and when they heard gunfire, from the direction of the meeting place or from any other direction, those rifles would be in their hands, and ready.

Sela checked the clock, paced in front of the dying fire, sat by Olivia for maybe half a minute before popping back up to continue her nervous pacing.

Nothing would happen. Ben would take care of the men who were planning to create their own criminal enterprise, and that would be that.

Nothing would happen. Ben would knock on the front door any minute now, and tell her it had been a piece of cake.

Nothing would happen. The universe would not be so cruel as to take away Ben when she'd just found him.

Sela took a deep breath, calming herself, then went to the fireplace to add some wood and poke at the embers to make them flare.

In the distance, she heard gunfire, a lot of gunfire. Olivia jumped off the couch at the noise, and headed toward the stairs to retrieve her .22. Sela whirled toward her own rifle, across the room. Before either of them could reach their weapons the front door was kicked in and Lawrence Dietrich stepped into the room.

Beyond him, through the open door, Sela saw Harley's still body. There was blood on the porch, on Dietrich's sleeve and boots, as well as down the front of his heavy jacket.

"Ladies," Dietrich said. He was smiling as he pointed his rifle at Sela.

Sela's blood froze, but somehow she kept functioning. She motioned for Olivia to go to Carol's bedroom, and after a moment's hesitation the girl obeyed, walking backward, taking small steps until she was inside the room. Carol shouted out, "What's going on out there?" Olivia whispered an urgent answer, and Carol went silent.

Sela didn't look at the .22 that was closest to her but she knew exactly where it was, and exactly how far away. It wasn't close enough, not nearly close enough. Even if she could reach it, she wouldn't have a chance in a close gunfight with Lawrence and his hunting rifle, which he was already aiming at her. Bullets went through walls. If he started shooting, the women in Carol's bedroom would be in the line of fire. There had to be another way. She didn't see it, but there had to be, if she could just keep calm and stay alive.

Lawrence kept the barrel pointed at Sela as he went to the back door and opened it, letting his brother Jeremy inside. While the door was open, she caught a glimpse of a still shoe. Darren was down, too. Dead or injured she couldn't know, not from that one shoe. At least Jeremy wasn't covered in blood.

At his brother's direction, Jeremy collected both .22s and placed them even farther away from Sela, propping them near the front door, while Lawrence edged around so that his back was to Carol's bedroom. Through the open door Sela caught sight of Meredith easing forward furtively. Good Lord, was that a *vase* in her hand? Meredith had guts, but—a vase? Sela caught Meredith's eye and shook her head slightly, warning her to stay back. This could go sideways fast, with one wrong move.

"I guess you heard those gunshots," Lawrence said. "I wonder what it means? Who survived? Your guys or mine? If it was mine, which I 'spect it was because I thought something like that might happen and we were ready, then your ass is in a sling. Oh, wait. Your ass is in a sling anyway because I've got this"—he lifted the rifle a little—"and you don't. Boo-hoo. Too bad for you I didn't trust Parsons. Wish I could have, I've always been a fan of doing things the easy way, but this time . . . this time it was a mistake."

He swung his rifle to the side and, for a moment, pointed it toward the front door before again taking aim at Sela. "I hope that son of a bitch Jernigan comes running to the rescue, any minute now."

Sela lifted a stilling hand, as if she could ward off a bullet. "Why?" she asked. Talk. Get him to talk, keep him talking. She needed to buy some time.

"So he can watch me blow your face off before I take him out," Lawrence answered with a sly grin. "We were going to have to do something about him ASAP, anyway. Once he got involved I knew he'd be a huge pain in my ass."

"No, why do any of this? You and your friends were all going to get a share of the gas. We've gone to a lot of trouble to make sure that everyone will get by. It won't be easy, but if we stick together we can all survive this." She tried to sound merely bewildered, not angry, not threatening in any way.

She had just lied. Not everyone would survive. Even in the before world, with electricity and modern medicine and conveniences, not everyone survived. Now their existence was much more precarious.

But Ben was a survivor. In any halfway even fight, she'd put her money on him. Lawrence thought his guys had won, but she didn't. Ben was on his way, she knew it. If she could just stall Lawrence long enough . . .

Dietrich laughed. "Your pissy little five-gallon limit of gasoline was going to work magic? We need more gasoline than you were going to give us. We need to be able to make short trips into other areas, and we'd like to be able to get home again."

"Trips?" Raids, more likely.

He made a mocking half dip of his head. "Some of us need more than canned beans. My wife, Zoe, she needs her pills. She's a nervous wreck without them. There's a basement weed farm in Maryville I'd like to visit. And who knows what kind of stash some of the folks right here in Wears Valley have? With all the trauma and stress, why, we can make a small fortune in the weed business, and there's a fortune in meth—but I needed that gas, and you fucked up everything. Why couldn't you have stayed your ass at home, instead of sitting in the store in the dark? Now I'll have to go from house to house to get it. Some people are going to get hurt, and it's all your fault, but you're just a bump in the road. I'm going to get through this mess and come out the other side a rich man."

"But people will die—"

"Not my problem." He'd reached Carol's bedroom door, and glanced over his shoulder into the room. What did he see, what was going on in there? Was Meredith still holding the vase? Carol would still be in bed, and frantic, because they would all have heard what Dietrich had said. What was Olivia doing? Olivia was the wild card, and she'd been involved in the gunfight at the store. She might try to jump Dietrich from behind. But, thank God, after looking inside the bedroom Dietrich began edging away again, back toward where Sela stood in the middle of the room.

"Jeremy," he said, grinning at Sela, "take care of the ladies in the bedroom."

Jeremy steered well clear of Sela as he circled around, walked to the door, and looked into Carol's room. "You mean, tie 'em up?"

"No, that is not what I mean," Lawrence said sharply. "When you stage a coup you wipe out the previous administration. Take care of it."

"But—"

"Gut 'em or shoot 'em. Your choice."

Horror filled her at his words. Jeremy paled, and it wasn't her imagination. She knew nothing about him other than he was

Lawrence's brother, and she wouldn't have known that much if not for Ted. Was he the kind of man who would do as his brother ordered, no matter what?

She had to do something, anything. She tensed, nothing on her mind except blindly rushing Lawrence and taking her chances with that rifle. If she could distract both men for just a little while, not even a minute, maybe the others could escape, maybe they could barricade the door—*anything*.

Jeremy let his arm drop to his side. He was still holding his rifle, but he wasn't aiming it at anyone. "I'm not killing a bunch of old women and a kid."

Lawrence erupted in fury, spinning toward his brother. "Damn it, you always were a pussy. I'll do it myself!"

Planning required calculation, and she didn't have time for that. She simply leaped, driven by desperation. She tackled Lawrence from behind, driving her shoulder into his hips. He staggered but didn't go down; she grabbed at his legs and jerked, lost her own balance, and sprawled hard on the floor. Her face was nauseatingly close to the blood-splattered boots. He stumbled again, recovered again, and still didn't fall. She grabbed one of his ankles and jerked, then drew her legs up and kicked as hard as she could, catching him behind the knee.

He grunted and stumbled forward again, but *the son of a bitch still didn't go down*. Sobbing, desperate, she tried to scramble to her feet.

Lawrence turned around and pushed her, hard; she landed on her back, the breath knocked out of her. He kicked her in the side, on the thigh, cursing at her with each blow. The pain was excruciating, paralyzing. Dimly she thought she should fight through it, but at the moment all she could do was curl up and cover her head with her arms.

Jeremy backed away from the bedroom door, hands up in a way

that indicated he wasn't getting involved. Over Lawrence's shoulder Sela glimpsed a blur of movement. Meredith rushed forward with the vase in her hand, while Barb—Barb!—was swinging one of Carol's crutches. Olivia had the other one.

Sela rolled away, somehow finding the strength, desperately hoping Lawrence's attention would stay on her and he wouldn't notice the poorly armed women. She came to a stop against the couch and could go no farther. Lawrence came toward her like a demon, his expression twisted with rage. She closed her eyes, waiting for the gunshot that would end her, or another savage kick. Maybe she hadn't been able to save herself, but maybe the others could make it out, somehow. *Ben.* His name echoed in her mind.

The sound of the blast was deafening.

She didn't feel anything. What—?

She opened one eye and saw Lawrence in a boneless, awkward heap a couple of yards away. Weakly she struggled to her knees, not understanding and wanting nothing more than to get away while she could. Then there was a blur of movement and Ben dropped down to wrap his arms around her, hugging her tightly to him.

"Are you hurt?" he asked, his voice raw and close, so wonderfully close.

"I thought he was going to kill me," she said numbly, still dazed and not with the program at all.

"Are you hurt?"

"He was going to kill us all, Carol and Olivia and—"

"*Are you hurt?*" Ben bellowed.

She blinked, looked up into those blazing, beautiful green eyes. "No." That was a lie. Her side was on fire where Lawrence had kicked her, and her leg was numb. She expected that would change any minute now, and she'd really miss the numbness. But she wasn't dead, she wasn't shot, and both of those were big pluses.

He helped her to her feet, never letting go. That was fine with her, because her leg wouldn't hold her weight right now. She had no intention of letting go of him anytime soon, anyway.

Lawrence was definitely dead, half of his face missing. Sela turned her face into Ben's shoulder, sickened by the sight. Jeremy stood to one side, disarmed, pale, his focus on the rifle Trey held on him, rather than on the raised vase and wooden crutches that were also threatening him.

"Lawrence told Jeremy to kill the others, but he wouldn't do it," she said into Ben's shirt, afraid they were going to execute Jeremy on the spot. Maybe they should; she didn't know what else he'd done, if Darren was injured or dead, if Harley, who'd been at the front door when Lawrence had arrived, was alive or dead. All she knew was that if Jeremy had done as his brother ordered, Ben and Trey wouldn't have arrived in time to save anyone.

The stench of death was strong in the room. Olivia rushed at her, crying; Ben didn't release her, just pulled Olivia in and held her, too.

Sela tried to think of practical matters, tried to turn her thoughts away from the death that surrounded them, but for right now she was both numb and filled with a relief that pushed out everything else. Ben was alive. Carol, Olivia, Barb, and Meredith were all alive. She'd been prepared for the worst, the worst hadn't happened, and she hadn't yet adjusted.

It was Barb who sucked in a deep breath, surveyed the dead man on the floor, and said, "It'll take forever to get this mess cleaned up."

In the bedroom, Carol was crying with harsh, throat-scraping sobs. Olivia pulled free and ran into the bedroom to her grand-mother. "It's okay, Gran," they heard her say. "It's over. We're fine."

"Fine" was a stretch—a big stretch.

Other men, both members of the patrol and their own close neigh-bors, came into the house, one after another. Ben deposited Sela at the table, and Barb brought her some water. Sela listened to their whispered conversations. Darren had been coldcocked but would be okay, and was sitting up . . . but Harley was dead. Lawrence had cut his throat; he'd never had a chance.

Harley . . . Tears stung Sela's eyes, and she stared down into the glass of water. He'd been such a good guy, always willing to help in any way he could. He'd been the one who would stop on the highway to aid strangers with car trouble, the one who smoked briskets and took them to families in need.

If Lawrence could die again, she thought she'd tear him apart.

Jeremy's hands were bound with zip ties, and a couple of the men roughly took him out of the house. Sela didn't know where they were taking him and didn't care.

Meredith looked around the room, her eyes wide, her expression drawn with worry. "Where's Ted?"

Ben took a deep breath, then sighed. He reached out and put his big hand on her shoulder. "He's been shot."

Meredith sucked in a ragged breath and slow tears dripped down her white face. "How bad is it?"

"Bad," Ben said reluctantly. "He's still alive, but—I'm sorry."

CHAPTER TWENTY-FIVE

The valley community reeled in the aftermath of the violence. Five of the six who'd plotted to take over were dead, but what would they do with Jeremy? He'd refused to kill the women at Carol's, but he'd hit Darren in the head hard enough that Terry Morris, the medic, was worried. So far Darren was hanging in, but if he died that was murder. They were all hoping it was no worse than a concussion, something he could recover from.

Losing Harley hit Ben hard. He'd lost too many men in combat, but Harley had been a civilian, and that made it harder. He'd never intended to get to know any of the people here, yet here he was, up to his neck in their lives. He'd liked Harley. The man had been willing to do anything and everything for the community, and he'd paid for that with his life, in the same way any soldier might.

Living in a world where there was no law had its challenges. No, there still had to be law. Somehow, some way. These people were his people now. Sela was his, her family was his, her community was his. As bad as it had been driving down the mountain in the dark when he'd heard gunshots at her store, that was nothing compared to how he'd felt when he'd come through the door and seen her on the floor, Dietrich aiming a rifle at her. His vision had gone to red mist, and his heart had stopped. He still wasn't over the sheer terror of that moment, especially now that he knew Dietrich had kicked her and she was hurt. She was moving around, but gingerly. He'd been kicked a few times himself, and it was brutal. He wanted to pick her up and hold her on his lap, just hold her, but after a few minutes of shock she'd gathered herself and taken charge in that quiet but quickly decisive way she had.

Carol's house was a mess. Harley had died a bloody death on the front porch, and Lawrence's brains were all over the living room. Sela had organized having Carol transported to her own house, where they would all stay until Carol's house could be put to rights, which the neighborhood women were taking care of as fast as possible. The big tattooed woman named Carlette had shown up and was moving furniture like a man, pulling up blood-soaked carpet, packing up personal belongings and hand-carrying heavy boxes down to Sela's house. Ben made a note to recruit her for the patrol.

Ted was hanging in, but it didn't look good. They'd moved him to a house not far from the building where the firefight had taken place, put him in bed, kept him warm, and dressed his wound. Someone donated a bottle of antibiotics, to try to fight off infection, but Terry Morris had done a quiet triage and given a small shake of his head. There was no point in wasting the pills. Ted had lost a lot of blood, he had some severe internal injuries, and they didn't have the medical facilities or equipment to treat him.

Mike and Darren were taken to the same house, at least for now, to make it more convenient for Terry to see to their care. Both men were on cots in the living room, where they slept and grumbled and were coddled by their wives as much as possible. Darren was in and out, but woke every time they tried to rouse him. Mike's wound, painful as it was, was much less serious.

Night fell. Dawn came and went. A half dozen people, including the couple who owned the house and had gladly allowed it to be turned into a field hospital, gathered in the den and waited. Meredith didn't leave her post beside Ted. She prayed, she quietly cried. Sometimes Ted roused and said a few words to her, and she held his hand.

When Meredith had to use the bathroom, she asked Sela to take her place watching over Ted. Ben was still not willing to let her out of his sight for long so he went into the bedroom with her.

Ted's breathing was laborious, and getting slower. He opened his eyes and frowned in hazy confusion when he looked at Sela. "Meredith?" he asked, his voice barely audible.

"She's gone to the bathroom," Sela said, taking his hand.

He drew a shallow breath, focused on her. "Take care of her," he whispered. "She's . . . my heart."

Sela wanted to say he'd be fine, but couldn't bring herself to lie to him. Tears stung her eyes. "I will."

Ben put his hand on her shoulder. He saw death in that bed. God knew he'd seen more than his share, and recognized it. Ted wouldn't last another hour.

Ted closed his eyes, drifted off again. Sela sat there, still holding his hand, until Meredith returned and took her place.

She stood and went into Ben's arms, rested her head on his chest. He wouldn't swear to it, but he was almost positive she whispered "I love you" into his shirt.

He walked her out into the dim hallway, lit by a single candle, and once more folded her close. "Move in with me," he murmured, resting his chin on the top of her head.

"Okay," she said without hesitation.

Half an hour later Ted quietly died.

A joint funeral was held for Ted and Harley, the afternoon after Ted died. It was a cold, gray day, with another dusting of snow on the ground. Trey had built the two coffins, and a handful of local men who hadn't volunteered in the past dug the graves at the edge of the cemetery, using nothing more than shovels and their own strength. They were alarmed by what had happened and had been pretty much shamed into making the decision to become involved.

There was strength in numbers, and they now added themselves to the list to be called on.

Most of the valley community turned out for the funeral. Sela studied the faces in the crowd. Some she knew, many she didn't, but almost everyone who'd heard what had happened attended. Many wore black. Most had walked, while a few had used precious gasoline to drive here. Sela had driven herself, with Barb, Meredith, and Olivia in tow. She couldn't see either of the older women handling the walk well.

Meredith had stopped crying a while back, though her eyes were red and she trembled. She had been Ted's reason for everything and, imperfect as he was, he had been her center. Barb stood to one side of the new widow. Leigh Kilgore was on the other side, a steadying hand resting on Meredith's arm. Harley's widow had similar support, both physical and emotional.

Carol had insisted on attending the funeral, but Sela and Barb had insisted more urgently that she stay in bed—at Sela's house, until the evidence of violence in her own home could be cleared away—and rest. There were too many gentle hills in the cemetery, too many potential pitfalls. The last thing they needed was for her to take another fall.

As the preacher's words came to an end, Barb stepped forward and began singing a hymn in her sweet voice, a familiar one most of the funeral goers would know. People began joining in, their voices rising in the cold air. Sela tried to join in but her throat was too tight, and she couldn't get the words out. She reached out, grabbed Ben's hand. He threaded his fingers through hers and held on tight. His hand in hers grounded her, and when the time came she was reluctant to let him go.

When the funeral was over, Ben hung back while Sela made the rounds, hugging Meredith as well as Harley's widow, offering her condolences and her prayers. Olivia got a big hug, too, many of them, from a lot of different people. She was a kid and she'd had too many harrowing experiences in the last few days. There was a new look in Olivia's eyes, an older, fiercer expression. Death had touched her at a young age, when she lost her parents, and now this.

Ben stayed close behind Sela and the others as they walked toward the car, sharply watching over his . . . well, hell, his *family*. They, and Meredith, were crowded into Sela's small house. No one wanted Meredith to go home alone, to that empty house on the mountain. It was a nice house, but it was also isolated with all those empty rental cabins in the neighborhood. Ben's house was the closest one that was occupied, and wasn't exactly easy to get to.

Sela fished her keys out of her pocket; Ben reached out and snagged them from her and she gave him a surprised look. "What——?"

"Olivia," he called, and the girl turned toward him. He tossed the keys to her.

She deftly caught them, her gaze flaring with joy. "Yes!" she hissed, clutching the keys.

"Ben!" Sela said in alarm. "She's fifteen!"

"Has she had driving lessons?"

"A few. She got her learner's permit a few months back. But——"

"Think she can handle the short distance to your house?"

"It's not that far," she conceded. "And Lord knows there isn't much traffic." There were a lot of pedestrians, though, and she wasn't sure how much of a danger Olivia would be to them.

"Let her drive. You come home with me."

Come home with me. That phrase was as tantalizing as the *When we have sex* that had haunted her for . . . well, hours, before it had actually happened.

"I really should see everyone settled."

"You really should come home with me and let me take care of you for a while. Olivia can handle the rest. We'll come down and check on them tomorrow morning. Promise."

Olivia had been listening. She spun around and mouthed to Sela, "We'll be fine. Go!"

Sela nodded, and as the women got into her Honda, Ben lifted her into the passenger side of his truck. She was definitely sore from Lawrence's kicks, her side and thigh deeply bruised. Barb had made a couple of poultices that had helped ease the soreness, but she still felt it.

"The community patrol met this morning," Ben said as he pulled onto the road.

"I didn't know. I would've been there."

"You needed your rest," he grumbled. "We voted on what to do with Jeremy. Tomorrow morning a group of us will escort him a few miles out and see him on his way. He'll have a couple bottles of water and some food, but from there he'll be on his own. I voted against the food, but I was overruled."

"Banishment."

"Yep."

"A bullet to the head might have been kinder." She could not imagine being on her own in this world.

"I brought that up, too." His voice was grim. "If Darren had died there probably would've been more votes for execution, but he's going to recover."

Just ahead, Olivia carefully guided Sela's SUV onto the side road that would take her and her passengers home. She even used her turn signal. She likely wouldn't see—Sela hoped she was paying attention to the road instead of watching her rearview mirror—but Sela gave her a thumbs-up.

"We've also decided to block off all the roads coming into the valley," Ben continued. "That won't keep everyone out, but we won't have anyone driving in once that's done. And we're going to set up lookouts."

She could only imagine a group like Lawrence and his friends with a handful of vehicles, goodness knows how many weapons, and plenty of gas. The damage they could do would be unimaginable. Access to the valley had to be controlled, because their lives could depend on it.

Ben turned onto Covemont Lane and they headed home. *Home.* She hadn't moved her things there, not yet, but she had no doubt that whatever they had was important, and permanent, and that his home was now hers.

Maybe it didn't make much sense, given what had happened in the past few days, but Sela knew she'd be fine. Carol and Olivia would be fine. Josh would come home when he could, and he'd be fine. They couldn't know what the coming months would bring, but with Ben by her side she could do anything.

She had never felt so strong.

He deftly steered the truck over the big rock, then they crested the steep drive and reached the house. "Stay there," he said, and came around the truck to lift her out of it.

"I'm okay," she said mildly. "Sore, but okay."

"Humor me."

They went up the steps to the porch, and the spectacular view took her attention. The valley spread out before them. "I should've packed a bag," she said as she walked the porch to the prime spot where Ben had positioned a couple of chairs. They would sit here a lot, she imagined.

"Tomorrow," Ben said. "I have an extra toothbrush and I promise you won't need pajamas."

No, she wouldn't. "What's the condom count?"

"Zero." He didn't sound concerned.

She sure wasn't.

The valley below looked so peaceful from this vantage point. It wasn't, not really, and wouldn't be for some time. They would have quiet days and days that were not so quiet.

Practical matters intruded on her thoughts. When Carol's house had been set to rights and she, Olivia, and Barb had moved back into it, Meredith could stay and live in Sela's house. She might want a roommate, and it wouldn't be impossible for her to move in with Carol, but it would be crowded. That would be up to the women involved, not her decision at all, but she could certainly offer her house to the new widow. She knew she herself wouldn't be living there anymore.

Harley's widow had family in the area, but still, it was only right that others help her out, when and if she needed it. Did she have heat? Plenty of food? Sela had known Harley a lot better than she knew his wife, but now the widow was on her list of responsibilities.

The Livingstons hadn't been at the funeral. That wasn't reason for concern, but she did want to check on them. Maybe tomorrow, when she went to her house to collect a few things.

Ben wrapped his arms around her. "What are you planning?" he asked, rubbing his chin against her temple.

"What makes you think I'm planning anything?" She folded her arms over his, burrowing into the heat of his body.

"The expression on your face," he said. "Besides, you're always planning something."

"Not always." She turned in his arms and looked up, smiling.

He narrowed those laser green eyes at her and pulled her closer.

"Turn those skills to planning our wedding. I expect your crazy aunt will get involved, so be strong."

Despite the sad day, Sela laughed and tilted her head to kiss the underside of his jaw.

"You'll have to keep her distracted, Stud Muffin."

EPILOGUE

September again, and as usual the summer heat was holding on. The best part of the day was when the sun had set and the day cooled. After sundown was the time for magic. Their work was done for the day, the breeze through the open windows cooled the house, and they could just be together.

Home. This was home.

Dinner dishes done—after a meal of fish, tomatoes from the garden, and wild greens, again—they sat on the porch and watched the sunset fade. Sela absently stroked her stomach, which seemed to be swelling more by the day though Carol laughed at her and insisted she was barely showing. She could feel the baby moving now, flutters and light kicks, and it still made her breathless with joy. A baby! She was having Ben's baby! This time last year having a family was a dream she'd given up on, and now she had a husband who made her breath catch in her throat, and a baby on the way.

This wasn't the way she'd always imagined her pregnancy—if she ever had one—would go. There was no ultrasound, no way to know if their baby was a boy or a girl. Terry Morris did keep track of her blood pressure and so far that was okay, and she tried to eat a lot of fruits and vegetables, but that was the extent of her prenatal care.

She should probably worry more, but what good would worrying do? In a perfect world she'd have an obstetrician, prenatal vitamins, and cute maternity clothes. She'd have weird cravings for ice cream and pickles, which would be immediately satisfied. After a summer where the gardens had been very productive she could manage the pickles. Ice cream was another matter.

She sighed. Who was she kidding? This *was* a perfect world. She was happier than she'd ever imagined she could be.

Ben sat beside her in the growing darkness, holding her hand. Yeah, this was perfect.

"I hope the power comes back up before the baby is born," she said wistfully. There still wouldn't be a functioning hospital, but lights, heat . . . boiled water.

"Howler says grids are coming up every day," he assured her. "We'll have power before you know it."

Ben and Cory checked in with each other about once a week. Some of Howler's news was good, some wasn't. In the year since the CME a lot of people had died—not the ninety percent the powers that be had initially predicted, but still . . . millions. Hundreds of millions. The world they'd known was gone, blasted to smithereens by a blast from the sun. Civilization might recover function in a decade, but not the way it had been before. The best and the worst of humanity had been revealed, not just in Wears Valley but around the globe. Survivors had found a way to do just that—survive—and many, like her and Ben, had made the best of a world turned upside down.

Howler's wife, Gen, was pregnant herself. Maybe, eventually, their babies could play together, be friends, grow up, and bond over being one of many CME babies. What a generation they would be, a whole new Boom generation. As Brother Ames had said, people had to entertain themselves somehow, and going by the baby boom here in the valley, Sela knew what form that entertainment had taken.

The past year had taken a toll. A number of valley residents had died from accidents or illnesses that would have been preventable or treatable before the CME. Their retired veterinarian had died in his sleep, throwing all their medical care on Terry Morris. Still, the number of losses had been smaller than one might've predicted, but each one had been deeply felt. A few strangers had wandered in, in spite of the community patrol's barricades. None of them had been what anyone would call upstanding citizens, except for a nurse and his family, who they had gladly welcomed. He had joined with Terry Morris to provide medical care for the valley. The other wanderers had been sent on their way, encouraged sometimes by Ben's shotgun. He had a way of looking at people that made them *want* to be elsewhere.

Sela's family was doing well. A fully healed Carol had reclaimed her position as community leader, with Meredith—who had moved into Sela's house just days after Sela had moved in with Ben—at her side. They made a kick-ass team.

Their school system, while not sophisticated, was up and running. Barb taught cooking classes. Helping Carol oversee the community wasn't her idea of fun, but she loved cooking.

Meredith walked to Ted's grave, with flowers in hand when she could find them, once a week. It was a long walk, but Meredith was stronger than her husband had ever given her credit for. A couple of widowers had asked to keep her company, but she wasn't ready for that, might never be.

The Livingstons had survived the winter, though Mary Alice was noticeably more frail. Sajack was a pretty awesome guard dog, as if he knew the old couple was his responsibility. Ben checked on them at least every other day. He imagined one day Sajack's job would be over, and the dog would come home with him.

Olivia had turned sixteen, and they'd managed to throw her a sweet sixteen party, complete with a cake Barb had cooked in her iron skillet over an open fire. With icing. It hadn't been a pretty cake, and there hadn't been much icing, but . . . cake.

Thanks to Ben's ham radio and Howler's military connections, they'd gotten word to Josh that his family was well and being cared for, and they'd gotten word back that Josh was busy but okay. There was no way to know when he'd be able to make it home, but hearing he was safe made them all feel better.

They sat on the porch until darkness had completely taken over the sky, then went back inside. Bedtimes had adjusted to the daylight hours, which suited her just fine.

She snuggled against Ben's hard, warm body, her arm curled around his neck, their child a gentle swell between them. "We need to pick a couple of baby names," Sela said sleepily, already relaxed.

"Not until I see his face," he said, not for the first time.

"Or *her* face."

Ben grunted. The idea of having a daughter kind of terrified him, which she thought was hilarious. He was already charmingly overprotective.

"I want at least three," she said, just to tease him.

"Babies?"

"Little girls."

Again that grunt, followed by a sweet kiss to her temple.

She was likely the only person who had ever called her husband sweet.

"I'm going to miss this," he said. "Once the power is on again, we won't be isolated. We'll have to let the world back in."

"Air-conditioning, functioning hospitals, running water, refrigeration, television, football . . ." she argued.

"Yeah, yeah, I get it."

"Oreos," she continued, "potato chips, ice cream, beef that doesn't come from a cow whose name we know."

He laughed. She loved that she could make this hard man laugh.

She stroked his face, so full of love she could barely contain it. He remained cautious where other people were concerned, and he probably always would. He'd never be gregarious, and neither would she, but both of them had been changed for the better by loving one another.

"We'll be fine, no matter what," she said.

He kissed her again, this time on the mouth. The power of that kiss never ceased to amaze her. It was electric. Now that she was over her morning sickness—which had been bad—she responded eagerly to him and they made love as they did most nights. He was more inclined to have her on top, but she could still tolerate his weight and loved it.

Afterward, she rested with her head on his shoulder and began drifting to sleep, so content she felt as if she were glowing.

The lamp came on.

It was what Ben called their canary-in-the-mine lamp, the one he'd plugged in when Howler began talking about some of the grids coming back online.

The light went off, flashed on again . . . and stayed on.

"We'll deal with this tomorrow," Ben said, then reached out and turned off the lamp.

ABOUT THE AUTHORS

Linda Howard is the award-winning author of numerous *New York Times* bestsellers, including *The Woman Left Behind*, *Troublemaker*, *Up Close and Dangerous*, *Drop Dead Gorgeous*, *Cover of Night*, and *Killing Time*. She lives in Gadsden, Alabama, with her husband and a golden retriever.

Linda Jones is the acclaimed *USA Today* bestselling author of more than seventy novels, including *Untouchable*, *22 Nights*, and *Bride by Command*. She lives in Huntsville, Alabama.

COMPLETE HANDBOOK
FOR TEACHING
SMALL VOCAL ENSEMBLES

COMPLETE HANDBOOK
FOR TEACHING
SMALL VOCAL
ENSEMBLES

Orlando Moss

PARKER PUBLISHING COMPANY, INC.

West Nyack, New York

© 1978 by

PARKER PUBLISHING COMPANY, INC.

West Nyack, N.Y.

Library of Congress Cataloging in Publication Data

Moss, Orlando
    Complete handbook for teaching small vocal ensembles.

    Includes index.
    1. Choirs (Music) I. Title.
MT88.M87   784.9'62   77-29232
ISBN 0-13-161273-5

Printed in the United States of America

DEDICATION

To my wife, Ollie, and our children,
Frederick, Karen, Orlando, Jr., and
Iris, in gratitude and affection

A WORD FROM THE AUTHOR
ON THE PRACTICAL VALUE
OF THIS BOOK

This book will provide you with the procedures and techniques you will need to build strong small vocal ensembles, and to improve the technical and musical skills of each student you teach. It will show you how to build the unique sound that is characteristic of each ensemble.

This book will also show you how to build, maintain and classify small ensembles, and at the same time, keep the interest of the students through a systematic plan that gets results. I call this plan the "Graduated Program." It begins with an informal group used as a bridge for worthy students to cross over from the full-choir program. When a student graduates to the next highest ensemble, usually at the end of each semester, his skills in the area of performance, vocally and theoretically, should be greatly improved. The personnel in each ensemble of the Graduated Program is kept in accordance with the number of voices needed to maintain the ensemble's special sound and color.

Let's look at one example of how the voices are "graduated" from one ensemble to the next: when a number of singers have developed the vocal skills from the techniques in the informal choir, you may permit them to move to the all-male or all-female choirs. Similar numbers should move from the above choirs to the chamber choir. At the same time, it would be necessary to permit a similar number of students to cross over from the full-choir program to the informal choir. When a student "graduates" from the entire program, his skills in performance should be of the highest quality.

Results of the Graduated Program first came to light during the 1968–69 school session when my a cappella choir was rated superior at the Louisiana Music Educators Association's State Music Festival. The music performed by the choir was as follows:

> Frere Jacques, arranged by Salli Terri
> Tu Es Petrus by Palestrina
> Alleluia by Randall Thompson

We were proud of our acquired techniques which permitted us to perform this difficult music. In order for small vocal ensembles to reap this kind of reward, techniques, as outlined in the Graduated Program of this book, must be worked on constantly. Without development of the different techniques in the program, you will not develop strong small vocal ensembles.

In later years, a teacher crossover program was instituted in our city. I became director of choral activities at a school where the choir program consisted of a concert choir, a girl's choir and two music appreciation classes. I continued the Graduated Program at this school by using some of the basic techniques found in this book. After twenty days of drill and hard work, I took the choirs to the district festival. The concert choir received a superior rating.

The year after that, I chose certain members of my concert choir to function as a unit in after school rehearsals to work on some materials and techniques found in this book. This ensemble became the first informal choir at the school. It aroused a great deal of curiosity and interest among the students on the campus. I carried the ensemble through periods of "acceleration" using the different techniques in each ensemble until it was able to perform skillfully. Finally, the ensemble was introduced to the school community in a concert. The concert was successful. As a result, the choir was placed in the school curriculum for the first time.

The following year, we received superior ratings in "tough" festival events. The news of these ventures spread rapidly, and the members of this choir received recognition from many sources in the community. But the most important event that happened as a direct result of our participation in these festivals was that a large number of students joined the choir program.

I then expanded the program by graduating students to other ensembles. I had the chance to use the Graduated Program to motivate these students to increase their interest in choral music as well as improve their individual talents. The work helped me to move students more quickly into the different ensembles.

Presently, these ensembles, the all-male, all-female and the informal choirs serve as beginner groups to help those students who come to our program for the first time. These units are moving toward musical perfection. There will be other expansion of them later. The chamber and a capella choirs and soloists give superior performances each year.

Here are three "case examples" of what the Graduated Program has accomplished for individual students:

- Bobbie King, a graduate from the chamber choir, received a superior rating in the solo festival. She also was chosen for all-state honors. Bobbie had taken the Graduated Program for granted and had never realized how it actually helped her. But the real surprise came when she was offered a scholarship to sing with the University Singers, a collegiate ensemble.
- Susan Hatcher met me at the door of the college auditorium where she was attending school and told me how excited she was that she had won a part in a musical play through an audition. She attributed her success to her studies in the Graduated Program.
- Brad Ingles, a graduate from the a cappella choir, graduated from college during mid-semester. He was immediately employed by the school system as a substitute teacher. He is also employed frequently for singing engagements. He attributes his success to the work he did while he was a student in the Graduated Program.

The aim of this book is to expand the ensemble program, giving it an added dimension to aid students who are moving from one musical level to a higher one in positive ways. It will show you how to teach the different musical levels to your students, leaving no room for mediocrity on the part of directors and students alike.

Here are some special features of the book's Graduated Program which will prove useful to you. . . .

- Procedures in the informal choir section of the book will acquaint you with techniques for teaching the high-arched and medium *ah* vowel sounds and projectional resonance for students to become familiar with the different small vocal ensemble tonal patterns.
- Special drills and vocalises are introduced to teach singers how to conserve the breath in order to shape the beauty of long musical phrases. The developed skill will eliminate the

use of staggered breathing which limits fine vocal performances.

- Special techniques designed to show you how to blend light vowel properties in tenor registrations are introduced in Chapter 3 dealing with the all-male ensemble.
- You will be shown how to add the necessary color to the baritone quality.
- You will learn how to teach mixed quality in the all-female choir.
- You will be shown how to develop the chamber choir's tonal unity and color by mixing tonal ingredients between the alto and tenor sections.
- Phrasing in polyphonic music has never been discussed from a technical point of view. This book will take you through several pieces and will give you specific directions for teaching effective phrasing.

Most successful full-choir programs need another outlet to give students the opportunity to achieve their maximum capacities. Many of these students have the ability to become very fine singers, but do not have the opportunity to develop their voices properly in the early musical stage, establishing firm foundations.

This book will meet the needs of these students by permitting them to train their voices with other students who have had similar musical experiences. Their need to be above the average musical performance will be met when they develop the techniques for each special ensemble. Once this has been achieved, these students can enjoy small vocal performances, and will be prepared for other higher musical forms.

Orlando Moss

ACKNOWLEDGEMENTS

The author offers thanks to Dr. Edward Deckard, Director of Choral Activities at Northeast Louisiana State University in Monroe, Louisiana, for his encouragement and help through conferences and clinics, and the Caddo Parish School System for the use of materials and resources, and also John Gilliam III for his assistance in typing the manuscript.

The following institutions have kindly given permission to reproduce copyrighted material:

The Folger Shakespeare Library, Washington, D.C.

Parker Publishing Company, Inc. West Nyack, New York

Contents

How to Train the A Cappella Choir (*continued*)

10.   **How to Prepare Small Vocal Ensembles for Festival Participation** **205**

CHAPTER 1

SUPERVISING THE SUCCESSFUL SMALL VOCAL ENSEMBLE PROGRAM

In this chapter, you will learn how to keep records for each of your students in order to move him or her to a higher ensemble. You will find forms that will be invaluable in helping you to organize your small vocal ensemble program in an orderly manner. This kind of order will help you to promote the program in the community. This information is compiled so that you can learn as quickly as possible the manner in which you can encourage community leaders to support you in building an effective small vocal ensemble program.

You will receive preliminary instructions on the special make-up of each small vocal ensemble, its character, and, in the case of the all-male and all-female groups, a contrast between them to help you understand the special nature of each.

The Graduated Program has been used successfully in training many outstanding students in many areas. You will be shown how to develop it to the fullest extent so that your students can become the finest singers you are capable of producing.

Every choral director is expected to be a good organizer, teacher and director, in that order, when he or she is hired by a school system. It has been proven by a number of cases that the ability to organize a program effectively is the first step in building a superior small vocal ensemble program. But, if the director lacks the ability to organize, the program will not have a strong foundation, which will cause many failures among the students. In some cases the program will not have the support of the school community. It is true that poorly organized small vocal ensemble programs do misdirect many talented students. This sets the stage for a dying program. It can be characterized as one that is not able to offer encouragement to the highly gifted and the highly motivated students to join its ranks. This, of course, will be reversed if the choral director has the ability to be an effective organizer.

Good organization involves purposeful and meaningful planning on your part. This means that you must utilize the time that is alloted to classes and your ensembles wisely. You can begin in the spring of each year reviewing and, if necessary, restructuring your plans for a new school year. If there are some weak parts to your plans, you should revise them.

Good planning for the students in your small vocal ensemble program must include points to help build character and develop good musicianship as well; these two concepts must bear the brunt of your decision to include certain materials for study in your plans.

BUILDING THE GRADUATED PROGRAM

The word "motivation" is one of the most prominent terms in your plans for effective teaching. Its usage in the teaching field is widespread because teachers and students alike want to excel in their work. In other words, after some form of motivation has been used to help us, we are moved emotionally, and thereby, achieve the best that is in us.

The Graduated Program represents one form of motivation. You can use it to help your students move away from the "average performer" status and develop those skills necessary to rate with those who sing in a superior manner.

Beginning Steps in the Program

Begin the program by providing proper training for the gifted and highly motivated students in the full-choir program. Training for these special students can begin during the summer months, or after school during the first semester. Actually, these students can be moved to the informal choir during the second semester if you begin in the manner stated above. Meanwhile, other students in the full-choir program can be trained in the same way the starters began. You may have to accelerate the program in its first year by permitting some "graduated students" to move to a higher ensemble during the mid-semester. This is necessary since you are working to build your ensemble program to full strength as soon as possible. Do not permit these students to neglect their membership in the full-choir program. This experience will be the base from which the small vocal ensemble program receives its strength.

Do not become discouraged if the small vocal ensemble program does not meet all requirements during its first year of existence. If you will continue to help your students develop the skills they need, full fruition can be realized the following year. But let your students go as far in their development as they can so that they can reap as many benefits from the program as possible. These benefits include skills, involvement, more knowledge and improved musicianship.

Illustration 1.1 graphically shows development toward the Graduated Program. Notice how the students are receiving training through solo and small ensemble experiences. This training, along with that of the concert choir, serves as motivation for those students to earn the right to participate in the small vocal ensembles of the Graduated Program. Many of these students had the opportunity to participate in a similar program during their junior high school years, and the development received there helped them to receive special recognition in the full-choir program above. In a sense, these students have already moved above the full-choir program level and will need to move into another developmental plateau similar to the Graduated Program of this book.

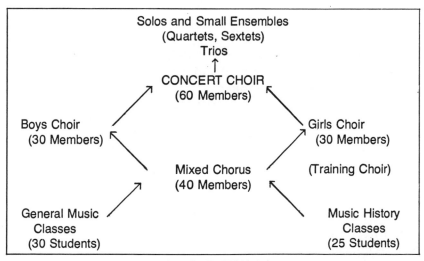

ILLUSTRATION 1.1

If the director has kept proper oversight in the program above, other students in each segment could be placed in a position to move to the Graduated Program. Motivation becomes the important element to get the program moving and expanding into the Graduated Program.

Recruiting

The influence of the successful choir director in recruiting students for his choral program can be measured when younger brothers and sisters of his present students decide that they will become members of the choir when they reach high school. Later on, you may want to know exactly who these people are, and what schools they are now attending so they can be referred to the choir directors of their schools. Periodic checks on these students will encourage them to keep their interest in the choir program. These students, in time, will lead others to your program.

Presenting mature musical performances is another fine way to recruit students for the choral program. This is reason for you to follow the procedure presented in the section "Planning Performance Schedules for Small Vocal Ensembles" as closely as possible. It is said that news travels far and fast. . . . This is true! There is no doubt that your students will receive recognition from the many sources suggested in that section, if the quality of singing is satisfactory.

Record Keeping

Keep up to date records for each person in the small vocal ensemble program. All dates for auditions, technique development, voice classification, range, school and concert attendance, completed assignments and attitudes should be a part of the records. These will be beneficial in helping you to select the most qualified students for your small vocal ensembles. The forms in Illustrations 1.2 to 1.5 can be used to help you keep records in an orderly manner.

Start a new set of forms for each student who enters the program for the first time. Once the form is added to a student's folder, it should become a permanent part of his records. However, your files should be kept so that they are never exposed. You may, upon request, show them to parents, school officials, or other persons in authority. Be specific when you add data to your files. Sometimes, one word is not enough to describe a certain situation; you will need to use a phrase that can be understood at a later date. If a time comes that you are absent, another person will be able to interpret the data and become familiar with each student in the program.

AUDITION FORM

Name_____Grade_____Address_____
School_____Telephone_____
Date of Audition_____Satisfactory   Unsatisfactory
Recommendations_____

Voice Classification_____Range_____

ILLUSTRATION 1.2

TECHNIQUE DEVELOPMENT

Name_____Grade_____Date_____
Address_____School_____Tel._____
Reading Skills   Tone Quality
   1. Rhythm_____   1. Vowel Color_____
   2. Pitch_____   2. Resonance _____
   3. Speed_____   3. Breath Control_____
                             4. Diction_____

Voice Classification_____
Recommendations_____
_____

ILLUSTRATION 1.3

PERFORMANCE RECORD

Name_____Grade_____Date_____
Address_____School_____Tel._____

Sept.____ | | | | ____   Feb.____ | | | | ____
Oct.____ | | | | ____   Mar.____ | | | | ____
Nov.____ | | | | ____   Apr.____ | | | | ____
Dec.____ | | | | ____   May____ | | | | ____
Jan.____ | | | | ____
Recommendations_____
_____

ILLUSTRATION 1.4

CONFIDENTIAL STUDENT FILE FORM

Name_____Grade_____Home Phone_____
Mother's Maiden Name_____School_____
Father's Name_____Business Tel. _____
Number of children in family_____ Ages_____
Date_____
Student's attitude toward school _____
_____
Changes, if any_____
_____
Student's attitude toward peers_____
_____
Changes, if any_____

COMPLETED ASSIGNMENTS

_____
_____
_____
_____
_____

Recommendations_____
_____

ILLUSTRATION 1.5

INTER-GROUP COMPETITION

Friendly competition among the students in solos and the different small vocal ensembles can be encouraged to motivate them to excel in those areas that are difficult to develop. Many students do not develop certain skills simply because they were poorly motivated. It becomes necessary, then, to devise a method to help them learn these skills and keep interest high at the same time. You may want to name this method after your school's music department. At any rate, it should be an inter-group festival.

First, prepare each ensemble as you would for competition in any major music festival. You will need to gain support for the affair from some sources in your community. Then, secure support for the affair through newspaper articles and advertising. Check those advertising agencies which offer free publicity to some non-profit organizations. Usually, a few local radio and television stations offer this service to schools free of charge.

You may have to arrange for transportation to and from the festival for a few students, but for the most part, this chore should be taken care of by your parent group. Preparations should be made at least a month in advance. It will be wise to set up a series of meetings with your parent group to brief them on the procedures to use to organize every aspect of the festival.

Programs

Formal printed programs may or may not be used, depending upon the amount of money you have to spend or the expectation of your school's community. But some type of program of events should be planned. A booklet organized by your parent group will be most impressive. These can serve as a source of pride for many years to come.

A Unifying Technique

You may want to ask other directors in charge of the community's music programs to take charge of your small ensembles and direct them in the festival. In this way, you will be able to acquaint them with your ensembles. This contact will help strengthen the relationship among the directors and will be a step in the right direction to bring greater harmony to the music programs in the community.

Awarding the Students

An awards ceremony can be held for the ensembles, at a later date. It is important to present each ensemble an award. Of course, the most prestigious award must go to the winners of the festival. It is obvious that the higher ensembles will perform with greater skill, but the idea here is to make each ensemble feel that musical progress is being made among its ranks.

PERSONNEL SELECTION

When you make final selections for your small vocal ensemble program, you are truly teaching all students in your school the value of possessing high moral character, good peer relationships, and scholarship. If, however, you admit students to your program who do not measure up, you will be teaching the concepts above in reverse. This is the reason why the first step in planning and selecting the personnel for your small vocal ensembles should be based upon proper record keeping, using the concepts above as criteria for the final judgement. You should involve other teachers in the school if you expect your selections to be valid. You may ask them to evaluate the students you have chosen. If one chosen student has trouble in adjusting to group demands, you may find this out through the evaluation of the other teachers.

After you have completed your records concerning voice character, vocal range and quality for each student, begin planning and assembling in sequential order all materials for your ensembles to advance in voice development. These should include sight-reading exercises, vocalises for the improvement of tone and technique, etc. Assign solo material to individuals who need specific help in areas such as rhythm, proper breathing, vowel formations, mixed quality, resonance blending, or the covered tone. Many individual problems can be worked out successfully through solo material that has been selected carefully.

ARRANGING SUMMER STUDY

Make a schedule of the music you will recommend for each ensemble to study. It should include music for performance and developmental purposes as well. Ask your section leaders and accompanists to check the music out of the library to help the other students become familiar with it during the summer months. Be sure to make recommendations for certain students who are having problems in certain areas when they study with the section leaders. These recommendations can be in the form of specific explanations about rhythm and articulation, or other problems that need attention. In case some students are not up to par in their development, encourage them to acquire the services of private vocal teachers in the community. On the other hand, encourage *all* of your highly talented students to seek out private instruction from reputable teachers to further their development.

Make contact with your co-workers in the junior high school program to make recommendations to you for those promising students who will be attending your school in the fall. You may ask the junior high school choral directors to set up private instruction for these students.

QUALITY TEACHING

Your ability to engage in successful teaching is important to your small vocal ensemble program. It is through this medium only that you can motivate your students to attain high levels in character and musicianship. It is true that a poor teacher encourages poor performances among his students, but good teachers do likewise if this planning is inadequate.

Quality teaching, then, is the ability of a person, by demonstration and explanation, to motivate the students to learn. Those techniques and skills unattainable for the moment can be learned by these elements and properly used instructional tools. But the techniques that must be learned immediately should be taught by demonstrations.

FINANCING PROJECTS

Rarely does the choral department receive enough funds from the public school system's financial department to finance the entire choral program. The money that is received and spent is managed in a way that each choir in the music department can receive some materials. Needless to say, only the minimum materials and equipment can be put into the budget. Some directors have long range plans to help save enough money to buy those necessary items such as music typewriters, or recording equipment for their departments. For the most part, it takes two to five years to save enough money to purchase the expensive equipment mentioned above unless there is help from another source. It would be well to organize a parent group to help out in purchasing equipment and other materials for the choral program. Be certain that you set specific goals for this group. If you wish for them to purchase materials, include the cost and work out the details for raising the funds. This, in many locales, must be done according to the guidelines of your school system.

One method to raise money could be a musical jamboree held in the spring, organized by the choral teacher group in your city. The proceeds from such a venture could be divided equally among the participating schools. Since the money will be divided equally, the parents in each district should be told of this and asked to support it fully. All efforts should be made to have the program well organized. Include as many students from each district to serve on the program in as many ways as possible. Include students from the full-choir programs of each district also since the entire choral program will benefit from this effort. Find a method to get the most talented singers from each district to appear as soloists and participate in the massed ensemble.

THE INFORMAL CHOIR

The students in the informal choir should have participated in the junior high school choral program, and spent at least one year in the full-choir program on the high school level. Your decision to place them in the Graduated Program can depend upon their musical maturity, the quality of their voices and proper peer relationships. The records from the junior high school can be a decisive factor relating the solo and ensemble experiences and awards. Be sure to add this information to the confidential student file form.

Members of the informal choir can be encouraged to perform in smaller units, but these performances should include the music that the students are already using in their development. In fact, these smaller units can be called upon to perform at different places in the community. To insure creditable performances, listen to these groups often and make suggestions for improvements. You could call in other teachers, or members of the higher ensembles, for special help.

Assign names to these small units of the informal choir such as "The Eaglewood Sextet." They will enjoy these titles of distinction. However, the names should be relevant to the importance of the ensemble and kept as permanent titles for future units.

Write weekly reports on the progress of this choir. Include accelerations in interest and attitudes. These reports will be helpful to you when you move those worthy students to higher ensembles. See Illustration 1.6 for a sample of this report.

THE ALL-MALE CHOIR

Choose the boys for the all-male choir directly from the informal choir. You can get your organization moving by using only those boys who have trained their voices well. In the beginning stages of the choir, you may have to start with a quartet, and, in many cases, this could be the ideal beginning for it because this gives you the chance to be selective in your choices for the all-male choir.

It is better to keep the standards high. Many boys at the high school level take pride in these high-standard organizations, joining

```
┌─────────────────────────────────────────────────────────┐
│                 WEEKLY PROGRESS REPORT                    │
│                                                           │
│  Name of Ensemble_____ No. of Students_____  │
│  School_____ Date_____    │
│  Outstanding Students With Accelerations In Interest      │
│  _____    _____  │
│                                                           │
│  _____    _____  │
│                                                           │
│  _____    _____  │
│                                                           │
│                                                           │
│       Students With Accelerations In Good Attitude Changes│
│              Toward The Ensemble Program                  │
│  _____    _____  │
│                                                           │
│  _____    _____  │
│                                                           │
│  _____    _____  │
│                                                           │
│                                                           │
└─────────────────────────────────────────────────────────┘
```

ILLUSTRATION 1.6

them, bringing prestige to a high level that grows with the years and making it a part of the group's identity.

Billy Evans was known around the campus for the disturbances he created in his classes. He had been in trouble with the school officials ever since he arrived at the school. One day, he decided to skip his third hour class to harass the all-male choir students as they practiced in the choir room. But, to his surprise, the choir sang some music that Billy had purchased from the local record shop. John Brody, a section leader, noticed Billy listening and invited him to join the choir. Billy did join the choir the following year and progressed rapidly. He was successful in singing a solo on the choir's annual talent show, and, as a result, his popularity increased and his entire attitude changed toward the school.

You can influence boys to become interested in the all-male choir by projecting masculinity among the members of the group. That is, you can show interest in the scouting program or the athletic program at your school. The music that you choose and the approach you take in teaching it must reflect the masculine attitude for it to be acceptable to most boys. Many do not participate in some choral programs because these do not offer satisfaction in this area.

Dress

Let the all-male choir have distinctive uniforms. Usually, robes are not effective for the members because they prefer uniforms that can be associated with a specific theme or title. When the issue of the uniform has been settled, at least fifty per cent of your problem with the masculine element will be eliminated.

THE CONTRAST BETWEEN ALL-FEMALE AND ALL-MALE CHOIRS

Many boys would rather think of their all-male units as "packs" or "clubs," but the all-female groups like to be thought of as "family types." You can take advantage of the situation by becoming the "leader" of your boys choir and maneuver in the girls choir as a "father type" or, in the case of sharing in the inner group feeling experience, become a "friend." Much can be accomplished under these conditions because students are responsive to directors with a "touch" of humaneness. They are not genuinely responsive to those who act as "lords" over them.

The general feeling among all-male groups is one of self-dependency, whereas, the all-female groups depend upon group strengths. These are the basic emotional elements which separate the two groups.

THE ALL-FEMALE CHOIR

The personnel for the all-female choir can be taken directly from the informal choir. If there has been a lack of training in the vocal process, you may improve it at this level in the Graduated Program: Use the group strength idea to encourage those girls who have weaknesses. Let them rely on those singers who are strong in the area of vocal techniques. But, as soon as these weak singers show signs of improvement, begin developing their vocal skills on an individual basis. They can be initiated in the quintet formations.

THE CHAMBER CHOIR

The personnel for the chamber choir can be chosen directly from the all-male and all-female ensembles. If you plan your ensembles correctly, you will have at least fifty students in the all-male and all-female ensembles from which to form your chamber choir. All of these students will have the kind of choral experience they will need to participate in the chamber choir, if you have permitted them to develop thoroughly the techniques needed in the all-male, all-female and the informal choirs.

The sight reading level of this group should be in the advanced stage. They must have a good foundation in theory, music history and directing. This knowledge will help you to present in-depth studies of the music to your students.

THE MADRIGAL CHOIR

The personnel for the madrigal choir should be chosen directly from the chamber choir. The auditioning of the students can be set up during a rehearsal session of the chamber choir. Generally, students look forward to the auditions since there are close relationships that exist between the two choirs in terms of abilities, interests and musicianship. The material used in the auditions can be chosen from any source. However, the best method for obtaining the personnel for the madrigal choir is to determine the amount of progress the students made in the chamber choir in the area of tonal control and color. If your students have developed the ability to control light and dark colors at will, they should be able to pass your examinations for entrance into the madrigal choir.

Devise a program of study for members of this choir. It can include bibliographies, general and specific objectives for the choir, a glossary of musical terms, specific vocal skills and remedies for their improvements. This will be beneficial to the students who will be required to have rehearsals and study sessions after school hours. If the madrigal choir is a regularly scheduled course in the curriculum, your program can serve in the capacity of a syllabus. In this case, you could also include a brief study describing how each composition you have chosen for study should be performed, the difficulties in performing them, and, the approximate time for learning the scores.

THE MODERN CHOIR

You can include the modern choir in your small vocal ensemble program to let your students learn how to use contemporary compositional techniques. This would include studying improvisational techniques as basic vocal processes.

The scope of your students' study of contemporary music can

	MON.	TUES.	WED.	THURS.	FRI.	TOTAL
High-Checkbone Resonance	5 10 15	5 10 15	5 10 15	5 10 15	5 10 15	
Low-Checkbone Resonance	5 10 15	5 10 15	5 10 15	5 10 15	5 10 15	
Ear Resonance	5 10 15	5 10 15	5 10 15	5 10 15	5 10 15	
The High-Arched Ah Vowel	5 10 15	5 10 15	5 10 15	5 10 15	5 10 15	

ILLUSTRATION 1.7

begin with Schubert, Brahms, Faure and Bruckner, then, end with the composers of the modern period.

OCTETS, SEXTETS, QUARTETS AND TRIOS

These small units will aid your students in developing projectional resonance that will certainly be needed when they are "graduated" to the a cappella choir. Naturally, the students will need to know how to use this kind of resonance correctly when singing solos. It is necessary for them to study it in these small units so that more individual attention can be given to each student as the need arises.

Use the plan outlined in Illustration 1.7 to help your students develop projectional resonance. Duplicate the work for each student on an index card. Ask them to circle the number of minutes they spend developing each technique.

USING THE SMALL VOCAL ENSEMBLE
RATING CHART

Each ensemble should be rated at least three times a year for their performances during class or rehearsal sessions. These ratings will help your students work for greater perfection and achieve it! The true worth of the rating chart can be observed when the third rating is higher than the first and second ratings. But, you should motivate the students in this direction. The best motivational technique to use here is your own enthusiasm about the outcome you hope your students will achieve as a result of serious study on their part.

```
SMALL VOCAL ENSEMBLE RATING CHART

Name of Ensemble ————————————— Period———— Date————
School ————————————————————— Number in Ensemble————
Names of Compositions & Composers—————————————————

    Ensemble Tonal Concepts.......................................................
    Rhythmic Precision...............................................................
    Technique (Posture, Phrasing,
        Diction, Intonation).........................................................
    Interpretation (Style, Tempo, Mood) ................................
    Balance and Blend................................................................
                                                    Total Points. . .
```

ILLUSTRATION 1.8

All results should be posted on your permanent bulletin board in the ensemble practice room for all students in the choral program to examine. It would be well to post the rating as it appears on the rating chart. The most successful rating chart is shown in Illustration 1.8.

Keep records of all ratings for each ensemble. You will find these invaluable aids to help you improve your ensembles in certain weak areas in the future.

PLANNING PERFORMANCE SCHEDULES
FOR SMALL VOCAL ENSEMBLES

It is difficult to keep the morale of an ensemble high in practice sessions without the expectation of a performance. You will be able to keep it high for the first two or three weeks of school, but, in the absence of a performance during the weeks that follow, your students will lose some of the initial excitement that goes along with the opening of school and you will have to resort to another method for keeping the morale high. For this reason, it is better to prepare your ensembles for performance as quickly as possible. This will be the greatest motivation of all, and your ensembles will work hard as you direct them to prepare for the concert.

It is always advantageous to let those ensembles perform that are prepared to do so. Of course, there is a disadvantage for you if you do not carefully select the places where the ensembles will perform. An audience that is rude during a performance can damage the morale of your ensemble, and it may take much time to repair it. Many of these performances can have harmful effects, especially if the student leaders placed in charge should bear the brunt of the criticism.

Set up the performance schedule during the summer months when you will have some free time. Write or call persons who are in charge of neighborhood house parties, business leaders, PTA clubs and other community functions where the children will be welcomed. Usually there are openings for high school singing groups at the places mentioned above, but you will have to make early contacts before their yearly schedule of activities has been formulated. These, of course, vary in different localities. You will be able to learn more about this with a few well-placed telephone calls to leaders in your community.

Suggested Performance Schedule

You will find below a suggested performance schedule for your small vocal ensembles:

- **A Cappella Choir.** School board meetings (district, county, state, small auxiliaries) conventions, concerts tours, festivals and performances with local semi professional groups such as little theaters and community ensembles.
- **Chamber Choir.** Small drawing rooms and den gatherings on special holidays, concerts and festivals.
- **Informal Choir.** Convalescent homes for the aged, elementary and junior high schools for recruiting purposes, concerts, festivals, community clubs and school assembly programs.
- **Madrigal Choir.** Visits to neighboring high schools for participation in activities of the humanities club and honor societies, concerts and festivals.
- **Modern Choir.** High school and college clubs, school and community banquets, concerts and festivals.
- **Octets, Sextets, Quartets and Trios**. Convalescent homes, weddings, civic clubs such as Kiwanis, Lions and the Optimist clubs, concerts and festivals.
- **All-Male Choirs.** School assembly programs, concerts for recruiting purposes at neighboring elementary and junior high schools (interchange with the informal choir) concerts and festivals.

- **All-Female Choir.** YWCA programs, school assemblies, concerts and festivals.

As you set up these performances, be sure that you brief your parent group about them so they can schedule themselves to help in organizing the project and provide proper chaperones and transportation for the choirs. It is your responsibility to provide opportunities for your students to perform, but it is also your responsibility to see that they are successful and safe while performing. If there are ever any doubts in your mind about a possible singing engagement, it would be in the best interest of the students to cancel it and wait for a better opportunity.

CHAPTER 2

HOW TO TRAIN THE INFORMAL CHOIR

It is impossible for a choral program to "start wrong" and "end right." It usually takes a fine director three or four years to reorganize a poor program and get it moving in the "right" direction. To help you in this realm, I will show you how to start the small vocal ensemble program correctly so that you will be assured of positive results later on.

You will find techniques in this chapter to help your students develop dark, medium and light vowel properties with specially prepared drills and vocalises. These developmental drills and vocalises are designed to help your students develop skills in accordance with the five basic performance skills that are introduced later in this chapter. In order for your students to be fine performers in an ensemble, each will have to develop these skills fully. Each skill is discussed and some remedies are introduced for their development among your students. These skills will be beneficial to your students when they begin the study of musical expression and style.

You will be shown how to teach the skills as fundamental points for successful performances, but the students must realize the length of time it takes to develop these into a syndrome of related parts. You can help by pointing out useful material to help them develop correctly. It must vary with each singer.

It is impossible for the singers to think of each skill separately while performing. Each of them must be developed singularly and sequentially in order for it to be effective as a part of the whole performing activity. In this chapter I will teach you how to develop needed skills thoroughly among your students so they will not be aware of them in action during a performance. Also, I will teach you how to blend the skills in with other developed vocal processes such as breathing and vowel formations.

You may permit any number of your students to remain in the informal choir for as long a period as they wish. Many of them will need the experiences this organization offers since the growth in vocal processes is dependent upon repetition of material. Each of your students will be encouraged to learn at his own rate of speed. No doubt, many of them may wish to remain for a longer period of time so that they can be certain to develop their talents fully. This is beneficial to your students since your higher ensembles require certain vocal technique development before an individual is accepted for membership.

INITIATING THE INFORMAL CHOIR

The informal choir should maintain sixty students in its ranks at all times. There should be fifteen singers in each section. This number permits you to advance singers as you have in a manner such as that suggested in Chapter 1. It is possible to divide this group, especially for performances held on the same day at different locations. But this is not always feasible since the students have not developed the necessary skills for outstanding performances. Actually, performance is secondary—becoming familiar with and developing vocal techniques further is primary. However, the students have developed some skills during full-choir experiences, and some performances should be permissible.

Tell your students before you permit them to graduate from the full choir to the informal choir, that working to develop their voices for better participation in the higher ensembles is the reason for being accepted in this choir; therefore, they must strive for perfection at all times.

Since the informal choir serves as a bridge for worthy students to cross over smoothly from the full-choir, only those students who rate superior on performance test and the Small Vocal Ensemble Rating Chart should be admitted to it. Make sure that your students understand this so that a pleasant atmosphere will exist at all times. On the other hand, you must have a good relationship with your students when you are teaching them techniques which could be considered "dull" if the students have little experience in this kind of work. Many of the compositions listed on the recommended music list should offer very few reading difficulties for those chosen for the informal choir.

VOWELS AND RESONANCES

But the portion of problems they will experience will emerge from the development of higher concepts such as vowel and resonance blending and the different *ah* vowel formations. The realistic hope is for your students to become familiar with the different vowel shapes and sounds, and the utilization of the *ah* vowel. The main emphasis is on understanding the purposes for which each is used: The colors of each ensemble are induced by the vowel as it comes in contact with the different resonances. Special colorings are achieved as a direct result of this combination and must be controlled by the singer in a most euphonious manner that is characteristic of each small vocal ensemble.

A Description of Dark and Light Vowel Properties

You should teach each member of the informal choir immediately how to achieve light and dark colors referred to in this book as vowel properties. They are developed by a mixture of two or more vowel sounds blended into one particular color. The technique involves adding or removing the color of a particular vowel sound to encourage the initial sound to change or maintain its color. There is further coloring from blended resonance on high or low vocal registrations. Further study of dark and light vowel properties will be found in Chapter 5. But be certain that your students understand coloration at this level in the Graduated Program and begin some developmental patterns.

Vowel Study

There is a multiplicity of vowels used in the English language, but most are modifications of the pure vowels *ay, ee, ah, o* and *oo*. It is always appropriate to develop the sounds of these vowels first, then move to modified sounds later on. You may want to isolate these sounds for your students. At any rate, they must understand both pure vowels and modified sounds. The vocalises in Illustrations 2.1a to 2.1d are provided to help them understand the difference in the sound patterns of the pure and modified vowels.

ILLUSTRATION 2.1a

ILLUSTRATION 2.1b

ILLUSTRATION 2.1c

ILLUSTRATION 2.1d

Vowel Unity

Vowel unity should be worked out technically among the sections of your informal choir at the beginning of its development. Mouth and lip formations should be somewhat the same throughout the sections. Work these formations out on every vocal level. Note the natural color of the vowels as they change from dark in the low register, to light in the upper register. Do not try to adjust these changes until your students become acquainted with them and can sing them spontaneously.

Five Rules for Blending the Resonances

Now, work to incorporate the sounds of the different resonances in different registrations of the voices of your students. You may want to work in blending the resonance if your students are ready at this point. If they are not prepared to blend the resonances, you will have to work at it on an individual basis to complete the study of vowel unity. Here are five rules for blending the resonances:

1. Blend low chest tones with nasal resonance by sending air toward the upper teeth.
2. If the vowel *oo* is sung with chest resonance, blend the *o* vowel to get the proper connection between the chest and the mouth area.
3. When singing the *ee* vowel, use the inner smile to blend the sound of the *oo* vowel.
4. Hum in the middle register to develop nasal and mouth resonance.
5. Keep all tones in the center of the mouth. This aids in keeping an open throat and in uniting all resonances at the same time in the top register.

Adjusting Vowel Unity

You can follow a prescribed order when adjusting vowel unity in certain compositions in the following manner:

- In close harmonic structures, permit your singers to use the same vowel structure throughout the ensemble.
- In open harmony, permit your singers to use the natural color of the vowel along with blended resonance in low or high registrations. This means that the sopranos could use a different color of vowel in contrast to the alto section when each is singing at different extremes in their vocal ranges. In many instances, the light voices will use a different vowel color when they sing in high registrations. In any case, you will have to make adjustments in lip and mouth formations (usually an inner or outer smile) or change blend status of the vowel by adding or taking away the effect of another.

Practice with your inner voices often in achieving vowel unity. Correct color in SATB music depends on the vocal beauty of these two lines. Let these students read through the music to learn its true character, then begin constructing the vowel unity with your altos and tenors. Use the unisonal drills above to aid in the proper development of the resonances.

The Definition of Resonance

Resonance is a reverberation of sound that is transmitted by the vocal cords to the different resonating chambers (chest, throat and mouth area, nose, sinus and head cavities) that can be developed among high school students through properly constructed vocalises. However, you must use caution when teaching your students how to develop resonance because many of them, in their exuberance to please you, will force the tone quality trying to give more than is actually needed. Tell them that proper resonance is achieved by the proper branching of the breath stream to the cavity areas.

Let your students practice the drills above daily. You will note, each day, degrees of improvements in resonance and tone production. Do not expect quick results, but work so that those students who will develop resonance at this point in the Graduated Program can use it to great advantage in higher ensembles. The results will crystalize faster among the females in the ensemble. You can expect some results among your boys, but full realization comes for a few of them only during their last year of study in high school.

DEVELOPING THE FIVE BASIC
PERFORMANCE SKILLS

Although the five basic performance skills will be developed among your students as you work them in your developmental plan, you must insure it further through solo material for each student. Again, you will have to depend on students in your higher ensembles to help out in this area. Naturally, you will not have enough time to hear each individual, but you should provide directions to your student helpers by telling them exactly what to do to encourage the correct development and what the outcome should be in each case.

Here are the five basic performance skills each of your students need to develop in order to become fine performers in an ensemble, or when singing a solo:

1. Each student must be able to measure and control the amount of breath pressure that is used for completing the musical phrase.
2. The correct tone quality is the product of blended vowel color and resonance.

3. Each student must have a knowledge of each musical, histori-cal period in order to interpret music correctly.
4. Each voice must be developed enough to get the proper vocal response to sing different compositions correctly.
5. Aside from the development of vowel and resonance blend-ing techniques, students must have a good theoretical background in order to transmit the composition's character to the audience.

Keep written records of the progress your students make so you will know when all the skills have been developed. It is advantageous to get the group started in developing these skills as soon as possible. A sample form for keeping reports on your students as they make progress in developing the five performance skills is provided in Illustration 2.2.

FIVE BASIC PERFORMANCE SKILLS
PROGRESS REPORT

NAME _____ GRADE _____ ADDRESS _____
SCHOOL _____ HOME PHONE _____

1. Uses correct breath pressure.   YES ____ NO ____
   Recommendations _____

2. Blends the resonances and vowels correctly.   YES ____ NO ____
   Recommendations _____

3. Has completed the study on the music
   historical outline.   YES ____ NO ____
   Recommendations _____

4. Has a good vocal response.   YES ____ NO ____
   Recommendations _____

5. Has a knowledge of music theory.   YES ____ NO ____
   Recommendations _____

_____
DIRECTOR'S SIGNATURE

ILLUSTRATION 2.2

Measuring and Controlling Breath Pressure

Your students learned how to fill the lungs and administer proper breath support during full-choir experiences. This, of course, was taught to them for a good reason. However, at this point, the abdominal muscles should be developed enough to let a slow stream of air flow evenly toward the vocal cords for proper phonation. It is time now to begin utilizing only that amount of air that is necessary to sing the musical phrase; but you must provide some instances, either by vocalises, or stopping places (cadences) in the composition you are working on with your students.

Let each student become familiar with his own air capacity so that he, not you, will be the judge as to the amount of air that is needed to sing certain musical phrases. One thing is certain: Taking in too much air into the lungs at this point in the Graduated Program is wasted energy. An increased amount of air is needed only when more volume is needed, or longer phrases are present in the composition. But even in these cases, you should teach your students to eliminate tension. There should be a definite advancement in relieving it at this stage of their development. Teach them that too much of a relaxed attitude is also detrimental to the effectiveness of the musical phrase.

Permit your students to practice the exercises in Illustrations 2.3a and 2.3b in spare times at their homes. These must be practiced on an individual basis, but other students can be present to encourage the singer. Ask your singers to work on one exercise at a time. When they can sing it successfully, that is, with a decreased amount of air and abdominal (breath) pressure, let them progress to the next exercise.

ILLUSTRATION 2.3a

ILLUSTRATION 2.3b

Your students should breathe at the end of the dotted line only! Now, proceed by using the same amount of air and breath pressure that they used during full-choir experiences. Then, proceed to decrease the amount as they sing in the two exercises above. Be certain that this process is not rushed. Permit your section leaders to check for development each day. Ask the section leaders to help by carrying the students through the following drill: Tell each singer to place his hands on each side of his body two or three inches below the ribs. Then, the section leader should place his hands on the hands of the singer with the intent of checking his breath pressure. This should be accomplished while the singer is in the process of singing. On the other hand, the same results will be achieved if the singer simply releases the air slowly in a hissing manner while the leader counts slowly to eight.

While it is important to develop the correct usage of the breath pressure, do not forget to articulate consonants clearly and quickly during the process.

Blending Vowel Color and Resonance

The blending of vowel color and resonance is very difficult to develop among students because it is a mental process rather than a physical one. But it can be developed if the singers "think" the process. It is hoped that you have permitted your singers to begin the development of vowel color and resonance separately. If they have not quite developed the usage of these, do not rush the process here. Rather, encourage them by permitting each to sing some parts of the composition that you are working on to help in the development of the skills in the shortest time possible.

Begin the process by blending resonance in the upper chest

register of all singers. Be sure to give perfect demonstrations with your own voice, or you may want to call in a local professional or use a recording. In any case, you should make your students aware that the pure vowels are mixed with chest and nasal resonance. Use the same unisonal drills for all voices. When a suitable mixture has been achieved, move the notes higher or lower so the students can hear the blend patterns at different musical levels. When the blending process has been fully achieved, practice for development through appropriate vocalises.

As soon as possible, begin work in the upper head register with a normally supported tone using the *o* vowel. Your students should get the sound of natural resonance. Now, blend carefully the nasal resonance by adding an *n* making the word sound similar to *on*. This will be achieved when you tell the students to try to feel the *n* sound at the nose level while singing the *o* at the mouth level. Be sure there is resonance present from the chest in this process. Be certain that the tones strike a medium between the chest, mouth, and nose area.

The air that is branched toward the chest, mouth and nose completes the fusion and creates a suitable mixture. When your students have successfully connected the different resonances, blend in all vowel sounds beginning with the *ay* and *ee* combination first. See page 103 of Chapter 5 to culminate this activity.

Teaching Interpretation

Teach your students all of the facets of interpretation so there can be a complete understanding of each. Some directors try to approach it through conducting alone, but this is never effective without the emotional aspect and a knowledge of musical terms. On the other hand, conducting is merely a sign language. It must have understanding from a verbal language to be truly effective:

• **Dynamics** The simplest way to teach dynamics to your students is out of musical context. Decide the proportionate extremes of loud and soft dynamic levels, then, include them in a pattern similar to the one below:

$$pp, p, mp, mf, f, ff$$

Practice other dynamic levels out of musical context also. There are no set rules governing the degree of loudness or softness for the dynamics, because these will vary among different compositions. But definite distinctions should be made for young students. This is one reason why you should train your singers to perform the music as thoroughly as possible in accordance with the correct style, mood and dynamics. In addition, study compositional trends, motives, text and the particular style of composers before you arrive at a manner of including dynamic proportions in the composition you and your ensemble are performing.

• **The Renaissance Style (1400–1600)** This music must be sung with restraint. It must be devoid of fast tempos. Since musical expression is characterized intensely in this period, expressive word character should be the main factor in determining the tempo, mood and dynamic proportions of the music. Avoid special effects and accents of all kinds. The music will sound authentic if you use only those accents and dynamic levels that are dictated to you by the natural rise and fall of the text and the phrase.

• **The Baroque Style (1600–1750)** This music can be performed with deliberate color. It is generally felt that tempos are more deliberate than those of the Renaissance period. In this sense, you will have more freedom of meter, but you should use restraint and never permit your ensembles to use exaggeration, rubato, or wide ranges in dynamic proportions.

• **The Classical Style (1750–1825)** This period brought about unity of design and more musical purpose than any other period in the historical outline. The elements of music were used in this period to bring more fabrication to the designed proportions of musical harmony; therefore, you should use tempos and dynamics with moderation.

• **The Romantic Style (1825–1900)** This period represented a venture into individualism in musical expression. Tempo, mood and musical coloration were used to characterize extremism in compositional techniques. Sudden fast or slow tempos were used for the first time, especially among the instrumentalists. Some choral compositions from this period should be approached with moderation, but most can be performed with freedom in musical expression and dynamics.

PROPER PREPARATION FOR A PERFORMANCE

Choose your music for informal choir performances with the following objectives in mind:

1. To increase the interest of the students.
2. To capture the attention and approval of your audience.
3. To be used as developmental showcase pieces.

All levels of difficulty can be chosen so that a suitable program of study can be outlined for your students. This is quite necessary since your audiences will be used to outstanding performances by way of television. If you expect audiences to attend your concerts, the level of your performances must be equal to that of the television medium. For this reason, every musical detail in the area of proper note-range structures, rhythm, harmony, vowel-consonant contacts, style, mood, proper phrasing, dynamic control, vowel color, and the articulation of consonants should be perfected at least two weeks before the concert. You may spend the remaining two weeks preparing your students psychologically for the performance, becoming familiar with the structure of the program and the ensemble formation.

It is never too early to begin working on the musical details in musical compositions you will perform. In doing so, you will be giving credence to the final musical product and will insure an outstanding performance by the ensemble. In the main, one outstanding performance is proper motivation for your informal choir to work toward another. It also serves to motivate your audience to return to hear future performances.

Talk to members of the informal choir often concerning good vocal and physical fitness to perform at concerts. During the remaining two weeks before the concert, tell your students to get enough rest so that they will be refreshed and have the proper amount of energy to perform at the concert. Tell them that no one can perform well without the proper amount of rest. Many performances do not go well because the members of the ensembles are fatigued and can not perform their best under such circumstances. Actually, a look of confidence and freshness during the concert will motivate your audience to pay close attention to every facet of your concert. If your students are tired and seem to be falling asleep on the stage, do not be surprised if your audience reacts the same way. There is a possibility that some will never return to hear your ensembles again.

Three Drills for Developing
Correct Breathing

One way to prepare your students for the strain and stress of a good vocal performance is to teach them how to develop correct breathing habits in singing. This idea alone will help your students present an ideal performance. If the breathing muscles are developed, they will be less likely to tire so easily during the performance.

ILLUSTRATION 2.4 Use all vowels.

Here are three drills that are effective for developing proper breathing. Drills one and two should be assigned to students to practice outside of class. Drill three should be practiced regularly in class.

- **Drill 1:** Place your hands on the sides of your body, thumbs pointing toward your back. Inhale as much air as possible without raising your shoulders. This process should cause expansion around your waist and in your back. Without moving, sing a low tone. Be careful that the air does not move toward your vocal cords too quickly. Practice daily.
- **Drill 2:** With your hands in position as in Drill 1, inhale air, feeling the expansion around your waist. Walk eight or ten paces while holding the air with your abdominal muscles. Then release the air slowly in a hissing manner while walking another eight or ten paces. Practice daily.
- **Drill 3:** Inhale as much air as possible, feeling the expansion around your waist, and sing the exercise in Illustration 2.4 very slowly.

Other drills similar to Drill 3 should be created to encourage good breathing. Many directors use phrases directly from the music to teach correct breathing to their students, but this often becomes practice for that particular composition only. Students need to develop good breathing habits from vocalises designed for the purpose of developing correct breathing. When thoroughly developed, these breathing patterns can be employed voluntarily in other choral compositions.

PLANNING THE PROGRAM

Some misinformed persons believe that high school students are not capable of performing the music in a creditable manner, or that amateurs cannot create the same kind of musical atmosphere as professionals do. But this is not true. It can be done, if you will follow this plan: Plan your concerts during the summer months when you have plenty of leisure time. Try to estimate the cost for each one. You will find that the only expense will be that of your programs. Actually, the expense of having all programs that you will use during the year printed on a once-a-year basis will be even less expensive than having them printed each time you present a concert. If you have access to career centers in your school system, you can save tremendously by permitting one to do the printing for you.

Include program notes on the programs. In this way, you can teach the audience some musical or historical facts about specific periods, composers and their compositions. In this way, you can inform them of the high caliber instructional programs you have instituted at the school. Aside from this, prepare the music your ensembles will sing to an excellent musical level.

Be sure to work the stage lighting instructions for the concert and permit a well-trained stage hand group to take full responsibility for this. Determine the amount of time it takes for an ensemble to arrive at its position on the stage and inform your stage crew about this so that they will know exactly where movement will occur in the program and will be able to control the lighting effects at those points.

Try to present several of your outstanding soloists on the concert. It is always a pleasant experience for the parents of these children to see them perform in this manner.

STAGE DECORUM

Ask your students to arrive for the concert at least thirty minutes before it begins to engage in warm-up procedures and to receive final instructions. Of course, it is good to clear up all details of the concert so that you and your students will present a smooth program exposition to your audience.

Start the performance on time! The audience expects this. Inconsistent timing is always a sign of unpreparedness and gives your audience the idea that the program will be mediocre.

If you permit small ensembles from the informal choir to perform on the program, let them make noiseless exchanges during the movement in a way that is not distracting to your audience. This can be executed well through a planned exchange, with each student knowing exactly where he is to go as quickly as possible. However, do not give your audience the idea that you are hurrying through the performance, rather, that you are simply obeying established rules of stage decorum; consequently, you should ask your students to walk to their positions gracefully.

Acknowledging audience response is a matter that must be taught properly during the informal choir experience. Teach your soloists how to smile and bow gracefully in response to the audience. Most high school students need lessons in this respect that most choir directors overlook, taking for granted that the students already know this common practice. But, do not leave this element to chance! Teach it correctly so that each student will execute it in the manner you prescribe.

Rather than permit the entire ensemble to bow with their backs and heads in a forward manner, ask them to smile and lower their heads at the neck level to achieve a better uniformity since some students are taller than others and the horizontal effect will be distorted in the former.

CREATING INTEREST THROUGH SOLO MATERIAL

The informal choir is, in a sense, a training choir in the Graduated Program. It is the beginning experience for those students who will be chosen for participation in the higher ensembles. For this reason, one hour a week can be set aside for individual solos. Each student in the choir should be given the opportunity to sing an assigned solo before members of the informal choir. The prevailing atmosphere for the occasion should be a sincerity of purpose for everyone. The soloists should be well rehearsed before they are permitted to sing before the group. Before the semester ends, each student should have performed at least once.

Teach these specific elements through the solo work: Tone spiralling, good attacks and releases, good interpretation, proper breathing, proper vowel formation, the correct articulation of consonants, resonance blending, proper stage decorum and correct posture. One word of caution: Never permit the students to be openly critical of each other. Rather, ask each to write his critique on a sheet of paper. You can discuss the points of the critique sheets with the performer at a later date. Give the performers remedies and examples by which they will be able to practice for the elimination of their faults. You can watch for improvements among these students during rehearsals of the entire group. But, find something good to say to these students behind an open analysis of their faults in order to encourage them to improve in their weak areas.

Some students may complain that they are not soloists. You should find a method to convince them that this is part of a method for improving tonal quality in the choir as well as preparing them for eventual graduation into higher ensembles. Once this idea is clearly understood by each student, you will have increased the chances of having a good atmosphere in which all of your students can perform regardless of differing abilities as soloists.

IMPROVING SIGHT READING

Your students in the informal choir should not experience too many problems in sight reading since they have received prior choral experience in junior high school, but improvements are always in order for the young singer. The more experience he has in sight reading, the broader his scope will be in all musical activities. You can improve your student's sight reading ability with the following:

- Compose eight measure phrases for each day in the week for your students to perform at sight.
- Compose at least four eight measure phrases per key signature, including other eight measure phrases in the relative or the parallel minor keys.

You may vary the rhythmical activity of these phrases to correspond with the student's rhythmical understanding. You may choose the phrases directly from some choral compositions that your students are not familiar with. But, be certain to choose them in sequential key signature order, and according to the needs of the members of the informal choir.

It is necessary to find words for your phrases if you compose the music, because all sight reading experiences will not be effective without them at this stage in the Graduated Program.

Let each member of the informal choir learn to sing the pitches of the syllables representing the chromatic scale. Place these in a permanent place in the choral room. You can help the students learn these quickly by asking the choir to sing the pitches as you point them out indiscriminately each day. Create interest by using different rhythmic patterns each time. Of course, the development should begin slowly in the beginning, but pick up speed as progress is evidenced. Now, transfer the sounds of the syllables to the actual notes in every major and minor key. To eliminate some wasted time, work the transferred note sound out according to the scale-range of each voice and permit them to practice separately.

When you introduce new music to the informal choir, let the

pianist play through the music once with the voices. The second reading can be without the aid of the piano. Ask the students to circle all mistakes. Then evaluate each and give projections for correct performances of the music. Naturally, the third performance should include all necessary instructions for a perfect performance.

RECOMMENDED MUSIC LIST

The music chosen here can be used for the sight reading experiences your informal choir will need for development, or all of it can be used as exercises to aid in the development of vocal techniques. On the other hand, all compositions are suitable for inclusion on different programs by either small ensembles taken directly from the informal choir or the choir itself.

Title	Grade	Composer	Number	Publisher
Agnus Dei	D	Morley	1771	E. C. Schirmer
Adoramus Te Christe	E	Palestrina	EM6578	Carl Fischer
Autumn Reverie	E	Young	689	Somerset Press
Battle Hymn Of The Republic	M	Arr. Roy Ringwald	A-28	Shawnee
Black Is The Color	E	Arr. Luboff	3017	Walton
Carol of The Bells	E	Leontovich/ Wilhousky	CM4604	Carl Fischer
Cantate Domino	E	Hassler	ES18	Bourne
Cherubim Song (No. 7)	ME	Bortniansky	687	H. W. Gray
Christus Factus Est	D	Bruckner	748	G. Schirmer
Come Again Sweet Love	M	Dowland	81274	Flammer
Cry Out and Shout	ME	Nystedt	1974	Summy
Eternal Life	E	Dugan Stickles	322-40018	Theodore Presser

Title	Grade	Composer	Number	Publisher
Fa Una Canzone	E	Vecchi	556	G. Schirmer
Hospodi Pomilui	MD	Lvov/ Wilhousky	CM6580	Carl Fischer
Hosanna	D	Hennagin	2805	Walton
I Hear America Singing	MD	Kettering	SP694	Somerset
Let Nothing Ever Grieve Thee	D	Brahms	6093	C. F. Peters
May Day Carol	E	Arr. Vance	2022-7	Belwin
No Man Is An Island	ME	Whitney/Kramer/ Ringwald	A-195	Shawnee
Now Let Every Tongue Adore Thee	ME	Bach	30	E. C. Schirmer
One World	M	O'Hara/Wilson	1039-8	Bourne
The Lord Bless You and Keep You	E	Lutkin	1089	Summy
The Star Spangled Banner	ME	Arr. McKelvy	MF335	Mark Foster
These Things Shall Be	M	Henderson	CM7139	Carl Fischer

CHAPTER 3

HOW TO DEVELOP THE ALL-MALE CHOIR

In this chapter, I will show you how to develop the proper tone quality in each section of the all-male choir by discussing their characteristic sound pattern. You will be shown how to teach falsetto quality correctly to those boys who are ready to be taught. This will lead you naturally to a study of light and dark vowel properties which will help you achieve the correct coloring in the choir and prepare the boys for the work they will do in the higher ensembles.

I will show you how to get the proper connections between resonances through discussion and developmental vocalises. With this work as a base, I will show you how to achieve the correct blend when your singers are singing in either the low or high registers of the chest.

It is important to the success of the small vocal ensemble program for you to promote only those boys who can meet the qualifications for entrance into the all-male choir. This is complimentary to those boys who can earn good ratings for admission into the ensemble. Other boys, in time, will come to realize what such a program means, and will strive to become members of it in the future.

Since the all-male ensemble follows the informal group, it would be wise to keep the membership small. A good number to begin with is twelve—no more than twenty at full strength. The breakdown for the all-male ensemble is as follows:

2 1st Tenors		4 1st Tenors
2 2nd Tenors	*or*	4 2nd Tenors
3 Baritones		5 Baritones
5 Basses		7 Basses

Note how the tenors compare in numbers with the other sections. The rationale for this is that most baritones and basses of high school age have limited resonance power on an individual basis and cannot achieve a full supportive sound in the chest area. The head voice is more resonant than any other vocal region among these voices. You will have to make the decision to add strength to these voices by increasing the number of singers to each part. But you will achieve the proper balance between these voice parts and your tenor section because of the beauty of the mixtures that you will make among these as will be suggested to you in this chapter.

ACHIEVING THE PROPER TONE QUALITY IN THE TENOR SECTION

The tenor must use proper vocal control in order to sing the music as the composer intended it to be sung. He must maintain control because he is the "leader" in the ensemble as the soprano is in the mixed groups. He must also practice his part separately from the other sections to be certain that the correct tone quality is developed. This kind of practice is necessary when you begin teaching your students the correct use of falsetto quality.

Teaching Falsetto Quality Correctly

Falsetto quality is thought of as an extension of the head voice, and should be developed as soon as there is a noticeable change of quality in the male voice. Be careful when working in this region because most boys experience difficulty when learning to sing with this quality for the first time.

Explain to your boys that the falsetto range is an extra feature added to their voices that can be used to sing high notes without difficulties. Provide them with solos that capture the falsetto voice.

Begin this development among your boys in the following manner: Begin at the top of the range. This note usually lies on C5. Let the student sing slowly down the scale until he reaches the apex of the head voice. This note will vary among voices, but will generally fall around E, F#, or G above C4. It is better to continue the work at this point by permitting the students to imitate your voice, or that of another student. It is necessary for your students to hear a correct example. It renders a "stereophonic" quality to the all-male choir. Teach all members of your choir to sing in the falsetto voice.

Light Vowel Properties in Falsetto Registration

Light vowel properties are modifications of natural vowel sounds and are made when the performer uses the *ah* vowel formation and its appropriate blended vowel color to sing correctly. They are used to add strength as well as beauty to the tones in high-note registrations of TTBB arrangements. Some teachers use a wrong developmental approach when they try to get their singers to "send" the tones to the back of the room in order to add strength to them. This approach should not be used to develop falsetto quality. Rather, ask your students to permit the tones to blend naturally with the sound that is filtered by the resonating cavities of the throat, mouth and nose and the head cavities. When your students blend in the light vowel properties, the sound will be pleasing. The mixture is correct when the sound of the choir has an "echo" effect. Use the vocalises in Illustrations 3.1a and 3.1b to help your students develop this falsetto quality. Remember that the voices will sound an octave lower than the vocalises are written.

A poor falsetto sound will occur if you permit singers to sing without the air being branched toward the nose. This kind of singing will always sound as though it is below the true pitch level, and many times it will be. Humming with closed lips is an effective technique that can be used to encourage the correct sound. Once the problem has been eliminated, tell your students to never use nasal resonance alone. It must be blended with the other resonances to be effective on every vocal level.

ILLUSTRATION 3.1a

ILLUSTRATION 3.1b

ILLUSTRATION 3.2

Achieving the Proper Sound Between
The Head and Falsetto Registers

The excerpt in Illustration 3.2 can be used to help you teach your students how to sing light vowel properties in the falsetto registration properly. Continue the development through other appropriate vocalises.

It is evident in the first tenor line in the excerpt above that the proper connections between the head and falsetto registers must be executed evenly in order to keep the continuity of musical expression and harmonic beauty in this composition, especially while singing the F to D on the word "I've." You should teach the students to apply the *ah* vowel while maintaining its light vowel property. Be certain that the vowel form is not damaged while singing the slurred notes, and that the passage will not become muddled with too much dark quality when you permit your first tenors to blend the *uh* vowel. This is important to remember because the color character must be pleasing

ILLUSTRATION 3.3

in those areas where the slur occurs. To complete this phase of the work, articulate the consonant at the last moment before moving to the next word which has the slurring effect also. Move smoothly to the word "seen" by going to the vowel *ee* modified with the *oo* quality.

Let your students develop an even scale between the falsetto and head voices. Assign more work similar to the exercise in Illustration 3.3 to encourage this kind of mixture.

Instruct your students to lift the sides of the tongue (high-arched *ah* vowel) and keep its tip directly behind the bottom teeth as they move to light falsetto quality. If need be, tell them to release some of the air as they shift to this quality to present the correct color. Keep the *ah* vowel formation perfectly formed. Do not become alarmed if the sides of the tongue are not touching the upper teeth. Develop this formation by holding the jaw down lightly with the hand while singing an appropriate vocalise.

Achieving the Proper Connection
Between the Head and Falsetto Registers

There is one technique that every male singer needs to develop: an even scale, void of noticeable quality changes, between the chest, head and falsetto registers. Encourage your singers to undertake this task. First, let them listen to recordings of fine, all-male choirs. These recordings can help them understand why it is necessary to have an even scale at their command. Ask them to listen specifically to passages where vocal quality between the head-falsetto register is one distinct sound.

Second, study the passage with them in Illustration 3.4 to discover how to sing an even scale in the first tenor part, then move to other compositions for full development.

The first four notes in the first tenor line above can be sung with chest quality mixed with nasal resonance. Make the remaining notes sound exactly as the first notes by keeping the mouth open as much as possible, and by using an outer smile to solidify the light vowel prop-

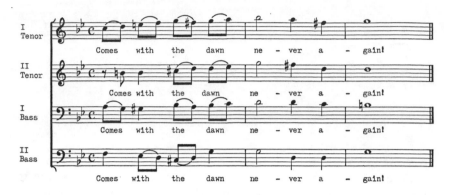

ILLUSTRATION 3.4

erties. Be sure that your students utilize an even breath flow in the process.

Study the vowel mixtures below and practice them with the aid of vocalises constructed in the falsetto register. Practice them often to become totally familiar with this quality:

> EE and OO
> Ay and EE
> Eh and Ih
> Ah and Uh
> O and OO
> Aw and O

Use the *ah* vowel formation as a base for developing the mixtures above. Without this development, a study of proper connections between the head and falsetto registers will be a complete waste of time.

Proper Articulation in Falsetto Registrations

Consonants should not be over articulated in falsetto registrations. Proper articulation should exist to permit time to execute the smooth interchange of qualities between the chest, head and falsetto qualities. Check your singers for proper breath pressure so there will be a proper amount of elasticity at the abdomen. Tension must not be allowed to build up before proper articulation occurs. Actually, it does not harm the falsetto quality to release some air pressure on certain syllables. However, if a clicking of the glottis is heard, the tone quality has too much consonant interference. It is okay to permit the clicking process in beginning voice classes, but limit its use as the voices move toward full development.

LEGATO DICTION

Let your singers develop singing correctly the style of completing the musical score by making the consonants effective at each word-end: Teach them how to release the note at the end of a phrase in order to prepare for another phrase, but apply the consonant between words as if it were an elongation of the note's sound. This process is called Legato Diction. To make the process effective, ask your singers to add the vowel *ah* at the end of every consonant, except when the word being sung ends with the consonant the next word begins with. But remember, this form of legato diction sounds good only among all-male choirs when every one in the first tenor section sings with falsetto quality.

USING VOWEL FORMS IN PIANISSIMO SECTIONS CORRECTLY

When singing pianissimo sections, many singers tend to open the mouth too wide at each corner, putting too much outer smile into the color of the vowel that intensifies its colorlessness especially when little attempts are made at blending the resonances. An inner smile is necessary to blend the correct color of vowels in pianissimo sections. If more light vowel properties are needed, let your students use either light natural head resonance, if the tones are written in that area, or projectional resonance if the tones are written in the low chest registration. This will place the tone quality at the cheekbone level, giving it the necessary color it needs for correct carrying power. But you must teach your singers to use proper vowel-lip formations when using projectional resonance, otherwise improper blend patterns will be the result. Of course, you can plan the kind of sound you would like to achieve in each phrase of the compositional texture so that tonal control will be assured. The phrase in Illustration 3.5 has been included here to influence your thinking when you prepare the tonal textural plan for each composition you may choose for the all-male ensemble.

Plan the kind of vowel color scheme you will need for an effective *oo* vowel for each voice in the composition. You may want your

ILLUSTRATION 3.5

first tenors to begin with the natural color of the *oo* vowel, blending the *o* vowel in falsetto registrations, or substitute soft natural head resonance with natural *oo* vowel quality in the high tessitura. This would be compatible with the first bass quality if you permit that line to use blended *oo* quality throughout the phrase. But you will have to regulate the resonance in this voice to increase the chance of achieving proper balance. The divided bass parts should be even throughout the phrase. Consequently, you will have to use a blended *oo* vowel in the bottom part, but a natural *oo* vowel sound in the top voice. So that the students will not become confused, let them write the pure vowel and its blended form beneath their parts. This will insure success in vowel blending. The inner smile approach should be set with the first vowel in the word and preserved until the phrase has ended. However, you can use the high-arched *ah* vowel sound with the appropriate words in the phrase. This kind of planning will add greatly to the correct sound of your ensemble and make it distinguishable from the barbershop quartet which has its own characteristic sound.

THE SECOND TENOR

The second tenor in the all-male choir sings an important line within the framework of good musical construction. The composer who writes or arranges for the all-male choir should pay particular attention to the following questions:

1. Does the line fit perfectly into the construction of the music?

2. Is it interesting?
3. Does it add support in making the melody attractive?
4. Are there instances when the line cannot be distinguished from the baritone line?
5. Are there allowances made for the use of proper resonances?
6. Is the melody given to this line occasionally?

Many second tenors are encouraged to sing their part creatively when some of the questions above can be answered satisfactorily. Would you schedule a composition for your all-male choir if none of the questions above could be answered satisfactorily?

A common misconception is that tenors are divided in terms of their singing abilities to execute the music well. Those who do not meet certain standards are moved into the second tenor section of the all-male choir. This practice is not a good one. The musical structure in the second tenor part is important in the musical scheme of the composition; consequently, your second tenors should have an active technique to enable them to sing the part creatively. You should make the same technical demands on the second tenors as you would on the first tenors.

Supporting the First
Tenor Properly

Tonal weight distribution is the process of blending the vowel sounds and singing them a degree softer or louder than the written dynamic level. It is most effective when used to increase or decrease resonance power and regulate volume and balance in the music. Generally, it affects the third and fifth of chords when they appear in certain positions. A lion's share of the responsibility for its effectiveness rests with the second tenor, especially when support is needed for the melodic structure in the composition.

Ask your students to begin supporting the first tenor by the same vowel forms and modification system as you have taught the first tenors. Then, teach them to think of tonal weight distribution in terms of equalizing the vowel sound vertically and horizontally.

Tonal weight distribution also involves voice weight which affects the make-up of the voices within the section. The distribution of notes in example one of Illustration 3.6 has the third of the chord in the first tenor. It is in a strong position according to the chord scheme; therefore, the second tenor must match the "strongness" of the third by a natural harmonic balance. No special color scheme is needed to support the first tenor because the C in the second tenor is

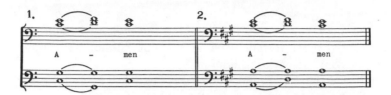

ILLUSTRATION 3.6

the root of the chord and will blend well with the third above it. However, because the D, that is the fifth of the chord, is a minor third below the first tenor, tonal weight must be applied to the D in the second tenor to create equality of sound within the chord. Other reasons for using tonal weight are: (1) When tonal weight is used correctly, the notes in the high registrations are effective. (2) It helps to preserve the blend between the chest and nasal cavities. (3) It also helps to achieve a better vertical blend in the chord structure. When such movement occurs in all-male choir compositions, this kind of scrutiny is needed to present a more satisfying musical experience for the singer and the audience.

The first chord in the second example has the third of the chord in the second tenor. Tell the students to blend the third by decreasing volume in this area. Once the "right amount" has been measured, let your students use the same amount each time they practice.

The second chord in the second example gives the second tenors the tonic, an octave higher above the bass line. Naturally, the tonic must be tuned perfectly between these voices. It is proper to increase the resonance power in the second tenor for proper support of the first tenor, and to present good vertical proportions among the lines for good musical results.

USING HIGH CHEST RESONANCE CORRECTLY

High chest resonance must be developed fully to permit the ultimate in artistic vocal production. The development of these two resonances, low and high chest, should be high on the agenda for all rehearsals. Do not expect quick results because many high school boys do not develop it fully until later in life. But, this should encourage you to nurture it and begin some correct developmental approaches at this level in the Graduated Program.

Compose other vocalises similar to the one in Illustration 3.7 to help your students develop high chest resonance. Work to blend nasal

ILLUSTRATION 3.7 Use all vowels.

and head resonance simultaneously. For good results, ask your singers to practice other than during class time. Choose compositions specifically for this purpose and give attention to as many individual voices as possible. The falsetto registration has been included in the vocalise above to help your students develop resonance in this area of the voice also. Be sure to present good examples for them to develop these vocal mixtures correctly.

UNDERSTANDING BLENDING TECHNIQUES

Interpretation, timbre and dynamics play important roles in the blending process. Each must be understood from a single viewpoint, then compounded for a production of the whole. As in all art forms, a feeling of completeness must be generated from the blend process to the person who is experiencing it. If poor intonation occurs, the timbre within the ensemble is faulty. If there are empty moments in the music, all three areas are faulty. However, if development and understanding are lacking, it is futile to employ blending techniques at any point in the composition.

Interpretation

The music must be understood from the director's point of view through historical data, good vocal demonstrations, terminology, and finally, proper directing techniques. In the historical realm, you can include some biographical material concerning the composer, other musical works composed by him, and some aspects of the period in which he lived. You may want to include other musicians who were contemporaries. On the other hand, include some descriptive material on certain compositions such as Negro Spirituals. Give specific instructions on how to achieve the correct, characteristic color for them. You can be specific by assigning certain recordings for the students to study and analyze.

At the last stage, you may ask the students to watch you carefully to help bring the correct meaning to the music, or you may recite the text of the music in an expressive manner, calling attention to specific tone qualities and phrasing. Progress is made when students can recite the text with similar quality and understanding.

Timbre

All voices must share in the responsibility of changing timbre at different vocal levels. There must exist a variety of tone colors in the composition because variety exists at different emotional levels in humans. These emotions, expressed naturally and sometimes individually, influence the differences in tone colors in the music. But timbre, brought on by these emotions, can always be controlled and memorized through thorough practice, good motivation and positive directing techniques.

Dynamics

If you wish to practice the dynamic format out of musical context, it is better to practice the two extremes first so that the proper balance can be made with the others. The format has been simplified for your convenience in Illustration 3.8.

Soft	Medium		Loud (Firm)
pp p mp	mf	f	ff

ILLUSTRATION 3.8

You can plan how soft or loud your extremes should sound in the dynamic format above for each composition you may choose. With this format, dynamic levels for each composition can be described and placed in your files for a permanent record in this manner:

1. Name of the composition, composer and publisher.
2. The pianissimo levels in this composition should have light vowel properties, and must be sung just above a whisper. Each student can maintain a feeling of "calm repose" while singing this dynamic marking.
3. The piano level should be a degree louder than the pianissimo sections, but a change of color is more desirable.
4. More resonance and deep-set vowel color are needed to make the mezzo piano levels effective.

5. Increase the resonance power in the mezzo forte levels.
6. Forte and fortissimo levels call for much control, but the singers should open with as much resonance power as is needed to do justice to the music. These terms tell singers to sing firmly, not loudly!

Perform the music only after you and your singers have investigated its dynamic levels. Understanding, in the main, comes through this investigation.

ACHIEVING THE PROPER TONE QUALITY IN THE BARITONE SECTION

A natural phenomenon that helps to influence the all-male choir's characteristic sound is the color of the male voice and its natural ability to change color at different registrations. Teach your baritones how to use these interchangeably with the different resonances. One naturally colored area occurs between B4 and E4. It occurs when the larnynx shifts in an upward motion causing a blend of the head voice. Be sure to blend the baritone and tenor parts into a suitable mixture when they are singing in this registration.

Low Chest Quality

Teach low quality in this fashion: Ask the baritones to send the air toward the upper teeth when singing in low chest registrations. Utilize an inner smile as they approach the high chest region. Notice the definite change in quality between these vocal regions. Adjust the resonance so that the voices do not protrude and be heard above the ensemble. Forcing the tone will cause some structural damage to the music.

As you work to develop blend in the low chest register, a medium dark "edge" will begin forming in some voices. You will need to pay strict attention to this quality. It is the beginning of mature resonance. Nurture it carefully!

Do not let your singers use too much breath support in the low chest registrations. Tell them to use an increased amount of breath pressure only when it is necessary to increase the volume.

Using Control in the Quality Change Area

Use the *ah* vowel as a basic formation to achieve the correct color when you begin blending your students' resonances around the quality change area. Send the air toward the nose, then move back and forth a perfect fifth beginning with third space E and ending with B below middle C. Change the quality of the *ah* vowel from a vertical sound to an horizontal sound by changing from the high-arched *ah* vowel to the medium *ah* vowel sound. Let your students develop this quality change area through appropriate vocalises.

Achieving Upper Chest Quality

Although upper chest quality is natural, male singers should understand how it is achieved in this vocal region. Tell them to place the tone on the cheekbone, or near the ears. The head tone will be natural, but be sure that your singers blend nasal resonance also.

Lyrical quality can be utilized easily in the upper chest registration. When it is used, permit your singers to cover the tones and control the vowel color so that it is agreeable to the color character of the composition.

When you permit your singers to perform compositions of a robust nature, it is better to let the natural sound of the male chest voice sing through the music. In this case, tonal control is subservient to the style of the music.

Covered Tones Versus Vowel Color Ingredients

A covered tone is the result of vowels blended with *ee*, *o* and *oo* quality and sung with the resonance from the chest and nasal cavities. Proper breath support must be used with the covered tone so that vibrato can be controlled to prevent pitch variations in the music's structure. Tell your singers to let chest and nasal tones, blended into a suitable mixture, take control in the covered tone by raising the chest somewhat, feeling the sensation of sound at each resonating point. The covered tone is most effective in pianissimo sections and can be used to support the harmonic structure in the high tessitura of the baritone part.

Vowel color ingredients are mixtures that can influence tonal beauty. They are used to make the covered tone musically satisfying. You will be able to tell when the "right" mixtures have been achieved within the covered tone because a variety of shades ranging from the nasal-head in the high chest registration to nasal-chest in the low chest registration will occur in the music. Do not restrict the vowel color ingredients. This will cause the covered tone to be too thin. But, be careful that you do not use too many dark colored vowels. These cause the covered tone to be too somber.

THE ALL-MALE CHOIR'S TONAL PATTERN

The diagram below shows the scope of light to dark tonal patterns that should exist in the all-male choir. The bass line represents the darkest portion of the sound. It seldom moves out of the low chest region. Assign solo material to these singers so they can develop their voices throughout their ranges.

Study the diagram in Illustration 3.9 to help you understand the tonal pattern in your all-male choir:

1st Tenors	falsetto, head, chest	Tones are Light.
2nd Tenors	head, chest. falsetto (used sparingly)	Tones are Light.
Baritones (1st Basses)	chest, head.	Tones are Medium.
Basses	Low and high chest. Head used sparingly.	Tones are Dark.

ILLUSTRATION 3.9

Use the tonal pattern that is suggested in the diagram in all compositions. Now, teach your students how to make adjustments in the tonal scheme by studying the excerpt in Illustration 3.10 from "Goin' Home." The work that you will do to achieve the correct sound can be used to correct the tonal pattern in other compositions.

Each voice in Illustration 3.10 must use blended vowel resonance in the chest, head and falsetto registers to initiate the correct tone quality. The tenor part presents no major tonal problem if the singers use falsetto quality most of the time. If all of them are able to use the head voice, be sure that they use the covered tone to encourage a light tone quality, but you will have to help your second tenors make successful interchanges between the chest and falsetto register.

The problem in the first bass (baritone) part comes if your singers do not make a smooth octave change across the change of quality area at the word "day," then move smoothly into the high chest register on the word "I'm."

The primary function of the baritone in this excerpt is to coordinate musical schema between the tenor and bass lines. His upper

ILLUSTRATION 3.10

chest quality starting with "some still day" should be covered to complement the parts.

SOLVING BLEND PROBLEMS IN THE LOW CHEST REGISTER

Blend is a term used to describe homogeneity of sound in one section of the choir. It is effective when each singer's vowel form, tonal balance, manner of breathing, articulation of consonants, musical knowledge and experiences are equal. The basses in the all-male choir encounter a special kind of problem in blend that affects the other voices in the choir. To eliminate improper tonal balance, ask the basses to use a blended *oo-ee* quality with the initial vowel in low chest registrations. Uncontrolled resonance can cause improper tonal blend that affects the harmonic structure in compositions. Offer help here by increasing or decreasing the resonance power among the students. Test the voices to discover if certain voices are causing the problem. You may ask these students to use a quieter dynamic level. In many instances, you may have to measure the resonance so that it is equal throughout the ensemble. Do not try to eliminate it! No instrument is effective without it. But, it must be controlled so that proper blend will exist on every vocal level.

Improving Vertical Blend

Permit the bass and first tenor lines to sing their parts together excluding the other voices. Poor quality of octaves, fifths, thirds and other intervals can be improved when you permit these voices to work together. They will be able to "hear" each part thereby learning the character of it. This is vital to proper blend patterns throughout the ensemble. You will need to work on vertical blend with the other voices in the same manner.

FOUR RULES FOR BRANCHING THE BREATH STREAM IN THE LOW CHEST REGISTER

Your students will need to know how to control the breath stream to achieve the proper tone quality in their low chest registers. Many students tend to focus the expired air toward one resonating point. The results from this are: pinched and pointed tones, poor timbre, dull tone quality and improper singing!

Here are the four rules to help you teach your students how to branch the breath stream properly:

1. Blend low chest tones with nasal resonance by sending the air toward the upper teeth. This process will cause the mouth to open to the correct width for proper vowel action. The upper teeth are exposed on all vowel sounds, and have the tendency to sound bright. It will be better to let your students use modified vowel sounds to encourage the proper coloring in this low registration. Resonance will develop and increase in some voices. Use the *o, oo,* and *aw* vowels to facilitate its effectiveness.
2. When the *oo* vowel is sung, blend the *o* vowel to get the proper connection between the chest and the mouth area. Permit the air to travel to the back of the mouth. This will help keep the mouth open.
3. When singing the *ee* vowel, use the inner smile to blend the sound of the *oo* vowel. Permit the air to travel toward the front of the mouth to unite that resonance with nasal resonance. Do not leave your students alone to develop this low chest blend. The desired coloring in this area can be studied further by listening to recordings of fine all-male choirs.
4. Ask your students to keep just enough air in the lungs to permit proper branching of the breath stream in this low chest registration. Tell them that more control is needed as the line ascends.

SINGING LOW PEDAL TONES CORRECTLY

Tones that are held through a series of chords are referred to as pedal tones. The use of them adds another dimension to the music. They are especially effective when the blend within the section is somewhat the same, and quality resonance is evenly distributed. Caution must be observed when you permit your students to sing these tones. Generally, if a bass cannot sing a resonant F2 with proper musical style and judgement, you should not let him sing low pedal tones. Rather, let him sing the baritone part at those points.

Pedal tones often cause singers to tighten the throat muscles, causing constriction in that area and possible intonation problems. When this happens, you will have to remind your singers of the techniques and skills they have already studied to prevent them. It is reasonable for singers to become lax in certain vocal developments because some are long term elements and require more time for full development.

In other instances, pedal tones cause singers to muffle the tone when they inadvertently permit them to stop at the lips. Of course, the remedy for correcting this is simply to ask the singer to sing in the center of the mouth and straight up, keeping the breath moving at the same time. Tell the singers to utilize the lips for forming the vowels, bilabial and labio-dental consonants. This works well in helping to encourage tonal beauty in higher registrations as well.

RECOMMENDED MUSIC LIST

The following compositions are recommended for the all-male choir to aid in creating interest among the singers. You may include all of them in your yearly plan for concerts and festivals.

Name	Grade	Composer	Number	Publisher
All Glory, Laud And Honor	M	Bach	2135	E.C. Schirmer
Alleluia	D	Berger/Heath	11020	G. Schirmer
A-Roving	M	Luboff	1004	Walton
Aura Lee	E	Hunter/Parker/ Shaw	527	Lawson-Gould
Ain'-A That Good News	M	Dawson	104	Kjos
Behold That Star	M	Arr. Cunkle	10	Shawnee
Brothers, Sing On	M	Grieg/McKinney	6928	J. Fischer
The Boatmen's Dance	M	Copland/Fine	1908	Boosey

Name	Grade	Composer	Number	Publisher
Bonnie Eloise	M	Hunter/Shaw	528	Lawson-Gould
The Bachelor	D	Kodaly	1893	Boosey
Cantate Domino	M	Pitoni/Greyson	ES 56	G. Schirmer
Come Let Us Start a Joyful Song	M	Hassler/ Greyson	ES 1	Bourne
Dreams	M	Wagner/Scherer	436	Gray
Didn't My Lord Deliver Daniel	M	Genuchi	008	Ludwig
Down in the Valley	E	Mead	1716	Galaxy
Drink to Me Only With Thine Eyes	E	Parker/Shaw	530	Lawson-Gould
December	D	Ives	812-2	Peer
The Dodger	E	Copland/Fine	1909	Boosey
Dirge for Two Veterans	D	Holst	8323	G. Schirmer
The Erie Canal	M	Forbes	10732	G. Schirmer
Emblems	D	Carter	MP120	C. Fischer
Festgesang An Die Kunstler	D	Mendelssohn	615	King
Good Fellows Be Merry	D	Bach/Duey	2944	Boston
Good Night Ladies	M	Hunter/Shaw	531	Lawson-Gould

CHAPTER 4

HOW TO DEVELOP THE ALL-FEMALE CHOIR

In this chapter, you will find practical information on blending the melodic line horizontally. This material will help you to lead your students from the beginning stages to full development with the appropriate singing drills to aid in the process.

You will be shown how to control the female ensemble through the study of shaping the melodic contour. This is discussed with certain illustrations to help you teach it correctly to your students.

You will also be shown how to teach your second sopranos to support the melody line and the harmonic proportions properly in SSA compositions. This, of course, is strengthened through the study of the correct rhythmic timing that can be transferred to any composition you may choose. In the same realm, you will be introduced to a study of the consonant as it appears in the high and low vocal registrations.

The all-female choir is important in the Graduated Program because its members are provided the opportunity to work homogeneously on special vocal problems and develop their techniques properly. Some girls do not wish to work on drills and vocal techniques in the presence of boys. It is necessary for an organization to be provided for all members who need this type of experience to develop their voices in the most practical manner possible. This includes streamlining each voice in quintet formations for complete absorbtion into sections of the ensemble. Once this initial effort has been completed, processes to build strong female ensembles should begin.

AUDITIONING AND SELECTION

The soprano who becomes a member of the all-female choir should possess a light, floating tone in the vocal region shown in Illustration 4.1. Any note extending beyond this range calls for special attention, and must be studied further in the chapter on chamber choirs. Those girls who cannot sing the tones below with an easy flute-like quality, should be considered second sopranos.

ILLUSTRATION 4.1

Careful evaluation of each applicant should be done on the basis of attitudes, voice character and the student's ability to sing with mixed quality. This quality is a mixture of dark vowels such as *ee* or *oo*, sung with blended chest and nasal resonance. It is equivalent to the covered tone in the male voice and must be developed in the same manner.

When auditioning altos, look for those girls who are able to sing a vibrant G3. Although it is rare to find true alto voices in high school, you will find girls with wide ranges extending downard to G3. Listen to these unsettled voices carefully to be certain that the low range can be performed naturally. If it seems that the student is performing with difficulty, it would be wise to place her in the second soprano section.

Each prospective member should be required to perform one solo as a prerequisite for entrance into the all-female choir. These solos should be judged and critiqued on these specific points by a faculty group:

> Range Manipulation
> Voice Quality
> Tonal Coloring
> Musical Perception

Now, set another date when each participant will sing her solo again. However, give them a reasonable amount of time to work on and improve their faults. Choose thirty voices with even numbers of ten within each section. Once this has been achieved, some type of induction ceremony similar to the one suggested later could be conducted for final initiation into the choir.

A week-long activity can be planned for the members chosen. You may ask them to wear some type of unusual clothing for the entire week, or certain colored clothing that will get some attention from their peers at school. They could eat lunch together one day during the week when they will be required to perform a song of your choosing. Be certain that it can be sung successfully and without the aid of an accompanying instrument.

The induction ceremony can be held in conjunction with a concert, PTA meeting, or some other event where a good number of parents, teachers and community leaders congregate. A simple plan for the induction ceremony is as follows: Let the new choir members be dressed in similar attire, but different from the ensemble's original uniform. At least three compositions can be performed by these girls. If the first two numbers are sung to the expectation of the girls who are already members of the ensemble, they will proceed to the stage and sing the last selection with the neophytes. This act will be an indication that the girls have been accepted for membership into the All-Female Choir. These can be carried out by the director and senior members of the choir.

BLENDING THE MELODIC LINE HORIZONTALLY

Ask your students to mark the phrases, fifth and thirds of chords found in the voice lines of the composition with a red pencil, then practice the lines separately to become thoroughly familiar with each. Be sure that perfect blend exists among the singers. This can be accomplished by providing good examples for your students to emulate.

- First, adjust the resonance to a suitable level. Unify each vowel sound in the total line and improve intonation.
- Second, assign vocal partners within the sections to work as teams in resonance and proper blend development.
- Now, work to improve balance through quintet sectional rehearsals. Be certain that each quintet formation develops identical blend patterns.

Since blending the melodic line horizontally in SSA compositions is dependent upon perfect blend and balance within the sections, you should present the techniques for improving them in the ensemble daily. They include horizontal and vertical balance, proper tone production, phrasing, rhythmical timing, pronunciation and enunciation, proper breath control and dynamic control. Discuss each of the techniques with your students so they can become fully aware of their importance. In order for this work to reach full development, let your section leaders become familiar with the techniques first. Acquaint them with the methods you have designated for teaching these elements correctly to your students. It may be necessary for you to visit the sessions your students are having in their homes to make sure the correct teaching procedures are followed.

Once blend and balance are developed, begin practicing unisonal compositions and check development and spontaneity in range manipulation. Do not assign part singing until the problems affecting proper blend and balance have been eliminated. The drill in Illustration 4.2 can be used as a unisonal exercise.

ILLUSTRATION 4.2 Use all vowels.

Choose simple two part songs that are totally equal in pitch and rhythmic levels. You will be able to solve your musical problems better with these simple pieces.

Each soprano must be able to sing an even scale. She must also know how to effectuate tonal weight in the melodic line. Begin developmental work on these two elements as soon as possible. The exercises in Illustrations 4.3a and 4.3b will aid in the development.

Teach your students how to control volume by bringing the intercostal muscles into action. The drill that follows will aid in strengthening these muscles. Place your hands on the sides of your body, thumbs pointing toward your back. Inhale air, feeling the expansion around your waist. Walk eight or ten paces while holding the air with your abdominal muscles. Then release the air slowly in a hissing manner while walking another eight or ten paces. Practice daily.

The problem of blending nasal and head resonance properly in the first soprano section so that it agrees with the tone quality of the

ILLUSTRATION 4.3a Use all vowels.

ILLUSTRATION 4.3b Use all vowels.

other voices in the ensemble must be worked out technically. Shown in Illustration 4.4 is the approximate range where the problem usually occurs:

ILLUSTRATION 4.4

Ask your sopranos to make every effort to unite the vowels and "feel" the sensation of uniting all resonances in this range. Every one should make a special effort to articulate the end consonants carefully. They must not be over-articulated. Ask them to study the kind of interplay between breath, lip formation, vowel sound and rhythm that is needed for a suitable mixture of vowel-consonant action also. As a follow-up, let the sopranos hum their parts in these sections of compositions in order to understand the proper blending process. Make tape recordings of the performances so your students can hear the difference between good and bad vertical blend in this problem range. Now, ask them to sing and utilize the resonance in the manner the exercise was hummed. This problem should be brought to your students' attention each day to insure full development.

SHAPING THE MELODIC CONTOUR

Since the soprano is considered the "leader" in the phrasing process among all-female groups, she must have a keen sense of melodic contours and be able to respond with knowledge and understanding. This means that you must acquaint your students with musical styles of all historical periods. Actually, this work should begin in the full-choir program with full understanding reached at this point in the Graduated Program.

Let us study the contour of the melody in Illustration 4.5.

Teach your students how to manipulate the shape of the line by way of a diagram. Let them think of the shape of the line as always moving from one spatial outlet to the next one. You can make influences here by using hand signals or descriptive word phrase softly. But think of it as a curve as it moves upward and comes to a soft landing as it descends. As you talk, move your hands in the description of the phrase also. These kinds of devices help to create understanding readily.

Your students should become absorbed in the message that the phrase conveys by way of the text. Then, move to a good singing position and sing it with good style.

ILLUSTRATION 4.5

ILLUSTRATION 4.6

Diagramming Melodic Lines

Diagrams are necessary to help your students acquire a mental picture of the music. Each musical phrase should be taken out of musical context and diagrammed. These diagrams should not be drawn on the scores, but prepared for permanent records and kept to be referred to when the need arises. However, each student should make them become definite parts of the music just as they do the dynamics. Study the melody in Illustration 4.6.

Your students must have an active technique in order to sing these kinds of phrases perfectly. Teach them how to sing staccato, marcato, forte and pianissimo techniques out of musical context. Teach them also, that rests, as in the line above, are not always breathing places, but are rhythmical rests. In order to sing with the proper style that will be interpreted partly from your directions and partly from experience, the students must use more breath support to make these effective. In addition, measure the vowel sounds among the students and be sure that they receive the same amount of color each time. You will have to instruct the students to use a downward and outward "push" of the diaphragm in order to sing the marcato technique successfully. It is necessary to increase the amount of air when singing forte, but pianissimo, staccato and marcato need no increased amount.

Note how the line explodes with the advent of the accent markings. Be sure your students prepare the breath stream sufficiently and initiate an increased amount of air with a small increase in breath pressure to sing these kinds of phrases correctly. Let your students place the hands on their sides with the thumbs pointing toward the back to help develop the process. Control intonation by holding still and being sure of the sound and character of the part.

In other melodic contours, you will have to employ the rhythmic beat and count in terms of the "unwritten note" introduced in Chapter 5. It adds life to the musical phrase and helps to make each note important in the musical structure. Study the composition carefully. Note those sections where the rhythmic count will be strengthened by the natural rise and fall of the voice in the melodic scheme. Be sure that your students use correct breathing patterns in order to control the musical flow of the melody.

PASSING TONES IN OPEN HARMONY

Care must be taken to preserve good tone quality while singing passing tones in open harmonic structure. This can be done by utilizing good tonal spiralling techniques, accentuating the passing tone, and using correct rhythmic timing with good quality carefully unified by each voice within the section. Let's look at each element mentioned above as it affects the passing tones in the excerpt in Illustration 4.7.

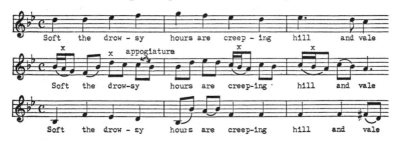

ILLUSTRATION 4.7

Tonal Spiralling

The proper method for good tonal spiralling in the second soprano above should be performed as outlined in the Chapter 5. The second soprano line also represents a sweeping horizontalism that is equal to the melodic line in the first soprano. It must be practiced out of musical context to be effective. Give special attention to each of the following details:

- Use one *t* between the words "soft" and "the." Keep the breath moving and avoid using the *h* sound to aid in singing the second sound on the word "soft." Permit the air to go straight up when singing the last sound on the word "the."
- Be careful that the jaw is not tight in going from the word "the" to "drowsy." *Blow* the air gently between the syllables in "drowsy." Send the air toward the upper teeth in the last syllable. If your students experience difficulty, ask them to hold the jaw down lightly with the finger tips.
- The word "hours" is difficult to sing at any vocal level because the double consonant *rs* will cause articulation problems. Tell your singers to articulate them at the very last moment, then get the jaw back down as quickly as possible to sing the *ah* vowel in the word "are."
- Keep the rhythmic-tonal pattern pure by practicing rhythm and tone separately.

Accentuating the Passing Tone

Always teach your students the importance of every tone in the composition. In some compositions, the structure is geared to include certain note-stress points. These must be accentuated correctly without damaging the composition's tonal image. Consequently, you must include in your teaching the analysis of chord structure and the correct identification of passing tones. Give the passing tones the correct nomenclature as they follow here: the suspension, neighboring tones, appogiatura, and the échappée. These represent the most common nonharmonic tones.

Your second sopranos must take a lion's share of the responsibility for singing passing tones correctly, even when they appear in the outer voices.

Accentuating the passing tone does not mean singing the affected notes louder than the other notes in the line. It means achieving the characteristic sound for those notes that are in style for a particular composition. It is proper, then, to give each passing tone a particular color according to the structure of the composition and the period in which it was written.

All nonharmonic tones are marked with an "x" in the excerpt above. When you choose compositions of this nature for your all-female choir, be sure to ask your students to form the vowels perfectly. Let them use feminine accents on the last note of the appogiatura when it is used in the composition. (See definition for the feminine accent on page 93.)

How to Achieve Correct Rhythmic Timing

Constant practice in rhythmic activity is essential in singing nonharmonic tones correctly. Each singer's vowel form must be somewhat the same, and vocal action must be timed perfectly to induce proper coloring, good articulation and intonation. If the rhythmic action is not worked out technically, the choir will experience problems in the specific areas stated above.

Teach your students to be responsive to basic rhythm patterns and the placement of beats between strict and rubato rhythms. Although this work started in the full-choir program, it should be continued here in this section of the Graduated Program. It will be beneficial to practice with rhythmic schemes similar to the ones in Illustration 4.8a and 4.8b.

ILLUSTRATION 4.8a

ILLUSTRATION 4.8b

In order to perfect this rhythmic action idea quickly among your students, consistency in practice is necessary. Do it by conducting them at first. Later on, you may permit them to practice without being conducted. Develop good rhythm among your students further by using certain parts of actual compositions which lend themselves to rhythmic action.

SUPPORTING THE FIRST SOPRANO
PART CORRECTLY

One fact must remain clear: The melody line must be heard and understood by your audience. All supporting voices must sing their lines with this thought in mind at all times. They must adhere to principles which support the soprano part as the most vital force within the composition. The second soprano, in this realm, has the chore of bringing the outer voices in connecting musical proximity and setting the principles of support in motion. Here are the principles you can use to teach your students how to get the job done in an effective manner:

• When there are a series of repeated notes in the melody, support this section of the composition by imitating the first soprano in voice quality and character, balance and line aggression. This device helps to keep good intonation and maps the musical strategy of this section in the composition. Tell your students to make every effort to keep the pitch constant. Otherwise, this process of imitation will be a waste of time.

• Many intonation problems arise when wide skips occur in the melody line. Again, the principle of imitation is useful. However, when they occur in the low chest register for the second soprano, ask her to use modified mixtures of *o, ee* and *oo* with existing vowel. There must be similarity between the second soprano and the alto quality. Be certain that neither quality is too dark.

• On occasions when parallel descension or ascension, or major or minor thirds occur between the first and second soprano, exact imitation is required in every respect of both voices. Mark the root of the chord when it appears in the second soprano and assign it more tonal weight distribution. Be sure the color in the voices is the same. There should also be an exact duplication of expression in music and the word quality.

• When the second soprano line occurs in high registration, permit the singers to use light vowel properties to support the first soprano part. If tonal weight distribution is not affected, except in those places where the root of the chord occurs in close note-range technique, it is permissible to use a dynamic level a degree softer than the first soprano when both are singing in the high chest register. This should be done also when the fifth of the chord and the third of the chord occur in close note-range between these two voices.

- In pianissimo sections, medium dark vowel sounds should accompany the melody line. This is done by blending the dark and light vowel properties together in a suitable mixture. The articulation of consonants takes new meaning in this section of the composition. Tell your students to be expressive, but not explosive when articulating the consonant, especially where the *s* and *t* are used.

- Since articulation for fast tempos is difficult to maintain in high note registrations, you should teach this method to your students to improve it and help maintain vertical balance between these voices: When the *r* appears in words such as "careful" or "mercy" permit the second sopranos to use a dark quality vowel, but move to the *r* and beyond it as quickly as possible. The first sopranos should use the natural vowel color. Sing through the vowel thoroughly, then articulate the *s* at the last moment. (Both voices) When the semi-musical consonants *b, d, l, m, n, ng, q, r, w, x* and *y* are included in the text of a composition, maintain the same pitch of the initial word-vowel. Do not exaggerate their semi-musical status when they appear at the end of words. Rather, articulate them quickly and clearly. Always connect these consonants to the next vowel-word through clear articulation and good rhythmic timing.

- The nonmusical consonants *ch, c, f, h, j, k, p, s, t, v* and *z* must not interfere with the sound of the vowel-word. They must be articulated with this thought clearly established among the singers. Provide much practice for them to improve articulation.

Roar rear near dear rear rear near dear roar rear near

roar rear near dear roar rear near dear rear rear dear

ILLUSTRATION 4.9

STRENGTHENING THE ALL-FEMALE CHOIR
WITH HORIZONTAL COLOR SCHEMES

Horizontal color schemes are not only necessary for all-female choirs, but chamber and a cappella choirs as well. Permitting your students to study these color schemes will aid in preparing them for the work they will have to do if they desire to become members of the higher ensembles.

The basic format for developing horizontal color schemes is the study and development of basic vowel color and the blending of the resonances. But it goes farther by capturing the different color changes of the female voice and blending them with the color and character of the composition into a satisfactory sound. This work, strengthening the all-female choir with horizontal color schemes, must be achieved at this level in the Graduated Program so that resonance power can be developed further to complement harmonic balance in higher ensembles later on.

To begin the work, let your students sing each of the vowels in the chart below to discover their character, color and sound:

Vowel Symbols	*Developmental Words*
	(Be sure to speak the words slowly in order to "hear" the correct sound)
ai	air, and, wear, map, hair, said, gap, bear, grass, laugh
ay	day, date, made, say, haste
ah	father, God, bother, hard
aw	saw, all, ball, law
ee	see, keep, knee, bee, tree
ih	him, kid, quick, is
eh	bet, bed, yet, let, never
o	go, home, road, low, no, door
uh	but, hush, rush, touch
oo	rule, you, moon, soon, too

ILLUSTRATION 4.10

Now practice singing each characteristic sound and color of the vowels in some appropriate composition. Once the students can sing the colors of each vowel with the same color character each time, they are now ready to begin the developmental processes provided in Illustrations 4.11 and 4.12. When the colors are developed thoroughly, they can be employed at will in choral compositions for further study.

Mixed Quality

This quality (see page 00 for a description of mixed quality)

ILLUSTRATION 4.11 Sopranos. Use all vowels.

ILLUSTRATION 4.12 Altos. Use all vowels.

ILLUSTRATION 4.13

must be used in the color scheme by the second sopranos when both sopranos sing in the chest register. The approximate range involved is that in Illustration 4.13.

Elements such as staccato, legato, marcato, crescendo, decrescendo, movendo and stringendo help to give mixed quality added dimensions of beauty and contrast. Isolating these in vocalises will be advantageous for your singers. Ask them to memorize the different mixed quality colors brought on by the elements above.

Feminine Accents

Feminine accents are natural accents formed at the end of slurred notes. It is not an explosive accent. The singer must use a "gentle" approach with them. Tell your students to acquire a feeling of holding back some of the stress, especially on the second note. Feminine accents are effective when singers use dark quality vowels to give them special colors. Ask your singers to use dark vowels when using feminine accents, especially when support is needed for the melody line. See Illustration 4.14 for an example of the feminine accent.

ILLUSTRATION 4.14

The Appogiatura

When the appogiatura occurs in the first soprano part, the second soprano and alto voices must be responsible for maintaining the chord tonality and character, rhythm and intonation. But in Illustration 4.7, the first soprano and alto are responsible for the elements mentioned above, giving the singers a special opportunity to control these factors. Since the appogiatura is not approached from the top voice, the problem of bringing out its important role must be dealt with in the following manner: When singing compositions utilizing nonharmonic tones in the middle voice of SSA compositions, permit that voice to use dark quality vowels and proper articulation of consonants. A similar quality and the same amount of volume must be maintained in the other voices to present the proper vocal form. Be sure to adjust the color and volume to a satisfactory level, but do not damage the compositional character.

THE ALTO

It is always good to choose some SSA compositions that will aid in the development of your alto voices in the choir. They should have the opportunity to sing in other registrations apart from the low chest area. The wise director can plan his activities to include proper management of the voices in the all-female choir. He will also schedule the performance of certain compositions to aid in the development of these voices. Like him, you should not permit your altos to sing each day in the same vocal register. Have them sing vocalises that will utilize both registers.

Do not let the music you choose totally dictate a certain manner of performance to the students before you observe whether the developmental needs of your students will be met. Choose your music carefully!

You may permit your altos to sing selected solos that you are sure will aid in the development of their voices. These, along with some proper vocalises, will be helpful. Be certain that some of these solos will aid in the development of the register change area. If this area has the slightest change, you may have to make an adjustment by placing the student in another section. This is permissible since the color character of the choir will not undergo drastic changes.

Developing the Correct Alto Quality

The alto voice must be nurtured each day with attention given to its high and low ranges. Do not permit this voice to become strident in either range. When this happens, the alto is forcing the tone, or utilizing the wrong vowel form. Sometimes, this problem comes from fatigue. Permit your youngsters to rest a few minutes before they attempt to sing the next composition. This will help them to conserve their voices so that the remaining techniques can be learned without tension.

The change of quality area is another problem point for the alto. Generally, it is the same area, an octave above the baritones and basses, and must be studied in a similar fashion.

Let your alto section form the blended *oo* and *ee* quality as a basic sound for performance in the all-female choir. This sound can be encouraged through vocalises composed especially to achieve it. Ask your students to keep the sound in the center of the mouth and sing straight up. Once the *oo* and *ee* vowels are blended into a suitable mixture, complete the development through actual compositions. As a last resort, tell the singers to set up the vocal apparatus with a round lip formation for all vowel sounds. Of course, this is virtually impossible, but the thought will encourage the blended *ee-oo* quality.

When all alto voices are singing in low chest registrations, you will have to blend the *o* and *aw* mixture with the vowels that are present in the text already. The rules below will help you teach your altos how to develop the correct quality:

- Use the "inner smile" approach when singing in the medium to high vocal registrations.
- Use the "outer smile" approach when singing in low registrations.
- All students must have similar lip formations in all registrations.

Balance

Teach all members of the all-female choir to think of their parts as melodic lines first. Then, add those musical devices such as dynamics and expression to initiate the different control skills (blend, range, color) in order to achieve group balance. Of course, technical drills designed to unify these skills should be assigned to the students for out-of-class work. Once this work has been developed, begin work on balancing the alto part according to compositional scheme and character. Be sure to assign tonal weight in each line, especially when the third and fifth of the chord appear. The alto voice should be careful when singing the third or the fifth because balance is difficult to achieve with the other voices. Ask them to decrease their resonance power if the other voices are performing at close range, but increase the power in open harmony. Be certain that vowels are unified and the correct color has been achieved.

Singing the lines in octaves with another voice is a good method for improving balance in the ensemble. If poor balance occurs between lines, do not permit your students to sing louder or softer. Tell them that it is best to check their breathing patterns, vowel forms, rhythm, posture and resonance power to correct the balance.

When your altos sing in the high chest register, and there are no special effects involved, tell them to use light vowel properties to create a natural color that will aid the other voices in this range. Be specific about color and resonance in this area of the composition. Give your students an example by providing the correct color with your own voice, or that of an advanced student. Commit to memory the mixture of vowels and resonances which lend to the specific colors you want at certain vocal levels. Inevitably, the adjustments in coloration you will make in your ensemble will affect the balance among the students.

RECOMMENDED MUSIC LIST

All of the compositions recommended for the all-female choir can be used for developmental purposes and performances. But the "starter" compositions listed below will help you to create the interest and enthusiasm needed to motivate your singers to develop their voices thoroughly.

Title	Grade	Composer	Number	Publisher
Mayday/Carol	E	Taylor	4872	J. Fischer
Bread Baking	E	Bartok	1669	Boosey
O Can Ye Sew Cushions	E	Britten	5213	Boosey
Lift Thine Eyes	ME	Mendelssohn	698	Willis

Title	Grade	Composer	Number	Publisher
An Offering	ME	Baldwin/ Watson	5W3362	Witmark
Calm As The Night	ME	Boehm/ Cain	2016	Schmitt, Hall & McCreary
Love At My Heart Came Knocking	E	Deale		Oxford
Lass With The Delicate Air	ME	Arne	515	Gray
Now Sleeps the Crimson Petal	E	Quilter	1678	Boosey
Music When Soft Voices Die	E	Clokey/ Cain	83121	Flammer
Younger Generation	M	Copland/ Swift	1722	Boosey
Waters Ripple And Flow	M	Taylor	5065	J. Fischer

CHAPTER 5

HOW TO BUILD SUCCESSFUL CHAMBER CHOIRS

The techniques in this chapter for building successful chamber choirs are designed to help you further develop the skills your students have already learned from informal, all-male and all-female choir experiences. The element that brings the techniques in harmony with others throughout the Graduated Program is tonal control. It is brought into focus when all singers in the ensemble contribute to the blend and balance characteristic of chamber units. If the techniques are developed sequentially as outlined in this chapter, tonal control, tonal beauty and the correct chamber choir sound will emerge.

You will be shown in this chapter how to develop special colors which lay the foundation for your choir's tonal unity. These colors, along with the numerical system in personnel breakdown, are key factors in establishing a firm base for the development of the chamber choir's tonal unity. Tonal unity aids in achieving proper blend and balance, evidenced only when this system and proper coloring are utilized. The strength of the system lies in the method of auditioning students for the choir. You will find the musical exercises offered for auditions helpful in selecting voices for the choir. They are designed to improve blend and balance on a continuing basis.

You will also find many techniques to teach your students the correct chamber choir sound, but distinctive chamber choir bass lines must be present to achieve it. Consequently, techniques are provided in this chapter for you to develop your bass section correctly. When the development is complete, you will have given the chamber choir the kind of bass section it needs to become a special unit.

KEY TONAL CONTROL FACTORS

The main factors which form a basis for proper tonal beauty and control are the ability to control the breath stream, sending it toward the different resonances, and the ability to equalize the color of vowels. You can teach your students proper branching of the breath stream with the following process:

> Take in air, feeling the expansion around the waist and in the back. Permit the air to escape slowly toward the mouth only. Try this again with the mouth closed, permitting the air to escape to the nose. With this process continuing, open the mouth slowly, permitting air to escape through the mouth and nose simultaneously. This process should now be developed through vocalise study.

Illustration 5.1 will help your students understand proper branching of the breath stream. These factors, proper branching of the breath stream and vowel color, must be emphasized at this point in the Graduated Program so your students will have a keen awareness of their importance in helping to create the special sound of your chamber choir.

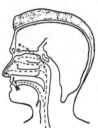

ILLUSTRATION 5.1

The Chamber Choir's tonal characteristic is an outgrowth of the following control skills your students developed during informal, all-male and all-female choir experiences:

- **Sectional Blend.** Each student should know how to sing the vocal line in a manner similar to that of the person next to him in the section. This skill should be in evidence when a person auditions for the choir.
- **Spontaneity in Range Manipulation.** Each student should know how to sing freely through both registers, executing upward and downward leaps. The quality change factor should be controlled so that different color schemes can be utilized successfully, especially when the fifth of the chord is involved.

- **Color Mixtures**. Light and dark colors are two extremes in voice development that are easily distinguishable. But you must teach your chamber choir students how to initiate the wide color scope of these changes as they occur in the composition. Illustration 5.2 will show you how to teach your students these changes correctly. Your students should carefully practice the initial vowels in the color pattern below. Notice how the vowels become brighter starting at the medium level. The *ah* vowel is the starting point from which the other vowels at the medium level receive their light status. Its formation must be blended with the vowels directly above it to induce light qualities.

MEDIUM

		o as in oh	uh as in but	ih as in kid	
					ai as in air
			aw as in all	eh as in bet	
DARK					LIGHT
oo as in moon	ee as in see	oo as in book	ay as in day	AH AS IN FATHER	

ILLUSTRATION 5.2

Effective Vowel Coloring

Teach your students how to develop each vowel in the color scheme above, then show them how to initiate the color by singing an appropriate line from a composition that lends itself to the scheme. Now let your students imitate your example.

You can teach your students to blend the following color schemes as a basis for developing the entire color format:

1. Sing the vowel *oo*, gradually blending the vowel *o*.
2. Sing *oo* gradually blending the vowel *aw*.
3. Sing *oo* gradually blending the *ee* vowel.
4. Sing *ee* gradually blending the *ih* vowel.
5. Sing the *o* vowel and blend *aw* for a lighter sound.
6. Use *ah* to make *uh* lighter.

7. In order to darken light vowel properties, remove the blend of the *ah* vowel.

The method of adjusting the sound of the vowel as it changes between the low and high range of the vocal line and those caused by rhythmic-word contacts, should be taught to section leaders first. Permit them to share in the responsibility of training your students. With their help, the results will crystalize faster.

Since the control factors above do serve as basic developmental patterns for the chamber choir's tonal character, failure to develop them will cause the final musical product of the choir to be of inferior quality. Be certain that your students develop all skills and techniques of each ensemble thoroughly.

SELECTING THE PERSONNEL

Final selection of the personnel for the chamber choir can be based upon the student's academic standings, his peer relationship and proper voice development. However, set the standards so the average student who rates highly among his peers and has developed his voice satisfactorily can have a chance to participate in the chamber choir also.

The only two workable numerical systems in personnel breakdown for the chamber choir are as follows:

3 sopranos		4 sopranos
4 altos		5 altos
3 tenors	*or*	4 tenors
4 basses		5 basses

The correct chamber sound will be achieved by permitting the dark sections of the choir to outnumber the lighter sections. This built-in system of light and dark qualities puts the final touch to the choir's special character and color. However, permit the dark sections to use light vowel properties to promote a medium dark sound at each vocal level.

You are not limited to selecting students from all-male and all-female choirs, but may make choices from the full-choir and the informal choir as well. But this should be done on a very limited basis and used as a special reward for the student whose growth in voice development is outstanding and who is mature enough to enter this level in the Graduated Program.

Once you have chosen the personnel for the chamber choir, you can begin nurturing the more talented students within the group. This does not mean that you should show partiality to any segment of the choir, but identifying the highly gifted students and encouraging them to proceed by way of private lessons would be appropriate.

Auditioning for the Chamber Choir

In auditioning voices for placement in the chamber choir, the following procedures have been found to be effective:

1. Audition one bass and one alto together. Follow the same procedure with tenors and sopranos.
2. Check to see if the students are using similar lip formations for each vowel. Correct where necessary.
3. Adjust the resonance in each voice to a similar level.
4. Use light vowel properties in the bass and alto voices to encourage proper chamber choir color.
5. Use less tonal weight distribution when the third of the chord appears in the line. However, do not permit the voice to lose its fullness.
6. Control the volume between the voices.
7. Utilize the exercises to develop flexibility.

The exercises in Illustrations 5.3a and 5.3b can be used in all auditions as assigned to the chosen members for further study. The pianist should be allowed to play the exercises with the voices at least once. Afterwards, the audition should proceed without the aid of the piano. In this way, you can check for, and rate, good or bad intonation, breathing habits, tonal control, spontaneity in range manipulation and good color mixtures. Most students who anticipate the audition with the proper attitude and training will be acceptable to you. They are usually willing to work on vocal techniques extensively in order to acquire the skills necessary for total participation. These represent the type of student needed in the chamber choir and they should be encouraged to develop to their maximum potential.

Since you know the vocal capability of each student who auditions for your chamber choir, use the above procedures and exercises to motivate them to greater musical achievement. Ask them to become vocal partners to study the audition exercises in spare times at their homes. You may wish to compose other exercises similar to the ones below. By all means, let your students become aware of the kind of perfection that is needed for the chamber choir to exist as a special musical unit.

ILLUSTRATION 5.3a Sing on **lah.**

ILLUSTRATION 5.3b Siing on **lah.**

DEVELOPING COMPACTED CHORD BALANCE
IN CHAMBER CHOIRS

Since the chamber choir is a compact unit, its harmonic balance between chords must be worked out technically to further encourage the characteristic chamber choir sound that is needed to perform in the types of settings as outlined in Chapter 1 under the topic "Planning Performance Schedules For Small Vocal Ensembles." A study of compacted chord balance is the only way to bring musical compositions into focus as chamber choir compositions, since it is possible to use any number of them interchangeably throughout the total choir program.

Vowel and resonance blending are necessary skills your students need for developing compacted chord balance. Teach them how to use these skills interchangeably, to effectuate compacted chord balance. If your students fail to develop these basic skills, their admittance into the chamber choir should be delayed.

Tonal Spiralling: The First Step

Tonal spiralling is the first step in developing compacted chord balance. Your students can develop it with the aid of the proper amount of breath pressure and learn how to project the sound of the chord so that it ends consonantly at the beginning of another, thus creating a vacuum for the operation of overtones, good intonation, and artistic musical conduction. Breath pressure is correct when it is felt, without rigidity, around the waistline, and especially in the back. This process will cause tension if used incorrectly! Check your students periodically. Your ability to make your students feel comfortable in the ensemble will help to ease some tense moments. For example, one soprano sang sharp at each entrance that required the use of the upper head voice. Naturally this caused intonation problems in the choir. Miss Ball, the director, took the necessary precautions to correct the situation with very few results. Finally, Miss Ball asked each section to sing its individual part. Each sang perfectly. She noticed Elsie Fikes, the soprano section leader, who did not sing, but listened intently. Elsie told Miss Ball after rehearsal that she was excited about the approaching festival and used too much breath pressure in the upper register of her voice. Miss Ball told Elsie not to worry, but always keep in mind the correct solutions for solving vocal problems. This is significant because the chamber choir personnel should be familiar with all basic problems and their solutions. Choir members should also feel that the director will help them solve the problem rather than blame them for creating it.

ILLUSTRATION 5.4

In Illustration 5.4, correct spiralling of the tone between the first two chords can be successfully performed by articulating the consonant *m* in the first word as closely as possible to the *ah* vowel in the second word. Color the vowel, then close the lips, leaving the mouth open for the last half of the beat to articulate the consonant *m*. Then go directly to the *ah* vowel as quickly as possible. Be sure to scrutinize this process of consonant-vowel contact between every word and chord. To complete the process, permit the air to be "blown" rather than "released" between the notes. Proper attacks and releases are important here also. A good attack is initiated by correct rhythmic timing, and the release is taking in enough air at the end of the phrase to prepare for another. Let your students practice proper tone spiralling by studying this illustration, then move to other choral compositions for development.

Keep only that amount of air in the lungs that is necessary to sing the phrase. When the breath is activated in the spiralling process, keep it moving evenly toward the vocal chords. Increase the amount of air only when more volume is needed in the phrase.

So there can be a complete understanding of compacted chord balance, you should teach your chamber choir students how to construct and sing each major and minor key. Since much of this work was begun during full-choir experiences, technical details you will present should be easy for them to understand in this part of their development.

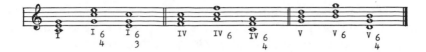

ILLUSTRATION 5.5

Duplicate Illustration 5.5 to teach your students how to recognize the root, third and fifth of each triad as quickly as possible. When they understand this process, begin teaching chord inversions and give reasons for chords having the same note make-up, but different fractional numbers. Be sure to show how these numbers relate in other keys. Transpose the triads to every major key and begin the teaching process again. When the major chords have been learned, complete the study by introducing minor, augmented and diminished chords in the same manner the process began.

Dominant seventh chords should be explained in terms of phrase endings and final cadences. Other references to them will be made in the chapter on the modern choir. If your students experience difficulty, permit them to analyze the chords in appropriate choral compositions.

When the students have learned to construct and sing the chords successfully, tonal weight distribution should be analyzed and distributed evenly throughout the chamber choir. However, do not permit it to become more important than the personnel make-up of the choir. Tonal weight distribution must be subservient to the choir's special numerical setup which determines its tonal character.

SINGING OPEN AND CLOSED HARMONY CORRECTLY

Closed harmony is most satisfying in the chamber choir when similarities exist in lip formations of all vowel sounds and correct usage of the resonances is in evidence throughout the entire ensemble. When these techniques are used with the special numerical make-up of light and dark voices in the ensemble, the natural beauty of closed harmonic sections of compositions will be very effective.

Open chords present problems in balance and create disruptions in vowel unity among the sections. To achieve the proper sound in the open harmony sections, tenors must use light vowel properties mixed with nasal and head resonance as outlined fully in Chapter 3 of this book. Use the inner smile to give the light vowel properties a special color for this section of the composition. Be sure that all voices blend within their sections, and with other sections vertically and horizontally. Open harmonic structures cannot be performed well without this technique.

The remedy for improving vertical and horizontal structure, including the proper tenor quality, is to stop on each chord and improve the sound by unifying vowels, correcting resonance and improving intonation. Move back and forth between the chords to be sure of proper blend and balance. Permit other voices to use the inner smile approach, but the jaw should be lowered comfortably so the process will be natural.

WAYS TO SKILLFULLY BLEND
THE ALTO AND TENOR SECTIONS

The alto and tenor lines in fine chamber choir music must be developed to support the melodic lines of the outer voices and the harmonic structure within the composition. To be effective in this realm, you must work to eliminate individuality between these two voices. If your singers can hear themselves individually, they have become soloists and not chamber choir singers. Modern composers use proper theoretical practices and compositional techniques to build these inner voices perfectly. But many chamber choir directors permit their singers to become soloists, destroying harmonic structure and chamber choir character. Others permit vibrato, uncontrolled head tones and loud singing, which are undesirable in any dignified choral ensemble. It is no secret that Bach, Handel, Beethoven and Brahms used the elements of theory and compositional techniques to great advantage, establishing rules by providing proper note-range structure and motifs suitable for characteristic light and dark qualities of the human voice and equated stringent vocal compatibility among them. It would be well for us to follow their trends in building the alto and tenor sections of the chamber choir.

Do not permit one of these vocal lines to overshadow the other. Imbalance will be the result! This one element will cause much structural damage to the music and cause numerous vocal problems that will affect musical continuity throughout the ensemble.

Without realizing it, many choir directors fail to pinpoint the specific problem their choirs are experiencing and place the blame on the music as in the following actual case study: Mr. Hall had worked on a section of music with the chamber choir for twenty minutes with seemingly very few results. Finally, with obvious resolution, he ordered the librarians to return the music to its proper place in the library. The music, in Mr. Hall's opinion, was too difficult for the choir. Cindy Banks, the alto section leader, told Mr. Hall she thought the music was going very well. "In fact," she said, "We were enjoying our part so well that I could hear every alto in our section."

The altos in Mr. Hall's chamber choir were so engulfed in their own part of the musical score that very little attention was paid to the other parts and musical details. They sang too loudly and individually! Although Mr. Hall had worked on proper vowel forms, diction, chord tuning, breathing and the articulation of consonants, these would not suffice in solving his problems.

Here are four approaches that would have helped Mr. Hall eliminate his problems in a positive way:

- Check the tessitura of each vocal line in the composition to discover its fitness to the voices in the choir.
- Permit each student to sing his line with his vocal partner.
- Analyze and assign tonal weight.
- Remind your singers to study the style of the music and think beautiful tones before they are sung.

Improving Color Schemes
Between the Tenor And Alto Parts

When the alto and tenor voices are in close proximity (major second to a perfect fifth) the tone between them should be as closely identical as possible. This can be done by permitting the tenors to use soft natural head resonance in the upper head register in order to sound similar to alto quality in their low chest register. Be sure the vowel sounds are unified, the resonance blending process effectuated and the tones supported with proper breath pressure. This remedy should be done on a one-to-one basis with each voice emulating the other to get the correct balance. This gives the singer the opportunity to study the coloring of vowels by analyzing his part out of the musical context of the composition.

If there is parallel descension in the composition, the color in both voices should be intensified somewhat by utilizing a slightly darker quality of the vowels. Be sure to maintain as much similarity between the voices as possible.

It is very important to choose music carefully for your chamber choir. Too many chamber choir directors choose music of the festival type with harsh dissonances, large chordal harmonies and vocal line doubling of parts. This kind of music is not suitable for chamber choir performances. Try to choose music where composers have built the inner parts specifically to complement and support the outer voices.

Improving Resonance

The medium *ah* vowel sound is correct when the jaw is lowered to the width of two fingers with a slight outer smile at each corner of the mouth, and the tip of the tongue placed directly behind the bottom teeth. This form of the *ah* vowel should be used when the alto and tenor voices sing it in their low chest registers. It is very important to have crisp articulation of the end consonants for proper word identification.

A mixture of chest, nasal, and head resonance should be used in the upper tenor head register especially when the fifth of the chord appears in that voice, or repeated notes, or when the line ascends from *mi* to *fah*, or *ti* to *do*. This type of mixture can be effective for the alto line as it makes contact with the tenor line constructed in the chest register around the quality change area.

The *ay* vowel is naturally white and colorless. When it is used in the low chest registers of the alto and tenor voices, it must have a mixture of the *oo* and *ee* vowels to give it the proper coloring.

CONTROLLING VIBRATO

As your students mature physically and musically, vibrato will begin developing in their voices. Aside from teaching them how to use it correctly, teach them how to keep it under control in the chamber choir by using the process outlined below:

> On the intake of air through the mouth and nose, the diaphragm moves downward and outward admitting air to the lungs. At this point, ask your students to apply only that amount of pressure at the waistline that is necessary to sing the musical phrase in Illustration 5.6.

ILLUSTRATION 5.6

Sing each tone in the exercise with resonance from the chest, mouth, nose and head cavities. Without proper resonance, constriction will develop and the tone will not have the kind of quality a chamber choir needs to be a special unit.

No one can eliminate vibrato completely because it is a natural

process expelled from muscle tonus. But students will develo
correct process that is necessary to control it if you presen
technique in the next paragraph in a meaningful way.

After your students have learned proper breath support, tell
them to let their vibrato be absorbed by the similarities within each
section. As the phrase comes to an end, tell them to control vibrato in
the center of the tones, permitting the initial vowels to vanish, leaving
a natural replica of the blended vowels. For example, if *ee* has been
blended with *ay*, the vanishing sound should be closer to the *ee* sound
than the *ay*.

BUILDING THE IDEAL SOPRANO SECTION

Chamber choir sopranos must be taught how to sing a light,
lyrical quality that is used for every composition. It can be encouraged
by elevating the tone directly above the throat at the exact moment of
phonation. You can explain this further by asking the students to lift
the breast, then, apply the breath and acquire a feeling of being
elevated as they sing. This technique is especially effective when singing a series of repeated high notes. Lyrical quality is further developed by asking the students to listen to each other to see who comes
closest to the desired tonal quality, then emulate her in quality and
technique. Be certain that the tone quality is correct. Recordings of
great chamber choirs, or the director's own voice, can be advantageous in establishing the correct sound.

The articulation of end consonants should be assigned to one
soprano in the section so that no tonal quality will be sacrificed among
the others. This works well in slow lyrical compositions. But in fast
pieces, permit each soprano to articulate each consonant for greater
uniformity and natural choral beauty that comes from certain tempos.

When sopranos sing in the low chest area, permit them to send
the air stream toward the upper teeth. Do not permit the tone quality
to become nasal at any point in this register, but blend the resonance
from the chest area to give the tone more power and beauty.

Here are four rules that will help you build the ideal soprano
section:

1. Never scoop below or dip above the tone.
2. If a note is held for more than one count, sing different
   shadings of "loudness and softness" to enhance coloring.
3. Never overuse the jaw when singing repeated notes in the
   upper register. Keep the mouth open as much as possible.
4. Hold still when singing rapid passages.

Most young sopranos do have the tendency to sing out of tune on passages calling for sudden crescendos, decrescendos, staccato, repeated notes and descending or ascending scale tones. The first step in solving this problem is to be cognizant of the correct amount of air that is needed to sing these passages. Secondly, the passage must be well practiced so the students can be very familiar with the sound and character of it. Thirdly, the process of holding still while performing delicate passages is most important.

Note in Illustration 5.7 how the quarter note tenuto is contrasted with the eighth note staccato. The only remedy that works successfully is to hold still while singing this part, with total concentration on the character of the entire composition.

High Note Registration

Be sure your students know the sound and character of their part in the high tessitura of the line. The method below will help your students eliminate tension and permit them to become familiar with certain high notes in their part:

> "Girls, the high A in your part has the sound of *mi* in this
> key. Let us sing that section in the lower octave to study and
> learn its true character."

Singing in the lower octave will relax your students. Once they are allowed to study the part in a comfortable octave, the chance of singing out of tune lessens. When they understand the true character of their part, you may permit them to sing it as written. One word of caution: Do not permit your sopranos to push the tone in high note registration, rather, ask them to simply apply the right amount of breath pressure and open or release the tone gently.

High Note Modification

Never permit your sopranos to sing above or below their normal range. This can cause much damage and eventually ruin their voices. Know the range limitations of each person in the section and choose the music for your chamber choir accordingly.

ILLUSTRATION 5.7

Every high note your chamber choir sopranos perform must be subjected to some modification. If the composer includes any note above high G5, let only those girls whose ranges extend a minor third above it perform in this section of the music. Be sure that the final sound blends well with the rest of the ensemble. This can be done by testing the problem notes in the soprano part with the tenor part. If compatibility exists between them, your problem has been minimized. However, you must test further for development so the singers will use the same amount of breath pressure each time.

The mouth must be opened to a formation similar to the *ah* vowel formation at all times when singing in this range. Some sopranos try to use the chest cavities alone in this range, but without nasal and head resonance, poor blend will result among the sections. Of course, every choir director knows that using the chest cavities alone will limit the voice and eventually ruin it.

Permit your sopranos to practice often in this range using the consonants *ch, r, s, t, n, ng,* and *m* as initial and end consonants. Practice the exercises in Illustrations 5.8 and 5.9 until there are effective sounds with clear consonant articulation. Do not explode the consonants in this range, but work for a smooth natural flow of the vowels.

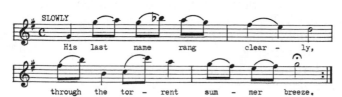

ILLUSTRATION 5.8

ILLUSTRATION 5.9

If stridency occurs in this range, you may check to see if your sopranos are using too much of the chest and mouth resonance and very little air is branched toward the nasal cavities, or whether there are variations in lip formations.

Here is a good rule to follow in teaching your sopranos how to sing high notes correctly: Think the tone quality, apply the proper amount of breath pressure, drop the jaw and form the vowel.

You can control emotional points in high note registration also by directing as calmly as possible. Too much stress will cause your sopranos to over-react creating other vocal problems. Students generally know how important these kinds of passages are and will respond by singing with proper quality and technique.

Each soprano in the chamber choir should commit to memory all vowel formations needed to sing at this level in the Graduated Program. A description of these formations are found in the section titled Vowel Study in Chapter 2.

Rhythmic Modification

Rhythm is another factor that must be modified in high note registrations. Each note within the composition's high range should be measured and equalized among the sopranos, and other sections as well, to present all in good musicality. It is from the director's point of view that each beat within the measure is modified in this high range. So that your students will understand, tell them another name for rhythmic modification is "the unwritten count." Developing this idea will certainly discourage improper breathing and phrasing. Let your students develop it in the musical exercises in Illustration 5.10. You may write other exercises to help in the process. Do not permit them to release any tone until the proper amount of counts have been observed.

RHYTHMIC BEATS			RHYTHMIC COUNTS
Whole Note	o	=	o ⌣ ♩
Half Note	♩	=	♩ ⌣ ♩
Quarter Note	♩	=	♩ ⌣ ♩
Eighth Note	♪	=	♪ ⌣ ♪

ILLUSTRATION 5.10

You may sing the exercises in Illustrations 5.11a and 5.11b with syllables or vowels.

The hour has come to tell you just how
much I love you, how much I love you.

ILLUSTRATION 5.11a

Sing me a song of to - mor - row: a
mo - ment's joy to come fer-vent-ly;
Free this lone - li - ness quick - ly;
drive these cares a - way!

ILLUSTRATION 5.11b

Rhythmic figures such as that in A (below) should be modified in the high range to that in B in order to give more space for tonal beauty.

A

B

UTILIZING AN EVEN SCALE IN
DEVELOPING CHAMBER CHOIR BASSES

It is essential that the bass and alto sections develop compatibility by practicing their parts together regularly. Of course, tenors and sopranos should do likewise. In this way, you will improve the two main color schemes that already exist in the special make-up of your chamber choir. However, the vertical and horizontal sound of the choir can only be improved when your basses sing the characteristic chamber bass sound. It can be characterized as a medium dark sound, full of resonance at both extremes of the voice. This sound must be easily produced by each bass in the section. Help your basses develop this potential by studying the process in Illustration 5.12.

ILLUSTRATION 5.12

Bass quality change occurs on fourth space G. Begin the developmental process at that note working downward. Do not try to rush the process. Develop a perfect fifth, then add the next lower note for development. When the octave between first line G and fourth space G is developed, encourage perfection by practicing daily the drills in Illustrations 5.13 and 5.14. Construct other drills to help arouse more interest among your boys.

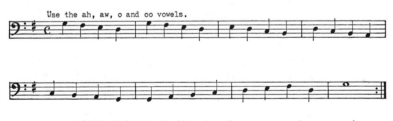

ILLUSTRATION 5.13 Use the **ah, aw, o,** and **oo** vowels.

ILLUSTRATION 5.14

ILLUSTRATION 5.15

ILLUSTRATION 5.16

ILLUSTRATION 5.17

When low chest quality has been smoothly connected to the change of quality area, include the notes in the upper chest and head registers by working downward again. The drills in Illustrations 5.15 and 5.16 will aid in this development. Utilize all initial vowels.

Practice the drills in Illustrations 5.17 and 5.18 slowly, utilizing the *ee, o, oo,* and *ah* vowels. When the drills have been memorized, increase the speed.

Be sure to use the covered tone idea that was introduced in Chapter 3. However, modify its usage by blending light vowel properties to maintain chamber choir character. The color is correct if clear overtones can be heard between the basses and sopranos. If there is incompatibility between these voices, the following problems will surface, and you will need to review all preceding techniques with your students.

ILLUSTRATION 5.18

- Poor intonation on open fourths, fifths and octaves.
- Stridency in either of the voice lines.
- Improper tonal mixtures and resonance.
- Breathy tones in the bass line and thin tones in the soprano line.

Chamber choir basses must be especially careful when blending their line with the other parts. They must develop the skill of balancing their quality within the confines of the total compositional character which will cause them to be heard as effectively as low tones on a very fine organ playing a Bach fugue.

RECOMMENDED MUSIC LIST

These titles are included here to help you complete the training your students need to become fine chamber choir singers. You will also find all of these selections to be suitable for public performance. All of them can serve as developmental showcase pieces. However, the following compositions can be used to help your students develop choral balance and tonal control.

Title	Grade	Composer	Number	Publisher
Come Soothing Death	M	Bach/ Christiansen	172	Augsburgh
Four Chorales from the Saint Matthew Passion	ME	Bach/ Ehret	686	Lawson

Title	Grade	Composer	Number	Publisher
There Is a Balm in Gilead	M	Dawson	105	Tuskegee
Onward Ye People!	M	Sibelius/ Lefebve	938–10	Galaxy
The Lord's Prayer	MD	Robertson	1.1199.1	Galaxy
In These Delightful, Pleasant Grooves	M	Purcell	8	Novello
Sure on This Shining Night	MD	Barber	10864	G. Schirmer
Let Nothing Ever Grieve Thee	D	Brahms	ES929A	Associated
Hodie Christus Natus Est	D	Willan	Cm469	C. Fischer
Rise Up, My Love My Fair One	M	Willan	94P306	Oxford
The Eyes of All Wait Upon Thee	M	Berger	1264	Augsburg
In the Bleak Mid-Winter	M	Sateren	A470	Hope
Rainsong	M	Bright	A–269	Associated
Cry Out and Shout	ME	Nystedt	1574	Summy
Were You There	M	Burleigh	N.Y.423	Ricordi
The Evening Star	M	Wagner/ Christiansen	1198	Schmitt, Hall McCreary
Cherumbim Song (No. 7)	E	Bortniansky	687	H.W. Gray
Wasn't That a Mighty Day	ME	Work	6835	J. Fischer

The following pieces will be especially helpful in developing the tonal character and color your chamber choir will need to be a special unit.

Title	Grade	Composer	Number	Publisher
I Saw Three Ships	E	Parker/Shaw	10188	G. Schirmer
Lost in the Night	MD	F. Christiansen	119	Augsburg
Hosanna	MD	F. Christiansen	57	Augsburg
Ride On! Ride On!	M	Thompson	1154	Gray
Linden Lea	ME	Williams/Salter	1401	Boosey & Hawkes

Title	Grade	Composer	Number	Publisher
Songs Mein Grossmama Sang	MD	Pfautsch	562	G. Schirmer
Onward Ye People!	M	Sibelius/Lefebve	938–10	Galaxy
All Breathing Life	D	Bach	7470	G. Schirmer
Sing and Rejoince	M	James	2079	Fitzsimons
Sanctus	D	Bach/Damrosch	5654	G. Schirmer
Dedication	M	Franz/Riegger	81043	Flammer
O Sing Your Songs	M	Cain	81154	Flammer
Hallelujah, Amen	ME	Handel	304	E.C. Schirmer
Nunc Dimittis	M	Gretchaninoff	7039	Kjos
Anthony O Daly	D	Barber	8909	G. Schirmer
E'en So Lord Jesus, Quickly Come	M	Manz	98–1054	Concordia
Kyrie Eleison	ME	Dieterich	1931	Boosey & Hawkes
Come Soothing Death	M	Bach Christiansen	172	Augsburg
Soon Ah Will Be Done	M	Dawson	101	Tuskegee
Daybreak	ME	Gastoldi Greyson	ES26	Bourne
Cantate Domino	ME	Hassler Schroth	5336–6	Kjos
Madame Jeanette	ME	Murray	PT 1542	C. Fischer
Pater Noster	M	Stràvinsky	1833	Boosey & Hawkes
Listen To The Mocking Bird	D	Kubik	M18	Southern
Stars Are With The Voyager	M	Bright	A513	Shawnee

CHAPTER 6

HOW TO DEVELOP THE MADRIGAL CHOIR

High school students may not develop fully all techniques that are needed to participate in the madrigal choir during their stay in lower ensembles. Consequently, they need specific instruction in, for example, learning how to sing the musical phrase in contrapuntal structures properly. You will find information in this chapter on teaching the phrase properly. You will also learn how to deal effectively with two kinds of stress points which influence correct phrasing.

You will learn how to blend vowel color, correct breathing, consonants and variety into unifying skills. But, most of all, you will learn how to organize these into simple patterns that can be taught to your students easily. I have also included several examples that will show you how to teach dissonances as functional theoretical processes that can be put into simple patterns for your students.

The madrigal choir can be considered an extension of the chamber choir. The members of both choirs should develop close, interpersonal relationships because of the close ties of the music each sings. In addition, since the madrigal choir will be restricted to the performance of the music of the Renaissance, the members should study the history of the people who lived during that period. These studies can be used to help build the mutual relationship that is needed to help the members of the madrigal and chamber choirs acquire musical kinship between these groups. Of course, you will have to plan a study guide centered around the group concepts that were learned from the study of the Renaissance. This plan should help your students gain knowledge and experience to carry the choirs to their highest level of musical achievements.

AUDITIONING AND SELECTION

Choose your madrigal singers directly from the chamber choir. I hope that you have taught your students how to maintain discipline in the musical process. They should have high regard for musical expression and development. Be sure that you have given good training in these areas under the most purposeful conditions. Actually, promoting the students to the madrigal choir will present no problem since the membership begins with three, and no more than sixteen singers at full strength.

The personnel breakdown for the madrigal choir is as follows:

4 Sopranos
4 Altos
4 Tenors
4 Basses

The numbers above represent the ideal numerical breakdown in personnel for the madrigal choir. The only other breakdown that will help you maintain the Renaissance character among high school groups is as follows:

3 Sopranos		4 Sopranos
3 Altos	or	3 Altos
3 Tenors		3 Tenors
4 Basses		3 Basses

The election of officers for the choir is most important! Ask your singers to choose the persons who can render the most effective service for the organization. The section leaders who are elected must have some directing techniques at their command, and should be able to express musical ideas in the appropriate musical terms and language since many rehearsals will take place under their supervision.

Much publicity should be afforded this group by way of the school journals and newspaper, radio and television. Coverage of all performances and activities of each ensemble by representatives from these sources will be stimulating to your singers. Special news items on school bulletin boards, or in weekly newsletters concerning ensemble activities serve as a source of pride for members of your ensembles.

THREE WAYS TO DEVELOP PROPER MADRIGAL TONAL CONCEPTS

If the correct madrigal tonal concepts are understood and developed thoroughly by your students, they will be able to experience the ultimate in singing these compositions. But you will have to devise a plan that will help your students learn the following concepts thoroughly.

Pure Vowel Modification Concepts

Let your students modify each pure vowel, with the exception of the *ah* vowel, with the dark qualities of the *o, oo,* and *ee* vowels in the high vocal ranges for all Renaissance music, and use the light vowel properties of *ay,* and *ah* in the low chest range. This technique will reap dividends when you permit your students to make vertical and horizontal lip adjustments during vowel formations. It will also let the music differ in color scope from other compositions.

Do not modify vowels such as *ih, eh, uh, ai* and *ur.* These need no modification because they are already modified. Their sound pattern is already conducive to the Renaissance musical character and will move quite well, providing other musical phenomena such as rhythm, good articulation and proper style are worked out in the music.

The Correct Tuning Concept

It is possible that intonation problems will arise, but these can be worked out when you teach your students to sing a perfect horizontal line as it occurs in the music. If poor intonation occurs at cadences, work these out by tuning the chords vertically, permitting each person to become familiar with the sound and character of the notes. Since bar lines are recent additions to this kind of music, tuning cadences will help the students understand why they were added and the importance of the phrase in this music. To further enhance the proper tuning kept in accordance to polyphonic structures, let two voice lines, preferably the alto and bass, then the tenor and soprano, practice their parts together while other students listen critically for missed notes. Missed notes are the reason for many intonation problems!

The Correct Tenor Quality Concept

The tenor in the madrigal choir should possess an even scale beginning with C3 through A5. Permit them to use falsetto quality only if it becomes absolutely necessary! But, pure vowels blended with lyrical quality presents this voice in good form for correct madrigal singing. Do not permit your tenors to use head resonance alone! It will destroy characteristic madrigal singing! Be certain that they use good mixtures of the other resonances to render satisfying performances.

You can introduce the technical vocalises in Illustrations 6.1a and 6.1b to aid in developing an even scale among your tenors. In order to realize crucial benefits from these vocalises, first, ask them to practice blending vowels and the lyrical quality. When there is evidence of development, employ tonal spiralling techniques with proper on-the-breath attacks.

ILLUSTRATION 6.1a Use all vowels.

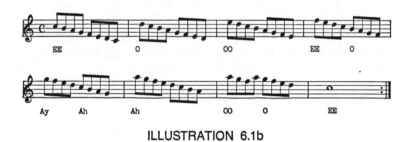

ILLUSTRATION 6.1b

BUILDING GOOD QUALITY IN THE CHOIR

Let your singers continue the partner system that was introduced in the chamber choir auditions. In fact, the same drills that each team used to attain vocal unity in the chamber choir can be used here in the madrigal choir for the same purpose. The underlying principle is to control dark and light vowel patterns in different sections of the compositions, especially in the bass and alto sections when they are singing in their upper head voices. The same principle holds true when the soprano and tenor sections are singing in their low chest registers.

You can give your singers good experience when you permit

them to become familiar with the light and dark color patterns as they occur in the music. Be prepared to offer examples to include the correct tonal character at these points in the composition.

Correcting Improper Line Movement

Do not permit a deterioration of fabrication in line movement as the voices move in close or open voice annexations. The identity of each line must be maintained! Keep the fabric design in each line of the composition pure and identifiable.

1. Keep special nuances, colors and effects out of the music.
2. Analyze note/word stress points to discover the natural color of the words and the music.
3. Study other stress points which effect the elongation of the rhythmical count of the notes, then assign the manner for performance to each person in the ensemble.
4. Study each line to discover where the different blended resonances will be utilized, and assign these to the affected lines.
5. Give detailed instructions to your students concerning imitation, fugue, canon ostinato and cantus firmus.

Word Stress Versus Musical Expression

Do not let your madrigalists become confused concerning the application of word stress and musical expression as they relate in Renaissance music. Outline their meaning in clear terms, and secure recordings to help the students understand them. You may choose those words in the musical phrase that can give you clues for proper musical expression, and to help you discover the "right" rhythmic and emotional stress points. Then, say the entire word phrase poetically to give you the clue to its musical meaning. Now, sing the music with the correct stylistic approach. When this process has been inculcated in the students, let them breathe at the phrase ending only! One student who will be allowed to enter the musical stream after taking a breath in the middle of a phrase interrupts perfect line movement, causing possible intonation problems, foreign uninhibited vowels which cannot be controlled successfully by the ensemble.

Be certain that your singers understand the importance of employing musical expression with similarity throughout the ensemble Tell them that proper word scrutiny and technical perfection will always eliminate the possibility of damage to the fabrication in contrapuntal textures.

Acquiring the Proper Background

Your students in the madrigal choir must be knowledgeable about inversions, augmentations and diminutions. These must be pinpointed for discussion whenever the opportunity presents itself. Do not permit your students to sing through this music without the proper understanding of its background. You will need to study with them a list of Renaissance composers whose works will help enlighten them on canon, imitation and stretto.

UTILIZING PROPER PHRASING TECHNIQUES IN CONTRAPUNTAL STRUCTURES

Imitation is used universally as a contrapuntal process. It can be taught from the theoretical standpoint at first. This will help your students understand it as it appears in musical compositions under the auspices of repetition. Begin teaching this process by constructing a two part canon on the board. Then, point out the relationship between the "leader" and the "follower" in the music for your students. Find other compositions of this nature to perform and let your students add variety to them by using a tonal spiralling technique to initiate the lines properly. In those places where the composer has employed sequence, strengthen this process by permitting the singers of each line to make entrances with the same amount of vocal stress. Remember that vocal stress influences emotional stress, and it occurs from the power and influence the text has upon the singers.

The color of the vowels in the sequence pattern must be identical in each voice also. This means that all vowel formations must be shaped somewhat the same by every singer in the ensemble, and proper blend patterns must be in evidence in each line.

The proper line contrast will occur when you permit your madrigalists to use the natural dramatic stress that comes from the expressive quality of the words within the text. Each phrase interpreted in this sense will lead the singers naturally to another phrase. Of course, stretto is the only contrapuntal process that does not need the same amount of vocal stress put forth by the singers because it has its own built-in pressed points. Encourage the students to sing these with perfect balance.

Unifying Skills

To keep the imitative texture of polyphonic music unified, be sure that the following skills are definite parts of your student's vocal technique. They must be unified in the polyphonic process.

• Vowel Color. Strict uniformity should exist throughout the ensemble. Each voice line must be clearly defined using the same color ingredients and rhythmic stress.

• Breathing. Staggered breathing concepts are not satisfactory for the performance of Renaissance music because the correct madrigal tonal concept cannot be maintained with it. Teach your students these drills in order to learn proper breathing:

1. Stand erect, place the hands on the sides two or three inches below the ribs.
2. Take in the air, feeling expansion around the waistline.
3. Let the mouth remain partially open and permit the air to escape slowly while the teacher counts to eight. Repeat this drill.

• Consonants. Do not permit your singers to over-articulate consonants at the expense of ruining the vowel form.

• Variety. Other forms of variety should be included by the singers. These are:

1. Rhythmic-word continuity.
2. Balance and blend
3. Musical continuity
4. Dynamic control
5. Tonal control

These skills can be taught through solo material, or you may want to work in sectional rehearsals to develop them. At any rate, they must be developed and unified to render proper phrasing in polyphonic music.

Initiating the Phrase Properly

A good musical phrase occurs in contrapuntal textures when all sections of the ensemble initiate their individual lines with good coloration, rhythm, balance and blend, and when, according to style, they have been scrutinized from a vertical as well as a horizontal sense. If proper note/rhythm and line contact have been made and the rhythmic-word stress is satisfactory, the phrase has been sung properly.

Now, let us study Illustration 6.2 to see how all of the skills above relate in contrapuntal textures. The lines in each excerpt have been marked to indicate its structure. The dotted line means that the note must be carried over to its full count. Only at that point can a phrase end successfully in contrapuntal textures.

ILLUSTRATION 6.2

By permission of the Folger Shakespeare Library, Washington, D.C.

In measure three there is an overlap between the alto and the tenor. That is, the alto line descends below the tenor. The continuity of the alto line must not be interrupted at that point. It would be well to permit the tenors to use resonance from the chest and nose (covered tone) which will let them keep their identity at that point. Let your altos use an outer smile for a special coloring of the root of the chord. Strategically carry over the existing sound with good tonal spiralling technique to the D major chord in this measure. Do not release the notes of the alto, tenor and bass in measure eight too quickly. The Bb in the soprano line is the third of the chord and affects the D major textural setup in that measure.

Rhythmic rests are important in contrapuntal textures because they provide stopping places for the music, but not necessarily for the singer. There is one provided in measure nine for the sopranos. It is wrong for the sopranos to breathe at that point because they would be taking a chance on destroying the effectiveness of the *ee* vowel in the word sweet. Actually, the entire phrase will be destroyed, making a possibility for the good madrigal concept remote.

Dissonances and Proper Phrasing

Many students are not aware of the importance dissonances have in polyphonic music. You can bring about an awareness by telling your singers the exact function of the dissonance in a specific composition. You may also acquaint your students with the theoretical process and deal specifically with the dissonant factor. If they are not understood by the students, the music, in many instances, will suffer.

Since the problem of tonal weight distribution has been worked out by the composer, it is unlikely that you will have to disturb the harmonic process in any respect. When you let the students practice, be sure to identify the places where the dissonances occur.

Note how the dissonances tend to electrify the excerpt in Illustration 6.3 taken from "Oh Had I Wings Like to a Dove." Use a lighter vowel quality in the high vocal range to make a vacuum for the successful operation of overtones and the initiation of the dissonances. But be careful when you prepare a vertical mixture of high and low tones. You may have to delete or add some vowel color among your students to enhance the dissonant factor.

Composers of this type of composition were aware of the problems the singers would experience. This reasoning is assured in the fact that not all who sang this music were professionals, and needed the built-in elements such as displaced accents and canon to help overcome poor breathing habits and inconsistent musical phrasing.

ILLUSTRATION 6.3
By permission of the Folger Shakespeare Library, Washington, D.C.

Ask your singers to always mark their music similar to that in the excerpt above. This practice will help them to understand proper phrasing in the music of the Renaissance.

Stretto

Another device used in contrapuntal textures is stretto. An example of it in Illustration 6.4 has been taken from "April Is in My Mistress' Face" by Thomas Morley. Note how the vowel *ur* and *uh* are utilized here. Let your singers set the vowel form so that no drastic vertical changes can be heard between them. If you allow this to happen, an unnatural sound pattern will be heard.

Since the stretto begins on different pitch levels of the note D, you should use every effort to "tune" these notes up perfectly. There should not be a modification in color scheme between the soprano and tenor lines. However, you can permit the bass line to use more resonance here. Do not sacrifice it to achieve a similar blend with the soprano and tenor sections. Rather, the blend will be achieved with the "right" rhythmic stress among the voices. But a definite intoned diagonal interchange must be heard to encourage the characteristic madrigal sound.

ILLUSTRATION 6.4
By permission of the Folger Shakespeare Library, Washington, D.C.

Matching the Voice Lines

One of the best methods for teaching proper phrasing in contrapuntal textures is to allow each voice line to sing the part with the
bass line without the other voices. In this way, you can check vocal
technique more closely and shape the lines by way of a matching
process. This process is necessary to show the singers how closely
related each line is with the other.

Here are seven steps you should use in matching the voice lines:

1. Hold the count of the last note in each measure over to the
   first count in the next measure.
2. Help your students develop a keen sense of rhythm by clap-
   ping their lines often.
3. Let the students become familiar with the color schemes of
   the composition by isolating them.
4. After you have permitted your students to practice the color
   schemes out of musical context, work for extreme uniformity
   throughout the ensemble.
5. Avoid dramaticism and special effects!
6. When singing diphthongs, the first vowel must be held
   throughout the duration of the note with the last vowel articulated quickly. Equalize the vowel-lip formations throughout
   the ensemble.
7. Set a definite pattern for the articulation of consonants.

DEVELOPING SENSITIVE GROUP MUSICALITY

Members of madrigal choirs can have common interest in the customs and characters of the people who lived during the Renaissance. Each singer can be assigned the task of searching for, and relating to the group, some particular point of interest that took place during this period. This assignment can serve as a basis for becoming acquainted with the Renaissance world. It also gives each person an opportunity to share in building group interest. Actually, each person can learn how to cooperate with others by serving on research teams and working assignments out together. However, the end results are to develop a trend in motivation and initiate an interest in the Renaissance period so there can be good reasons for developing sensitive group musicality.

All madrigalists must be able to sing certain compositions at sight. One person should be responsible for getting the choir started, cueing and ending phrases successfully. But the singers must be able to perform without a formal director, each individual "feeling" the pulsation of the beat, and doing his part to keep the music from "falling apart."

It is obvious that adjustments have to be made after the first reading. But you should choose music that is on the reading level of your students. Once the music is read by the students, they must have a feeling of being successful. Remember, nothing works like success in developing the singer.

Rhythmical Development

Try to get your students to be responsive to each other through rhythmical activities. These should be designed for part of the group to answer the other rhythmically from question-answer situations similar to the ones in Illustration 6.5.

As the last stage in your students' development in rhythmic activities, you may combine all questions and answers into a composite pattern to be performed simultaneously. Use different dynamic and speed levels. Try to get as much spontaneity as possible. Exchange the patterns among the groups when there is evidence of development.

The four exercises were provided to help you develop a smooth rhythmical flow among your singers. You can continue this development by providing other rhythmical activities similar to the ones in Illustration 6.5. Try to maintain the same level of difficulty.

When the rhythmical flow is developed evenly among your stu-

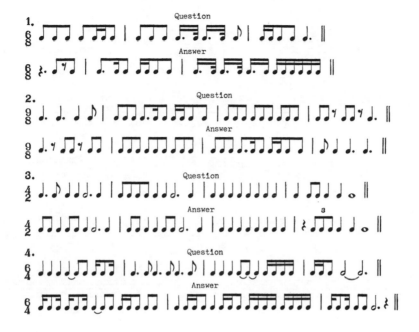

ILLUSTRATION 6.5

dents, introduce compositions similar to the ones in Illustrations 6.6a and 6.6b. You will need other compositions of this nature to help develop an acceptable rhythmical level among your students. Since these short compositions are more suitable for the initial development, compose your own, using the different techniques that are related to this type of composition.

It is imperative that each student be left alone to learn the musical score. Each must have this skill at his command. Learning parts is secondary to rhythm at this point in their development. I do not mean to minimize the importance of learning parts, rather, permit melody to simply exist and be developed as a result of good rhythmical expression. You can point out to your students that rhythm and melody, in balance, are most important in developing group musicality.

Speaking Choruses

Use speaking choruses to finalize your plans to develop sensitive group musicality. Aside from choosing material for the individual

ILLUSTRATION 6.6a

voice, use sections of the text taken directly from one of the compositions you are working on. If you choose to use materials such as poems, or essays, mark the text with different musical symbols similar to the setup below:

ff
Were you there that night?

pp
Were you there that night?

There are many ways to set up the simple text for your students to practice individually, or as a group. You may even try making up the words yourself, or ask your students to try writing some original poems.

When there is evidence of some development, you may begin utilizing those compositions that will help you and your singers reap full benefits from the group's musicality.

ILLUSTRATION 6.6b

THE MADRIGAL STYLE

Rehearsal sessions should be held in formations similar to the formal concert formation you will use. But at some point in the student's development, he or she should be placed in a practice formation so that the face will be exposed to the group. This can be achieved by practicing around a table, or standing in a circle.

Time can be spent at trying to arrive at the proper setting in which the correct interpretation of the music can be understood by all. Of course, the composer spent many hours composing the music; you and your students should spend many hours studying and determining exactly how it should be performed. Each ensemble in the Graduated Program should be assigned this same task. Each ensemble will be able to get the correct musical message if its members search deeply for it. The true musical meaning from any composition will come only after the proper time of study and the amount of talent you and your students have in the musical process.

Counterpoint

Teach your students the basic elements of counterpoint, then introduce melody-making. You may, at this point, let them make some of their own. When there is a definite development in melody-making, ask them to prepare two-part canons utilizing the melodies they have made. Do not permit your students to rely heavily upon chordal harmonies, but create harmony as a result of the melodies moving into contact with each other. You may have to help your students with these in the beginning, but let them work as independently as possible. The idea should be to acquaint your students with the simple mechanics of counterpoint for a better understanding of the music that they will be singing.

The Text

Ask the students to make up the text for their melodic creations. Although many students may experience difficulties in composing words for their melodies, you will have to encourage them to keep searching deeply within themselves for their texts until one has been formed. Be sure that these texts are original.

Tell your students to begin searching for word-clues that will produce specific ideas for a title. The title will help them to classify their material into a composite thought structure. They may now begin searching for words which rhyme with other key words. The texts should now be well on the way to becoming sensitive and poetic in quality.

Accents and Rhythm

Accents and other stress points should occur in Renaissance music only as a direct result of the text. However, you must be certain that your students understand the marks in Illustration 6.7 as those of a later period, and must not be confused with accents in early polyphonic structures.

ILLUSTRATION 6.7

Think of the accents in the illustration as a mixture of the vocal as well as the emotional stress points in music. But the accent in contrapuntal music is created as a result of a "displaced" beat in many instances. Do not let the students use too much vocal stress. Rather, let the words and the power of the note sing through at those points where accents would be normal in later compositions. If confusion occurs among your students, it is always a sign that they have not had enough study of the text and the music which have great influences on the character of the music itself. Proper study will bring about a greater understanding of accents and rhythm, thereby increasing the chance for having a better fusion of music and text, and proper style.

Achieving the Correct Tonal Character

There are two extremes in achieving the correct tonal character in the madrigal choir:

1. Modify each pure vowel in the high range with *o, oo,* or *ee* quality with the exception of the *ah* vowel.
2. Modify the vowels in low ranges with the light vowel properties of *ay* and *ah.*

The color from the two extreme ranges above should be practiced often so that the students will have the chance to hear, understand and develop the correct tonal character. Be sure to ask them to keep the mouth open as much as possible when singing.

Let your students study the works of the composers in the Renaissance era to become acquainted with the true musical character of this period. Through this study, the seemingly intangible conotation of style, character and form will take shape and give to the students an understanding of the music.

RECOMMENDED MUSIC LIST

Some choir directors select music specifically for concerts and festivals with little attention paid to the developmental aspect of their choirs. The list below has been prepared to help you make selections to develop the correct madrigal tonal concept.

Title	Grade	Composer	Number	Publisher
Fa Una Canzone	E	Vecchi	LG 556	G. Schirmer
Weep O Mine Eyes	E	Bennet	ES 30	Bourne
O Eyes of My Beloved	E	Di Lasso	1146	E. C. Schirmer
I Have Longed For Thy Saving Health	E	Byrd/Whitehead	1679	Gray
Allon, Gay Bergeres	E	Costeley/Shaw	10178	G. Schirmer
Ecce Vidimus	E	Palestrina	1883	Chorale Press
Agnus Dei	M	Morley/Dart	603	Galaxy
Alma Redemptoris	M	Palestrina	921	McLaughlin
Jesu Dulcis Memoria	M	Victoria	5573	G. Schirmer
O Admirabile Commercium	M	Palestrina/Sargent	354	Oxford
Ave Regina Coelorum	M	Di Lasso/Richter	A–406	Associated
April Is In My Mistress' Face	ME	Morley/Churchill	748	Bourne
The Silver Swan	D	Gibbons	ES 18	Bourne
Fire, Fire My Heart	D	Morley	ES 65	Bourne

Title	Grade	Composer	Number	Publisher
Sweet Honey Sucking Bees	D	Wilbye	GS 8781	G. Schirmer
Your Dancing, My Dearest	D	Costeley/Mason	7017	Walton
Surrexit Pastor Bonus	D	Di Lasso	7685	G. Schirmer
O Magnum Mysterium	D	Victoria	ES 20	Bourne

CHAPTER 7

HOW TO DEVELOP THE MODERN CHOIR

There are nine basic skills which should be taught to the members of your modern choir: the portamento, syncopation, dissonance, repetition, imitation, rhythmic variations, resolution, quarter tones and nuances. In this chapter I will show you how to teach their special effects to your ensembles. The influence of syncopation is dominant in the modern choral composition. For this reason, I have included it in several musical settings, examples and discussions. I will show you how to bring out its full character in modern compositions through the development of dissonant and consonant factors. When you develop this with your students, their knowledge of theory and singing techniques will be greatly improved.

Diction is very important in the training of any vocal ensemble. It is especially important in the modern choir because so much emphasis is placed upon the fusion of words and music. Therefore, I will show you how to build the special character of the modern choir through the study of proper rhythmic-word action and the articulation of the consonant.

BUILDING THE SPECIAL CHOIR

Give your students as much freedom as possible in the area of self expression and creativity while they are studying in your modern choir. Let them do much research for the music this choir can perform. You may also permit them to bring in recordings that will accentuate those techniques they may wish to develop. However, you should control the situation so that only the music you wish for the singers to perform will be researched. This is important since there are numerous types of modern choirs which could be developed. Of course, all kinds of modern choirs can benefit by studying the techniques found in this chapter.

Selecting the Personnel

The modern choir will help you prepare your students for the musical excellence they will need to participate in the a cappella choir. It will also help them to project the vocal techniques in a special way to your audiences.

The students who are chosen for this choir must come directly from the madrigal choir. They should not be accepted from any other source, and their stay in that choir can culminate with at least one semester of training before they are allowed to graduate to the modern choir. It is possible that all members of the madrigal choir could graduate to the modern choir if enough members are moved from the chamber choir to take their places.

The membership of the modern choir should not exceed twenty singers during any semester. This will help you to maintain the membership of each small vocal ensemble and give you ample time to help your students develop thoroughly the techniques found in this book.

Involving the Students

I have found that it is a good idea to let your students visit college programs which have developed modern choirs. Encourage them to look for new ideas that can be used in your ensembles. Be certain that positive theoretical processes and proper rules of acceptable writing techniques are observed. This is important since the students may wish to include these in some of their own compositions later.

TEACHING MODERN VOCAL SKILLS CORRECTLY

Modern choirs should represent the extension of a dignified musical experience for your students. The seriousness with which they study the techniques while in the choir will be of great value when you move them to higher ensembles.

The key skill areas are: the portamento, syncopation, dissonances and repetition. They and their components—imitation, rhythmic variation, resolution, quarter tones and nuances—are provided here for study so that you and your students will have success in performing the music similar to that found on the recommended music list at the end of this chapter.

- **The Portamento.** Be careful when you teach this skill to your students. It is wrong to assume that there are no definite note patterns involved. Indicate the notes in the portamento by placing them on your board correctly. Encourage the singers to sing the notes as rapidly as the tempo of the music dictates. If the notes are sung too slowly, that is, accentuating the sound of certain notes, you will have difficulty in differentiating between the portamento and other passing tones. When all of the notes are sung correctly in the portamento, permit it to be sung with an "on the breath" approach. Do not let improper breathing, resonance, or other vocal problems destroy the purity of the vowel in the portamento. Proper vocal production must be maintained at all times. Study the portamentos in Illustrations 7.1 and 7.2 that are represented by major and minor thirds. The idea of identifying the notes of the portamento as they are above helps your singers to eliminate guess work in the note proportions.

ILLUSTRATION 7.1

ILLUSTRATION 7.2

- **Syncopation.** The only rule for using this skill is to shift the accent to some normally unaccented beats. But you will discover many additional rules to improve and evaluate the increasing number of innovations in syncopated styles. Notice

ILLUSTRATION 7.3

how accents affect the text and the music in Illustration 7.3. The accent mark on the first beat of the measure gives the phrase a special character, just as well-placed accent marks change the character of similar rhythm patterns in snare drum solos. But the voice is distinctive; consequently, varied characteristic vocal sounds can be created. Of course, the change in the word-vowel scheme offsets the accented situation in the example above between the first two notes, but is intensified by the accent on the fifth note.

Using Breath Support Correctly
In Syncopated Rhythms

Since a speeding up of the breath stream is needed to sing syncopated rhythm, ask your students to control the air stream by holding as much of it back as possible. An increased amount of air, however, will cause more diaphragm expansion. You will need to alert your students to use more breath support. Tell them to keep the tone quality pure by keeping the mouth open as much as possible.

Correcting Abnormal Blend
In Syncopated Rhythms

If abnormality occurs in the blend of your modern choir, you can probably trace it to uncontrolled vibrato, faulty breath control, incorrect vowel forms or poor resonance blending. You will have to test each person in each section to correct it. Look for faulty breath control first. This will help you eliminate uncontrolled vibrato if it is an offending element. Now, work for the color you desire by adjusting the vowel formation and resonance blending. Ask your students to hold still when singing difficult patterns in syncopated rhythms. The process of not permitting the mouth to move excessively, especially in using good vowel forms, will aid in a smooth translation of all syncopated rhythms.

- **Dissonances.** The results you can create from proper use of dissonances in modern music are identifiable horizontal melodic schemes solidified by your student's ability to project the correct tonal textures that are involved. These textures will relate to repetition, imitation, rhythmic variations, resolutions, quarter tones in rare cases and nuances as they occur in compositions. These textures represent a conglomerate of techniques that modern composers have used in their music, and ones that you can let your students become acquainted with to further their vocal development. They are used in the dissonant proportions of some modern compositions to add another dimension to musical art. Let each section of your modern choir practice carefully those phrases where dissonances occur. Be certain that each person can identify the melody in the phrase. The dissonants that are composed beneath or above it should be sung as an adjunct, not overemphasized, but measured vertically and horizontally in a pleasing manner.

- **Repetition.**   When repetition occurs, especially among short phrases, permit your singers to use different vocal color patterns. Sometimes the composer offers help in this area by using alterations in one of the phrases or changing the dynamic format. Be careful when you teach this kind of repetition to your students! Good vowel coloring must be planned so that preservation of the music's character will be assured. But in those cases where exact repetition is used between two long phrases, it would be wise to plan a totally different color format for each of them. Again, be sure that the composition's character is preserved! When repetition is used as in the example below, you can let your students hear the composition in its entirety in a recording, or by a professional group in your community. This will help the students to gain an understanding of the true character of the piece, even to discover the composer's construction techniques. So these two elements, character and construction, should be analyzed in compositions that make use of repetition.

Achieving Contrast in Repetition

The repetitive rhythmical outlay in the alto line in Illustration 7.4 is important despite the part it plays in creating the dissonant effects within the excerpt. Although the outlay is, in a sense, simple, it nonetheless carries a symbolic message that makes it equal to the

ILLUSTRATION 7.4

other lines. For this reason, you will have to teach the students how to use light vowel properties in the alto line as opposed to a medium dark sound in the soprano line. This kind of vocal interplay will be balanced after you work out the harmonic balance in the male sections of your modern choir. The contrast that should be made between the male lines comes from the natural sound of the voices in both registers. You may use more resonance in the second bass part since this will help to strengthen that voice in the vocal process of this kind of composition. Let your tenors use some projectional resonance in their

ILLUSTRATION 7.5

registrations. Once the horizontal aspect has been attained, be sure that the vertical harmony is effective also. This can be improved through proper intonation and singing the correct note.

- **Imitation**.   This technique is the repetition by one voice line of a theme or motive that was sung or played previously by another voice line or instrument. It is used in some modern compositions to place emphasis on certain melodies or phrases, to add interest to the composition, or to show the inventive skill of the composer. Study Illustration 7.5 to see how you can teach your students a good method for singing imitation devices with understanding. Notice especially the alto and tenor parts beginning in the same octave. Do not adjust the color scheme between these voices. The composer has created the line so that they complement each other by way of the tonal arch that occurs at different intervals in the lines. Be sure that the bass line is effective by using light vowel properties. But be sure to keep the balance in the composition by using proper tonal weight distribution.

Practicing Imitation Correctly

When preparing music with imitation as in the example above, let your singers sing through the music to pinpoint those places where it occurs. Identify these by writing "imitation" directly above the area. Now, let one or two voices within a section sing the theme that is used in the imitation. Give directions to them to sing it correctly. Add other singers as each sings the line similar to the others in the section. Be sure that light vowel properties are used throughout the imitation process in this example. As each voice line enters the musical stream, you may, in the framework of the dynamic level of the imitation section, allow the students to state the line somewhat louder than the other voices. Be careful that you do not destroy the blend with special effects unless the music specifically calls for them.

You may have to use dark vowel sounds in the imitation process. In this case, all voices must follow this trend. There must be complete unity in performing the music when imitation is involved.

● **Rhythmic Variations.**   These are necessary to create distinct dissonant character in the modern composition. Rhythmic variation in Illustration 7.5 is caused by the imitation process itself. It adds another dimension to the syncopated structure in the composition. Notice the elongation of the dotted quarter note as it comes in contact with the syncopated structure. You will have to give identity to these areas by using modified vowel sounds. If rhythmic variations used in different sections represent a basic structure in the composition, you must tell your students how to color the pattern each time it occurs. You can do this by experimenting with different colors until you find one that is correct for that composition.

● **Resolution.**   This device moves a musically dissonant factor from that state to a musically consonant one. When this occurs, permit the dissonant factors to change to consonant ones with a definite change of tonal quality. This means that you will be able to use "legitimate" vocal approaches similar to those in the informal and chamber choirs.

- **Quarter Tones.** Teach each of your singers in the modern choir how to sing quarter tones. If these can be sung correctly, your students will become more adept at staying in tune because they will have a better knowledge of the distance between such intervals as major and minor seconds. This work is demanding, but your efforts will not go unrewarded.

- **Nuances.** Nuances (tempo variations, tone color, dynamics and phrasing) are evidenced more in the twentieth century than ever before. They are used to create better fusions of text and music. But in modern compositions, dissonant harmonies serve as an adjunct to articulate this fusion without restrictions as was the case in earlier periods. However, it remains necessary for the singer to maintain a well-rounded technique to perform the music which requires rhythmic changes at a moment's notice and subtle vocal color. Vowel color and quality must be studied and developed for successful performances of this music with its varied shadings during one composition.

THE CONSONANT

One of the major goals of twentieth century composers is to bring about a greater fusion of the modern text and the music written for it. This goal is becoming a reality in many contemporary compositions. For this reason, the singers in the modern choir have to pay strict attention to all rules governing the proper articulation of consonants. The rules are as follows:

1. Consonants that are produced with the aid of the vocal cords are voiced. They are: b, d, g, l, m, n, r, ng, w, x, and y.
2. Consonants that are produced without the aid of the vocal cords are voiceless. They are: th, ch, c, f, h, j, k, p, s, t, v and z.

For clarity, refer to them as semi-musical and non-musical.

The chart below will show you how these consonants are to be formed. You should have each student memorize each formation.

Rules for articulation of the consonant are: (1) When the consonant precedes a vowel maintain the same pitch of the vowel if it is semi-musical. (2) Provide the correct formation for the vowel, holding it the duration of the note and articulate the consonant at the last moment. Although this is basic development for all kinds of ensem-

THEORETICAL NAMES	CORRECT FORMATION	SEMI-MUSICAL	NON-MUSICAL
Bilabial	Formed with the lips	b,m,w,y	p
Labio-dental	Lower lip and upper teeth		f,v,
Dental	Tongue against upper teeth		th
Alveolar	Tongue against upper gum	l,r,n,d, ng,g	t,j
Gutteral	Back of tongue against soft palate	q	h,k,ch
Sibilant	Tip of tongue behind upper teeth	x	c,s,z

ILLUSTRATION 7.6

bles, the work you will do here in the modern choir is special in creating its special sound.

Selected Solo Material

When your students have successfully memorized and demonstrated each consonant through vocalises or music you have chosen for this purpose, complete the development through the solo material below:

Title	*Composer*
Under the Willow Tree	Samuel Barber
Across the Western Ocean	Arr. Celius Dougherty
Symphony in Yellow	Griffes Op. 3, No. 2
Music When Soft Voices Die	Gold
The Buckle	Arthur Bliss

*From the book, *Developmental Procedures for Advancing Choirs* from April 1971 *Music Teacher's Workshop Journal* by Orlando Moss. (c) 1971 by Parker Publishing Company, Inc. Published by Parker Publishing Co., Inc., West Nyack, New York

It Must Be Me (From Candide)   Leonard Bernstein
The Lonesome Dove
  (From Down in the Valley)   Kurt Weill

All of the songs above can be purchased in the bound collection titled *20th Century Art Songs* published by G. Schirmer.

Title	*Composer*
Beau Soir	Debussy
A Dissonance	Borodine
Do Not Go, My Love	Hageman
Lilacs	Rachmaninoff
Love's Old, Sweet Song	Molloy
Nur, Wer Die Sehnsuckt Kennt	Tchaikowsky
Then You'll Remember Me	Balfe
Were My Song with Wings Provided	Hahn

The songs above can be purchased in a bound volume titled *56 Songs You Like to Sing* published by G. Schirmer.

Improving Rhythmic Word Contact

Start the study of the rhythmic activity of a particular composition very slowly. Decide the correct rhythmic timing for each pattern including the timing of the consonants. Let the students clap the rhythm and recite the text simultaneously for the entire piece. Show them stress points in terms of the size of the note. For instance, the quarter note receives more rhythmic stress than the eighth note because it is a half-count larger; consequently, the composition will have a number of these stress points for you to work on especially in those places where emotional stress is indicated. You may permit your students to find these stress points, both from the note and emotional standpoint, by speaking the words again in rhythm. Ask them to separate the words equally and clearly through proper articulation of the consonants, carrying the count of the note to the beat of the next note.

Achieving Clear Enunciation
Of Words Formed with the Consonant *R*

Many young singers experience difficulty in articulation when the pronoun *I* follows the consonant *r* as in "for." Never permit the *r* to become a part of the next word, for in doing so, the word becomes "rye"! This is most distasteful in any vocal art form. Rather, spend time in working for clear enunciation of the word and clear articulation of the consonant. Begin very slowly at first, then increase the speed when progress is evidenced. The r is a difficult factor in articulation because it causes your singers to anticipate the next vowel sound too soon; therefore, let your singers work this consonant in the framework of good rhythmic timing.

Achieving Rhythmically Balanced Consonants

In the main, an understanding of rhythm must accompany properly articulated consonants in the modern choir. This fusion will take place if there is unity in the attack on each word-vowel in the composition, and the vertical balance in this respect has been worked out at each vocal level. In addition, if the students have developed unity of word-note and emotional stress points, and have become acquainted with the character of the voice lines, work should begin on the fusion of melody, text and rhythm. Improvements in this area take place when you teach your students to attack a word in rhythm, at the same time and balance the consonants vertically throughout the ensemble.

DEVELOPING IMPROVISATIONAL SKILLS

Today's vocal students, more than ever before, are studying composition and improvisation in high school. But it is difficult to schedule theory and composition classes for these students during regular school hours because they must spend this time in other academic studies. The ensemble program is needed for these students who want to excel in other areas in the music field. Rather than let these students give up in despair, the wise choral director finds time to teach theory and composition techniques to them other than during class time. One good way to begin this kind of study is to purchase texts in this area for each of the interested students. Assign homework each day, and check it with the students the following day. I have prepared a list of texts that will be beneficial to you.

Title	Author	Publisher
Form in Music	Wallace Berry	Prentice-Hall, Inc.
Adventures in Music	Howell	National Textbook Co.
Musical Interpretation	Matthay	Books for Libraries, Inc. (Also pub. by Greenwood Press.)

Publisher

Introduction to Musical Knowledge	Jones & Barnard	Schmitt
Introduction To Music	Bernstein & Picker	Prentice-Hall, Inc.
The Mechanics Of Music	Jenni	Schmitt
The Gist Of Music	Wedge	Schirmer Books (Macmillan)
Principles of Harmonic Analysis	Piston	E.C. Schirmer Music Co.

Developing improvisational skills is the most successful method for stimulating interest in the creative process among your students. This is one of the main reasons why the modern choir has been included in the Graduated Program.

Rhythmic Time Values

It is important for each student in the modern choir to be responsive to the rhythmic time values which make the music sound complete. Their feelings in this respect should be strong. The slightest alteration or distraction in the rhythmic aspect of the music should not go unnoticed. For example, if the Star Spangled Banner is performed out of its original rhythmic context, your students should note immediately that the rhythm is "wrong" because it is not what their ears have been accustomed to hearing. They should be able to tell if the notes in the composition have been rearranged or modified. This type of distortion should be rejected by your students when they begin vocal improvisations. Tell them to give the compositions their best effort when composing the rhythm. In addition, tell them that being able to "feel" the rhythm is a basic skill for learning how to improvise.

Building the Improvisational Format

To begin the process for developing vocal improvisations, let your students compose a series of rhythms for the prose or poetry you may choose for this purpose, then let them compose different melodies to complement each rhythmic pattern. When the melodies are composed, ask your students to go to work building the appropriate chord scheme for the melodies. These should be restricted from the tonic to the dominant seventh harmonies. Be certain that the compositions do not duplicate each other rhythmically or melodically. In other words, offer encouragement to those who seek new ideas and originality in their compositions. When you have approved this work, duplicate each composition so that they can be sung by the class.

Developing Vocal Improvisations

Ask one student to sing arpeggios in the chord scheme, while the remaining choir members sing the chords in block harmony in each composition. When each student can sing the arpeggios correctly in every major and minor key, ask them to sing the same arpeggios with spontaneous rhythms. To encourage this, you may have to provide examples to get the students started. Use the example in Illustration 7.7 as a guide and compose eight measure phrases to help your students get started:

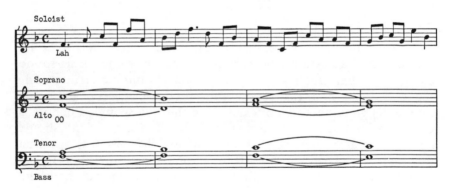

ILLUSTRATION 7.7

Embryonic Improvisations

When you are certain that a moderate level of success has been achieved in improvisations among your students, let them work to develop their individual styles. Your work can be in the capacity of an overseer rather than a teacher. Your students will always need your advice, but it is more beneficial to help them realize that they can depend on their own ability to create the material for improvisations. These, in many respects, will be embryonic at first, but they can be improved in areas such as chord construction and musical form. You may offer suggestions to improve the melodic structure if your students have made errors. Otherwise, permit them to grow with these embryonic experiences they will create. Encourage them! Tell them their work was sufficient at this time, but will need to be improved as time goes along.

Here are some suggestions you can give to your students to be used in their embryonic improvisations:

1. Use sixteen measure phrases.
2. Add non-harmonic and passing tones to the melody line.
3. Use some superimposed chordal tones.
4. Use repetition, sequence, variations, chromaticism and counterpoint to expand and strengthen the improvisations.

You will have to explain each of the items above, in terms of their relationship to good compositional techniques. Give your students specific assignments to write a few measures employing each as a technical device. When these have been constructed, let them memorize the techniques to enhance their improvisations. The first attempt must be sung slowly, but increase the speed as development is evidenced.

Developing Embryonic Improvisations

Encourage your students to use limited chord progressions at first in order to learn all techniques and skills under this condition. Later, other progressions can be used when they are able to improvise at an acceptable level. At this stage, you may permit them to change key signatures often, and use different tempos and dynamic levels. You may also permit them to write some of their musical ideas down on manuscript paper to be referred to later in their development. Of course, being able to write music is the basic reason for studying improvisation.

Expanding Improvisations

It is evident from those musicians who are good improvisors, that proper musical construction could not exist without the use of chromaticism. It is used effectively in contemporary music by many composers in different ways. But let us begin our study of it in a manner that can be understood by the high school student. Permit your students to begin the construction by adding chromatics to some of their compositions they have composed already. When they have made some progress, let them continue in the manner prescribed below.

• **Chromaticism.** The melodic structure can be expanded by using chromatic intervals with the chord scheme of the composition.

Motivic elements can either begin or end with them, but should not be written in ways to cause the singers to damage the tonal character of compositions. You will find in Illustration 7.8 a method to add color to chords by using chromaticism, but it does no damage to the character of the piece. Teach your students to use it in this manner.

ILLUSTRATION 7.8

When you permit your students to add chromatic coloring to compositions they have already composed, ask them to build the coloring in the same manner the neighboring and passing tones are used in compositional structure.

Let your students expand some of their earlier melodies in a similar fashion to that in Illustration 7.9b. Of course, the original sound pattern of the melodies should be recognizable when the expansive chromatic technique is used; consequently, the major note proportions in the composition which give them identifying marks similar to the beginning note and the eighth note figures in the melody in Illustration 7.9a should not be distorted. It is better to leave some notes as they were in the original melody.

ILLUSTRATION 7.9a

ILLUSTRATION 7.9b

Let each student sing spontaneous improvisations to test the skills he or she has learned so far.

Using the Seventh Chord Correctly

Your students can add the seventh tone to any chord in order to expand the scope of their compositions. Generally, modern music is not so modern unless seventh chords are used in some way. The most positive aspects of dissonant harmonies in modern music occur through the usage of the seventh chord, therefore, it would certainly be to your students' advantage to learn how to deal with them effectively. (See Illustration 7.10.)

ILLUSTRATION 7.10

Any combination of the circle of fifths with an effective inclusion of seventh tones can be used to create improvisations. For the younger singer, it is better to write them in original compositions first, then move to spontaneous improvisations when the students are familiar with them. Do not let your students be misled in making distinctions between written compositions and the spontaneous improvisations. Both are legitimate, artistic expressions and can be used to help your students become fine composers and singers.

Using the Original Motive

Encourage your students to keep their motives. It does not matter if they consider them to be bad or good. Any of the motives can be improved by using the "right" techniques. You will have to give your students help in this area, especially in rhythmical variation and motive development that include repetition and sequence.

The Meter

When development in improvisations are in evidence, ask your students to change meters frequently among their compositions. However, simple meters will serve in a better capacity than the compound meters because the students will be familiar with them, but do not neglect to introduce the compound meters at a later time.

Using Key Signatures

When a student's composition has met all of your requirements, let him transpose it into all major and minor keys. It is most important for them to be able to improvise in every key.

RECOMMENDED MUSIC LIST

The titles below have been chosen to help you teach modern vocal techniques correctly to your students. You will find at least one composition that will help you teach the portamento. Others are heavy in the area of providing syncopated rhythms for study. However, all of them are excellent for inclusion in public performances.

Title	Grade	Composer	Number	Publisher
And Will You Leave Me So?	M	Baksa	5816	Boosey
Credo	MD	Allcock	5853	Boosey
Music, When Soft Voices Die	ME	George	ESE–1878–8	Greenwood
The Zihualtecan	ME		NY 2592	Colombo
Three Contemporary Madrigals	ME	Butler	SP 687	Somerset
Canticles Set II	M	Rorem	5841	Boosey
Michie Banjo	M	Freed	5777	Boosey
Never Weather Beaten Sail	MD	Binkerd	5847	Boosey
My Soul, There Is A Country	D	Binkerd	5845	Boosey
Snowflakes	M	Trubitt	ESE–1688–8	Westwood
Flower of the Town	MD	Sitton	FC 2781	Colombo
The Gallows-Tree	D	Nelhybel	FC 3600	Colombo
Johnny Has Gone For a Soldier	E	Dooley	FC 2798	Colombo

Title	Grade	Composer	Number	Publisher
A World I Never Made	ME	Raksin	60847	Belwin
To a Lady Who Asked for a Cypher	M	Beeson	5749	Boosey
Calico Pie	M	Ives	AP 30	Belwin
Winter	M	Kirk	5769	Boosey
Swift as an Indian Arrow Flies	M	Billings	2215	Walton
Three Contemplations of Anne Bradstreet	M	Boyd	ESE–1518–8	Westwood
Garden	MD	Binkerd	5764	Boosey
O My Nation's Grieving	MD	Kodaly	5752	Boosey
Rainsong	MD	Bright	AMP–95624–6	Associated
I Fear Thy Kisses, Gentle Maiden	ME	Russell	2605	Walton
Bitte	M	Madison	2600	Walton
La Cucaracha	MD	Hennagin	2803	Walton
Wir Sind Die Treibenden	D	Binkerd	5731	Boosey

CHAPTER 8

HOW TO DEVELOP PERFORMANCE SKILLS IN OCTETS, SEXTETS, QUARTETS AND TRIOS

It is difficult to teach all of the vocal techniques at one time to all of your students in one ensemble. So one of the best teaching devices is to break the ensemble into smaller units. In this chapter you'll see how to organize these smaller units in order to help you teach difficult vocal techniques to your students.

For example, I will show how to teach projectional resonance to your students to solidify their techniques for solo and ensemble work. You will also be shown how to perfect the high-arched *ah* vowel that is so useful in solo and ensemble work. Your students will need the time to work this formation out in smaller units such as those described here in the Graduated Program.

ORGANIZING THE DEVELOPMENTAL FORMAT FOR THE SMALL ENSEMBLE UNITS IN THE GRADUATED PROGRAM

Small ensembles in this chapter should be thought of as distinctive units, not offshoots of their larger counterparts, because the techniques herein are designed specifically for their development. The students chosen to participate should have earned the right by showing interest and cooperation, and by developing thoroughly all the skills that are found in the preceding chapters.

In some cases where students need more vocal experience, let the smaller units serve as "stopping places" for learning those necessary skills. In the process, these students will become better prepared for the a cappella choir experience.

Do not leave these students alone to work out their problems. Rather, they should be supervised by students who are already in the a cappella choir. Be sure that the "supervisors" keep close contact with you on every vocal problem. It is important for the "supervisors" to be courteous to their students at all times. No supervisor should be given the authority to reprimand another student at any time. Their attitudes should be that of a helper, not a boss!

Engaging the Help of Parents

You should plan all singing engagements and rehearsal schedules and select the literature to be used when your ensembles are asked to sing in different locales in the community. Although you may ask your parent group to help set up these engagements and chaperone the students, you will be held responsible for the quality of the performance and the discipline of the students as long as they serve under the auspices of the school. For this reason, you may permit your parents group to be present at some rehearsals to establish lines of communication with the school's administration, the students, other parents and the choral music staff.

Choose certain parents to act as sponsors for the different units. At least two sponsors per unit can be chosen to take the responsibility of organizing parent patrols for the units during rehearsals and concerts. Since you will also be supervising other ensembles, or planning your next day's work, these parents are needed to chaperone the students to and from singing engagements, and to raise the necessary funds for the small vocal ensemble program.

SELECTING THE STUDENTS

The personnel breakdown for the entire small unit program should be kept at thirty-six singers. The suggested unit breakdown is as follows: two octet units, one sextet, two quartets and two trios. The rationale for the number of singers is to have enough highly trained students who will be capable of performing in the a cappella choir. It will also help you to motivate your students to work for greater achievement in vocal techniques. Notice that there are six students over the number needed in the a cappella choir. You may tell all of your students to try to avoid being in these numbered "spots" by working constantly to improve their vocal skills. However, tell the students who have been left in the numbered "spots" to continue developing their vocal skills so they can "graduate" to the a cappella choir at a later date.

Using Records for Proper Selections

Keep the records for each ensemble up to date. (See Chapter 1.) You will need the information that will provide you with references to student development and involvement. From this, you will be able to make the best possible selections for your smaller ensembles.

Records of performances, awards, and any innovations that were used successfully to secure group recognition or solidarity should be kept by the parent sponsors and reported to the director who adds these to his own records and files. You do not have to be present at many of these performances, but good record keeping will give you some insight into the nature of the development among the students during these performances.

Here are five questions that must be answered positively for each student who is being considered for membership in one of your smaller units.

1. How well does the student follow leadership? Parents who serve as sponsors for ensembles do like for the students to exhibit freedom of expression. But, they feel that the behavior of the students should be under strict control. The sponsors will not have enough time to "train" your students in this respect. In fact, many would prefer not being bothered with students who have little self-control.
2. Are these students able to implement ideas presented to them? Parents who volunteer to be sponsors usually have excellent ideas for involving other parents in the community. Your students will benefit from this experience if they use their time to help the sponsors. Generally, this would come in the area of making telephone calls and running errands.
3. Are the students loyal to school precepts? These students must love the school they attend. If this is true, every act committed by them will be in accord with the rules and regulations of the school.

   Enforcing Rules. No one should be permitted to break rules of the school while on tours and concert trips. Rules should be strictly enforced by the director, student leaders, sponsors, teachers and chaperones. If a student breaks school rules, he or she should undergo some type of punishment for the infraction. In some school districts, dismissing a student from the choral program is not considered too harsh.

4. Are the students able to meet rehearsal and concert schedules? Your records should verify this. In the main, if they have missed two concerts without giving satisfactory reasons, their inclusion into the smaller units should be deferred.

5. How well does the student get along with his peer group? It is obvious that students ought to be able to render their best service under the best circumstances. These exclude hindrances and attitudinal problems from anyone.

Securing the Support of Other Teachers

Each student should be able to keep up with work assignments in all of his classes. Often a teacher is critical of the choral program in school because the students seem to be interested in that program alone. You can help in this matter by encouraging your students to strive for perfection in all school subjects. When other teachers find out that you are helping students solve problems concerning their subject areas, they will be more tolerant of your ensemble program, and will support you in fund-raising activities, concerts and festivals.

DEVELOPING THE HIGH-ARCHED *AH* VOWEL SOUND

There are three forms of the *ah* vowel that can be used in singing. The initial *ah* vowel sound that is necessary for the beginners in vocal art is described here:

Place the tip of the tongue behind the bottom teeth and drop the jaw so that two of your fingers with the thumb pointing down or up can be placed in the mouth. Maintain this formation when the fingers are removed. Let the tongue lie flat when you sing the vowels *ah, o* and *oo*. This form of the *ah* vowel should have been developed during full-choir experiences.

A Description of the
High-Arched *Ah* Vowel

The formation for the high-arched ah vowel should is as follows:

Place the tip of the tongue behind the bottom teeth as you did in the initial formation of the *ah* vowel. Drop the jaw so that two fingers can be placed in the mouth with the thumb pointing down or up. Remove the fingers, keep the formation constant and add an outer smile, then gently lift the sides of the tongue toward the upper teeth, making an arch in the center of the tongue. Practice in front of a mirror.

Actually, you should simply let the students look at the formation a couple of days just to get accustomed to it. After this period, utilize the vocalises in Illustration 8.1 to aid in its development. Be sure to ask the students to study and practice slowly at first and increase the speed as technique develops.

Studying the Sound and Character
Of the High-Arched *Ah* Vowel

When your students have memorized the exercise in Illustration 8.1, let them practice further n in the keys of D, E and F#:

Begin the practice at the mouth and chest areas only. Be sure to open the mouth to the width of two fingers. Notice the hollow sound of the vowel as your students open their mouths to form the vowel correctly. Now, ask them to use an outer smile to blend the resonance of the nose and head. The sound pattern is now correct.

ILLUSTRATION 8.1 Low voices—alto, baritone, bass.

You may want to use low or high cheek resonance to create more tonal beauty. This is okay. However, be sure to maintain the hollow sound of the chest and mouth in the blend pattern.

The Final Stage in the Development
Of the High-Arched *Ah* Vowel

Your students will need a great deal of material to help them

ILLUSTRATION 8.2 High voices—soprano, tenor.

develop the high-arched *ah* vowel sound. You can compose the music by using Illustrations 8.1 and 8.2 for your pattern. Be sure that the notes in your music follow the stepwise order found in the illustrations. You may use some intervals of thirds, but wider intervals will cause wider mouth formations. This is a correct vocal procedure, but the resulting change in the color scheme is not understood by many students. Consequently, wider skips should not be attempted until they have heard the sound pattern of the high-arched *ah* vowel on different musical levels composed in simple patterns similar to Illustrations 8.1 and 8.2.

Transpose the vocalise in Illustration 8.2 to the keys of B, D and Eb and follow the instructions above. When the development is complete, the sound pattern should resemble the blended chest and mouth resonance in the low register and resemble blended *ah-uh* mixtures in the high register. When progress is evident, encourage your students to sing selected solos to continue the development of the high-arched *ah* vowel sound.

UTILIZING PROJECTIONAL RESONANCE

Projectional resonance is used to help carry the sound of these smaller units to the audience. The sound is magnified because the singers use the resonance of the mouth, nose, ears and cheekbone blended into a suitable mixture. The cheekbone structure of the face helps to give projectional resonance its true color. Be sure that your students use the resonance of the chest in the development of projectional resonance. Ask them to practice slowly.

Developing Ear Resonance

Place one finger directly beneath the ears on each side of your face and let the sound travel to these points by way of controlling the breath stream. Utilize the three forms of the *ah* vowel sound in this process. You may permit your students to practice with other vowels later on.

Developing Low Cheekbone Resonance

Place one finger on each cheekbone, then, move the finger to a lower level near the corners of the mouth and pretend that the sound is traveling through your fingers to these points. You will have to practice slowly through vocalises in order to perfect this kind of resonance.

Developing High Cheekbone Resonance

Place one finger on each side of your cheekbone at a higher level, even with your nostrils. This should place your fingers on the cheekbone itself. Now, pretend that the sound is traveling through your fingers to these points. Practice through vocalises to perfect this resonance.

Do not let your students overuse the voice while developing this resonance. It is better to encourage them to practice for shorter periods of time at different intervals rather than trying for perfection on longer intervals. The young voice must never be forced. The idea is to *let* the voice perform rather than forcing it.

Nurturing Mature Resonance

Once the singers develop projectional resonance, you will notice a mature sound developing among the voices in your smaller units. This is the time to assign some of your most difficult solo material, now that your students are developing the vocal maturity needed to perform this music. But you must be extremely careful that the singers do not overuse the throat muscles. Tell your singers to simply let the developed voice perform this difficult music. This will help relieve some tension that your students will experience when they discover the difficulties in the music.

Identifying Abnormal Breath Pressure

Be sure to check for abnormal pressure at the throat among your students by placing your finger at the neck level while they are singing. The small amount of pressure you will feel should come from the natural pressure of the breath stream. Some students show readily that too much pressure, caused by using the throat muscles, is being used at the throat level when their veins protrude on either side of their necks. This is always a true sign that too much pressure is used. In almost every case, you will find that the student is breathing incorrectly. For quick results, ask the student to practice correct breathing patterns in front of a large mirror. If you allow him to continue singing with abnormal pressure, it will eventually ruin his or her voice.

Natural Head Resonance Versus
Projectional Resonance

Do not be afraid to permit your students to use natural head resonance. This has been called "loud singing" by some choral directors. You can encourage it by placing one finger on either side of the head even with the eyes. Now, sing some vocalises using *ah, uh,* a mixture of *o-oo* and the *o* vowel in the upper register. It is called natural head resonance because the other resonances will be blended automatically. It is not effective when you use it in your smaller units, but when used correctly, it helps to create good horizontal balance in larger ensembles.

When you permit your singers to use projectional resonance, be certain that they blend the other resonances. This is not a natural process. It must be developed through properly constructed vocalises for full development.

SEVEN PERFORMANCE PITFALLS TO AVOID

The pitfalls below will cause your ensembles to fail to develop their maximum potential. They may become second rate as a direct result of these errors. In addition, your administrative staff will certainly become concerned if there is evidence of inconsistent planning in your area.

It is true that some choral directors inherit poorly organized ensemble programs. But a genuine effort can be made to correct the situation as suggested below:

• **Poor Organization.** Good organization is the sum total guiding your small units to success with proven techniques that get results. One facet of improper organization occurs when you permit your students to arrive at their concert destination too early, then permit them to move about aimlessly without proper directions. Begin your instructions concerning the total festival or concert at least a week in advance, with references made to specific things you would have the students do from the time of their arrival to the time of departure.

1. Use Time Wisely. When preparing your small units for performances, choose the music during summer months when school is in recess. When you begin your practice, spend only one or two weeks in positive preparation of the music. Too much time in this direction will cause some loss of interest among the singers. If your students have developed all

techniques in the Graduated Program successfully, they will be able to spend only this necessary amount of time in actual preparation of the music.

2. Initial Preparation for the Program.   The officials at the concert site where the ensembles will be performing should be contacted concerning the type of program that will be needed for the occasion. When this has been attended to, some kind of program format can be planned and presented to the officials for their approval.

3. Costumes and Props.   Plan the kind of costumes and props you would like to use and present your ideas to the concert officials. Most people take pride in knowing and planning every aspect of the program so that it becomes a part of their effiency patterns. Use as much simplicity as possible in creating costumes and props in order to cut down on expenses that will be involved.

4. Arranging the Musical Portion of the Program.   It is wise to let your ensembles perform at the beginning of the program in order that the organizations which have invited them to perform can have ample time to attend to their business affairs. This will also give your students the chance to return to their classes as early as possible, or, to their homes to review their assignments for the next day.

• **Inadequate Transportation.**   Some directors wait until the last moment to arrange for transportation to the concert. This is poor planning! Arrange transportation for your trips at least a week in advance. Be sure that proper maintenance is performed on the vehicles to insure the safety of the members of your ensembles. Proper planning includes filling in the information on the correct forms that are required by your school, and acquiring proper chaperones for the students. Parents must be assured that the safety of their children has been secured. If extra materials are to be transported to the performance site, you will need to plan for their delivery as well.

• **Ill-timed Arrivals.**   Let the members of your smaller units arrive at least forty-five minutes before the concert begins to set up the props and go through a vocal warm-up period. If you do not have enough time to take care of these necessities, you will create some tense moments for the concert officials as well as your students. Most likely, your concert will not go as smoothly because of your poor judgement in time.

If at all possible, try to arrange for some parents to accompany the students to the performance site. This will relieve you of this responsibility and will permit you to drive to the concert in some tranquil moments. You will need these to think through some details concerning the performance.

- **Group Alienation.** Although high status can be attached to the smaller units, they should be a definite part of the development scheme in the total small vocal ensemble program. It is better to keep the importance of these units on an even basis with the other ensembles. This keeps the competive nature of each ensemble high when you show special concern for each group. Actually, group importance can be kept by making a special effort to acquaint the entire school community with the activities of each group in the Graduated Program.

1. Praising an Ensemble Improperly.   One of the elements that a choral director can use that will cause problems in the group process is over-praising the ensemble as in the following case study: Mr. Murray had organized his small units satisfactorily. In fact, the units had performed successfully at a nearby shopping center, and had won several outstanding awards in the local ensemble festival. Mr. Murray had stated on several occasions that these units were the best trained he had had the privilege of teaching. Some members of the ensembles stopped practicing because they thought that all had been accomplished. Mr. Murray sought desparately to get the students to begin practicing again with little results. Their performances took a downswing! By the end of the year, the performances were poor, all because of overpraising!

2. Praising an Ensemble Constructively.   Praise the students when they deserve it, but inform them of their weak points as well. This kind of balance will aid in keeping your students working. It is rare that young singers perform flawlessly regardless of the amount of training they have. Because of this, you can always find some points to criticize in order to keep the singers alert and working toward perfection.

3. Promoting Group Value.   Do not cause one group to be alienated from the others by permitting a deterioration in one group's musical value. This can happen if you do not make the right choices in the music for performance. Students have intergroup discussions concerning group values and progress. They also discuss the music in terms of their likes and dislikes. It would be to your advantage to choose music that

your students like and can relate what they like about it to others. So that each group will respect the other for the music it sings, you may establish a student committee to help you make the "right" choices.

• **Disobedience.** Some students will not have to be reprimanded more than once for breaking rules. But there are those who repeat violations often, and should be referred to their parents for correction. Others can be placed on suspension or probation. If there is a continuation of these infractions, these students should be placed in a lower ensemble as in this case study: Martha Harvey, an alto in the sextet, sang the soprano part in rehearsal. Her explanation to Mr. Hall, the choral director, was that the soprano part was prettier than the alto part. Mr. Hall explained that he needed her to sing the alto part since he had capable sopranos already. After the singing had resumed, Martha continued singing the soprano part. Mr. Hall referred Martha to the school counselor and had her removed from the sextet and placed in a lower ensemble. Mr. Hall would have been justified in dismissing Martha from the choral program entirely. If such flagrant disobedience is allowed to go unchecked, it will influence others to react in a similar manner. It is good to try to help your students through emotional and personal crises, but never dismiss disobedience at the expense of inviting chaos to the smaller units or any segment of the small vocal ensemble program.

• **Poor Mental Attitude.** Some poor performances can be attributed to poor mental attitudes among your students. They can be caused by improper rest habits, but primarily through poor motivation. It will be impossible for you to check on each student in these respects, but, some individual "on the spot" poor habits can be referred to school counselors and the parent group for special help. Do not overwork your group! This always causes mental anguish among students. Certain song materials bring about poor mental attitudes also. Always include some music that you know will arouse the interest of your students.

• **Inattention To Musical Details.** Since none of the smaller units is in need of a director until rehearsal sessions, each student should be asked to memorize musical details such as proper attacks and releases, phrase endings, dynamics and other elements that are usually given interpretation by directions. You can bring much attention to these kinds of details by referring to the skills found in Chapter 6 under the heading "Developing Sensitive Group Musicality." As in the madrigal group, each person in the smaller units should be able to "feel" what the other singers will do before the initial group action. In any case, full development of this technique can reap benefits at this stage in the Graduated Program. You can devise other rhythmically patterned songs that your students can study to develop this technique further. Utilize them as you did in Chapter Six.

INFORMING PARENTS CORRECTLY
ABOUT THE PERFORMANCE

A letter well in advance of the concert should be sent to the parents of the students giving specific details of every aspect of the performance beginning with the kind of costumes that will be worn, the departing time and the return trip, the names of the bus drivers and chaperones. The parents will certainly appreciate this effort.

ACHIEVING PROPER PRE-CONCERT CONTROL

Many choir directors prepare their students well in all areas of performance, but the area of pre-concert control is sometimes taken for granted. The director assumes that the students will know how to conduct themselves. This is not always true as the following case study shows: Bill Jackson, the student director, assumed the task of directing the ensembles to their singing positions because the singers were losing valuable minutes trying to get the job done themselves. Aside from this problem, one alto wore a set of extra-long earrings. Bill took the responsibility of asking her to remove them. This act created some confusion. Lucy Attock, the alto section leader, began giving directions to her section that were different from Bill's direction. All of this was done in the presence of some members of the audience who had arrived early for the concert. Everyone become confused, and as expected, the concert was of poor quality.

One cannot expect the high school youngster to act alone unless he has been given specific instructions. He is not an adult! You should always make sure that your students have adult supervision with the correct instructions to insure proper behavior.

Review the rules below periodically with your students:

• **Walking on Stage.** Ask the students to walk to their positions on the stage at a normal pace, not in a military fashion, yet, orderly and sophisticated. Give them permanent standing positions. Find the time to inspect the stage before the concert, and if necessary, permit your singers to hold at least one practice session there.

● **Talking.** There should be a minimum of talking among the singers on stage, or for that matter, between a singer and the director. All directions should be given before the date of the concert. Usually, one class period will suffice to give directions and instructions to insure a smooth concert performance.

ACHIEVING THE CORRECT SINGING POSITION

Once the students reach their singing positions on the stage, the proper posture should be maintained in performance. The correct guidelines are as follows:

1. Lift the chest to its natural position.
2. Place one foot several inches in front of the other.
3. Let the arms hang naturally in line with the foot that was placed several inches in front of the other.
4. The spine should be straight, but not rigid.
5. The position is correct if the singer can sway back and forth without losing his balance.

CHOOSING THE PROGRAM OPENER

Good programs are sometimes started with a patriotic composition by one or several of the units combined. Some interesting folk songs usually follow this special number very well, going from the lighter moods to the serious. Many folk songs do deal effectively with intangible subjects such as hope, love, beauty and joy. Be certain to include these on your programs through the appropriate compositions. Your students and audience will reap the fruits of these experiences when they follow a good program opener.

PROGRAM DISTRIBUTION

One of your parent sponsors can be held responsible for passing out programs to your audience if this chore has not been given to your host organization. It is standard procedure for these smaller units to have their own programs made and to see to it they are distributed to the audience. It is better for you to make this kind of plan so that every detail, including everything from the production of the programs to distribution to the audience, happens under your supervision.

RECOMMENDED MUSIC LISTS

The music listed below will be useful in helping you train the girls you have chosen for your sextet groups. Many of the techniques such as the ah vowel formations and projectional resonance can be developed by using the compositions below.

Title	Grade	Composer	Number	Publisher
Adoramus Te	M	Di Lasso	1508	E.C. Schirmer
Come In	M	Thompson	2539	E.C. Schirmer
A Joyful Song	M	Duro	CM6742	C. Fischer
Love Lives Over The Hills	M	Rowley	8320	G. Schirmer
Enchanting Song	M	Bartok	1954	Boosey
A Lover and His Lass	E	Forsbald	6080	Kjos
Recordata	M	Palestrina	NY2033	Colombo
Greetings	M	Brahms	2503	E.C. Schirmer
Pater Noster	E	Gevaert	2502	E.C. Schirmer
Lass with the Delicate Air	E	Arne	515	Gray
Fain Would I Change That Note	M	Vaughn Williams	636	Gray
Now Sleeps The Crimson Petal	E	Quilter	1678	Boosey

The music below can be used to help you develop all of the skills that your students failed to develop fully while "graduating" through the small vocal ensemble program. For this reason, the octet formations have been included in the smaller units. Be sure to call to the attention of your students the specific techniques you want them to develop.

Title	Grade	Composer	Number	Publisher
Hallelujah, Amen	ME	Handel	2020	E.C. Schirmer
To Music	E	Schubert	5575	Summy
Weep O Mine Eyes	E	Bennett	ES 30	Bourne

Title	Grade	Composer	Number	Publisher
April Is in My Mistress' Face	E	Morley/Churchill	748	Bourne
Farewell My Love	E	Hirt	CM701	C. Fischer
Adoramus Te	E	Palestrina	769	Belwin
Fa Una Canzone	E	Vecchi	LG 556	G. Schirmer
Scarborough Fair	M	Arr. Henderson	1099	Kjos
Oh, My Love Is Like a Red, Red Rose	E	Arr. Henderson		Kjos
Come Again Sweet Love	M	Dowland	81274	Flammer
I Know A Young Maiden	E	Lassus/Hirt	CM7039	C. Fischer

All of the music recommended here can help you develop the head voice among your male quartets, and you will be able to do some work in the change of quality area also. But the most significant group of pieces is represented in the three-part choruses for male voices. You will find a wealth of material among them to help you continue the development of the covered tone among your students.

Title	Grade	Composer	Number	Publisher
Three-Part Choruses	ME	Arr. Wilson	44	Hall & McCreary
Smokes Gets In Your Eyes	E	Kern	500–1	Harms
The Riddle	ME	Arr. Jenkins	N.Y. 2433–6	Colombo
Mattinata	M	Leoncavallo/ Burleigh	N.Y. 881	Ricordi
Nobody Knows The Trouble I've Seen	M	Arr. Burleigh	N.Y. 845	Colombo
Aura Lee	ME	Poulton/Hunter, Parker, Shaw	527	Lawson-Gould
Everyman's Handyman	MD	Beeson	5817	Boosey

Title	Grade	Composer	Number	Publisher
Ezekiel Saw The Wheel	ME	Arr. Burleigh	700	Colombo
My Lord What A Mornin'	ME	Burleigh/Vene'	F.C. 1713	Belwin

You will need some compositions which utilize lots of open harmony so that you can teach the three forms of the *ah* vowel correctly. Two such pieces that you will be able to use in this respect are "Fire, Fire My Heart" and "Ave Maria" listed below. The other compositions can be used to develop all of the skills referred to in this chapter.

Title	Grade	Composer	Number	Publisher
Fire, Fire My Heart	ME	Morley/Greyson	3140–6	Bourne
Ave Maria	E	Arcadelt/Greyson	2548–5	Bourne
Mister Banjo	ME	Scott	83253	Flammer
Who Is That Yonder	MD	Arr. Woollen	ESE–705–4	World
Could My Song Go Flying	ME	Hahn/Ringwald	B–85	Shawnee
Who Hath Seen The Wind	E	Christiansen	348	Schmitt
Solfeggio	ME	Maxwell	SH 3875–4	Robbins
A Bird in Spring	E	Atkinson	354	Schmitt
Matchmaker	E	Bock/Leyden		Sunbeam

CHAPTER 9

HOW TO TRAIN THE A CAPPELLA CHOIR

In this chapter you will be shown how to achieve the special character and coloring of the a cappella choir by training it through quartets. Since the characteristic group coloring depends upon the special color of each line in the choir, you will be shown how to achieve it through the study of the proper tone production that is characteristic of each section.

You will also be shown how to blend the color of the vowels and resonance through the *ah* vowel formations. This development leads you naturally into the study of inner voice drama, which is the product of musical expression. You will also find two sections on musical expression, so you can help inner voice drama to be developed naturally among your students.

A PREREQUISITE FOR GAINING MEMBERSHIP IN THE A CAPPELLA CHOIR

Before you assign students to the a cappella choir, the development of all vocal skills is necessary and should be exhibited by each one of them. In fact, if the students have learned each technique that you have taught, as outlined in this book, there should be very few vocal problems of any magnitude. I hope that you have followed each procedure mentioned. It is possible to dissect the program, studying and developing each ensemble separately, but the success of the program is assured when it is followed sequentially.

SELECTING THE PERSONNEL

As in each ensemble, the number of students involved affects the character and sound of the choir; therefore, anywhere from twenty-five to thirty students should be utilized in the a cappella choir with the following personnel breakdown:

Sopranos	8		Sopranos	9
Altos	9		Altos	11
Tenors	4	or	Tenors	5
Basses	4		Basses	5
	25			30

The color of the a cappella choir can be characterized as rich and sonorous. One reason for this can be attributed to the vertical, full-voiced sounds in the bass and tenor sections, and the vertical light and dark colors in the female voices. You can begin the work through quartet formations to achieve the tonal setup on a smaller scale at first. It is advantageous to let these quartets remain active with the same personnel as long as possible. Although this may vary in some groups, at least three weeks of practice in the quartet formations is needed to let your students become familiar with the correct sound of the choir. When there is evidence of development, let the students continue it through the appropriate choral literature.

USING THE PIANO

It is always better to develop the a cappella choir without the aid of a piano. Many directors use it simply to give the correct pitches to their students and maintain musical continuity during the first reading of a composition. Once the students have learned their parts, a pitch fork can be of great value since it can be used to check pitch levels while the music is in progress without disturbing the choir's color and character. The piano is a necessary instrument for accompanying the solo voices, but it must be used sparingly in the training of the a cappella choir.

TRAINING THE CHOIR THROUGH
QUARTET FORMATIONS

You may form these SATB quartets among your students and assign each quartet a leader who will take charge of rehearsals at their homes. However, during the initial stages in developing the correct a cappella choral concept among your students, keep the girls segregated from the boys until the color characteristics are developed and the students understand them. Now, set up as many after school rehearsals as possible for these formations.

If you choose twenty-five voices for your a cappella choir, you should be able to form four quartets among the girls with one alternating with another in the section and two quartets among your boys. On the other hand, if you choose thirty singers, you will be able to form five quartets among the girls, and two quartets among your boys with two boys alternating with other singers.

Achieving the Initial Color Scheme

Begin developing the correct color schemes for the a cappella choir in the low chest registers of all singers. You must be cognizant of developing the correct sound between octaves in this register. The work should begin among members of one section. You should use persons from different sections when you begin the work in higher registrations. Let two singers hum the octaves at first. Then, move from the dark vowels to the light vowels utilizing the inner smile approach on each vowel level in the low register. Be careful that you do not go below the ranges of your young singers. Let your basses use an outer smile in their low registers to achieve the correct color between octaves.

Achieving the Correct Color
In Different Registrations

Ask all of your singers to begin developing the upper chest register beginning with the medium colored vowels found in Illustration 5.2. Be certain that your altos use full resonance in their low and upper chest register, although you may require them to use light vowel properties in the upper chest to blend acceptably with the tenor quality. Do not be confused here about color in the different registers. If you use the vertical approach in each vowel formation, blending other vowels and the different resonances, the color in the a cappella choir will be appropriate. Although the highness and lowness of the vocal lines induce different colors among the sections, you will have to shape each vowel sound so that the quality of the pure vowels will sing through each time. All mixtures, vertical quality, blended vowels and resonance should be developed from, and maintained through, the color of the pure vowels *ay, ee, ah, o* and *oo*.

Exchanging the Resonances Properly

Use some projectional resonance among your male singers when all singers are performing in the chest register. However, if too much darkness occurs in the music, you may have to exchange this resonance for blended head resonance among your tenors and the covered tones among your basses. Like the basses, the altos should use similar resonance. But in many cases, they may use projectional resonance when the root and third of the chord appear in their voice line.

Identifying The A Cappella Sound Principle

In registrations where the light vowel properties are required, the principle of singing in the center of the mouth and straight up will be the cog from which the a cappella choir operates musically. This principle will also help you to maintain the vertical quality and the special colorings in different registrations.

Achieving the Correct Color Through The Correct Posture Development

Some directors use the term "round tone" when referring to the a cappella choir's tonal character. This caption is characteristically correct since it captures the correct sound pattern of the choir. You must work to develop this sound in the following manner:

- Let each quartet, segregated and SATB, practice with their backs against the wall. All material should be sung from this position. However, do not permit any rigidity in their postures. Ask them to "feel" moments of being elevated especially when singing in the upper chest register.
- When development is assured, permit each member to sing a selected solo, maintaining the developed posture in front of the entire ensemble. On the basis of the number of superior solos, the best quartet should be chosen and given a name of distinction. Usually, the numbers 1, 2 or 3 will suffice for this purpose. When the quartets are equal in development, discontinue the number system.

Now, you may let your quartets sing in SATB formations permanently. Be certain to maintain these quartets in concert formations for your a cappella choir. These types of formations usually eliminate most intonation problems. But your singers must develop their individual talents thoroughly through daily drills and vocalises. Be sure to offer encouragement in this direction.

PROPER GUIDANCE TO ENCOURAGE
THE PROPER PERFORMANCE

Some musical problems arise because your students either do not have the technical training necessary to sing the music, or they are not familiar with the technicalities of the musical score. But good performances can be obtained if you have taught your students to work hard in the two areas mentioned above. Tell them to practice regularly and keep their interest high each time they practice, in order to perfect the composition. In order for them to be successful, you should offer continuity and orderly sequence in your technical assignments. This means that if you are working in a certain technical area such as vowel coloring on a given day, you should continue in this realm, using motivational techniques, until the work has been completed.

Studying Vocal Composition Character

Here are ten elements that are used in compositions from which you can let your students form some questions and answers.

1. Key Changes
2. Rhythm
3. Rhythmic Rests
4. Modulations
5. Color Changes
6. Meter Changes
7. Rhythmic Modifications
8. Divisi
9. Mood
10. Style

It would be well for you to review all techniques that have been developed by your students at this point so there will be no confusion when they form their questions. Be sure that the questions and answers are relative to your particular realm of study.

To help you influence your student's thinking, here are ten hypothetical questions that you may want to use as examples.

1. Does the color of the vowel change in measure five of this composition? Why?
2. Is it necessary to use tonal weight distribution?
3. What is the basic formula for the singer to perform rhythmic rests?
4. Are there occasions when the baritone section should use the covered tone?
5. Are diphthongs helpful in creating color in the composition?
6. Is it customary to change the speed of the music at the time the meter changes?
7. Will rhythmic modification harm the character of the music?
8. Is it feasible to use different color patterns among the voices when there are divided parts?
9. How are somber tones created?
10. Is the construction in this composition polyphonic or homophonic?

DEVELOPING LISTENING HABITS IN QUARTET FORMATIONS

Your students will develop a keen aural sensitiveness to each other if you let them study some basic rules to help them learn how to compose legitimate music by acceptable standards. First, begin by teaching the students the overtone series. Second, let them construct scales, all kinds of scales—major, minor, modal, pentatonic and chromatic, in all keys. Once this work has been completed, you may continue with chord construction as it is utilized in beginning composition, then introduce these basic rules:

1. Double the root in the first chord.
2. Do not double the third of the chords.
3. The seventh degree of the scale goes up and becomes the tonic of the I chord.
4. Parallel motion of the chords must be avoided by using contrary or oblique motion. Keep the common tone between chords when possible.

You can expand these rules later as your students gain experience. But these four are included to help you get the students started in harmonizing simple melodies. Let your students work independently in this work, however, make periodic checks to make sure that they are doing the work in a creditable manner. In almost every case, you will have to make certain suggestions for the students to improve, but for the most part, praise them for the work they are doing.

Developing Listening Skills
Through Singing Scales

Each student should be able to sing all major and minor scales. Their knowledge of these scales and the ability to recognize them will add greatly to their listening skills. To insure this, set aside a time during each rehearsal to permit your singers to learn the names of the notes of each chord you construct on the scale tones. When this work has been learned by your students, let them construct and sing all forms of the minor scales in every key.

Following Up

Your students should now be able to work out many vocal problems because they have studied the scale work mentioned above. Consequently, all of the compositions you choose should include all of the scales and vocal techniques you and your students are studying. If problems arise in your rehearsals with the entire group, send the quartets back to their SATB formations to correct them. Be sure that you pinpoint the problems so that the students will know exactly what to study. Also, be certain that the problems have been eliminated before you permit the quartets to reassemble into your concert formation.

CULTIVATING THE CHARACTERISTIC
GROUP COLORING

The entire scope of colors for the a cappella choir can be drawn from the sound patterns of the pure vowels *ay, ee, ah, o* and *oo*. Although other vowels will be utilized, they must be skillfully blended with the pure vowel sound patterns. But you will have to experiment with the sound patterns and plan the kind of tonal varieties you want in different compositions. In other words, you will have to inspect the composition and plan the coloring of the a cappella sound pattern so that it agrees with the total character of the composition.

Achieving Tonal Varieties

The method for maintaining the a cappella choir's sound pattern is as follows:

1. Controlling the breath stream.
2. Using the vertical vowel quality.
3. Blending the resonances.
4. Using the pure vowel sounds as the basis for the a cappella choir's tonal character.
5. Having the correct numerical make-up of the ensemble.

Be sure that these blended patterns for the a cappella choir are a part of your students vocal technique:

1. Blend a mixture of the *oo* and *ee* vowels.
2. Blend a mixture of the *ay* and *ee* vowels.
3. The *ah* vowel should always have a mixture of the *oo* and *uh* vowels especially when singing in the chest voice.
4. Blend the *o* vowel with the *oo* vowel to achieve a vertical quality in the head register, and the *o, oo,* and *aw* vowels to neutralize some of its dark quality in the low chest register.

You may wish to compose vocalises for the blended vowels above and assign them to your students to practice outside of class. It is certainly beneficial to practice them each day in class using unisonal and harmonized drill to aid in this development. Change these drills periodically so your students will not tire of them. When this happens, very little progress is made in the area of vocal development. Compose enough material so that you will be able to spend at least five minutes each day during the entire school session to develop the blend patterns above.

ACHIEVING THE CORRECT SOPRANO TONE QUALITY
IN THE A CAPPELLA CHOIR

Your sopranos should develop a light, flute-like tonal quality. Again, the approach for developing this quality must be from the vertical mouth position: Keep all tones in the center of the mouth and sing straight up. The different resonances, proper breath management and support, vowel formations and personnel make-up will give you the necessary tonal color varieties you will need for your correct soprano quality to emerge.

Achieving the Proper Connection Between
The Nasal and Head Resonances

Keep all of the pure vowels blended as stated above, but use an inner smile to get the proper connection between the nasal and head

ILLUSTRATION 9.1 Use **ay, ee, ah, o,** and **oo**.

resonances. Do not allow your students to sing this blended resonance with thin, unsupported tones. To prevent this from taking place, and to assure development, practice with your sopranos daily with vocalises created especially for this purpose similar to the one in Illustration 9.1.

Achieving the Proper Blend in The Soprano Section

You will be able to detect development in the soprano section when it sounds as if one giant soprano is singing. This means that each person in the section must shape the vowel with the same type of lip formation, even the same type of facial make-up of the vowel. You will have to give the girls a perfect example for each vowel-lip formation with your own vocal make-up. Ask your girls to form these vowels exactly as you are doing at this moment. However, male vocal teachers may have to change keys if the tessitura of the line goes to high for their falsetto quality. But, it is essential for you to give the example with falsetto quality to sound exactly as a female would sound. Be sure that your example, and the eventual sound of your soprano section, is derived from the correct sound of the pure vowels.

Placing the Sopranos Properly In the Section

Height and weight of the girls in this section play important roles in helping to achieve the correct soprano sound. Generally, the heavier girls are able to sing the firmest tone. It is also true that the taller girls usually equal the heavier girls in singing firm tones. When you find this to be true in your soprano section, place the heavier and taller girls near each other so there can be a better sound for the smaller girls to emulate. But you have to be careful, because some of these smaller girls have naturally firm tones and you will have to place them correctly in the section and help them conserve their voices by using the correct vocal techniques. By the same method, you should keep the smaller sopranos with less resonance power from pushing their voices. Many of them do this trying to emulate the firm sound of the larger sopranos. Ask these smaller sopranos to emulate the correct vocal quality, not the degree of firmness exhibited by the larger sopranos.

Achieving Tonal Unity Among the Sopranos

Tonal unity in the soprano section will be strong when you place the larger girls in the middle of the section. The smaller girls can be placed on either side of the section. If there is one soprano who has a problem blending with the section you may use the following remedies to alleviate the problem:

- Always keep the resonance of this person subdued. Ask her to sing softer than the other girls in the section.
- If the above remedy does not work well, use her as a soloist.

When you have eliminated all the problems in each section of the a cappella choir, using the same plan that helped you to improve the soprano section, sectionalize it into permanent SATB formations.

Rhythms and Speeds

Aside from describing and giving examples of the blended vowels, insist that the rhythm and speed of the composition be studied so that the correct timing, especially at breathing places, will be understood by each soprano. Since they are the "leaders" in the ensemble, they must set the pattern for a smooth translation of the rhythm and the speed of the composition for the ensemble. The best method for developing a set pattern is to set your metronome at the proper speed and permit your sopranos to sing their line appropriately. If some girls have difficulty in the development of this skill, check the following faults:

- Poor breathing habits.
- Poor breath support.
- A rigid jaw.
- Poor vowel forms.
- Unrhythmically articulated consonants.

- Poor understanding of the compositional character, especially its melodic and harmonic make-up.
- Poor posture.

Of course, if these elements are allowed to go unattended in the a cappella choir, the attempt at trying to achieve the characteristic group and sectional tone quality and blend will be a complete waste of time.

ACHIEVING THE CORRECT ALTO TONE QUALITY IN THE A CAPPELLA CHOIR

The alto in the a cappella choir represents a vertical extension of the soprano section, but also unifies the vertical sounds of the tenor and soprano sections with those of the alto and bass sections. Since the alto's role in the a cappella choir serves a twofold purpose, a greater number is needed in the high school choir to be effective. But, you must be careful that you do not create an overbalance of that section. Rather, a distinct alto line should be heard equal in color to that of your bass section. However, the alto color must be complimentary to the tenor section and different from the soprano section because it is darker.

Achieving the Proper Blend In the Alto Section

Work for a perfect tonal blend that agrees with the vertical quality of the ensemble. Be certain of this blend by developing the alto quality beginning with G below middle C. The quality you need from this note ascending to E on the first line is the naturally dark hue that blends well with the tenor section. You must maintain as much of this quality in the range starting with F in the first space to the highest note for the alto line that is used in the composition. Although the quality will be different in this range, the dark appeal will give you the necessary color that blends well with the other voices in the choir. Now begin development by working downward on appropriate vocalises each day. First, work with vowels, then include words so that the singers will become familiar with the articulation of the cosonants with this quality.

If some of your singers experience difficulty in the low range, permit them to sing the first alto parts on other compositions which have divided parts, or simply do not let them sing out of their ranges.

Balancing the Alto and Tenor Parts

The tonal quality among your altos in the low range is similar to that of your tenor section when it sings in its high chest register, and the alto change of quality area should sound similar to your tenor's falsetto quality. Let your altos develop correctly in this area by imitating your tenors when they sing with the correct falsetto quality. Remember, the vertical approach should always be present. If too much dark quality occurs, permit the alto section to use light vowel properties and adjust the resonance suitably.

ACHIEVING THE CORRECT TENOR QUALITY
IN THE A CAPPELLA CHOIR

Let your tenors vocalize daily with the syllable *yo*. It is used initially to help the tenors achieve the correct a cappella tone quality for all vocal levels. When you let them vocalize with the pure vowel, be sure to ask them to maintain the quality of the *yo* syllable. But the section as a whole will need more support when singing with this quality in the low chest area. This is needful to achieve the correct sound. Too much breath support in the low chest area is unnecesary while singing solos, but this is primarily the reason for using more support in this area for the tenor so that he will not become a soloist, but will be able to control the tone and maintain the ingredients of the *yo* syllable.

Controlling Resonance in
The Tenor Section

Your tenor section will need to control the resonance when they are singing in the high chest register. This can be achieved better by permitting them to use the covered tone. As was discussed in Chapter 3, this kind of tone is created by blending nasal and chest resonance into a suitable union. Be sure to adjust the resonance at different pitch levels, either more or less, whichever affects balance and blend positively. But stridency usually occurs in any section when force is used in singing certain tones and when improper resonance blending techniques are used.

This fact must be uppermost in your mind in blending your tenor section correctly in the a cappella choir: Tenor resonance that is subdued too much is not suitable. Rather, a firm base must be established so that flatting will not occur. This means that the correct tenor resonance level is even with that of the other sections within the choir, but never under it!

ACHIEVING THE CORRECT BASS TONE QUALITY
IN THE A CAPPELLA CHOIR

The basses should be able to sing an even scale with the proper vertical quality. There are similarities that exist between your chamber and a cappella choir basses. But the main difference between the two is that the a cappella choir basses sound darker on every vocal level. This kind of quality can be encouraged by vocalizing with the syllable *yo*. However, if the quality becomes too dark, use light vowel properties with a vertical approached to achieve a lighter status. The a cappella choir relies on the basses for its strength in the vertical sense because that line supplies the firm foundation extending the correct coloration as well as the harmonic proportions of the composition. The harmonic condition in the choir can be widened if there are boys in the bass section who can sing low E2. If so, you can include this note in your daily warm-up and voice development procedures, but, permit only those boys who can actually sing a resonant E2 to perform it. Do not allow other boys to strain for this note. The initial *ah* vowel should be used to help develop this sound.

Teaching the Correct Bass Quality
In the Low Register

Do not let the basses use too much breath support in the low register because this condition will not permit the tone to be resonant. The breath must move faster in low registrations in order to produce a sound similar to the vertical quality that the other voices are using, but do not allow tension at any point in this low register. Ask the singers to relax. Also, ask them to send the air toward the upper teeth using as little breath support as possible.

If the note is used for a pedal tone, it would be better to eliminate the use of the words at those points and sing a vowel sound while the other voices above sing the words.

Here are three rules to follow in training the a cappella choir basses to sing in low registrations:

1. Use an outer smile when singing in the low register.
2. Use the inner smile when moving toward the upper register.
3. Too much support will cause tension in low registrations; therefore, work to achieve the correct vowel sounds and proper branching of the breath stream.

UTILIZING AN EFFECTIVE *AH* VOWEL

The *ah* vowel is difficult to develop because two elements, vowel formations and resonance blending, are required to be unified in its development for all ensembles. Adding to this, two forms, the medium and the high-arched *ah* vowel sounds, are used interchangeably, the medium *ah* vowel in the low tessitura and the high-arched *ah* vowel in the high tessitura among the voice lines in the a cappella choir. The difficulties emerge when the high and low musical levels in the composition utilize the *ah* vowel but require changes in voice character, rhythm and, inevitably, variety in the vertical color scheme among the voices. Voice changes in the vertical scope add variety to the compositional structure. So you see why it is important for your choir to develop vowel and resonance blending and the two forms of the *ah* vowel. Practice them often out of musical context and discover the different color schemes that will emerge in the a cappella choir composition. Be sure that this is done in a vertical framework, but the *ah* vowal must remain constant, unyielding in its formations and character. In addition, all voices must use the same mouth and lip formations for the vowels except when the voices are in different registrations. In this instance, ask your singers to have as much similarity as they can, to permit as much tonal unity as possible. Don't forget to adjust the resonance in your choir among the sections, but do not harm the vowel forms in the process. This kind of elasticism of do's and don'ts will give your a cappella choir the kind of sound it needs to exist as a special unit.

The Medium *Ah* Vowel

Most high school students are familiar with only the initial form of the *ah* vowel, and have only the minimum training to develop further forms of it. The manner in which it is used in their speech habits is based upon the sound they are accustomed to hearing from other people with whom they associate. The imitation is correct in some instances, but with a total lack of understanding. Consequently, this reason for the development of the medium *ah* vowel should be given to the students so that a good attitude will form the base for proper development: the medium *ah* vowel goes farther in scope and is beneficial to the tonal character and color in the a cappella choir. It gives the *ah* vowel sound a lighter hue because it has the basic blend patterns of *o, oo, aw, uh* and *ee*, and it can be used as follows:

- When a melodic line is written in the low tessitura.
- When divided parts occur in octaves, the medium *ah* vowel can be used in the lower octave. A description of the medium *ah* vowel is found on page 111 in Chapter 5.

The *Ah* Vowel Interchange

In some cases the medium and high-arched *ah* vowels should be used interchangeably when all voices are singing in the high or the low range. Whether it is more expedient for one voice than it is for the other would be speculation since the process has been known to vary in different ensembles. But it can be used to encourage more tonal beauty in your choir if you experiment with it to get the best results.

On the other hand, when the female voices are singing in the low range while the male voices are singing in the chest area, the female voices should use the medium *ah* vowel when it is necessary, and the male voices should use the high-arched *ah* vowel sound.

Using Resonance Correctly in Pianissimo Sections

Some directors let their singers sing too softly in pianissimo sections causing some loss of color. Without color, some variety will be lost, and with variety goes audience interest and mental participation. The remedy here is to measure the degree of softness you want to attain, but make sure that the proper vowel and resonance blending can be at a satisfactory level in these pianissimo sections.

UTILIZING INNER VOICE DRAMA

Inner voice drama is an expressive vocal phenomenon brought on by the musical beauty of the melodic line and the creative abilities of your singers to give it meaning and purpose. The composer is responsible for creating interesting vocal parts so that the singers will be motivated to be creative. The composer should also use some techniques to give the singers and the director clues to perform the music creditably. The main clue is the expansion of the composer's writing techniques which can be identified in almost every composition he writes.

Since you know your students, choose the music according to their experiences and abilities, and in terms of their sight reading skills. Sight reading is necessary in order to experience success in studying inner voice drama which will lead your singers into developing spontaneity in musical excellence.

Singing Parts Creatively

When your students learn the parts to the composition, the work in proper performance begins. It is not only proper for them to simply learn the sound of parts, text, rhythm and the melodic character in order to sing creatively, but they should also understand style, mood, texture and compositional character as they relate to the total composition. When your students understand all of the elements above they will be able to move the vocal lines with surety. Tell them to emphasize their lines with vocal agressiveness, following the creative schema of the director carefully.

Following the Expressive Melodic Idea

Teach each singer in the a cappella choir to think of his vocal line as the cog around which the entire composition revolves. This is important because it will help your students to understand the expressive element that brings about inner voice drama. Tell your students to find a central thought for each musical phrase, then help them to color the phrase accordingly, utilizing the correct vowel formations and blending techniques. Now connect the phrases through emotional stress points, proper instructions concerning the piece, motivation and creative conducting.

Permit some discussion among the students in order to bring about a unity in understanding the expressive elements. These will take name clues such as romantic, joyful, melancholy, robust or grotesque. These terms can be understood by your students and their reactions to them in singing the melodic lines will produce the inner voice drama that is so necessary to the tonal life of unaccompanied music.

Teaching Musical Expression

In order to carry your students further into the intangible realm of musical expression, place a section of the music on your overhead projector to discuss some expressive elements. When your students reach this level of understanding, you may begin using those descriptive phrases similar to the one that follows: "Altos, don't destroy the mood of the composition by singing too loudly at measure twelve. Listen for each section and emulate what they are doing." But these types of teaching phrases can only be used when the students understand what singing with expression means.

RECOMMENDED MUSIC LIST

Each of the compositions listed below can help you develop the special coloring of the a cappella choir. However, it is better to begin this development by using the easy compositions first; they are limited in difficult construction, but contain the elements your students will need to test and improve the concepts in this chapter. Then, advance to the medium and difficult compositions to solidify the developed skills.

Title	Grade	Composer	Number	Publisher
Why Has Thou Cast Us Off	E	Hovhaness	A–205	Associated
O Clap Your Hands	E	Glarum	CM7164	Fischer
My Heart Is Fixed on Thee O God	E	Arkhangelsky	2103–5	Walton
Cantate Domino	E	Hassler/Greyson	ES18	Bourne
Adoramus Te	E	Clement	352–00126	Mercury
Through the Desert of My Sorrow	E	Goudimel	7564	Fischer
All Ye Who Music Love	E	Donato	60650	Belwin
When Rooks Fly Homeward	E	Baynon	1870	Boosey
Lovely Heart	ME	Robertson	8595	G. Schirmer
The Eyes of All Wait Upon Thee	ME	Berger	1264	Augsburg
I Will Lay Me Down in Peace	ME	Willan	98–1231	Concordia
This Sweet and Lovely Siren	ME	Gastoldi/Greyson	ES103	Bourne
O Music Loveliest Art	ME	Widmann	7386	C. Fischer
Tutto Lo Di Midici	ME	Lasso/Klein	11961	G. Schirmer
Star, Moon, And Wind	ME	Bright		Shawnee
Two Festival Chorales	M	Bach	S.C. 24	Plymouth

Title	Grade	Composer	Number	Publisher
O Lord Increase My Faith	M	Gibbons	Oct. 2171	Belwin
The Lord's Prayer	M	Robertson	1.1199.1	Galaxy
If I Should Die	M	Arr. Ahrold	W 3556	MPH
Hodie Christus Natus Est	D	Willan	CM 469	C. Fischer
Crucifixus	D	Lotti	6396	G. Schirmer

CHAPTER 10

HOW TO PREPARE SMALL VOCAL ENSEMBLES FOR FESTIVAL PARTICIPATION

Many ensembles do not have successful performances at festivals because the music was not chosen with care, or the students did not prepare it well; consequently, their attitudes could not possibly have been conducive to a good festival participation. These factors result in poor performances in any musical ensemble. In this chapter I'll show you how to prepare your small vocal ensemble students properly.

You will also be shown how to improve the festival performance through a series of six workable, tested techniques. These include learning how to take advantage of the taped and drill sessions, memorizing the music, seating arrangements, teaching by example and conducting tips.

When your students begin to show signs of growth in voice development, review all of the techniques in this book with them, and, if necessary, reassign some material to those students who may be having some particular problem. There is always a possibility that some of your students will not remember all of the things you teach them and will have to review those techniques to develop certain skills. Reviewing some material with your students is part of the process of training the mind as well as the body for proper singing techniques. You ought to memorize all the techniques so that you will be able to readily spot the vocal problems your students are experiencing.

ANTICIPATING VOCAL WEAKNESSES
AMONG THE STUDENTS

It is not good to wait for a special time to warn your students about their faults. Rather, you should plan your work in vocal technique with the idea in mind that some students will be weak in certain areas of voice. Actually, you should be so familiar with your students that you will be able to tell which ones will be weak in certain skills. If you develop the ability to do this, your choirs will not have to suffer some embarrassing moments as the choir did in the following case study: Mr. Brown's a cappella choir was popular in the community for its excellent concert performances. Much publicity had been given to the choir in the radio, television and newspaper media. In fact, the choir was in demand to sing at different community gatherings during the entire year. Naturally Mr. Brown was very proud of his choir and wanted it to live up to its reputation in the community. He would ask the members of the choir to learn new music in case there would be people in the audience who had attended the previous concert and would not want to hear the same music over again. Many persons thought very highly of the choir until it received a second division rating in performance at the festival. Everyone, including Mr. Brown's principal, wanted to know what had gone wrong. For years the choir had received first division ratings at all festivals and second division ratings were never thought of by members of this choir. It had a firm foundation for securing the best voices in the school, and the vocal techniques among the members were superb. The reason for the lower rating was that Mr. Brown had permitted the choir to become too involved in concertizing, and he did not encourage the students to continue the development of vocal techniques. The choir met each day to sing compositions with very little attention to musical details. They sang through the festival selections, but failed to work out the problems that would be present for any choir, regardless of each member's musical ability to sight read the music and make the harmonic parts blend into a pattern. Mr. Brown, assuming that his students were musically perfect already, simply neglected to follow the training patterns that any normal high school choral ensemble should follow to become an outstanding choir. Naturally, the school board was asked to find a replacement at this school for Mr. Brown.

Eliminating Vocal Weaknesses

A choir director should never assume that the young high school choral group has "completed" training activities. Rather, he should strive to continue musical development at every rehearsal. This means that he must remain alert, planning for and measuring the skills that have been learned by his students and devising additional avenues by which he can carry these skills and others to full development among them. He can take advantage of this in every available opportunity including each musical event in which the students participate. He must challenge his students to excel in every vocal area. This can be achieved through written examinations, question and answer sessions and solo work.

DEVELOPING PROPER ATTITUDES
TOWARD FESTIVALS

Do not tell your students that you are taking them to the festival to receive a first division rating. They will be expecting to receive this rating and will be disappointed if they fail. Actually, festivals go much farther than receiving a rating and a trophy. The participants come from other schools with different ideas and training that can be exchanged among the school directors. The singers can hear other ensembles and receive an assurance that their own ensemble is productive and meets their aesthetic needs.

Rather than talk about the ratings your ensembles might receive, tell your students some of the experiences others had while attending festivals. Tell them that it will be a fun trip and an educational experience as well.

PLANNING THE FESTIVAL TRIP

If the festival is held on a college campus, or in a neighboring city, you can familiarize your students with the history of these institutions. There may be places along the route which have some historical significance. Let the students visit these, and, if necessary make special reports when they return to school. Encourage them to think of the festival as a continuation of the learning experience and the festival rating an expressive part of that experience. It should never be thought of as an end in itself.

Examining Reasons for the
Festival Participation

You should examine your reasons for taking the students to the festival. Do you wish to observe other directors in action? Many of them will be eager to share some "trial and error" approaches with you. Are you trying to create interest among your groups? Assess your reasons and weigh the valid ones with those you consider invalid. If the invalid ones outweigh the valid ones, you may be wasting your time and that of your students as well.

Building Group Solidarity

You can help build group solidarity on festival trips through discussions of certain group topics as in the following case history: There had been some discussion at school concerning dress codes the day before Mr. Hugh and the a cappella choir left to attend the district festival. Mr. Hugh had recently been appointed choral director at the school and needed this opportunity to become acquainted with the students, but the conversation always seemed to drift back to the school's dress code. Finally, one student asked Mr. Hugh to give them his opinion about the dress code. He told the students that it was his duty to uphold the school in policies relating to the school, and, since the school represented an expression of discipline that affected the lives of previous generations as well as their own, it would be well for them to uphold the school in trends which help to mold traditional aspects of the lives in the total community. He also told them that future generations will be looking at pictures of this present generation and will decide whether it was rational or irrational. The students agreed with Mr. Hugh and applauded him for bringing them together on what they considered a vital point. They also applauded him for helping them to receive a superior rating at the festival.

CHOOSING MUSIC FOR THE FESTIVAL

You should choose music that you are familiar with from a theoretical point of view as well as an historical one. Do not make the mistake of choosing the same compositions year after year. This does not project a picture of growth on your part.

Try to choose your festival music well in advance of the actual performance so that you can memorize it before you begin teaching it to your students. You may wish to have the nearest college group perform it for you at first. Be certain that the music is not too difficult for your students; let it represent the kind of training you have given them.

Effective Programming

When you begin searching for the "right" compositions for your ensembles, try to choose three compositions with varying degrees of difficulty ranging from difficult to medium levels. Try to make those choices which present challenges as well as aesthetic qualities for the students. Test these with your students. If during normal rehearsal periods, your students seem to tire of these selections, it may be that the musical value of the pieces is not equal to their level.

Here are two ways you can enhance your festival program:

- **Proper key relationships.** Proper key relationships lend themselves to the aesthetic values once the music is set in its performance order. You may want to utilize one common key between two compositions, but this should not be attempted when the two compositions are related in textures, styles or moods. In this case, it would be better to change keys in order to create more variety.
- **Maintaining the ensemble's character.** Your choice of music should reflect the special character and color of your special ensembles. This means that your modern choir should not sing, let us say, a composition from the Renaissance because the character cannot be maintained through this music, but, your madrigal choir's character and color can be maintained. Choose that music for each ensemble to complement its special character. Among the choices that you make for the festival should be at least one selection from the a cappella choir recommended music list.

FIVE WAYS TO INSURE
GOOD FESTIVAL PERFORMANCES

The items below represent some important elements you will need to check very closely when you make final choices for your small ensembles to sing:

- **Repeated notes.** Memorize the places in the composition where these occur. You will need to alert your students to these. However, avoid overemphasizing them because students usually lose control during the singing of repeated tones. The reason is that they fear them, especially when they occur in the upper register of the voice. Have them learn the sound and character of the entire passage in a lower octave or in another key.
- **The seventh degree of the scale**. Many students experience difficulty in singing the seventh degree of the scale especially when it leads to the tonic. Again, memorize the places where

these occur and be on the lookout for students who will offend here.

- **Wide skips.** Vowel color and resonance blending are affected when wide skips are sung in the composition. The problem rests with creating the correct color. You may have to isolate these for special work among the sections of your ensembles.
- **Modulations.** Establish the identity of the keys which are used in the composition. If it is possible, discover reasons why the composer used these in his compositions.
- **Dynamics.** Young singers have a tendency to sing flat when moving from loud to soft in certain passages in the high range, and sharp when moving from soft to loud in the low range of their voices. Try to secure a good recording of the composition and let the students hear good examples of these dynamics, then record your ensemble and permit the students to compare the differences that exist between the choirs. If this does not eliminate the problem, check for improper breathing patterns, poor vowel forms, tension and poor rhythmic timing.

Some directors choose music that is too difficult for their students. Various reasons have been given for this. But it is better to make choices that are comparable to the students' musical abilities. A difficult composition can be forced upon them, and, the students could perform it with a degree of success, but, the time that you spend perfecting it could have produced immeasurable success with a composition on the students' musical level.

EIGHT QUESTIONS TO HELP YOU CHOOSE FESTIVAL COMPOSITIONS

If you can answer the eight questions below concerning the compositions you have chosen for your students, it is likely that you will have success in teaching them.

1. What is the central idea in the text, and does the music relate to it?
2. Are there mistakes in the music? If so, can they be easily corrected by you and your students?
3. Are the parts easy for you to sing? If not, your students will have similar difficulty.
4. What difficulties will confront your students in the preparation of the music?

5. How much difficulty will your students experience in the first reading?
6. Do you believe the students will like the music?
7. Does the music make musical sense void of the text?
8. Will your audience like the music?

These are pertinent questions which must be answered before you make the decision to add the festival compositions to your repertoire. If one of the questions cannot be answered affirmatively concerning the music you have chosen, it may be wise to delete it from your performance list and add it to your sight reading list.

SIX METHODS FOR AN IMPROVED PERFORMANCE

Motivate your students to work diligently in the practice sessions in the hope of receiving a first division rating at the festival, because it is only from the success of these practices that the first division rating can be won. In other words, if they work hard for a first division rating in the rehearsal hall, they can expect to receive the trophy at the festival.

Some students have had bad experiences at festivals as in the case study that follows: Mr. Bell was having an after school rehearsal to practice a composition in which a number of problems had risen. He was confident that his students could work them out because each had had a wide variety of choral experiences. In fact, many of them had participated last year with the chamber choir when it received a first division rating at the festival. But, Mr. Bell had serious doubts when he found that the students were not taking their problems seriously. The section leaders laughed and told Mr. Bell that he had nothing to worry about, the ensemble would perform as expected. Mr. Bell knew that there was very little he could to to solve the problems with this kind of over-confidence that existed among the students. He also knew that they needed the shock of the lower rating they were sure to receive at the festival to eliminate the feeling of overconfidence. Unfortunately, the ensemble did receive a low rating, but the students learned that overconfidence destroys the will to practice.

Taped Sessions

The tape recorder could have been used to an advantage in the case study above. It would be well for you to follow the instructions which are given here: Set up your tape recorder at the beginning of your rehearsals and record the entire session. This will be an invaluable technique to help you show your students a big picture of what you were working for during the rehearsal. The students will be able to hear their mistakes, but they will also be able to hear you correct them. If you were successful, they will know it, if you were not successful, they will know it, and you will be able to point out specifically what is wrong. The taped session is a good way to create a certain amount of motivation to eliminate faults such as overconfidence and give you more room to make necessary improvements in the music.

- **Planning the taped sessions**.   Too much of anything soon becomes "dull" and "uninteresting." It is necessary then, to plan your sessions in advance. Know the problems the students are having and work out a definite plan to solve them. Your students will be excited about having their ensemble taped and will prepare themselves for it mentally. In this instance, you will be setting the tone for a serious study of the music. Plan no more than six recordings during the semester, but be sure that you plan for specific problems to be worked out with the final elimination during the last taping session.
- **Creating variety in taping sessions**.   Call sectional, quintet or quartet rehearsals and tape these separately. You can encourage the competitive element among the students in this way. Be sure to date all taping sessions. You may want to refer to them at a later date.

Drill Sessions

Many times, we tell our students their faults, give them remedies to improve them, then leave it up to them to solve them on their own. Do not leave the student alone to work the problems. . . . Organize drill sessions with section leaders in charge. Allow for a certain amount of time in which to work on the problems. Then bring the sections together and work on special problems such as intonation, diction and posture. Now, let each quintet or quartet sing each selection standing before the group. Call this session a "try out" sing. In reality, it is another form of a drill session.

Learning and Memorizing the Music

Try not to let your students begin memorizing the music before they learn its true character. Discuss the music with them. Let them recite the text. Mark the scores at phrase beginnings and endings.

You may want the students to make a special critique sheet to help them become familiar with elements which cannot be written on the score. Then drill work must be initiated. After this work is completed, the learning and memorizing processes can operate from a true base. When the students are confident that others will be pleased with the music, they can begin truly memorizing the music and you will be creating the music as it was meant to be.

Seating Arrangements for
Effective Rehearsals

Use a seating plan for your ensembles so the students can hear each section. Much memorizing and learning can take place in these types of seating plans. Some of the most successful ones are printed below.

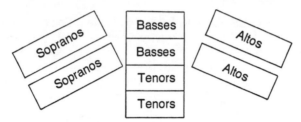

ILLUSTRATION 10.1 The Informal Choir.

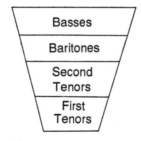

ILLUSTRATION 10.2 The All-Male Choir.

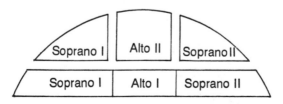

ILLUSTRATION 10.3 The All-Female Choir

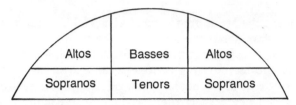

ILLUSTRATION 10.4 The Chamber Choir

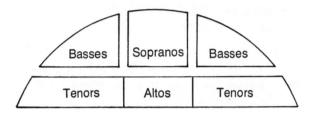

ILLUSTRATION 10.5 The Modern Choir

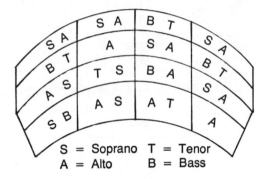

ILLUSTRATION 10.6a   The A Capella Choir (30 members)

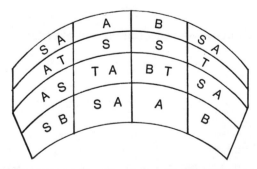

ILLUSTRATION 10.6b   The A Capella Choir (25 members)

Try not to deviate from the suggested seating arrangements that are printed above. If you permit your students to sit in these formations daily, you will be able to solve your vocal problems easily. You may want to move a voice to another position for a particular reason, but for the most part, these formations will bring good musical results.

Teaching By Example

Use your own voice to perform some demonstrations. It is to your advantage to show your students how to sing at forte or pianissimo levels rather than depending on a professional or a recording all of the time. If you do this kind of teaching by your own example, this will give your students more confidence that you know your job well. As the festival date draws near, you will need to do quite a bit of this kind of teaching to expedite time. Call it "on the spot" corrective measures, or "quick draw" methods, but it pays to teach by example some of the time.

It is true that some choir directors do not possess solo voices; they will have to learn to sing as best they can. They may have to take voice lessons from some colleagues. This is needful to help them do what should come naturally for a choir director—sing!

Conducting Tips

You should practice conducting each composition in front of a large mirror to eliminate your faults. Much of your own personality will emerge in your conducting. This is okay. But, be certain that you follow the fundamental beat patterns of conducting. Some directors confuse their students by using extraordinary beat patterns in their conducting. This is permissible for the professional conductor since he has established himself with these kinds of special conducting patterns.

Study the tips below and acquaint your students with them:

- **Smooth.** A rebound should not occur in the conducting pattern. Strive to connect each rhythmic point of your beat pattern so that the form will be correct. Be sure to control the volume in your ensemble by increasing or decreasing the space between your beats.
- **Detached.** The hand and arm should move together in detached patterns. You can use the word "stop" at each end of a beat to help your students understand the meaning of this word.

Here is a good rule to teach your students: when the directing arm stops, all tone stops as well.

- **Rebound.** This term applies to the "curve" at the end of a beat pattern. It is most effective in fast tempo. Be sure to control it in terms of its relationship to the beat pattern permitting it to be in preparation for the beat that follows.
- **Subdivision.** Every high school director should use subdivided beat patterns when conducting compound rhythms, or when cueing the parts which begin on the last half of a beat.

Teach your students how to conduct these patterns also. In order for the conducting language to be understood by the students, they must have some knowledge of all its vital parts.

STIMULATING INTEREST IN THE FESTIVAL

Permitting your students to hear other outstanding ensembles is a good stimulant to create interest, excitement and the competitive spirit among them. However, it is not a good idea to let them listen to other ensembles just before going on stage if it creates tension. It would be better to let this ensemble arrive at the festival fifteen or twenty minutes before their scheduled performance and spend that time in practice on warmup material. On the other hand, it is good for some ensembles to hear others in the actual performance at festivals: Mr. Hyde and his a cappella choir arrived an hour before their scheduled performance. When everyone had been seated in the auditorium, a neighboring ensemble with a good reputation began performing one selection Mr. Hyde had chosen for his choir. The performance was superb! Afterward, in the warmup room, the members of Mr. Hyde's choir were inspired by the performance they had heard. Many expressed their appreciation to him for permitting them to hear such a fine choir. Although the a cappella choir's rating was not a first division, it did represent a better one than had been expected of the group.

The Pre-festival Performance

Try to arrange for the other students at your school to hear the selections your ensembles have prepared for the festival. This experience of singing before an audience the day before the festival will help to relieve some of the tension for the actual performance. Be certain that your ensembles are well trained before you try to create this kind of interest for your festival debut. It may turn out to be a traumatic experience if your students are ill-prepared.

PREPARING AN ORGANIZATIONAL
PLAN FOR THE FESTIVAL

Many parents are eager to entrust their youngsters to your care if they feel that you are a competent teacher who has proved that you can plan well to insure the safety of the children in your ensembles. You can obtain this trust by explaining your plan to the parents, then formulating the plan so that it can be sent to each parent for his records. Be sure that the plan includes educational experiences as well as safety precautions.

It is apparent that festival trips are necessary because the children look forward to participating in them and meeting children from other schools; consequently, you should include in your plans instructions for the students to limit their movement in the festival area. Festival chairpersons can provide you with some of these restrictions.

Overnight Trips

Hotel accommodations must be made in advance since most operators require this. Also, your parent group will need to have this information to make preparations for their youngsters' financial needs for the trip.

Most high school groups will stay up late unless they are told specifically when to retire for the night. Insist that your students retire early in order to be refreshed for the performance the following day. Try to have planned activities similar to the one below:

5:30 p.m.	Arrival time
5:30–5:45	General instructions
5:45–6:00	Room assignments
6:00–6:15	Unpacking and getting settled in rooms
6:15–8:00	Dinner and relaxation
8:00–10:00	Reviewing music and working out school assignments (A rehearsal can be held in a conference room if necessary)
10:00 p.m.–6:00 a.m.	Sleep
6:00–6:30	Dressing for the festival
6:30–8:30	Breakfast and relaxation
8:30–9:30	Briefing, preparation for the festival
9:30–10:00	Ride to the festival site

Chaperones, section leaders and ensemble presidents should take the responsibility of carrying out the schedule above. You may spend your time visiting the festival site to hear other ensembles or checking your assignments for the festival. This information can be given to your students at one of your briefing sessions.

Outlining the Organizational Structure

You will find below, a diagram of the order in which responsibilities and the general organizational structure can be outlined for a smooth trip and festival participation.

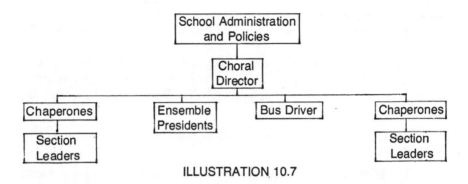

ILLUSTRATION 10.7

The policies of the school are administered by the school administration and should be respected by the pupils in that school as long as they are functioning under the auspices of the school; consequently, each person(s) in the outline above must carry out the school policies and see to it that the pupils adhere to them.

THE FESTIVAL PERFORMANCE

Generally, students reflect the attitude their directors have toward the festival. If a director seems to be nervous, his students will react in the same manner. For this reason, project a calm attitude so that your students will have a good example to emulate. Any changes in your attitude that are different from those you present each day will certainly have adverse effects upon your students. If they are nervous, ask them to settle down. You may calm them by relating some kind of humorous anecdote. But one thing must be clear at this point: If you have permitted mistakes to go uncorrected in rehearsals, they will still be there at the festival performances. Usually, adjudicators will overlook inherent faults such as nervousness which may induce false starts, however basic, technical problems in voice production will not be overlooked.

Utilizing the Warmup Period Correctly

Your warmup period should consist of vocalises and two or three short chorales. If time permits, you may include one selection from your program. The warmup period is intended simply to warm the voices for performance, it is not designed to resemble another rehearsal period.

Initiating Control During the Festival Performance

Remain in complete control during the concert. Avoid spontaneous movements and gestures in your conducting that you did not employ during normal rehearsal periods. Yet, the seriousness of the occasion must be translated to your students in terms of positive directional signs and demands with your hands and face. Being exact in your directional sign language means cueing entrances correctly, shaping words and phrases, building the correct style and the mood of the composition.

In order to keep your ensemble alert between selections, say something to this effect: "Kids, you did very well on the first selection, let's do that again in the following selections." This kind of attitude toward your students' performance will encourage them. If there are criticisms to be made, these will be on the adjudicator's critique sheets, and you will have time to make your own upon your return to the rehearsal room.

INDEX